# THE CABAL

## Catriona King

This is a work of fiction. Names, characters, places and incidents are used fictitiously and any resemblance to persons living or dead, business establishments, events, locations or areas, is entirely coincidental.

No part of this book may be used or reproduced in any manner without written permission of the author, except for brief quotations and segments used for promotion or in reviews.

Copyright © 2017 by Catriona King
Photography: Verve

Artwork: Jonathan Temples: creative@jonathantemples.co.uk
Editors: Andrew Angel and Maureen Vincent-Northam
Formatting: Rebecca Emin
All rights reserved.

ISBN: 978-1979845038

Hamilton-Crean Publishing Ltd. 2017

**For My Mother**

# About the Author

Catriona King is a medical doctor and trained as a police Forensic Medical Examiner in London, where she worked for some years. She returned to live in Belfast in 2006.

She has written since childhood and has been published in many formats: non-fiction, journalistic and fiction.

'The Cabal' is book sixteen in The Craig Crime Series. Each book can also be read as a standalone.

## The Craig Crime Series So Far

A Limited Justice
The Grass Tattoo
The Visitor
The Waiting Room
The Broken Shore
The Slowest Cut
The Coercion Key
The Careless Word
The History Suite
The Sixth Estate
The Sect
The Keeper
The Talion Code
The Tribes
The Pact
The Cabal

The seventeenth Craig Crime novel will be released in 2018

The author's fantasy/ mythology novella, Aurora, was released in August 2017.
She has also written a science fiction novel set in New York City, entitled The Carbon Trail.

# Acknowledgements

My thanks to Northern Ireland and its people for providing the inspiration for my books.

My thanks also to: Andrew Angel and Maureen Vincent-Northam as my editors, Jonathan Temples for his cover design and Rebecca Emin for formatting this work.

I would also like to thank all the police officers I have ever worked with, for their professionalism, wit and compassion.

Catriona King
November 2017


Discover more about the author's work at: www.catrionakingbooks.com

To engage with the author about her books, email: Catriona_books@yahoo.co.uk

The author can also be found on Facebook and Twitter: @CatrionaKing1

# Chapter One

**Monday, 27th June 2016. 7 a.m.**

If the opening of one eye was painful then the opening of two was agony as Marc Craig's dry, sealed lids ripped apart and he struggled to make sense of his world. The exercise was futile, the sterile hospital room so ubiquitous that he could have been anywhere, but nowhere would make sense unless he first accepted that he'd been injured and was able to recall how and when.

His long minutes of confusion seemed over finally when the room's half-glass door opened inwards, and a starched nurse entered with the quietness typical of her work. Soon he would find out which Northern Irish hospital he was in, and then he would claim his clothes, phone for a taxi and head straight for home.

As he croaked out "Where am I?" in a parched voice, the detective was already trying and failing to leave his bed.

A soft reply of "Dresden" was all it took to knock him back against his pillows again.

****

**Two Weeks Earlier.**

**Docklands Coordinated Crime Unit, Belfast. Monday, 13th June. 11 a.m.**

"It is a truth universally acknowledged, that a single man in possession of a good fortune, must be in want of a wife."

D.C.I. Liam Cullen's pale eyes widened as he read from the wooden plaque on PA Nicky Morris' desk, his surprise as stark as if he'd just seen the Chief Constable flying past the squad-room's tenth-floor window on the back of a unicorn. When his shock had subsided sufficiently to allow further speech, the few members of the murder squad who were present knew that they were in for a treat.

"Who writes this bollocks? A single man with dosh is in want of a trip to Vegas with his six best mates and several crates of beer, not a wife!" He waved a long arm expansively around the floor, almost clouting a passing Andy Angel on the way. "Everyone agree?" He didn't wait for an answer, continuing his diatribe under the PA's narrowing eyes. "And anyway, isn't all that marrying for money stuff anti-wotsit?"

Andy obliged with a translation, completely missing Nicky's ire turning his way.

"Anti-feminist?"

Liam nodded enthusiastically. "Aye. That. And seeing as you lot can earn more than us nowadays *we* should be marrying *you* for your dosh." He turned the knickknack over, searching for its origin. "Who is this Jane Austen bird anyway?"

It was too much for D.I. Annette Eakin on several counts. One, she wasn't long back from maternity leave after the birth of her second daughter and she was missing her baby, Carina, like hell, and two, she was torn between taking her other half, pathologist Mike Augustus, up on his suggestion that as he earned enough to pay the bills she should stay at home for a year if it made her happier, instead of forging higher in her career, so the last thing she'd needed to hear said anywhere in her earshot was 'anti-feminist'.

The third thing annoying her was the idea that a big culchie like Liam thought he could diss a genius like Jane Austen and get away with it; it offended her literary and every other sense. She was just about to let rip and say so when the ripping was done for her by Marc Craig entering the open-plan office, crossing the floor stealthily to where his deputy was holding court, and snatching the ornament that Liam was brandishing out of his hand and then smacking him with it, not so gently, right across the back of his head.

Liam's objection was predictably noisy. "OW! Who did

that?" His one-hundred-and-eighty-degree turn was accompanied by both fists curling. They swiftly uncurled when he saw his boss.

"Oh, it's you, boss. What'd you hit me for?" One of the uncurled fists rubbed his embryonic bald spot for emphasis.

Craig handed the knickknack back to Nicky and then leant against her desk.

"Would you just like the immediate cause, or a list of all your transgressions in the past year?"

It was said in a tone so dry that no-one present could tell if he was joking but it spurred Davy Walsh, the team's lead analyst, to start typing a list of everything he thought Liam might have done, just in case. When he got to the tenth point he gave up and sat back to watch the show.

Liam's mouth was still opening and shutting like a puppet's when Craig beckoned him into his small corner office.

"Shut the door, Liam. Coffee?"

The D.C.I. was about to refuse in mock offence but his ever-present thirst won out.

"Aye, and one of those biscuits I can see sticking out behind the mugs. Just for giving me such a whack."

Craig obliged then took a seat with his back to the best view in the building, leaving Liam free to watch the boats meandering down the Lagan on the fine summer's day. After a moment's silent sipping the Head of the Murder Squad gave the reason his deputy had been invited in.

"We've been asked to consult."

Liam lurched forward in his chair, suddenly enthused. It had been a boring few weeks for the team, all apart from their sergeant, Jake McClean, who'd just returned from a gruelling two months' rehab dealing with his steroid addiction and its cause, his attempted murder by his now incarcerated other half, Aaron Foster, recently sent to Maghaberry Prison for seven years.

Everyone else had either just been doing paperwork, giving evidence in court, or, in the case of Annette and Ash

Rahman, their junior analyst, had been away. In Ash's case that had meant New York, for training as part of a CIA task force set up to look at the vulnerability of space satellites to hacks.

Added to that all the thugs, drunks and domestic abusers in Belfast seemed to have decided to take a holiday, so there hadn't been a juicy murder in weeks; juicy was added shame-facedly for decency's sake, even inside the D.C.I.'s head. All of that explained Liam's sudden forward propulsion, so fast and unexpected that it made Craig push back his chair.

"Calm down, Liam. It's not a murder."

If someone had been recording them, Liam's tut of disgust would have been a tabloid journalist's dream, his follow-up whine even more so.

"Ach, you're kidding me? So you mean no-one's been topped?"

Craig stifled a laugh. "Sorry, but no." He was just thinking how dark police humour was when he remembered some of the things his girlfriend Katy, a hospital physician, had told him doctors said. He pushed the police into second place and added. "It looks like a kidnapping."

Liam raised a sandy eyebrow. "Kidnapping's not our thing."

"It is when the Chief Constable's the one doing the asking. Anyway, it could have been worse; until yesterday it was just a missing person's case."

He glanced at his watch and then waved towards the door.

"Gather the troops and I'll brief in ten minutes." As he spoke he slid his mobile phone from his pocket. "I have a call to make first."

Strictly speaking he didn't, *have to* make it that was. But he wanted to, and as Liam went to close the door behind him the softening of Craig's tone told him exactly who he'd just dialled.

****

**Belfast City Centre.**

The once groomed woman winced with pain as her wrists and ankles burned from their bindings, the chafing from days of restriction biting into the raw, torn skin below with every twitch. She would have shouted out to have them loosened except that she'd tried that before many times, until finally she'd given up calling, crying and begging the day before, each utterance falling on the increasingly deaf ears and growing fierceness of her captors, so fierce that she was terrified her next plea might be her last.

She slid down the wall of the empty space she was being held in, thankful that at least the room was warm; in every kidnap movie she'd seen there had been sodden floors, rubbish and rats to add to the victim's ordeal. She'd been spared that, but she wasn't being spared the anguish of not knowing who'd taken her, constantly worn hoods guaranteeing her captors' anonymity, or at whose behest she'd been dragged from her office God only knew how many days before.

But she *could* tell that she was in a city, and probably in its centre from the traffic noise and differing languages of passers-by. Her two guards' accents said that they weren't locals either, but her rudimentary knowledge of geography couldn't pinpoint them closer than coming from Europe somewhere.

She sighed, acknowledging that she should be glad they were hiding their faces; if she couldn't identify them to the police perhaps it implied that she had some chance of a future life. She disagreed with herself suddenly and as she did her heart sank in her chest. Why was she wasting her time hoping? Her jailers would never let her go, and she knew exactly why.

****

## The C.C.U.

"Right. Settle down everyone. We have a case."

Craig allowed a moment for the usual mock-disgruntled murmuring and a sneered-at cheer of excitement from Aidan Hughes, the Vice Squad D.C.I. who had joined them temporarily on a terrorism case three months before and was now a permanent member of the squad. Hughes was still new enough to display some enthusiasm for work, a behaviour that Liam promptly rewarded by knocking his elbow off his desk.

"OK. As Liam has no doubt told you this isn't a murder case-"

"Yet."

"Thank you for that, Liam. I'll be sure to tell the victim's family how you wished her dead."

"Ach, I didn't mean-"

"And I was cracking a joke. Remember those?" Craig motioned to his PA. "OK. Nicky, show us the first slide, please."

The secretary tapped her computer and the image of a glamorous middle-aged brunette appeared on the LED screen beside her desk.

"This is Mrs Veronica Lewis. Fifty-one, divorced and-"

Aidan Hughes cut in. "A madam."

Craig's eyes widened. "What?" He shuffled through some pages that no-one had noticed in his hands. "There's nothing about that here." And why the hell was the C.C. putting them on a Vice case?

"That's because she's very special." Hughes gestured towards the screen, rising. "May I?"

"Fire ahead."

When he was beside the image he restarted. "OK. Veronica Lewis. Her age and marital status you already know, but her stated occupation..."

He paused, waiting for Craig to read out what he had.

"Is as an occasional consultant in beauty and fashion at Marches department store."

Nicky nodded like a woman who knew her beauty products, as that day's deep purple lipstick and matching nail polish attested to.

"That's the big place in High Street."

Craig didn't want a debate on the relative merits of Belfast's shops so he moved swiftly on.

"OK, Aidan, you're clearly saying that's not her real job."

Hughes nodded his blond head. "Correct. It's a front for her more lucrative business. Mrs Lewis runs a high-class escort agency, and I'm talking serious money here. Some of her girls charge a thousand quid a night, and they get it as well."

Everybody's eyebrows shot up at the figure so Craig asked what they were all thinking.

"Who in Northern Ireland can afford that kind of cash?"

Hughes was about to answer when the squad's newest inspector, seconded Intelligence Officer Kyle Spence, who until then had been displaying his usual brand of jaded boredom, lounging back in his chair with both feet propped up on his desk, thudded them to the floor as interest enlivened his angular face.

"I'll tell you who. Powerful men with access to considerable money."

Craig turned towards his old university flatmate. "Business men?"

"And the rest. Diplomats, politicians, high-level criminals, maybe even some spies-"

He was cut short by Liam scoffing. "You see spies around every corner!"

"Only because they're usually there."

Craig cut the spat short and waved Aidan Hughes on again with a question. "Did you ever arrest Lewis when you were in Vice, Aidan?"

"Nope, she was far too slippery. We could never get anything concrete on her, just rumours here and there.

There was a sighting of her once on a raid apparently, but she skipped through a side door."

"Where was that?"

"A house in Bangor. Ruthie Brompton's place; she's another local Madam, although not in Lewis' league. We arrested Brompton and got a fair haul of directors, bank managers and middle-grade execs, but no punters above that level and not a single girl. They all ran."

"Back to wherever really rich men go to get their rocks off."

Annette gave a loud tut. "Thank you for that vivid description, Liam. Remind me to get you to write my Christmas cards."

Craig sighed. It was going to be a challenging case.

"Annette's right. Rein in the rhetoric, Liam, and that's an order. And while I'm on the subject, I don't want to hear the words: hooker, prostitute or even worse used during this investigation. Everyone's a sex-worker from now on. OK, carry on, Aidan."

The D.C.I. perched on Nicky's desk, making her wonder, and not for the first time, how much it would cost her to build a barbed wire fence.

"OK, so all we had on Veronica Lewis was that she occasionally turned up at Marches to do private beauty makeovers. We were pretty sure it was a front for recruiting new girls so we sent a W.P.C. in under cover, but all she ended up with was a blow dry and a fake tan."

Annette smiled. "I'll volunteer for that job, sir."

"I was thinking of sending Liam."

Hughes continued through the laughter, gesturing at the photograph again.

"Last time I saw Veronica she was blonde. She'd been a red-head at some point as well. Sometimes with short hair, others with long."

Nicky interjected. "Maybe she has a selection of wigs."

The Vice D.C.I. nodded. "That's what we thought. There's a file on her downstairs so I'll dig it out, but I know she's not from around here. Dublin possibly, but it could have been elsewhere down south. The W.P.C. said her accent was neutral southern and she was nicely spoken as well. Anyway, we were sure Lewis had a business base somewhere-"

Craig cut in. "A brothel?"

"That was the assumption although we never got any detail. High class was all we knew, with tight security."

Kyle nodded. "Maybe somewhere for the great and not-so-good to go, away from prying eyes? It could be in the country somewhere. Possibly looks like a farmhouse or manor house from outside."

Craig thought fast. "Nicky, set up a meeting with D.C.I. Sheridan in aerial support. I want to see what they have on their surveillance photos. If this place exists, there'll be some signs of extra security."

It was left to Andy Angel, their resident renaissance man, to bring them back to the important point.

"Liam mentioned she was kidnapped, chief."

Craig seemed surprised for a moment, then he gave a wry smile. "Timely reminder, Andy. Yes, while we need to know as much about Veronica Lewis as possible it's only to help find her. We're not pursuing her for any crime, she's a victim here. So...she was reported missing-"

Annette interrupted. "By whom? And why is it a kidnapping instead of a missing persons case?"

"Not sure. But someone must have reported her missing so, Nicky, can you find out who that was, please? Her son might know. Apparently, he uses her apartment to do his washing."

Nicky asked before anyone else could. "How old is he?"

"Twenty-four, but still a student so he often used her machine. Anyway, when whoever it was got to Lewis' place of work she wasn't around and none of her mail had been opened. Some of it was days old and still lying on the mat. They did the usual phoning around but no-one had seen her since Friday, so they reported her missing."

Liam screwed up his face. "So she went missing from a brothel?"

Craig scanned the pages in his hand then shrugged. "Her place of work is all it says here."

Annette pressed another point. "And why *kidnapping*?"

"Sorry, Annette. The truth is I don't know, so find out for me, please. But whichever label we put on it Lewis has been missing for three days."

Liam asked two questions. "Ransom demand?"

"None yet."

"OK. So why the C.C.?"

Craig turned to stare at him. "What?"

"This is a woman who's been missing for a few days. Sad, but not that unusual. So why is the Chief Constable of the PSNI getting personally involved?"

The obvious answer horrified Craig and he shook his head and turned away, trying to cover his shock. No way had Sean Flanagan been one of Veronica Lewis' punters; he just couldn't see it. Flanagan was happily married, more than happily; he'd seen him with his wife and it was real love. When he said as much it was Liam's turn to shake his head.

"Sorry, boss, your loyalty's laudable but even happily married men have been known to go over the side occasionally, and why else would the Chief be getting involved?"

Craig nodded heavily. "You're right, Liam, we have to check it out. But I still say the answer will be no."

Liam's finger shot up to volunteer.

"Not you, Liam, sorry. Kyle, you're skilled in subterfuge. See what you can suss out about the C.C. getting involved."

Spence rubbed his hands together in anticipation; poking around in other people's business was his forte, and digging through the C.C.'s dirty laundry was the stuff of dreams. When he stopped rubbing he gave a grudging shrug.

"To be honest I don't think I'll find anything. I did the force's top-level security screening for years and there was no dirt on Flanagan. Not even a rumour. It's more likely he's been *told* to stick his nose in by someone else."

"You mean someone higher up is worried."

"More than likely. Madams are the holders of men's secrets and a high-class madam equals very powerful men, like we said. My guess is someone in government, ours or somewhere else, is bricking it in case Lewis has been kidnapped for that information and that's why Flanagan's been tasked to investigate."

Craig made a face. "So why not do it himself? It would have kept things secret."

"And risk people lower down putting two and two together to make five about his personal life if anything got out? Nope. Too risky. The Chief Con trusts you, and trusts that you can keep all of us quiet as well."

Craig raised an eyebrow. "And can I?"

Spence adopted an innocent look. "Why, boss... How can you even ask?"

The response was a wary grunt. Craig knew Kyle Spence too well to be reassured.

"OK, let's see what we've got so far. Aidan's going to dig into Lewis' file, Annette will check out why her disappearance is now being labelled as kidnapping, Liam and I will check aerial surveillance and go on the hunt for the pleasure palace, and Kyle will investigate why the C.C. is getting involved."

He shifted his gaze to Andy and found him gazing longingly at a chocolate bar on his desk. He'd had the good sense not to start eating it, which was progress of a sort; six months before it would have been smeared all round his mouth, briefing or no briefing.

"Andy, since Jake's back; welcome Jake." There was no pause for comment in the circumstances. "I want you two to interview the son and look around Lewis' home." He turned back to his deputy. "Liam..." He'd been about to say, "interview some of the escorts" when an image of Liam getting a slap across the face for being vulgar stopped him dead in his tracks. Instead he turned back to Andy, tacking on the task for him and Jake, and then returned to look at Liam's now disappointed face.

"Liam. Can you think of anything else we need to do?"

The D.C.I.'s chagrin turned swiftly to pleasure, never one to hold upset for long. "Yep. Who's been protecting Lewis all these years?" He glanced at Aidan as he asked it, adding. "How many years has she been active anyway?"

The word active made Craig wince, certain as he was that it would be followed by a bawdy joke. For once he was wrong and Liam kept a studiously straight face as Hughes replied.

"At least thirty, that I know of, but I'll check her file."

"Well, OK then. So, who's been protecting her during those years? And so successfully? No hooker, no matter how high-class, could stay out of jail, hospital, or the tabloids that long unless *someone* was covering her back."

The twinkle in his eye told everyone that he'd really wanted to say 'ass'.

"Good catch, Liam. Opinions, everyone?"

Davy Walsh had been sitting quietly since he'd given up on his list of Liam's transgressions, now he pushed back his long EMO black hair, normally controlled in a ponytail but making a rare bid for freedom that day, and ventured a suggestion in his soft, slightly stammering voice.

"S...Surely her wealthy clients have the power, and a vested interest in protecting her, chief."

Nicky smiled proudly at the analyst, her tendency to view Davy as her surrogate son undiminished by his advancing years and the just over a decade between them. She'd responded to his suggestion before she realised what she'd done.

"That's a very good idea, Davy."

Craig smiled. "As Nicky said, good idea."

But Aidan Hughes wasn't so sure it would lead them up the hierarchy. "Normally the person organising protection would have a financial interest in the business."

"A partner in her escort agency?"

"Possibly. Or if not, maybe she hired a body guard herself."

"OK, but what's to stop one of Lewis' wealthy clients being her partner? Lots of people avail of their business' benefits."

Hughes shrugged. "Nothing, I suppose."

Davy hadn't finished. "Once we locate her business w...we can find out who owns it. That might give us a name."

His tone of voice said even he was dubious it would be that easy.

"More likely it'll be a shell company, but it's worth a try."

Liam had another suggestion. "What if her place is just one of a chain of brothels? Owned by someone elsewhere, with protection thrown in. It would make sense if a criminal gang was involved, or even if some of the bigwigs who used the place wanted to ensure absolute privacy. Like that time in Fermanagh, remember? All those weirdos auctioning girls off in that tower place."

Craig shuddered as he recalled the case from twenty-thirteen when they'd cracked a ring of people traffickers who'd specialised in selling young girls. Liam was still talking.

"If a gang is involved they could have just let Lewis run the place, paid off the cops and press for her, etcetera, all for a cut of her profits." He paused for breath before continuing. "Or maybe it's a franchise? Sort of Orgies Incorporated, run by different madams in different places but always in the same way. Like some central coordination thing."

Craig rolled his eyes. "Now you're just stretching credibility." He was suddenly serious again. "There's nothing to stop the partner or gang possibilities, but we'll need to find plenty of evidence, especially if you're insinuating that Sean Flanagan is one of those paid-off cops."

Liam shook his head. "I wasn't thinking of him, actually. It's more likely to be someone at ground level who's taking a bung. D.C.S. level or below. The higher ups would be too busy attending their fat boy dinners."

It was hard to argue with considering the size of some businessmen.

When there were no more suggestions Craig nodded to wrap up. "OK. Kyle, put out some feelers in Intelligence to find what there is about organised brothels and bought off cops, and Aidan, dig deeper at your end." He glanced at the clock. "This should keep everyone busy for a few hours. We'll reconvene at five o'clock."

# Chapter Two

**Whitehall, London.**

The elderly man rotated his crystal tumbler slowly, not forcefully enough to smear the ice-chilled liquid inside up its sides, but just enough to make a satisfyingly gentle clink as the cubes of frozen water touched. It was his ritual before an event: gin, no tonic, just three cubes of ice and a wedge of lime. Sour enough to reflect his mood and sharp enough to keep him alert, the clink's very sound enough to warn his subordinates that something was afoot.

Ritual over, he drained the glass, pulled out his phone and rose from his seat at the private club's bar, murmuring into the handset as he strolled past the scurrying flunkies towards his chauffeured car. Making calls was an everyday activity in his privileged life, but this one was the signal to let the first domino fall.

****

**The C.C.U.**

When Ash Rahman strolled into the squad-room an hour after the briefing had dispersed, his swagger was as loud a call for attention as anything Nicky had ever seen. That was, until the analyst realised that the only audience present comprised the PA, a pre-occupied Davy whose head was so far buried in his semi-circle of computers they'd have to send in a St Bernard to get him out, and a grey pigeon pressing its face against the office's tenth-floor window from the outside.

His entrance's impact not so much lessened as non-existent, the newly-returned-from-New-York analyst down-graded his saunter accordingly. Nicky gave a knowing smirk and then walked past him murmuring. "Tea?"

It proved better than a rescue effort in ensuring that Davy's eyes lifted, and as a side-effect granted Ash a watered-down version of the welcome that he'd craved. Davy stood up at his desk and gave a nod.

"You're back, bro."

In the shorthand of Generation Y Ash answered "Yo."

Davy's eyes narrowed suddenly as he noticed his subordinate's garb, and his next words weren't, as Ash had expected, 'tell me all about the project', but a typically ego-deflating Northern Irish. "What the hell have you got on?"

Ash glanced down at his baggy trousers and responded with a cool scan of Davy's skinny jeans, waistcoat and narrow tie. As a comment on whether he thought US or UK fashion was better it spoke loud. When Nicky reappeared with the tea she threw in her two-pennies worth on Davy's side.

"Hate your sweat shirt and baggies, Ash, but I like the red, white and blue Mohican. Very Free World. I'd just be careful where you wear it in Belfast though. Some people might think you're a Union Flag."

With his readjustment period over and the junior analyst yanked firmly back down to earth, everyone lifted a mug of tea and Nicky returned to her desk to let the analysts talk. There was no point in her eavesdropping as most of it would be in acronyms and computer-ese, but when it gave way to police business after ten minutes she turned her bat ears back on.

Ash leaned over his boss' desk, squinting at Davy's central screen.

"What're you working on?"

"A kidnapping."

Ash's response was to the point. "Why?" *We're the murder squad* didn't need to be said.

"Because the C.C. asked the chief to, that's w...why."

Ash gave a slow whistle. "Something's rotten on high."

"Exactly."

"OK. So that explains why you're running UK

kidnapping data for the past five years."

Davy responded with a non sequitur. "She's a madam."

"And *that* explains why you're cross referencing it with Vice arrests." Ash pulled up a chair and stared at the two results. "Have you got anything?"

He already knew the answer; there was a red-flash alert scrolling along the bottom of the page. Davy clicked it and a page opened, displaying two names.

"Where-?"

Before Ash could finish the question, a map of the UK appeared with two cities highlighted, so he read their names aloud.

"Manchester and Edinburgh. Two women kidnapped. One in March and one in April this year, both known prostitutes."

"Sex-workers. The boss says so."

Nicky gave up eavesdropping and walked across to the pair.

"Were they madams?"

Ash screwed up his face. "Is that important?"

"It might be if you're looking for similarities with what we've got. Well, Davy?"

Davy's lean fingers flew across the keys and after a moment of silence he gave a half-surprised nod.

"One was. In Manchester. The Edinburgh one was a high-class escort who apparently w...worked out of her own flat."

Nicky warmed to her theme. "The madam. Low or high class?"

"It doesn't say. But that doesn't matter so much. If we can establish a pattern, then there's nothing to s...say the level wasn't being tailored to the customers in the area they served."

"You're saying the important link is kidnapping and sex work."

He nodded and began typing again. Nicky's face fell.

"You're checking to see what happened to them."

Ash was in the right position to see the search results and it wasn't good news.

"Both found dead! After how many days?"

Davy clicked again. "The Manchester one after five, with the Edinburgh one it was a w...week. They died soon before they were found, so that means they were held somewhere first."

Nicky flopped down on a nearby chair. "Our one's been gone three days already. You need to tell the chief right away."

The analyst had already done so, sending an alert to the whole squad's phones with one tap. When it had gone he pushed back his seat, frowning.

"What's the connection between kidnapping a sex-worker and killing them?"

"Were they rape-murders?"

Davy shook his head. "The files say there was no sign of sexual assault on either woman." He gestured to his right-hand screen. "And the database says that violence connected with sex-workers is normally one of two sorts: s...spontaneous attacks during a dispute, over money or jealousy, or in a minority of cases weirdos who target them for sex attacks and kill them right away. Why go to the trouble of holding them for days?"

Nicky shook her head primly and stood up. "That's what we have detectives for."

\*\*\*\*

When the text appeared on Craig's and Liam's phones they both missed it, too busy leaning over a map table trying to make sense of some aerial views, with Liam asking the D.C.I. in charge so many questions about marks and anomalies that Craig could see the jump-suited man winding up to throw a punch.

He intervened quickly. "Liam, for the last time, it doesn't matter what that white line is! It's obviously not a building and that's all we're interested in."

He cast an apologetic glance at Theo Sheridan and stepped away from the table to take a seat, hoping that his withdrawal would encourage Liam's newly discovered geographic nerdiness back into its box. When it didn't the small, muscular helicopter pilot pulled up a chair beside Craig and gestured at Liam, whose large nose was now pressed flat against the horizontal glass screen.

"Doesn't get out much, does he?"

Craig suppressed a smirk, torn between his liking of Sheridan, whom he'd known since he'd moved back to the province from London eight years before and often encountered since at courses and the force's football tournament, and his loyalty to his deputy of all those years. He plumped for the second.

"Let's just say Liam's a man of wide-ranging enthusiasms."

This time he couldn't stifle his laugh.

Sheridan nodded sagely.

"If you say so. But it would help if you told me exactly what you were both looking for, and why."

Craig's expression said that he wished he could; it would be useful to bounce ideas off someone outside his team.

"All I can say is what I've already told you. It will probably, but not definitely, look like a house. A large one, like a farmhouse or a mansion house. Somewhere secluded, probably with only one approach road, and with heavy security."

"Any idea what sort of security? High-level with electrified fences, dogs and guards, or just a low level domestic alarm system?"

"What differences would you see from the air?"

The pilot thought for a moment.

"Well...there'd be the obvious physical infrastructure; guard posts, dog kennels, double fencing, with power boxes if they're electrified. And then there's the human element, moving vehicles, patrolling men, maybe even armed guards."

"You can make guns out from the air?"

"You'd be surprised what we can see using different lights and lenses. But don't forget the men's postures will also show if they're carrying a rifle or machine gun. If there's a lot of security then it'll be easy to spot, although you might want to get your analysts on to the power companies, searching for any unusually high power usage by non-commercial properties."

He stood up again. "We'll scan the country for all that and get back to you, but if the place just has domestic alarm type security then there won't be much for us to see. I mean, we can generate a list of properties that fit for size and access, but your best bet would be searches of the alarm companies' databases and-"

He was cut short by a loud whoop.

"I can see my house, boss! Look."

The repeated jabbing of a sausage-like forefinger told Craig that he'd better look before either Liam cracked the glass or Sheridan cracked him.

He glanced at the map and then pulled his deputy away.

"That's great, Liam, but we're going now. We've things to do back at the ranch."

"Aw. I was enjoying myself."

"I'm sure Theo will let you come again."

The combined head shaking and blade-drawn-across-the-throat signals from the jump-suited D.C.I. left no doubt what would happen if he did.

\*\*\*\*

**The Police Intelligence Section. Malone Road, South Belfast.**

Kyle Spence wasn't a man who took the trouble to be subtle unless there was a direct quid pro quo involved for him. Subtlety required more effort than secrecy, his forte, and inevitably had to be tailored to its audience. If there'd been a guaranteed-to-work, one-size-fits-all subtlety level then he might have flicked the switch to turn it on now and then, but there wasn't so he didn't. Thus it was that the D.I. marched brashly past a guard he knew well at the entrance to the Police Intelligence Section, flashing his badge so quickly that she didn't have time to register it no longer held an up-to-date stamp, and was in the lift and along the upper corridor rapping on the door of his erstwhile boss before anyone caught on and kicked him out.

On the same brisk theme, Spence didn't wait for a shouted 'come in', opening the door and planting himself in a seat before D.C.I. Roy Barrett had even had a chance to speak.

"Hi, boss. How are things?"

The D.I. had answered his own question with "Good. Now I need to ask you something" before the Director of Intelligence's open mouth had time to shut.

"What do you know about high-class hookers?"

Roy Barrett was rarely surprised by anything in life, a trait his mother had said had been present since the day that he'd been born. Apparently he'd been unsurprised by his abrupt entrance into the world, not howling as new-borns normally do, but instead staring at the midwife as coolly as if she had merely asked him the time. Things had continued in the same vein at school, with the first kick in the head he'd received at the end of a classmate's rugby boot being greeted with the same insouciance as an aunt's invitation to afternoon tea, and when he'd received his first-class law degree when he'd only expected a two-two it had barely caused his eyebrows to rise.

So it was that his one-time protégé, Spence, who had left him for what he considered the navvy-like existence of a murder detective, barely raised a blink with his blunt question about recreational sex. Instead the grey-haired Barrett merely indicated the kettle and on the D.I.'s nod he rose to make them both tea.

When the genteel arts of brewing, milking and sipping had been completed, the Director set down his Royal Doulton cup, rested back in his well-worn leather chair and folded his hands in front of him on the desk, while Kyle Spence tried his utmost to make his teeth grinding frustration not generate an audible noise. He should have known better than to approach Roy Barrett like a bull in a china shop but his impatience and disdain for the niceties had made him do it anyway, and he knew that this enforced period of waiting was his well-deserved penance. Finally, Barrett hinted that the punishment was almost over, inhaling deeply and at length before he spoke.

"You would, I take it, like to know about the sexual proclivities of Northern Ireland's great and good?"

"Yes." It emerged through Kyle's gritted and slightly nicotine-yellowed teeth.

"May I ask why?"

"It's confidential, sir."

"Well then." The smaller man rose to his feet. "My answer shall remain confidential as well. You can show yourself out."

The D.I. didn't move, instead emitting a frustrated sigh. He'd wondered if Barrett would adopt this approach all the way from the C.C.U. to his office door, but he hadn't been certain, just as now he couldn't be certain that if he'd approached the man with some deference he mightn't be helping him more now.

Spence waved his old boss back to his seat and regrouped, starting again in an entirely different way.

"This is highly sensitive, sir."

"As am I, as you well know, Kyle."

Spence really couldn't argue with that; the man was telling the truth. Even under pain of torture Roy Barrett would never reveal something passed to him in confidence.

He nodded.

"I know that, sir, it's just that D.C.S. Craig won't be happy if this gets out. He was entrusted with it personally."

It told the Director all he needed to know. Only one person warranted such secrecy and he was known to have relied on Craig a good number of times.

"So this is a direct request from the Chief Constable."

"It is."

He could truthfully tell Craig that Barrett had worked it out for himself.

"Well, as D.C.S. Craig is head of this section as well as Murder, and by logical progression my boss as well as yours, you can be assured that it is not in my interest to get on his wrong side." Barrett gave a shrug of futility that would have done a Parisienne proud. "However, unless you're prepared to give me more information my hands will still be tied."

Kyle Spence thought about it for a moment, running through the probability tree of how telling Barrett meant that something could go wrong and land him in the shit. But the likelihood of things going nowhere at all and him having to return to the squad and admit the horror of having no useful information loomed even larger, so over a fresh cup of tea and a chocolate covered snack the D.I. told his old boss the minimum that he needed to know to keep his new boss off his back.

\*\*\*\*

## The C.C.U. 2 p.m.

"Ah, now, that's what I like to see. The teenage geeks hard at work."

The insult was delivered in as loud a voice as Liam could muster and with all the subtlety of a truck, yet it didn't sound offensive to anyone's ears but his. Davy didn't hear him, so embroiled was he in his searches, and all Ash had registered was 'teenage', and in his book, anything that pointed out his youthful appearance had to be a good thing. Offended by their lack of offence, Liam had another go, while Craig checked the messages Nicky had just handed him and poured himself an espresso so strong that her teeth were pained even by the look of it.

"Of course, it'd be hard to tell which of you two had the crappiest dress sense. The Smurf with those baggy things he's wearing, like that MC Hammer guy, or the boy for wearing jeans so tight he can hardly walk without his knees joined."

Liam had christened Ash the Smurf during his blue hair phase, and he saw no reason to alter the title now. This time the insults hit their mark; not on Davy with his ineffable cool, but on Ash's image of himself as a transatlantic style icon because of the comparison to a nineties music star. The colourful analyst was just drawing himself up to his full five-foot-nine when Craig decided that Liam had had enough fun. He walked across to Davy and pointed at his screen.

"And that is?"

Davy smiled, not looking up. "Already on your phone."

It prompted Craig to quickly check his mobile, which he'd had on silent all day, hence the messages Nicky had just passed him accompanied by a reproachful look.

"Sorry, I missed it. Explain."

"I decided to search kidnap victims who were prostitutes in the UK and Republic, so far I've found four, including ours. Manchester, Edinburgh, and Dover on the south-east English coast."

"And?"

Liam had just read his message. "All dead, boss."

Davy nodded. "Five days for Manchester, the others after a w...week."

Liam strode across, looking for attention. It had taken two insults to get even a slight rise from Ash, so he would have to get his limelight in another way.

"A week till they were found, or a week till they were killed?"

Craig nodded. It was a good point.

"Both. They were killed just before they were found and none of them were s...sexually assaulted. I'm still trying for more details. Getting info from other forces is harder than getting Ash to wear normal clothes."

Liam tutted; there'd be no fun to be had soon if the nerds began to insult themselves. Meanwhile Craig was frowning. Veronica Lewis had disappeared three days before so she mightn't have much more time.

"Let me know if you need me to apply any pressure, Davy." He gestured to the new returnee. "Ash, there'll be some addresses coming in from D.C.I. Sheridan in surveillance. When you get them, I need you to do some searches on alarms and power usages. Before then, you and I need a few words."

He moved away to let Davy get on with things and beckoned Ash into his office, taking a seat behind his desk and waving the analyst to one opposite. His amused scan of the younger man's hair made his next words no surprise.

"I take it you enjoyed New York then?"

Ash sat forward enthusiastically, expounding on how fast a New York minute actually was compared to their own until Craig diverted him.

"So, what can you tell me about Dudaev?"

Bakar Dudaev was a Chechen national who'd been linked with stealing American satellite codes and part of the reason the New York cybersecurity taskforce had been established.

Ash's cheerful expression was replaced by a scowl. "He's not proving easy to find, chief. After he left Amsterdam in April the next place he surfaced was Valencia in Spain, then Milan a month after and last week he was seen in Crete."

Craig looked puzzled, causing Ash to nod.

"Yeh, that's what we thought. Where the heck is he going?"

Craig rested back in his chair, steepling his fingers. The CIA had postulated that the market for US satellite codes would have three main buyers: Russia, Iran and North Korea. The last two had edged ahead when they'd realised Dudaev was Chechen, given the no-love-lost status between Russia and the republic, and yet Dudaev's trek was taking him away from all of them.

"I take it the CIA have tried geolocation algorithms to make sense of his journey?"

The analyst was impressed. Perhaps Craig's knowledge of computing was better than he'd realised.

The detective read his mind.

"Sorry. I wish I could take the credit but it came from the box-set of Homeland we watched last weekend. Still, it's true, isn't it? Their software *should* be able to make some sense of what Dudaev's doing? At the moment, it looks like he's deliberately spaghetti trailing across Europe to throw them off."

Ash screwed up his face, uncertain how much of the task force's work he was permitted to divulge. Once again Craig read his mind.

"I'm Head of Police Intelligence now as well, remember? I get written briefings on the taskforce's work every week, but I'm afraid I haven't read this week's just yet."

"Ah. OK, then. Yes, they think they may have some sense of where he's going, or rather where he's desperately trying to pretend he's *not* going. His trips since Amsterdam have all been in Southern Europe, so-"

Craig cut him off with a smile. "His destination is somewhere in the north. Given his Chechen nationality probably somewhere ex-communist Bloc. The Baltic States maybe?"

"Or East Germany, Poland, the Czech Republic, etcetera. Wherever he's going Dudaev's taking his time, trying to throw us off, but MI6 and the CIA have agents in every country, so he'll have his work cut out."

"Except that with the Schengen Agreement pretty much abolishing border checks inside the EU, he could have reached his destination already and we wouldn't know. Damn."

He jumped to his feet abruptly, taking the analyst by surprise.

"OK, keep me up to date, Ash, and check my Intelligence

briefings, please, in case anything's been left out. Nicky has them in a file."

With that he nodded towards the door and then turned to the window to look out at Belfast Lough, his thoughts returning almost instantly to their missing madam.

\*\*\*\*

## The Ormeau Road, South Belfast.

Jake McClean was less than amused to be heading for a sex-worker's apartment on his first day back at work, especially as that apartment was on the thirteenth floor of a tower block whose lift had given up the ghost. He glanced at Andy Angel with considerably less deference than his D.C.I. rank warranted.

"Couldn't we have asked the girls to come to High Street for interview?"

In between gasps for breath Andy summoned the energy to shake his gel spiked head. He *really* needed to go to the gym; there was Jake not even breaking a sweat and he thought he was going to die. He leant against a graffiti covered wall, wondering why the only variation between Belfast's Catholic and Protestant graffiti seemed to be whether to do the obscene things it suggested to the Queen or the Pope. Apart from the lack of creativity there seemed to be no respect for pensioners of any persuasion nowadays.

After a full minute of puffing he mustered an answer to the sergeant's question.

"They're not suspects so we'd like their co-operation, that's why. And judging by the outfit the last one was wearing when we knocked her door I'd say a trip to the station might have cut into her day's work. Plus, what Jack Harris would say if we filled his reception with hookers doesn't bear thinking about."

"Sex-workers. The chief said."

"Well, whatever you call them, Jack would choke on his

tea."

High Street Station was the closest nick to the C.C.U. and Sergeant Jack Harris normally welcomed the break from his daily tedium that the Murder Squad's interviews provided. But even his tolerance had a limit and Andy thought this case might breach it.

Semi-refreshed by his brief rest he gestured the politically correct sergeant towards the next flight of stairs, only to be answered by a shake of Jake's head and his finger pointing towards an aptly painted red front door.

"We're already here. That's Jennifer Wasson's flat. Apparently, she's one of Lewis' best girls."

Andy was certain he detected a twinkle in the younger man's eye as he said the words. Given that Jake was gay it was unlikely to be lechery, and lewdness wasn't his character type, so he asked the question.

"Why is that amusing?"

Jake laughed out loud, the first time Andy had heard him do so since he'd been sent to rehab months before.

"I was just picturing a flabby businessman clambering up these stairs and collapsing outside her door in a breathless heap. She'd have to be amazing at what she does to get any passion out of that."

Andy instantly glanced down at his own abdomen. Thankfully he still had his youthful wiry build, but one day all the chocolate he'd eaten would impact and he would turn into a giant whale overnight. He sucked in his stomach and marched towards the red door hand raised, only to have it open inwards before his fist fell.

The figure that greeted the detectives was unexpected. The petite redhead in front of them couldn't have been older than twenty-five, and dressed in jeans and wearing no make-up she provided a stark contrast to the negligée wearing, false-eyelashed seductress that they'd interviewed an hour before. A small hand shot out to shake Andy's.

"Jenny Wasson. Come in, Chief Inspector."

The woman turned briskly on her heel and was in the

small apartment's living room before the detectives had even entered the hall.

"Come along, then. I have to collect my kids from school in twenty minutes."

As Andy entered the tastefully decorated room she had another thought.

"In fact, perhaps you could drop me off there? It's only a mile away."

The D.C.I. nodded and took the indicated seat, while Jake remained in the room's doorway with both arms hanging by his sides. The woman gestured at him.

"What's wrong with your mate? Morals? Does he disapprove of me then?"

"More of the men who visit you." Seeing the girl was becoming embarrassed Andy's tone became unusually terse. "Sit down, Sergeant. Now."

As he turned back to her, his gaze fell on a framed photograph displayed on a bureau. It was of Wasson, dressed up and looking stunning and he suddenly understood why some men would pay hundreds of pounds for her time. The photo was surrounded by silver cups and a range of rosettes.

"Who won the prizes?"

She glanced at them. "Me. Horse-riding and piano."

Jake inhaled sharply, making her roll her eyes.

"Aren't whores supposed to have posh hobbies, then?"

It was then that Andy noticed her accent: modulated and middle-class. It said that she'd come from a very different place than this. She explained without him asking.

"My parents had money and I have a degree in Italian, in case you're interested. But they didn't like my husband so they cut me off. When he left me two years ago, proving them right of course, it was too late to mend things between us and I was flat broke with two kids. There are limited openings for an Italian teacher in Belfast." She swept a hand around the room sarcastically. "And so here you find me, in all my glory. Mouths to feed and only my winning smile to depend on."

As she rested back in her chair, Andy noted that at least Jake had the decency to look ashamed. There was no point being politically correct if you were also as judgmental as hell.

"Ask whatever you need, Chief Inspector."

"Thank you, Ms Wasson. Veronica Lewis. She's your madam, yes?"

The young woman shook her head instantly. "I work for myself." That established, her tone relaxed. "But Veronica organises high-end parties."

"How often?"

"Fortnightly or thereabouts. More often in the winter, between September and March." She gave a wry smile. "Party season. Dark nights."

Andy nodded. There was nothing like the cover of darkness to make someone throw caution to the wind.

"What sort of people attend?"

She stared at him coolly. "Men and women."

*Touché.*

"Let me rephrase that. You would be one of the women, yes?"

She nodded.

"How many other women would there be, approximately?"

"Thirty or forty of us. All in our teens or twenties."

It seemed that powerful men liked them young.

"Do you know the others?"

She shrugged. "Most, not all. Veronica's loyal. She always hires her regular girls first, as long as they know how to hold their knives and forks."

"But there are occasional additions?"

"New girls. Yes. They tend to be the teenagers."

Jake spoke for the first time since they'd entered. "Were you a teenager when you started with Mrs Lewis?"

Their hostess' green eyes swivelled towards him and Andy answered before she could.

"Ms Wasson's already explained she was married until recently."

She smiled at him, nodding. "I was, but my friend Hannah was a teenager when she started with Vero."

Jake pressed his point. "How old?"

It elicited a tut.

"Naughty, naughty, Sergeant. If you're trying to imply that Vero procures underage girls then you couldn't be more wrong. She insists on passports to prove we're eighteen. When Hannah first went to a party it was to supplement her student grant."

Andy took back the questioning. "So, when you fell on hard times more recently..."

"I contacted Vero looking for work and she helped me."

But Jake hadn't finished. "And the men? How many of them usually?"

"Ten to twenty. Vero likes a ratio of two girls to one." She gave a slow smile. "That way no-one feels lonely."

"Older men?"

She shrugged. "Mostly, but some of the guys have been in their twenties as well. It all depends."

"On their funds?"

"That and their kinks. Vero caters for some unusual tastes."

As Andy opened his mouth to ask another question she raised a finger, waving it from side to side.

"I'm not giving you any names, so don't ask. That's what they pay for. Discretion."

She glanced at the clock and jumped up. "We need to go. My youngest finishes soon. You can continue your questioning on the way."

They did, and by the time they'd reached the ground floor of the building they knew that Jenny Wasson had last seen Veronica Lewis fit and well at a party on Saturday, ten days before. All the sex-worker's queries on whether something had happened to the madam since were answered by silence, as were all the detective's requests for names and venues, so by the time they approached St Anselm's Primary School, the conversation seemed to have hit a dead end.

Wasson smiled at Andy in consolation.

"It's not that I *won't* tell you where the parties are held, it's that I don't know, and none of the other girls will either. We gather at one of our flats and Vero sends a car to collect us, then we're blindfolded when we get in. They're only removed when we're inside the party house. All I can tell you is that they're usually places in the country. A different place each time. One of them was huge, with a marble statue on the veranda and acres of grass. I should know, I tried to walk round it with a guest but we had to give up."

Andy switched off the engine and turned towards her. "Answer me this. Were there any street lights that you could see?"

"None. It was pitch black almost as soon as we walked away from the house."

He signalled Jake to pitch in. They only had minutes before the school bell went and their source disappeared to meet her son.

"Could you hear any cars or aircraft?"

Wasson shook her auburn mane.

"How long were you in the car going there?"

She smiled, revealing small white teeth. "That I can tell you. From east Belfast, that's where we gathered that night, it took just under two hours till we reached that particular house." She shrugged at Jake's raised eyebrow. "It was so long I checked my watch when we arrived. Also, it was in May so driving conditions were good, if that helps any?"

It gave them something at least. Andy became solemn suddenly.

"Can you think of anyone who would want to hurt Mrs Lewis? Girls, her son, customers?"

Wasson looked shocked and asked her earlier question again. "Has something happened to Vero? Tell me. *Please.*"

When he didn't respond she replied to his question in a

heavy voice. "None of the girls would ever hurt her, but some of the clients are really dodgy. Not ducking and diving dodgy, but sleazy and arrogant, like they're so rich they think they're entitled to do whatever they want. But you're barking up the wrong tree with her kid. Rupert loves his mum, and he would starve if it wasn't for Vero baling him out."

"He might be after her life insurance."

She shook her head firmly. "No. I *really* can't see it. They're the only family the other one has. He would never hurt her."

Just then a klaxon sounded, making Andy jump; it sounded like a nuclear bomb was about to drop! It made him nostalgic for his old school bell.

Wasson opened the door and went to get out, then she turned back, glancing towards Jake.

"You're not wrong you know, most of the men *are* scum, but well-connected scum that you really don't want to mess with. Be careful, you two. You're dealing with the top one percent."

Then she was gone, leaving Andy pondering their next move. His thoughts were interrupted by Jake leaping into the passenger seat and punching Rupert Lewis' address into the GPS.

\*\*\*\*

## 3 p.m.

Craig was still gazing out at the Lagan, thinking, when he heard Nicky answering the phone outside. Her words registered only as background murmuring so he returned to the questions pre-occupying his mind. Who was pressuring Sean Flanagan to investigate Veronica Lewis' disappearance? Who had the power to compel the PSNI's Chief Constable to do *anything,* except someone in government? But which government? Westminster or the

Stormont Assembly? And why would either care what had happened to some madam?

Covering up some politician's sexual misdemeanours was too simplistic an answer, and he honestly couldn't see Flanagan agreeing to it. The agenda had to be more significant than that to involve the police.

His questions would have to wait, not only because they needed information that they'd only begun to gather, but because Craig suddenly found himself being dragged unceremoniously out his office door. In the second that he took to register who was dragging him, not that there could ever have been much doubt, he had ripped his arm from Liam Cullen's hand and started to form a fist.

"You've got five seconds to tell me why you just manhandled me!" He ignored Nicky's elevated eyebrows as he went on. "And don't even get me started on why you couldn't have just *asked* me to follow you, instead of hauling me out like a resisting perp!"

Liam stared down at Craig's clenched hand and then at his increasingly irate face, then his gaze shifted reluctantly around the room as he registered everyone's astonishment at what he had just done. It was then that the penny dropped with a clang.

"Oh."

"Yes, oh! It's customary to knock the door and say, 'we need you out here', not grab me like we were in the middle of a scrum!"

Nicky raised a finger timorously. "I think that might have been my fault, sir."

A pair of angry eyes swivelled towards her. "How?"

"I took a call and panicked, so I shouted to Liam that I needed you urgently and-"

"He went into Incredible Hulk mode." Craig nodded tersely. "Leaving that aside for now, what was the call about?"

"It was from Hillsborough Castle, sir." The PA swallowed hard. "The First Minister's been shot."

# Chapter Three

**Hillsborough Castle, Hillsborough, County Down.
4 p.m.**

Northern Ireland's First Minister Peter McManus hadn't just been shot, he had a hole in the centre of his forehead the size of a fist, and as Craig stared down at a kneeling John Winter, the country's Head Pathologist, no-one else considered important enough by their self-aggrandised political orthodoxy to confirm that McManus had indeed been killed, he had the incongruous thought that whoever had done the deed had probably won shooting prizes in his youth, and that such accuracy said they were very well deserved.

No-one had seen the shot coming, and so far no-one could tell him where it had come from. All they did know was that McManus had been standing at the entrance of the historic castle, taking the afternoon sun and chatting to an advisor, when a soundless, unheralded missile had dropped him where he stood.

Craig broke the silence that existed within the bubble encompassing the body, John Winter and him, the chattering of his team taking early witness statements and the murmurings of civil servants and an unfortunate busload of Japanese tourists who had been touring the historical edifice, having faded into the background minutes before.

"Well?"

The pathologist glanced up at his best friend, shielding his bespectacled eyes from the sun with one hand; they didn't get much sunshine in Northern Ireland but, despite the evidence to the contrary lying at his feet, today was proving to be a perfect summer's day.

"Well what? You didn't need me here to tell you cause of death, Marc! The bullet went straight through his head!"

Craig shrugged. "Sorry about that. It wasn't my idea to drag you down here." He gestured vaguely towards the building's paned glass windows, hosting the crowd of the murmuring behind. "Someone in there insisted." His gesture shifted to the body. "Important man, McManus, even in death. Allegedly."

Winter's smile said that he shared the detective's cynicism about their political class. As he jumped to his feet an enormous shadow across the body told them that Liam was approaching, his bulk sufficient to block out the low-lying afternoon sun. Craig continued as if his deputy wasn't there.

"What *can* you tell me then?"

The pathologist stripped off his latex gloves as he spoke. "High powered rifle firing bullets of at least one hundred millimetres diameter. The defect's enormous, as you can see. I'm actually surprised that the man's still recognisable. Anyway, I'll know-"

Liam finished the sentence. "More after the P.M."

"Indeed. What I *can* tell you is that your shooter's a professional."

He pointed past the blue-lit police cars and across the wall that shielded the castle from common view, and with a waggle of his wrist implied additional distance.

"The angle of entry says it came from up there somewhere, but the size of the hole and the fact it went straight through means you're looking for something special. The bullet could be embedded anywhere around here so you'll really need to search. This wasn't just any old man with a normal gun."

His last few words fell on deaf ears as the detectives had already shifted, searching the building's frontage and driveway for the bullet that had got away. Craig beckoned some uniformed constables across.

"I need a fingertip search of the ground and walls." He pointed towards some nearby foliage. "And someone needs to get down in those bushes. Liam, cordon off the whole town."

As Hillsborough fancied itself as one of Northern Ireland's elite *villages*, even the words used to order such an invasion could be taken as offence.

A tall W.P.C. asked the pertinent question. "Searching for what, sir?"

Craig's reply was to nod to the pathologist. "John. Tell everyone what they need to know."

As Winter outlined the likely missile and the fact they might find it intact, flattened or embedded, Craig made his way back to the corpse, staring down at the hole in Peter McManus' forehead and the mild surprise in his still open bright-blue eyes. The breach was so large that he could see the driveway's gravel through it and he wondered if the MLA had seen the approaching missile about to end his life. No doubt Liam would perform some cabaret about the episode later for the entertainment of the squad, but for now their main task was to catch whoever had made the shot.

The detective turned the facts over in his mind. The bullet, gun and assassin might lead them somewhere, but the answer to *why* McManus had been targeted almost certainly lay in the dead man's life; the reason someone had wanted him gone badly enough to take out a professional hit had to be there.

Craig frowned as he ran through possible reasons; there were probably many but politics had to be top of the list. As well as being the First Minister, McManus had been the leader of the radical Independent Britain Party, and the IBP had pissed off a lot of lobbies in its short life, particularly with its stances on immigration and the environment. But while McManus' party manifesto might well turn out to be the answer it would be lazy to assume it, so what else had the First Minister got up to during his, relatively meteoric at forty, public rise? Or in his private life? Their job was to turn over every stone in their search for answers, regardless of how uncomfortable it made people or what nasty little creatures lurked beneath.

His thoughts were interrupted by Liam approaching again.

"We've started the search and the lads are taking quick and dirty statements. Anyone interesting we'll interview later in depth. But what about over there?" He pointed a chunky finger towards John's suggested direction for the bullet's origin. "We'll need to check out the shooting gallery."

Craig nodded. "Get Andy and Jake on that."

"They're still out interviewing on the kidnapping."

"OK. Aidan then, and ten uniforms. Ask Des for a quick trajectory analysis."

Doctor Des Marsham was Northern Ireland's Head of Forensics and he worked closely with John Winter at the province's Belfast-based Pathology Labs.

As Liam went in search of information Craig made a call to their base.

"Nicky? Has the C.C. been on?"

The PA stopped typing the email she'd been just about to send him, instead reading its contents aloud in an anxious tone. She wasn't sure why but the idea of the lead politician in the country getting shot in broad daylight agitated her, and she hadn't even voted for the man.

"I was just about to message you, sir. Chief Flanagan has organised for the Deputy First Minister, Gloria O'Rawe of The Whole Ireland Party ..." She stopped suddenly, confused. "Oh. No, well actually, she's the First Minister now, isn't she? Or will that be Roger Burke, Mister McManus' deputy in the IBP?"

Craig gave a sigh that moved her on.

"Well, anyway, he's arranged for her, the rest of the executive and the whole IBP to be sequestered temporarily, just for a few hours till he can upgrade their protection details. And he's asked for you to call and update him in an hour."

Craig nodded. Standard protocol. Secure the other politicians in case this was the start of an assassination spree. He doubted it somehow, if that had been the plan the assassin would just have waited till they could have killed the whole assembly at once, and their weapon of choice wouldn't have been a gun.

The idea brought him up short. Even though McManus was only one man, why *shoot* him? He could have been killed in far less obvious ways: poison, something that would mimic a heart attack, a road traffic incident, drowning; there were a million ways to kill a man that could have been dismissed as natural. The assassin could have achieved the same result and put nobody on their tail.

His thoughts were interrupted by Nicky's voice rising in volume.

"Did you hear what I said, sir? The Chief would like to meet you and Doctor Winter tomorrow morning at nine."

Craig shook his head to clear it. "Sorry. Yes, Nicky. That's all fine. I'll call him in an hour and we'll be there tomorrow. Just one thing. Who apart from the C.C. knows where the politicians have been sequestered?"

She was taken aback for a moment; she hadn't even thought of asking and she hated being caught on the hop. Craig moved on quickly, realising that she wouldn't know the answer, and that the question sounded suspicious even to him. He wasn't even sure why he'd asked it. It was unlikely that someone had killed McManus just to get the others sequestered so that they could take them out en masse, more likely that a weekend spent watching Homeland was making him paranoid.

"Don't worry, Nicky, I'll ask the C.C. when I call him. And could you push back the briefing to half-five, please. Thanks." He cut the call and made another one immediately. Sean Flanagan's PA came on the line.

"Hello, Donna. Is he there?"

Donna Scott smiled. She liked Craig. Mainly because he was handsome but also because he was polite; a rare combination in her experience.

"I'll put you through now, Chief Superintendent."

As Sean Flanagan's familiar warm boom vibrated the line, Craig took a deep breath for calm, knowing that if he revealed his paranoia he might scrap his credibility for ever more.

"Hello, Craig. Bad business."

"Yes, sir. We've almost completed the preliminary interviews and I've organised a fingertip search."

"For the-?" He cut himself short. "Hold on a minute."

Craig heard the door being opened, followed by some murmuring before Flanagan came back on the line.

"Call me back on this number."

As Craig scribbled it down the phone went dead. He redialled, registering the unmistakable buzz of a secure line as Flanagan started speaking again.

"OK, now we can talk. Your fingertip search is for-?"

"The bullet, sir. It was a through and through shot so Doctor Winter thinks it'll be embedded somewhere nearby."

Flanagan didn't try to hide his shock. "Bloody hell! Someone must really have hated the man."

Craig didn't comment, taking a different tack. "We've asked forensics for the likely trajectory and I've a D.C.I. and uniforms going to search along it now."

"What are you hoping to find? Casings?"

"Not sure yet. But I have to ask...why shoot him?"

Flanagan frowned at the obvious question. "Sorry, what?"

"Why bother shooting the First Minister, sir, when they could have killed him a million disguisable ways? Poisoning, an accident-"

The C.C. cut him off with another "Bloody hell" but he fell short of saying that Craig was wrong. "You think this is a political statement of some sort?"

"Or a distraction. They could have achieved their result in easier ways." Craig could hear his voice speeding up. "The truth is we don't know what it is yet, sir, but we'll find out. In the meantime, you've got the others sequestered?"

"Yes. Under armed guard. Just until we up their

protection details."

"Of course. It's just..."

"You think this might have been the plan all along? Get them together to take them all out at once?"

He'd obviously been watching the same box-set as him. Although he'd asked the question Craig surprised himself by shaking his head almost immediately.

"It's unlikely. If they'd wanted the whole assembly killed then they could just have planted a bomb during a major vote. But then again, maybe creating fear and uncertainty is part of their plan. It might just be an idea to split them across a few locations."

"I'll do that. If generating fear *is* part of their plan, it's worked short term." Flanagan paused, considering whether there was anything else that he needed to say. When he was certain there was nothing more he wound up. "I'll see you and Doctor Winter here at nine tomorrow. OK."

"Yes, sir."

Craig's line went dead just as John re-appeared.

"The C.C. wants to see us both tomorrow at nine."

The pathologist had taken off his black-wire glasses and was rubbing them on his sleeve. It was his proxy for annoyance or frustration and Craig wondered which one it was this time. He soon found out.

"Des sent me the trajectory analysis." He returned his spectacles to his thin nose and pulled out his smart-phone, tapping it to retrieve a map. The bullet's origin point was clear.

"Shit!"

"That's exactly what Liam said. It might make sense though, the bullet coming from the Travis. That place is as rough as hell."

The Travis Estate was one of Northern Ireland's roughest housing estates, of which there were many, mostly split along Republican and Loyalist lines. A sink hole that should have been demolished decades before, the Travis' walkways and stairwells were a breeding ground for vermin, including the human sort, and the poverty and disenfranchisement that had bred them was the perfect recruiting ground for violent gangs.

John was still pondering. "But actually, no, it doesn't make sense. Being the Travis I mean."

Craig frowned quizzically. "Why not?"

The pathologist was shocked that Craig didn't know and was tempted to bask in his superior knowledge for a moment, until the detective's warning glance moved him on.

"It doesn't make sense because the Travis is a *Loyalist* estate, and the IBP depends on that side of the community's vote. McManus was their man, so why would someone there kill him?"

A name sprang immediately to Craig's mind in answer. Tommy Hill, a Troubles Era Loyalist paramilitary and now petty criminal; also, a sometimes-useful source whose love/hate relationship with Liam had yielded useful information in the past. Tommy had been born and bred in an estate just like the Travis, the Demesne in east Belfast, and even though he lived in rural Templepatrick now to be close to his young granddaughter, his ears and his erstwhile gang were still close to Loyalism's ground roots.

Tommy might be able to help them understand why someone from his community would shoot their own man.

Craig dragged his thoughts back to the present.

"Can Des tell exactly where on the estate the shot came from?"

John nodded. "I gave Liam the name of the block and Aidan's there now with Armed Response."

Craig yelled for his deputy and Liam emerged from some undergrowth down the Castle's side.

"You called, M'Lud?"

"Any word from Aidan?"

"He's just got there. The Armed Response lads took a while to arrive." He ambled across to join them. "The block, Carson Tower, has fifteen floors. They're evacuating the residents then working their way up to the roof, clearing each floor as they go. The shooter must have taken the shot from there. It's the only place high enough."

"How far is it, John?"

"About a mile as the crow flies. A sniper rifle could have made the shot, but the shooter must still have taken a punt. He couldn't have seen McManus clearly through the intervening trees."

Craig sighed heavily. "None of our paramilitaries could have managed that accuracy. This guy's got to be ex-forces."

Liam was looking puzzled. "The thing is...none of this makes sense, boss. The Travis is Loyalist through and through and the IBP is a Unionist party, so why the hell would they shoot one of their own? I could see it if McManus had been a Republican, but..."

They all thought the same; a Unionist first minister shot from a Loyalist housing estate simply didn't fit. John raised a note of dissent.

"Just because someone shot from there doesn't mean they're *from* there. It would be the perfect cover for a Republican dissident, wouldn't it? Shoot McManus from a Loyalist estate so that the blame falls on them."

Liam's noisy snort saved Craig from stating the obvious.

"Are you kidding, Doc? Have you ever been on one of those estates? Everyone knows everyone and his wee brother. Within five seconds of a stranger walking through the gates he'd be spotted and the word would be out. Then it'd be all 'who's that?', and if the answer isn't 'our Jimmy's cousin' the stranger would find himself in deep shit."

Craig concurred. "Even more so if he was carrying a sniper rifle, John, even if it was well packed. Nice theory, but no prize. Sorry."

Just then a squeal pierced the air, and a small hand appeared from a rhododendron bush, with the rest of the W.P.C. they'd spoken to earlier following.

"I've found it! I've found it!"

Liam spoke for all three of them. "Leave it right where it

is! And don't touch it, there might be a print."

John was first into the shrubbery, followed by Liam and then Craig, who gasped in shock at the missile lying on the ground. Not at the bloody detritus of Peter McManus' cerebrum that still coated it, but at its sheer size.

"It's like an anti-tank missile, boss! It would have taken some gun to have fired that!"

"I need to know the type. Get Des on the line, John."

Within seconds the bearded forensic guru was waving at them on FaceTime and John was holding his phone above the armament. Des Marsham's long whistle confirmed what they thought.

"Holy God! That's a 12.7 by 108 millimetre. It's an anti-material round, usually used on buildings or vehicles. If it came from the Travis, there's only one weapon that could have sent it that far. A high-powered sniper rifle. Is there any of the victim's skull actually left?"

John held the phone at arm's length so that the scientist could see all three of them. "Not much."

Liam's phone buzzed suddenly and he put it on speaker. "Go ahead, Aidan. Everyone's here."

Aidan Hughes' normally loud voice whispered down the line. "We've thrown up a cordon, evacuated the block by tannoy, and now Armed Response are about to go floor to floor. Davy's checked out the known council tenants and there are no obvious candidates for our shooter in this block, but a handful of possibles on the estate. One-"

He was cut short by a loud crack that all of them recognised as a shot. As the call cut off suddenly the detectives raced for Liam's Ford, knowing that by the time they reached the estate the probable ensuing firefight would already be done. Liam hurtled down Main Street and Lisburn Street onto the Millvale Road with his lights and sirens flashing, while Craig took out his Glock and got ready to fire.

The shot never happened. As they screeched into the neglected estate, past the boarded up one-storey police station once manned by a PSNI liaison team but now abandoned in defeat, past the inelegantly worded murals inviting people to abuse Republican politicians and the acronyms celebrating a well-known gang that half of the residents wouldn't be literate enough to expand, they arrived at the row of liveried land rovers that ferried Armed Response and Tactical Support to and fro.

Aidan Hughes was perched on the running board at the back of one of them, his head hung low and rubbing a hand exhaustedly across the back of his neck. As Liam jerked the car to a halt Craig leapt out.

"What happened, Aidan? Anyone hurt?"

Hughes nodded slowly and raised his eyes. "One dead. Not ours."

As two armed officers manned the cordon around the building, preventing the disgruntled crowd of residents from moving away, a man that they all recognised appeared at Craig's elbow, wearing a solemn expression on his face.

"Your dead lad's called Billy Regent. Lives in number twenty-five Faulkner Tower."

Craig didn't hide his surprise. "What the heck are you doing here, Reggie? I thought that you just covered the Demesne."

Sergeant Reginald, 'Reggie', Boyd had been an officer for almost four decades and was more experienced than all of them. He'd chosen to put that experience to work as the resident officer on the Demesne Estate, fifteen miles away in east Belfast, the place where the teenage Tommy Hill had cut his terrorist teeth.

"I was here trying to show the residents how we dealt with the gangs on the Demesne, and to see if they'd let us reopen the branch station."

Liam scoffed. "Good luck with that."

Aidan Hughes cut in before Reggie snapped back.

"When the shooter's body was found I asked for Reggie's help. Reckoned if anyone could I.D. the lad he could, being as he knows every Loyalist in the country."

"A dubious honour indeed." The Donegal sergeant shook his head. "Billy Regent...it's hard to fathom, it really is. He wasn't a bad lad. Just a few minor transgressions when he was a kid: taking and driving away, shop lifting, that sort of thing."

Craig loosened his tie, the day's events starting to make it feel like it was strangling him. "Any gang involvement?"

Reggie made a face. "He flirted with the UK Ulster Force at one point, but he was never one of their big guns, if you'll excuse the pun-"

Liam cut in. "UKUF? That's Tommy's old crowd."

Craig nodded. He'd known Tommy would come in handy.

"Have a word with him, will you, Liam."

The veteran sergeant went on. "Regent joined the army instead of a Loyalist gang and went to fight in Iraq and Afghanistan. Two tours. He had trouble settling when he came back, I heard."

Craig frowned. An ex-military shooter. He'd been right. "The gun?"

Aidan beckoned to an energetic looking Armed Response officer. "You found the gun, didn't you, Jansen?"

The young man dropped his ever-raised rifle to his side and approached. "Yes, sir. Still on the roof if you fancy a look." He gestured towards the building. "It's an impressive piece of kit. Muzzle, scopes, the works. We found him lying beside it, brains all over the ground. Suicide. No question."

Craig's eyes widened. It couldn't have been suicide by rifle or they'd never have made the I.D.

Jansen shook his head, reading the detective's mind.

"Hand gun, Superintendent. The shooter must have brought it with him. Planned to kill himself all along and just waited till we arrived at the estate."

It was Craig's turn to take a seat. He perched on Liam's car bonnet.

"I don't suppose he left a note?"

"Not that I saw, sir. We'll be searching his flat next."

Craig shook his head. "Thanks, but no. You and your men take details from everyone inside the cordon then stand down. We'll follow up. Doctor Winter's team will take the body and we'll check Regent's home." He turned to Liam. "Liam, you and Aidan get those details across to Davy once we've viewed the scene, then organise a full search of Regent's apartment and any other linked abodes: parents, partner, whatever. I'll call John down now and then we'll head up to the roof to take a look."

It didn't take long to scan the tower's roof for the detritus of Billy Regent's day. A fit, still young man, in theory with everything still to live for, lay in one corner, with his charred head turned to one side and the brain matter that had held his every thought, hope and dream oozing beneath.

Craig raised his eyes to the summer sky trying to erase the image from his mind. After a long pause he returned to grim reality, and started to analyse the architecture of the scene. Against the roof's end wall sat a heavy rug, folded over several times and pushed into a corner, the corner from where Billy Regent had taken his marksman's shot. Craig pictured the young man kneeling on the blanket for elevation, focusing his sights and lining up every angle, before squeezing gently on the trigger for the bullet's release, incongruously gently for such a violent act.

The detective allowed his gaze to run along the ground towards the recumbent body, following the trail of the assassin's clear up: the removal of the shell casing and the dismantling of the rifle, until it lay there, half hidden in its black fabric bag. His gaze moved on, back to the bloodied body with its still held pistol, his eyes seeing exactly what Jansen had told them, but his logic screaming that something didn't fit.

But now wasn't the time to say what, or even to think further than this scene, and as the detective turned and left the roof silently, the man who could help quieten his noisy logic arrived. Within an hour Billy Regent's body was lying in a drawer in John Winter's freezing mortuary awaiting post-mortem, incongruously next door to Peter McManus, the man he'd dispatched earlier that day. Meanwhile Craig was back in his office watching the afternoon prepare to become evening, and wondering exactly what the two deaths meant.

# Chapter Four

**The Malone Road, Belfast. 4 p.m.**

Andy Angel wasn't sure what he'd expected a madam's son to look like but it certainly wasn't the young man who answered Veronica Lewis' elegant penthouse's front door. They'd headed to her home after trying the student address they had for Rupert Lewis, a run down, damp ridden room in a house in Belfast's Holyland district, and finding no-one but his flatmate there, nursing a hangover and grunting that he hadn't seen 'Rupe' since the day before.

Rupe suited the youth, as his impeccably modulated "Do come in, Officers. Would you like some refreshments?" suggested that mummy had spent a large proportion of her dubiously gotten gains sending him to a very good school. Add to the accent the youth's perfectly trimmed hipster beard, expensive jeans, and a leather jacket that could have added a new painting to Andy's collection of contemporary Irish art, and it was clear that Veronica Lewis' business had been going well.

The detectives took seats at either end of a velvet sofa, both shaking their heads in astonishment. Never one to wait on the order of rank, Jake decided to speak first.

"We'd like to ask you a few questions, Mister Lewis."

Lewis threw his long-limbed frame into a slouch chair and draped one leg over its arm. "Fire away."

It was said so cheerfully that the sergeant turned to look at his senior officer, wondering if Lewis had even been informed that his mother was missing, and deciding that if he hadn't then perhaps rank *did* matter and breaking bad news was one of its privileges. He sat back, staring Andy into action.

"Mister Lewis."

"Yes?"

"When was the last time you saw your mother?"

The young man wrinkled his tanned forehead. "Mum? Thursday afternoon I think. Why?"

Jake nodded inwardly. He *hadn't* been informed that she was missing and tomorrow Craig would roast whoever had failed to do their job, but for now, it fell to Andy to update the student. The D.C.I. swallowed hard. He hated this bit of the job. No-one was good at breaking bad news but some were better than most, so where the heck *was* Annette when you needed her?

"Is that usual? Not to see her for four days?"

The hipster shrugged. "Suppose so. She goes away a lot, so I just let myself in with my key. To do my washing mainly. Mum's cool with it."

Andy pressed the point. "Does she normally phone you when she's away?"

"Not always, no. Sometimes it's a week before I even know she's gone. She likes her little jaunts."

The words were accompanied by a chuckle that said he found such eccentricity endearing.

Now was probably the moment to inform him that his mother hadn't simply gone for a jaunt this time but had probably been kidnapped, yet something made the words die in Andy's throat. Jake understood why immediately; as soon as they told Rupert Lewis that his mother had been taken he would get distraught, and he for one wanted to know more about the jaunts' destinations before their duty of care to the boy became the first order of their day.

Andy read the sergeant's mind and nodded him on generously; he liked Jake despite his disrespect, and he'd been through a lot lately so he deserved a treat. As soon as he sank languidly into the velvet upholstery in a signal for Jake to proceed, the sergeant angled himself purposefully towards the son, who was still smiling about his mother's jaunts.

"How often does your mother go away?"

"Two or three times a month."

"Weekdays or weekends?"

"Mostly weekends, although sometimes she'll take off mid-week. Depends."

Jake's ears pricked up. "On what?"

"What time of the year it is. She goes away at weekends more during the summer. In winter, she tends to disappear mid-week."

It meant something, but what he couldn't yet tell. As the youth showed no sign of shutting down the questioning Jake decided to push his luck.

"Does she stay in Ireland, or..."

"Most of the time. The very odd time she'll go abroad, but mostly it's local or down south somewhere. I don't know where."

Suddenly Rupert Lewis sat forward, staring from one detective to another as if something was starting to dawn.

"Has something happened to my mother? Is that what you're trying to say?"

Jake squeezed in one last question before realisation hit. "What does your mother do for a living, Mister Lewis?"

The youth frowned as if the answer was obvious. "She's a design and beauty expert. Veronica Lewis Couture and Beauty. Surely you've heard of her?"

Andy's eyes widened as he suddenly placed their victim's name. He certainly *had* heard of Veronica Lewis designs, but if the clothes were as good as their appearances in the glossy magazines suggested then why did she need to be a madam? Either way it was clear that her son knew nothing about her side-line in sexual services and he was beginning to think that telling him wasn't a wise move. He took back the reins hastily.

"One more question and then we're finished, Mister Lewis. Does your mother own or rent any other properties? Residential or commercial?"

Lewis shook his head. "No. She works from home and sees people by appointment."

He rose and walked to an inner door that they hadn't noticed. Andy followed, reluctantly leaving his seat. He made a mental note to buy some velvet furniture; it was the most comfortable sofa he'd ever tried.

The door was opened to reveal a mirrored dressing table, a drawing board covered in dress sketches and a dressmaker's dummy stabbed with pins.

"Mum works in here."

The D.C.I. turned to leave.

"Thank you for answering our questions, Mister Lewis. We'll be in touch again."

He saw Jake's eyes widening and his mouth open to say something, but he grabbed the sergeant's arm, propelling him out the front door. They were at the car before Jake got his chance to speak.

"Why did you shut me up like that?"

Andy climbed in the driver's side, turning over the engine. "I'll tell you on the way."

As they headed back to Pilot Street he elaborated. "The boy obviously knows nothing about his mother's brothel, and saying 'your mum's a madam' then following it up with 'and we think she's been kidnapped' wasn't something I was prepared to do without speaking to the boss. What if Aidan was wrong and Lewis *isn't* a sex-worker? It would destroy the boy. You saw how much he loved her."

Jake wasn't persuaded. "And what happens if she turns up dead and we haven't even alerted him that she's gone? He'll be wrecked."

The D.C.I. considered for so long that they were parked in the C.C.U.'s garage before he answered.

"No. We did the right thing. We need to dig deeper into Lewis' background, find out where she's been going to on these jaunts and arrange searches of any premises we find. She may still be at one of them. Maybe she hasn't been kidnapped at all. Only when we've ruled out all the other possibilities do we destroy a son's image of his mum."

\*\*\*\*

## The C.C.U. 5 p.m.

Annette arrived back at the C.C.U. at the same time as the two detectives and Andy cornered her in the lift.

"So? Who reported Lewis missing?"

She stared at him coolly until he started the conversation again.

"Sorry. Hello, Annette. How was your afternoon? Did you manage to find out anything on the kidnapping?"

She nodded primly, shaking her new-baby bob up and down. "I did, thank you." Just then they arrived at the tenth floor and she stepped out. "And if you follow me I'll tell you at the same time as the chief."

She pushed through the glass double-doors and walked straight to Craig's office, collecting Liam and Aidan on the way, so that by the time Craig answered her soft knock and opened his door the pied piper detective inspector had four men trailing in her wake.

He took one look at the group and stepped out, waving them all to take a seat.

"OK. I *had* decided not to brief again as events had overtaken us today, but as John and I are with the C.C. first thing we might as well do a tidy up now."

He smiled hopefully at his PA for a coffee and when he had it in hand he waved Annette on.

"You were finding out exactly why this was labelled a kidnapping, Annette."

"Yes, sir. Well, I went to an office address that Ash found for Lewis-"

She was cut off by Andy raising a hand.

Craig sighed.

"Can't it wait, Andy?"

"It's just to say that according to the son Lewis doesn't have any properties but her apartment on the Malone Road."

"OK. We'll come back to that. Carry on, Annette."

Annette had used the break to check her notes. "The

address is definitely registered to her, and it's not rented. She owns an office at one thousand Lisburn Road."

Aidan nodded in confirmation. "I've just found out that's the address Vice has had for the past year."

Craig nodded sharply. "Fine, so Lewis has a place her son doesn't know about. Go on, Annette."

The D.I. folded her hands primly in her lap. "OK. Well. There were a couple of girls at the office, but it didn't look as if they actually worked there. The place was basically just a front desk with a computer and phone and a lounge behind, just somewhere people could have coffee. That's where the girls were when we walked in."

"Were they sex-workers?"

"If they were they were high-class ones. They wouldn't have looked out of place in the pages of Vogue. I didn't ask them outright, just took their details to follow up."

As Andy sat forward to cut in again, Craig stopped him with a shake of the head.

"Who reported Lewis missing, Annette?"

"It was a caretaker, Vincent Downs. He services the offices; there are six in the building. Most of them are hired by the hour, by visiting business people holding meetings. Veronica Lewis is the only permanent tenant. Anyway, Mister Downs puts out the rubbish, does odd jobs and looks after the place generally, and he noticed the door to her office open around eleven on Friday morning, so he went in and found the place in a mess. Papers across the floor, desk turned over. He knew Lewis had been in there earlier because he'd seen her enter at nine o'clock, so he panicked and phoned the police. Initially as a break-in, but he told the constable who attended that Lewis had been there at the time and was missing."

"She could have left before the break-in."

Annette nodded. "That's what I thought. Downs hadn't seen her for two hours, so she could easily have left and *then* someone broke in. They might even have been waiting for her to leave before they did."

Craig frowned, thinking. How had a reported break-in and a *possible* kidnapping worked its way up to the Chief Constable's ears?

Liam answered his unspoken question. "Someone must have had her name tagged, boss. That's the only way a simple break-in and possible missper could have worked its way up the chain."

Craig turned to their Vice detective. "Aidan? *Was* Veronica Lewis tagged for attention?"

The D.C.I. shook his blond head. "Not during my time, but I'll ask around."

Craig nodded. There was a lot of digging to be done all round.

"Let me know if you get something. Annette? Anything else?"

Her expression said she was tossing up whether the next thing she had was important enough to say.

"I'm not sure, sir...it's just...the caretaker had been there for ten years, and Lewis there for nine, and he seemed *convinced* that she was just running a fashion and beauty empire. I probed a bit and he said there were never any men in or out, just women, so I've got her computer coming over for Davy to check." She smiled in his direction. "Could we get her calls pulled as well?" This time Ash got the grin. "It could tell us a lot."

"Fine. Do that please, you two. Also, get any computers from her home. By the way, Davy, there'll be a list of names coming over from the Travis Estate soon, so I'll need you to run them for everything you can think of. OK, thanks for that, Annette."

He could see Andy and Jake both straining to speak and was tempted to change tack to the shooting just to wind them up. After a moment he relented.

"OK, you two obviously have something to say. Andy?"

"Well, it's just that the son doesn't know she's a madam."

Craig's eyes widened in horror. "Tell me that you didn't enlighten him. *Please.*"

"We didn't." The D.C.I. smirked an 'I told you so' at Jake. "But the boy supported the story the caretaker gave. That Veronica Lewis is a fashion designer. I thought her name was familiar; I saw some of her designs in last month's Vogue."

No-one queried why he was reading a woman's magazine, but it clearly wasn't for the fashion tips.

Andy was still speaking.

"Her son showed us her workroom in the apartment and said she saw clients there by appointment. There was a dressmaker's dummy and-"

Jake jumped in. "He also said that she often disappeared on jaunts. Weekdays during the winter and weekends in the summer time. He thought they were mostly here or in the south."

Craig frowned and Liam knew exactly what he was thinking.

"Summer's when the Assembly's on recess, boss."

"My thoughts exactly. And the rest of the time they're at Stormont, so they can't get away as easily for weekends."

Liam sniggered. "Convenient local weekday trysts for tired MLAs?"

"Probably. Andy, you said the son didn't know of Lewis owning any other properties."

Andy nodded. "He said there weren't any. He seemed convinced that she did everything out of the flat. I have to say, he seemed genuine, chief. He was a pleasant lad."

Jake confirmed the impression with a nod.

"OK, so we have a nice lad who thinks his mum's a designer-"

"Which she is, as well as whatever else."

Craig continued as if Andy hadn't spoken. "And who believes that the only property she owns is the apartment where she lives. What else does she spend her money on in his opinion?"

"Her jaunts away and him, I think. By his clothes and accent I'd say every other penny Lewis makes goes on the boy."

Craig considered for a moment.

"OK... so we have Veronica Lewis: dress designer, beauty consultant, high class madam and devoted mother. A multi-faceted woman, but apart from the risks attached to catering for the sexual needs of wealthy men she doesn't seem to have done anything dangerous. And nothing to make anyone dislike her, never mind kidnap or kill her. What did her employees say about her?"

Annette shook her head. "The two women in the office didn't admit anything-"

Jake interjected. "We interviewed two other women, both admitted escorts. They both liked Lewis, and said her son loved her. But they did say that she organised high-level parties for rich men where the ratio of women to men was two to one. One of them didn't think much of the customers and warned us to be careful investigating. She said they were the top one percent." He glanced at the analysts. "She also said the parties were held in the country and they were blind-folded all the way there, but one place had acres of grounds and a marble statue and it was around two hours' drive from east Belfast."

Craig glanced at Davy. "Can you do anything with that?"

The analyst gave the grin of a man who loved a challenge. "Leave it with me. The phone dump from her office might help us, especially if there are rural numbers on there."

Craig nodded his thanks. "OK, good. I see Kyle's gone AWOL again so we'll have to get his feedback tomorrow. For now, Liam's going to update you on the other little matter that took up our afternoon."

# Chapter Five

OK, so now she knew she was in Belfast, more familiar accents passing by the window as the day moved on, and more pertinently none of the faster, north-west voices that would have been heard if she'd been in the country's second city, Derry.

Central Belfast, judging by the traffic and the frequency of the buses rattling past the walls. But apart from the fact that meant she was so close to her own home and Rupert that the frustration made her want to cry, the knowledge advanced Veronica Lewis' escape cause not one single inch.

A few hours before she'd had the fear of being killed and anger at the man who she was certain had paid the goons sitting outside the door gnawing at her, but at least she'd had some tiny comfort that their desire for anonymity meant she might yet escape alive. Now, with the benefit of too many hours to think, she was sure that she was headed for the grave, and it was unlikely to be the marble headstoned one that she'd paid for through the Co-op.

The thought prompted a tear to start down her filthy cheek, its perfect mask of foundation and powder applied three days earlier replaced now by dust and grime mixed with blood from the split lip she'd received when she'd tried to run.

Her mind flew back to the moment of her capture; sitting at her desk completing the mundane tasks of running a business, two businesses to be accurate. One set of accounts had been for her design and beauty work, the respectable front that disguised her more lucrative enterprise. She needed the front, not because she was ashamed of how she earned enough to give her boy the small luxuries of life: a good education, designer clothes and a little nest-egg to help him when she'd gone, but because she wanted him to be able to hold up his head in front of his middle-class friends at university, friends whose parents held titles like Doctor and

Professor and who at one hint of her sexual services sideline would have side-lined Rupert as well.

The madam smiled to herself, lifting her cuffed hands to brush away the tear from her cheek. She'd achieved what she'd set out to do, give Rupert the start in life that he deserved, and she was proud of that, if not of what she'd had to do to make it real.

A sudden scraping outside made her jerk to attention, imagining that her captors were pushing back their chairs and readying to enter and finally end her life. A moment's vigilance yielded no second sign of her impending demise, and as her cell fell silent once more Lewis rested back against the wall again, her mind turning to other things.

She should never have taken his filthy money, she'd known it from the start. For years she'd run her business quietly and successfully, hosting small parties that catered for local men's sexual peccadillos, which truth be told rarely strayed beyond a bit of light S&M and the urge to be dominated while wearing a giant Babygro. It had kept her ticking along nicely, paying the mortgage and school fees, with her couture and beauty business providing the three holidays a year icing on the cake. Occasionally one of her regulars had brought along a tourist, a visiting businessman who'd got bored watching pay-per-view porn at their hotel, and she'd been happy to accommodate them. They'd been big tippers, and if anything, their demands had been even fewer than the locals', north and south. Until he'd come.

She shuddered violently as the man's image filled her mind. Good looking in a silver fox way, with close-cropped grey hair and blue eyes that shone out like search beams from his sixtyish, deeply tanned face. Every inch of the man had been muscle, rock hard and sculpted, as if he'd been hewn from a tree; only the inches that she'd imagined through his suit of course, the dubious honour of pleasuring him had been left to two of her best girls.

He'd been proof, as if she'd needed it at her age, that good looks do not an attractive man make, his coldness making her long for the soft dishevelment of the boys that she'd dated at school, their humour and kindness more than compensating for their inelegant clothes and unkempt hair.

But worse than his coldness, there'd been a callous cruelty behind the man's blue eyes. Something she didn't think she would have to worry about for long; he was a traveller, after all. An international businessman, in Belfast for only one week.

Their second encounter had taught her better. The Fox's sexual needs sated he'd come in search of her, backing her against a wall, speaking softly but insistently beneath his breath. Coaxing, cajoling, tempting her, not with sex but with something much more orgasmic, money; the promise of future wealth. It had cast her caution away, her common sense and animal instinct with it, and she'd agreed to his, what had seemed like then, simple proposition, although part of her had known from her first step backwards that he would never have accepted a no.

She was to continue to hold her parties, but more frequently and lavishly now and funded by him, seeking higher level customers amongst local politicians and Ireland's wealthy top one percent. That was to be her only task; he and his partners would do the rest. She'd never known his exact agenda but she'd sensed it was the beginning of her end as soon as they'd signed on the metaphoric line. But whatever end game The Fox had planned for her customers Veronica Lewis knew that hers would be over long before then.

\*\*\*\*

**The Operating Theatres, St Mary's HealthCare Trust. Tuesday, 7 a.m.**

Natalie Winter née Ingrams felt like hell, whatever that was supposed to feel like. She'd spent four hours the night before listening to her husband banging on about a hole in the First Minister's forehead, then annoying her by swearing her to secrecy about it at frequent intervals. As if she had nothing better to do than bore her theatre team with the detail of how Peter McManus' lights had been snuffed out!

It always irritated her when John did his secret squirrel act but last night's performance had kept them up till two, irritating her even more than usual and exhausting her, and as Natalie wasn't much given to introspection she was disinclined to blame any part of that outcome on herself.

The sudden clang of a steel kidney dish hitting the tiled floor made the surgeon swing round so fast that the nurse who'd dropped it jumped back with a "Holy God."

Natalie's response was caustic. "Not yet, but I'm expecting a promotion soon. Try not to wreck the place, can-"

The gimlet gaze of the theatre sister halted her mid-word.

"I'll thank you not to tell my nurses what to do, Ms Ingrams, unless you'd like your junior doctors to experience the same from me."

Natalie's planned acid retort was prevented by an unheralded light-headedness that made her reach for the nearest surface with a small, gloved hand. She was going to kill John! Keeping her up late and exhausting her when she had to operate all day. It was a threat that she would never carry out because life would get in the way.

\*\*\*\*

Liam was not a happy bunny, although were-rabbit would probably have been a better description based on his nature and size. Either way, he was pissed off at Craig. He'd been looking forward to a leisurely start to his day with a nine o'clock breakfast at The James Bar, timing his casual dander into the squad-room for fifteen minutes before he predicted the boss would return from his confab with the C.C.

Instead he'd been woken at seven by his mobile, while Danni was still dozing, warm and curvy beside him, and the fiends, as he liked to call his two young children, were still angelic looking, something they only ever managed to achieve while asleep.

His Pavlovian answering of the offending smart-phone was something that would probably take twenty years of retirement and a trip to his grave to halt, as it would his standard "Who's this?" response, something which his ladylike spouse had been trying to cure him of since he'd first invited her out on a date.

Too late, the words were out, followed by "at this unholy hour". All of which Craig ignored because he had information to impart.

"Haul ass and join me at Headquarters. John and I will be there just after eight for a pre-meet before we brief the C.C."

Liam shook his head and then realised that Craig couldn't see the joy that was his puffy morning countenance.

"You don't need me. The C.C. just wants you two."

That decided, he went to lie down again. Craig must have been psychic because his next words said that he could tell.

"Don't lie down and go back to sleep. He may not want you there but I do. Three heads are better than two."

Craig glanced at his watch, and then past it at his slumbering girlfriend, Katy, his mind shifting randomly through thoughts of the sex that he didn't have time for, to a far more practical one that was prompted by her right arm dangling over the side of the bed. His bed was too small, he needed a bigger one. He'd just muttered "Super King" when Liam countered with a bid of his own.

"How about I just meet you there at nine, then. I can come in and the Chief can ask questions of all three of us."

But Craig had already made up his mind, partly out of a genuine desire to hear Liam's input, and partly from the same adolescent devilment that makes boys shave off one of their sleeping friend's eyebrows for a joke.

"If we're up, you're up. Get your ass in gear."

As the phone went down Katy moved sinuously in her sleep, making Craig think that perhaps he did have the time after all.

\*\*\*\*

## The C.C.U. 9 a.m.

"So what's the latest on Dudaev, then?"

The question was asked casually, as if the questioner was only vaguely interested in the reply and the lack of one wouldn't bother him one whit. In truth Davy wanted to shake the information out of his junior, Ash not having rushed up to him the day before full of news about New York and the CIA taskforce making him almost blow his legendary cool.

Ash smiled inwardly and slid further down at his desk, making Nicky wonder if it was even possible for him to see his computer screen from where he was. The junior analyst decided to milk the situation.

"What was that you said, Davy?"

It made even Nicky want to pound him on his red, white and blue head. As a substitute for such violence she repeated Davy's question loudly, thwarting the international traveller's wind-up attempt. Other than saying he was deaf from his flight Ash had no further excuse not to reply, so he answered the question with what he'd told Craig the day before.

"His trips since Amsterdam have all been in Southern Europe, the most recent sighting was in Greece. So-"

Davy cut him off. "His destination is probably in the north somewhere. Scandinavia, Germany, The Baltic States; *they* must be a strong possibility because Dudaev's Chechen and they're ex-commun-"

Ash cut him off huffily, annoyed that he'd worked things

out so fast. The international stuff was his baby and he wasn't sharing it.

"We've agents in every country, so he won't be able to disappear."

Nicky chimed in. "Except that he has, hasn't he?"

Davy was still on the fact Ash had said 'we've'.

"Who the hell's *we*? Have you joined the s...spook brigade now?"

The junior analyst had the decency to blush. "You know who I mean! MI6 and the CIA."

"So. *Not* you then."

He made up his mind to get Davy's coffee order wrong for the next week, but his boss was already on to other things.

"Schengen's going to hammer them finding him, you know."

"We've already thought of that."

*Of course you have.*

"We've got facial recognition software working at all ports, border posts and airports."

Davy poured scorn on that fast. "He could just walk into another European country through some wood! You need it on traffic cams, trains, buses and the rest. Dudaev could get from Bulgaria to Finland and never trigger any of your checks."

The debate was prevented from getting more fractious by a ping on one of Davy's PCs. He broke off to read the message and then turned back.

"Veronica Lewis' phone logs are through."

Nicky nodded. "And her computers have just arrived downstairs. Des says, can you call him when you've had a look."

It was the signal for an hour of peace.

\*\*\*\*

## The Merchant Hotel, Belfast.

It was all going to plan. The First Minister was dead and soon Lewis would be back in place, the fear of God put into her, and even more importantly the fear of him. The Fox removed a cigarette from his pocket and tapped the stiff white column languidly against the coffee table's edge. He resented the law that prevented him lighting it but couldn't risk any unwanted attention till his job was done, his satisfaction from the panic the action provoked in nearby staff having to suffice for the moment, as his mind returned to his earlier thoughts.

The madam had never liked their arrangement, going along with it grudgingly from the start. And that had been OK. Sort of. He didn't need people to like him to do their job, few ever had, and despite all her moaning she had done what was required of her, and when it hadn't been sufficient Peter McManus had paid the price.

No-one could say that the politician hadn't been warned. He'd had warnings of what would happen if he didn't cooperate and, typical arrogant official, had chosen to ignore them all. Political deadlines might be elastic, Minister McManus, but in his world it was three strikes and you were out, so there was no point anyone complaining if they ended up dead.

But The Fox was also a realist. You might have been able to leave a trail of corpses forty years ago without being caught quickly, but nowadays Northern Ireland adhered to the strict rule of law. Already some thick-set plod would be investigating McManus' death, and if he'd been forced to kill Lewis as well they might have doubled their efforts and that was a headache that he didn't need.

He glanced at the espresso being set down in front of him and sent the waiter away with a nod, gazing languidly at his surroundings as he did. The velvet backed chairs and quiet elegance of the hotel's cocktail bar reminded him of Vienna; a timeless, dignified oasis in an over-heated world. He scanned a passing young waitress casually, bemoaning the fact that he didn't have the time before his flight to pursue his desire, it brought his thoughts reluctantly back to Veronica Lewis, and he speculated on ways to further subdue her should the need arise.

She was a woman and women were easily frightened, so the kidnapping might have done the trick, but the odd heroic member of her sex was still capable of causing an almighty fuck-up, so it might require more than fear for her own safety to guarantee the continued cooperation of the whore. The idea came to him gradually, growing until it had legs. If Madam Lewis showed the slightest hint of reluctance to run future parties exactly as he directed then she would lose her only child.

\*\*\*\*

### Police Headquarters. 9.30 a.m.

"Aye, well, that was a big fat heap of nothing!"

Craig stifled a laugh as they clattered down the stairs to the car park, John not bothering to stifle his at all.

"Don't you sugar coat it, Liam! Give us all you've got."

"You."

Liam stopped dead on the landing, his tone the verbal equivalent of putting his hands on his hips.

*"You."*

One hand was off the hip and pointing at Craig.

"Woke me up at seven this morning and dragged me down here, for a five minute How's Your Father that we could have put in an email!"

Craig stopped stifling and laughed. "Do you know what How's Your Father means?"

Liam shrugged. "A chat?"

Craig started down the next flight with a grin. "It means a quickie. You've just accused me of dragging you out of bed to have sex with the Chief Con."

The D.C.I.'s eyes widened and he set off in pursuit. "You've just made that up!"

John's shaking head said otherwise.

"Ach. Well, that's not what I meant and you both know it!" They stepped out into the fresh air. "The point is you didn't need me here, and he didn't need to see you two either. He'd already had a briefing on the shooting from Stormont House!"

Craig beeped open his Audi. "Maybe he just wanted company."

"Aye, and maybe you didn't want me snug in my pit while you provided it." Liam tried for a hurt look. "That's cruel and unusual punishment, boss. Danni was really upset that I had to leave."

Craig scoffed. "Both your wives were probably glad to get the bed to themselves for a few hours."

John shook his head as he climbed into the passenger seat. "Natalie was already at work, actually. But to be honest, even if she hadn't been I'd have been glad to leave. She was in a hell of a snit this morning. Blamed me for it too. She said I'd kept her up half the night talking about McManus' death!"

Craig swallowed his *'as if'* and started the engine. "Liam, follow us to the lab. We're going to look at the bodies."

*"Before breakfast?"*

It received the grunt it deserved and twenty minutes later they were staring down at the square-jawed face of Peter McManus, his forehead neatly covered by a drape.

"Let's see the wound, please, John."

The pathologist obliged, whipping off the cloth with the flair of a matador. Liam rolled his eyes and gave a noisy yawn.

"It isn't any different to yesterday, so what are we looking for?"

Lack of respect aside Craig had to admit that he had a point. He moved along to McManus' next door neighbour and waited for the pathologist to withdraw his shroud. It revealed the more youthful face of William H Regent, Billy to his mates, once Corporal Regent of the Mercette Regiment.

"How old was he, John?"

"Thirty-six in April."

"It was definitely suicide?"

The pathologist looked surprised to be asked. "Well, there's gunshot residue on his hand, a hole in his right temple, and a bullet that matches the handgun found by his side."

Liam had stopped yawning and started thinking a few seconds before. It produced a question that even Craig had to admire.

"How can you be sure the GSR came from the handgun, Doc? I mean, couldn't it already have been there from the rifle?"

It caught John on the hop but he resisted blustering out a defence, turning instead to a nearby stool to sit down. Craig shifted his eyes from the body to his friend, watching as the wrinkles on John's forehead did an elastic dance while he thought. Finally, Liam got his answer.

"The answer is that you're right, Liam, I *can't* be sure. So, well asked. I can speculate that the rifle's barrel is so long there was unlikely to be substantial GSR on Regent's hands from the shot that killed McManus, so it must have come from the pistol, but until we do tests on both I can't be certain at all." He stared at the D.C.I., narrowing his eyes inquisitively. "What's your thinking here?"

Liam perched on a nearby bench, leaving Craig to take the only other stool in the room.

"OK ... Well, let's say, just for the sake of an argument, that Billy here." The D.C.I. gestured casually at the corpse, "Took the big shot. He killed McManus, probably asked to do it by someone else, unless we find out that he harboured a secret loathing for the man. But then, when the job was done and he was packing up to go, and probably to collect his payment-"

Craig cut in. "So, you're saying Regent was paid to hit McManus?" It was said in a 'you're probably right' tone.

Liam shrugged. "To be decided, depending on what else we find out. But right now, let's say it *was* a paid hit. The rifle was only half packed away when we got there, but if Regent was a marksman and a soldier he'd have taken proper care of his equipment, so why shoot himself in the head before everything was neatly back in its box?"

John raised an eyebrow. "You're basing your theory on the fact that Regent was untidy?"

Craig intervened, halting Liam's impending retort. "Murder cases *have* hinged on less, John."

It was the pathologist's turn to shrug.

Liam picked up his theory with renewed vigour.

"But if whoever had hired Regent to kill McManus had wanted to tie up loose ends, he might have followed Billy up to the roof and taken him out with the handgun, then left it behind to make us think that Billy'd committed suicide."

Craig followed the thought through. "And even if the GSR *does* match the handgun, there's no proof someone didn't force Regent to hold it and shoot himself. Everyone was so busy clearing the tower they might have missed someone getting on and off the roof, maybe via the fire escape." He turned quickly to his deputy. "Is there one in that building?"

"Two. I saw them when I walked round. Although..." Liam shook his head. "Allowing that a second shooter *might* have managed to kill Billy and get down off the roof somehow, Hughesy had already chucked a cordon round Carson and its evacuees before we arrived. Remember? All the residents and the cops were standing inside it when we got there."

John was warming to Liam's scenario now. "So, you're saying that this second man went up to the roof after McManus had been shot, to kill Regent."

Craig nodded in confirmation but Liam had another idea.

"Or he was with Regent the whole time, and shot him when he wasn't expecting it. *After* McManus had been taken out."

"Wouldn't the locals have noticed a stranger?"

"Might have, but if he'd been with Billy the whole time he might've been given a pass."

Craig rose from his stool. "But someone might remember seeing him, either with Billy or hanging around on his own afterwards, inside the cordon. Good catch, Liam. OK, it's time for a door-to-door on the Travis. Tell Andy and Jake to get down there with some uniforms, plus give Reggie the heads up on everything. He needs to keep his ear to the ground."

Liam followed him to the exit with a reminder. "What about Spence doing something? That skiver always gets off light."

Craig tugged open the door. "He won't this time. I want him with us when we meet with Tommy. Text him the address and say that you and I are heading out there now." He turned back just in time to see John covering up the bodies. "John, can you chase up those GSR possibilities with Des, and get the rest of the details by this afternoon? I'm calling a briefing at three o'clock."

It cheered the pathologist up instantly. The only daytime outings he usually got were to inspect an unusual death at a scene, so a C.C.U. briefing with its promise of a pint at The James afterwards would be a welcome buffer for an evening at home that he was sure would see him being blamed for something new.

\*\*\*\*

## Templepatrick Village, Country Antrim.

Craig's tolerance of his team members' lateness had always been limited, but if the officer in question had the good sense to look apologetic when they eventually rolled up he would usually bite his tongue. Kyle Spence had no such sense, or sense of anything but his own importance it seemed, as his leisurely three goes at reversing into a parking space to ensure his new Alpha's paintwork didn't get scratched and the following walk around the vehicle proved. Liam could feel his lips widen into a grin as he saw Craig's always close-to-the-surface temper come to the boil.

"Inspector Spence! Get over here now!"

Craig stared pointedly at his watch, holding his wrist up and out in a way that made him despise himself instantly, reminding him as it did of a particularly nit-picking master he and John had once had at school. But Kyle Spence either didn't have the wit to know when to behave, or else he had so much wit that he'd spotted Craig's self-disgust instantly and decided to wind him up. Liam was torn trying to decide for a moment, but when he spotted the twinkle in the erstwhile Intelligence Officer's eyes he plumped for the second option and gave the D.I. a grudging tick for having the balls.

The ex-spook dandered across to the waiting detectives as if he had all the time in the world, his demeanour implying that sniffing a flower or two in the pretty cul-de-sac might even come next.

"Sorry, sir, am I late for something?"

"Your own funeral" was muttered beneath Liam's breath.

Craig's tanned skin darkened and what happened next would go down in the annals of C.C.U. history, not for the violence of it, Craig was too controlled for that, but for the sheer 'fuck you' blow that it delivered right between Kyle Spence's eyes.

"Get back in your car and down to the Travis, Inspector. D.C.I. Hughes has work for you on door-to-door."

As Spence's jaw dropped Liam could see his mind racing, as he tried to work out what to say to dig himself out of his hole. The last thing he fancied was a morning spent interviewing the public; knocking on doors that would either refuse to open, or worse, *would* open but then thirty seconds later be slammed in his face. Not to mention the risk of some wee thug scratching his new car or nicking his tyres.

As the other men watched, Kyle Spence composed his face in a mask of contrition so genuine looking that even though Liam knew the D.I. was a lying toe-rag he couldn't be certain wasn't real. Craig however had known Spence since university, and had seen every shade of the deception that had made him such an effective Intelligence Officer employed to full effect, whether lying to some poor girlfriend he was two-timing, or to a tutor about to mark him down for his assignment being late.

He had learnt the 'tells' that distinguished Kyle's lies from his truths and they were clearly visible to him now, but he let the D.I. contort his face anyway, his amusement rising in anticipation of the bullshit they were about to be treated to.

"I'm very sorry, Super."

*Using his rank? Tut tut, Kyle, that's amateur hour. Even for a sycophant.*

"It's just, when Liam gave me the message that we were meeting Tommy Hill, I assumed that he was still living in east Belfast. It was only when I arrived there that I found out he lived all the way out here, and that's why I was late."

Craig was starting to enjoy himself and he rested back on his Audi's bonnet and folded his arms, urging Spence on with. "And your parking?"

Liam almost laughed at his earnest tone, contradicting as it did Craig's incredulously raised brows.

Spence glanced back at his car and composed his face sorrowfully. Liam was really hoping that he'd cry, just to add the finishing touch.

"I know it took me a long time, but, you see..." Pause for effect. "The car was my great aunt's legacy to me. You'll remember that my grandmother died in March, during the jihadi case. Well, her sister died last week and left me some money. I bought the Alpha with it, so it's a sort of memorial to her, and I would hate for it to get marked, out of respect."

Liam shook his head in disbelief as Craig nodded sympathetically.

"Ah, yes. Which grandmother was that again? Your father's or mother's mother?"

What Kyle Spence possessed in chutzpah and imagination he sadly lacked in his power of recall, something that Craig was depending upon.

"My father's. She was ninety-one."

"And your great aunt's name?"

"Edna."

Instead of answering Craig pulled out his phone and after some leisurely tapping he turned the screen towards Liam, before then showing it to Kyle. The obituary of Edna May Spence, who had indeed died, but in nineteen-ninety, was emblazoned in bold on his screen.

He pocketed the smart-phone and shook his head.

"Nice try, Inspector, but no cigar. And if you try even harder you'll recall me going to that great aunt's funeral with you when we were sharing a flat. Report to D.C.I. Hughes on the Travis immediately and find some other dead relative to lie about next time."

Then he was through Tommy Hill's front gate with Liam following, praying that every door Spence knocked on that morning had an authority figure hater lurking behind.

If Kyle Spence was unamused they'd cheered up Tommy's day immensely. As Craig went to knock his front door he noticed the ex-paramilitary standing, arms folded, at his living room window, with as close as it ever got to a gleeful expression on his craggy face. Hill answered Craig's knock quickly, waving the detectives in and then standing in his pathway for a moment, giving Kyle Spence a big thumbs-up. As he closed the door behind him Hill snorted.

"Best entertainment I've hud in ages. An' after he parked his car so neatly an' awl."

He pushed past Liam and flopped into a well-worn

recliner, pressing the button to start the whirring that said it was extending itself. Craig had had enough of bravado performances for one day so he took the nearest chair without invitation, nodding Liam to do the same.

"We need to ask you some questions, Tommy."

Hill's response was to pull up both of his trouser legs, making Liam snort.

"Either you've taken up Morris Dancing, or you're showing us you're not wearing a tag."

As Tommy's natural state was to be on bail or probation for some offence or another, his ankle tag had been a permanent fixture for over a year.

"First prize! Give thon man a Teddy Bear. I'm tag-free, ye big ghost. Aff probation an' ye can't touch me."

Ghost had been Hill's nickname for Liam for decades, based on the detective's sandy-haired pallor. Sometimes the appellation was spat out, but today it almost sounded fond.

Craig raised an eyebrow. "Give him time, Tommy. He'll think of something to charge you with."

It made Hill jerk forward in his chair and repeat the whirring noise, this time to straighten the recliner up.

"I've dun nathin'! Ye pigs, yer awl the same. Give an old lag a bad name, ye wud. Yer jest lukkin' tee-"

Liam waved him down. "Aye, aye, you're a very misunderstood man, Tommy. We know. But you might want to hear us out. There could be some folding money in it for you."

Craig had agreed a maximum fee of fifty pounds for information, starting at twenty and working up depending on what Tommy knew.

Hill's eyes narrowed suspiciously. "Fer wat?"

"Information about the Travis Estate."

As the ex-paramilitary's body language softened, Craig knew that they'd caught his interest. Tommy had been born and bred on the Demesne, and he'd run one of Loyalism's most fearsome gangs long before The Troubles, soon spotting the opportunities for mayhem and profit that the political situation brought. In the late sixties, he'd cannily changed his gang's title from The Demons, a play on the Demesne's name, to the UKUF, and it had become one of the country's most feared paramilitary groups for the next three decades, making money from organised crime, and killing Catholics and police officers whenever it got the chance.

Neither detective had any doubt that the grey-haired grandfather in front of them would have put them both in their graves decades before if he could have done so. Now Tommy saw his knowledge of Loyalism as a financial opportunity, and Craig knew which of the two life approaches he preferred.

They watched as Tommy's creviced face shifted expressions from cynicism to calculation to smugness in a flash. The last one verbalised itself.

*"So ye need wat I knaw, dee ye?"*

Liam sighed. Pandering to terrorists was low on his list of preferred activities, but needs must.

"Yes, Tommy. We need something you *might* know."

The might became the insult Liam had calculated it would.

"*Might? Might!* Wadda ye mean, might? There's no wan knaws more abyte ar community thon me."

Mission accomplished. It was almost too easy to wind Tommy up nowadays; he was getting old.

"Prove it. Tell us about Billy Regent. What do you know about him?"

Tommy opened his mouth to answer and then thought again, shaking his crew-cutted head from side to side.

"Aw, naw... I'm nat fallin' fer that wan. How much?"

Liam shrugged. "Depends on what you tell us. Twenty for basic info, thirty for advanced."

"That means ye've gat fifty quid in yer packet, so I'll hav the lat."

Craig gave a grudging smile at his street smarts. "We'll see, Tommy. First the information. What do you know about Billy Regent?"

Hill rested back with his hands folded as if he was about to read them a story and all that was missing was the book. A smile touched his thin lips.

"Wee Billy Regent. I knew his ma, Eileen, ye knaw." His smirk said it had been in the biblical sense. "Man, she wus a lukker. Long blonde hair, an' legs right ap to her-"

Craig cut him off impatiently. "Her son."

"Ach, dun't rush me. I'm gittin' there. Aye, well, Billy. He was a cheeky wee skitter when he was young. Intee everythin'. He used tee hang around us wantin' tee play wi' ar guns."

An embryonic marksman even then.

"Did you let him?"

Hill shrugged. "Nye an' then." He added primly. "Wi' the bullets out, like."

Liam scoffed. "How very child protection of you."

The sarcasm passed Tommy by completely.

"Aye, well, we wurn't thugs, ye knaw."

Craig's glance at his deputy said not to take the piss, no matter how tempting it might be. He moved to the edge of his chair, urging Tommy on.

"So, was Billy ever involved in anything? With any gangs?"

Tommy shook his head immediately. "His ma wud huv red him the riot act. Eileen Regent wus wild strict. Naw, awl Billy wanted tee do wus join the army. Squaddie Regent we used tee call him when he wus a kid. We used tee let him practice his drills wi' a gun." An impressed look covered his face. "He cud strip an AK-47 by the time he wus ten. Sum goin'."

"His mother must have been so proud."

Craig silenced Liam's sarcasm with a glance and nodded him to hand over twenty pounds. It disappeared into Hill's pocket quicker than a Hobbit's ring.

"OK. What about as Billy got older?"

When Tommy's hooded eyes narrowed suddenly Liam

knew that he'd sussed them out.

"This is abyte McManus gettin' topped yesterday, isn't it? Ye think Billy Boy hud sumthin' tee dee wi' it!"

Liam's face gave him away and Hill lurched forward in his chair.

"I'm right! I am! Fuck me! Billy Regent drapped the big man!"

His grin of pleasure was soon replaced by a frown.

"Naw. Hang on a minute... why'd Billy kill McManus? He wus wan af us! Nye, if he'd topped thon bitch O'Rawe from Whole Ireland, I cud understand it, but McManus..." He shook his bullet-like head. "Naw. That makes no sense. No sense at awl."

Liam spotted something behind the words and jumped on it. "Why not, Tommy? Was McManus involved in paramilitarism?"

Hill shot him a 'that'll cost you more than fifty quid' look and sat back. Craig decided it was time to regroup.

"OK, Tommy. So, Billy had always wanted to be a soldier and we know that he became one. Two tours in Iraq and Afghanistan with the British Army. But what happened to him after he came out? Do you know?"

The grandfather considered whether the answer came under the fifty-pound mark and decided that it did.

"He wus in a reel bad way. Shell shack they used to call it."

Liam translated. "PTSD."

Craig nodded. Billy Regent had had post-traumatic stress disorder. No doubt they'd find confirmation of it once they got hold of his medical report.

Tommy shrugged. "Whatever ye call it, Billy hud it bad. Used tee wander around the Travis awl night I heered, howling at the moon, like."

Liam raised an eyebrow. "Really?"

It earned him a scathing snort.

"Naw, nat really, ye dickhead. He wusn't a bloody werewolf! He jest used tee get drunk an' shout a lat, an' he wus alays gettin' in fights."

It would be easy enough to check.

Craig pushed him further.

"How do you know all of this, Tommy? You've never lived on the Travis, I checked, and you haven't lived on the Demesne for years."

Tommy's only answer was a tap of his nose.

"That means his old gang still live there and they tell him everything."

Hill snarled a confirmation. "They'd bloody better! They knaw better than tee cross me."

Apparently there was no such thing as an ex-boss. There might be snow on Tommy's roof but the murderous instincts that had seen him sent down for two decades were obviously still there, as was the fear he engendered in his erstwhile followers. Craig was thankful that the man had a granddaughter to stay out of prison for now, or they might be looking at a fresh round of bodies piling up.

He asked another question to break the chill.

"OK, so Billy wasn't well when he first left the army. How had he been recently?"

As soon as the words were out Craig could have kicked himself. Tommy jumped on his 'had' like a piranha on raw flesh.

"Billy's dead, isn't he! Ye bastards topped him fer shootin' McManus!"

Craig knew it was time to take back control; they'd played Tommy softly because they'd needed what he knew, but if they gave him any more rope the skilled manipulator would use it to strangle them with.

He rose to his feet and loomed over the recliner, a shake of his head telling Liam not to do the same. When he spoke next his voice had an edge.

"Listen to me carefully, Tommy. You're right that Billy Regent is dead, but we most certainly didn't shoot him, and if you spread that dis-information before we've informed his next of kin and established the facts you'll do some major harm."

Tommy's triumphant expression disappeared and when he spoke again it was in a surprisingly soft voice.

"Eileen's at twenty-five Faulkner. Billy wus her only kid. His da wus killed years back an' far as I knaw she never remarried. Proper sorta wife, that girl."

His reverence suggested that their youthful dalliance had left quite an impact.

Craig sat back down and repeated his instruction.

"It's very important that you don't say anything, Tommy, and I'm willing to make sure that you don't."

Hill's eyes widened. "Ye're lakkin' me ap?"

Liam smiled, knowing the ambiguity was exactly what Craig had been aiming for.

The detective shook his head slowly. "Not unless I have to, Tommy, but I will if you mess us around in any way. Now, tell us everything you know about Billy's known associates and anything else he'd got up to since he'd left the army, for fifty quid. There'll be more in it for you if you put out your feelers and find us something useful, including what that look of yours hinted at about Peter McManus' extracurricular activities."

\*\*\*\*

**Belfast City Centre.**

The rain pelting against her small cell's high window was adding to Veronica Lewis' gloom. Not that it should make much difference what kind of day you died on; sunshine might make you feel that you were being cheated out of a nice one, and rain could make you think of the worms going in and out when they put you in the ground. But for some reason she'd long ago decided, in that place where people harbour their secret speculations about what their last moment on earth might be like and picture the people who've offended them in some way crying guiltily by their grave, that she would prefer to die when it was snowing. She wasn't sure why, but probably something to do with the angels she'd made in the cold, white powder as a child.

So, departing this life while it was raining wasn't on her agenda, but she guessed that she'd just have to go with it because it was the fifth day that her kidnappers had held her and she was certain the end was coming soon.

As if to prove how right she was there was a sudden clinking outside the door; the unmistakable sound of someone shuffling keys. Perspiration sprang to the madam's upper lip and forehead and a thin trickle of the liquid began to work its way down her back. The trickle became a stream when the searched-for key was finally inserted in the lock, and as it turned slowly and the door opened inwards a wave of nausea hit Lewis, making her turn her head politely so that her vomit didn't stain the entrant's shoes. That was the nuns for you; even when somebody's coming to kill you, you should always put their needs first. At another time she might have laughed at the incongruity, but as it was, as soon as her terrified retching had vented another wave threatened, as the hooded man in front of her hauled her to her feet.

"Please don't. Please, *please*. I have a son-"

The words were muffled by a cloth bag being yanked roughly down over her head, and Veronica Lewis held both her nausea and her breath as she waited for the shot that would undoubtedly spell her end.

\*\*\*\*

### The Travis Estate, Hillsborough. 11 a.m.

"Do you honestly think any of these muppets are going to tell us anything useful? Half of them wish us dead!"

Reggie Boyd lifted his eyes slowly from his clipboard, every fibre of him struggling not to use it to clout the whining officer in front of him around the ear. Instead he employed what his wife said was one of his most attractive attributes, his droll sense of humour. Not because the idiot in front of him was an inspector and theoretically he could be done for insubordination if he hit him, although Craig *had* phoned to say he had both immunity and carte blanche to thump Kyle Spence if he thought it might improve his work, but because he regarded physical violence as both beneath him and pathetic. If he couldn't manage a wee squit like Spence with his verbals then there was no hope for him at all.

"Well now, Inspector..."

Boyd's soft accent and quiet voice made the words sound like he was speaking to someone he loved, instead of to an arrogant spook who thought he was above real police work.

"I have no doubt that you're right, sir, and that most of the good folk around here *do* wish us an early demise, but that doesn't necessarily mean they're bad people."

He waved a hand around the water stained, grey concrete walkway on which they were standing, as if it was the most beautiful vista in the world.

"Who knows what sad experiences they may have had with people wearing uniforms: meter maids, waiters and the like. But it's *our* job to help them past those scars and *enable* them to help us. And to that end." He shoved the clipboard hard into Kyle's chest, apologising inwardly for his baser instincts as he did. "The Superintendent phoned and he'd like you to interview a Mrs Eileen Regent, the dead man's mother. She's in Faulkner Tower. Two floors up in number twenty-five."

A warning frown creased his forehead. "Be nice, mind you, sir. The woman's just lost her only son." He turned towards a short P.C. that Kyle hadn't noticed. "Just to be on the safe side I'm sending along Officer Donaldson here to hold your hand. It's not that I don't trust you, sir, you understand, but he'll be reporting directly back to me."

He turned to the uniformed constable. "Don't take any nonsense from the Inspector here, mind. The

Superintendent says he gets carried away sometimes and needs to be reined in."

His cool smile to Kyle was unambiguous, and as the D.I. walked away with Donaldson trailing after him he could feel the sting of Craig's revenge.

\*\*\*\*

It was going to happen in the countryside. She just knew it. No-one would bother to put you in a car-boot and drive for miles otherwise, especially when they could just have shot you in a room where the sound would have been well covered by city noise.

A sudden jolt banged Veronica Lewis' head against the boot's lid and a second threatened to knock her out. Her head swam for a moment before she recovered, thankful for the small mercy of the car moving on to a seemingly smoother road. The smoothness continued for what felt like an hour, the steady grinding of tyre against tarmac broken occasionally by the car's wheels wandering onto some cats' eyes and the noise of an indicator signalling as they changed lane. They were on a motorway, they had to be.

She broke her relentless anxiety by playing a game of 'let's guess where I am' and miles had passed before she realised it was a pointless pursuit; It would require passer-bys' voices or traffic stops to yield a clue and she'd watched too many episodes of Criminal Minds to imagine there would be.

The madam found herself dozing for a while and when she awoke she had the sudden urge to kick above her head. Perhaps if she could make enough noise some passing driver might hear her, but her legs had tired before she'd realised the idea had been nonsense anyway. They were going too fast. The only people who might hear her were the men inside the car and it would only serve to anger them. If she *had* to die she didn't want to encourage them to make the experience worse.

Eventually she lay back on the boot's carpeted floor, finding some sort of acceptance. It made the pulse in her head that had been deafening her with its pounding, subside for long enough to hear her captors speak. She listened closely to their words, strangely comforted by having human beings nearby yet at the same time realising the ridiculousness of finding comfort from the men who would cause her death.

One man had a low, warm voice, a voice that she might have found attractive on another day. His words flowed over her, speaking of sport and a concert that he'd been to earlier that week, his companion silent aside from "yes" and "hmm". Their exchange had a rhythm to it that made her feel sleepy and without trying to the madam felt herself dozing off, only to be woken some unknowable time later by the feeling of rain splattering on her hand, the light seeping through her hood's fibres saying that it was still day.

First one arm and then the other was grabbed, and she felt herself being yanked wholesale from the boot, and dragged by her assailants across rough, obstacle filled ground. She had no idea where she was. There were birds, she could hear them, and bits of twig snapping underfoot. A garden? A forest? The latter made more sense. Kill her in a remote forest and no-one would know where to look for her body. That's what The Fox had said months ago when they'd first met. *Cross me, Veronica, and they won't find your body for years.*

She hit the ground suddenly with a thud, something that she'd fallen against knocking the breath out of her chest, her captors' kicks to her torso ensuring its depletion. As she gasped for air, necessary for the renewed pleading she was planning on doing, the pounding pulse in her head made her deaf once again. So deaf that she didn't hear the footsteps moving away and almost too deaf to hear the car engine starting up, but clearing enough to hear the vehicle pull away and leave her alone. Wrists bound, head hooded, but still alive, biting back her tears of relief in case they choked her still-gagged mouth, and thanking whoever or whatever power had saved her for the sake of her son.

\*\*\*\*

**The Travis Estate.**

Kyle Spence knew that he was unfeeling and he usually considered it a gift. Not for him the shirt-rending, soul-searching pangs of anguish that many of his contemporaries suffered when faced with the worst that humanity could do. He could stare at a victim and walk away, and smile at the dead body of a villain, noting anything that the police marksman might seek to improve upon next time. Not for him the wondering about how they'd embarked upon their criminal path: the bad childhood, the poverty, the influence of the other sad sacks that they'd encountered on their way. As far as he was concerned it was their own stupid fault that their life had ended with a bullet; they should've worked harder at school and joined the boy scouts.

So, unfeeling was the order of Kyle Spence's day. He balked at calling himself callous, carrying as it did the implied urge to seek opportunities for sadism, which he didn't. In truth, he would far rather be drinking a good wine and seducing some lovely than shooting a man in the head, but he had chosen a job that served his country, so in that light his lack of empathy was a distinct advantage in his book. What the lovelies thought was a different thing entirely, but as he never dated anyone for longer than a fortnight as a matter of policy, and they all knew that going in, no-one could ever cry about their hurt feelings or imply that he'd led them astray.

It was with that same cool detachment that Spence knocked on the door of number twenty-five Faulkner Tower, his clear eyes unburdened by any feelings of pity engendered by the poverty around him: the peeling mustard paint covering the apartment's narrow door jamb; the dried-out planter on the balcony outside, some futile attempt at brightening the small piece of real estate Eileen Regent called home; the drunken stainless steel five, hanging only by its bottom screw at an angle, saying that she lived in number twenty what?

No, the D.I.'s mind was unclouded by sentiment as he listened to the strangely light footsteps of the lady of the house approaching, and it remained unfogged as the snib was turned and the door crept back, threatening only to mist up when a tiny, triangular face appeared several feet below him in the sparsely furnished hall. A face belonging to a small girl, not older than six or seven, her thin, mousey hair clamped flat against cheeks which widened slowly into a hesitant smile.

"Daddy's not in. Granny's gone to see him."

Whether it was her chirpy tone or her innocent opening of the door to a complete stranger, one who was only now showing her his badge, or the high-pitched voice designed by evolution to make adults want to protect her, or the naiveté that said she believed Billy Regent was merely out instead of dead, Kyle Spence didn't know. But something made him want to pick the girl up and hold her, to tell the young daughter that none of them had been aware Billy Regent had had that everything would be OK, and that same something made a tear form in the unsentimental inspector's eye, and fall unbidden down his pale and normally unfeeling cheek.

\*\*\*\*

## The C.C.U. 12 p.m.

Craig walked straight past his PA as she waited in front of the squad-room's double doors, her posture hinting that she'd rushed there as soon as she'd heard the lift. She had in fact, so desperate was she to impart the information that Kyle had just given her, so she was less than impressed when Craig waved her away, with. "Later, Nicky. I need to check something first."

Nicky Morris was not a woman accustomed to being ignored and Liam decided to capitalise on that fact, as his immediate halt by her side and fake-concerned expression proved.

"You can tell me, you know. Always happy to chat."

"NO. It's for the chief."

He jutted out his bottom lip in a show of hurt but Nicky wasn't taken in.

"And you needn't try that one on me. Our Jonny holds the prize for guilting." She turned on her heel, shooting Craig an annoyed look all the way back to her desk. "But if we're talking about people offending other people, we'd have to travel a long way to beat *him*."

If Craig was aware of the tableau playing out behind his back he pretended not to be, pulling up a chair to sit down at Davy's desk.

"Have you got Veronica Lewis' phone records yet, Davy?"

Without looking up Davy waved towards his junior and Craig shifted his chair across to Ash, wondering when the shy EMO analyst who'd once been afraid to speak without being spoken to had become so blasé. Ash's smooth tenor stopped him following through the thought.

"I've got the outgoing calls from her office since January, chief." He tapped his smart-pad and a list appeared on his computer screen. "The company's dragging their feet a bit on the details on the incoming ones." He gestured to the phone. "But I'll chase them up again."

"Do that." Craig stared at the screen. "Anything interesting on the incomings, even without the details?"

"A lot of withheld numbers, just like you'd expect from people calling a madam. We're working on getting them uncovered, but my bet is quite a few will be from throwaway phones."

Craig thought about what he'd said for a moment before

shaking his head.

"People are lazy. Someone will have used their own phone and just concealed its I.D., and one number might be all we'll need." He pointed to the smart-pad. "Particularly if it matches an outgoing call."

Ash nodded his colourful head. "I'm working my way through those. So far, there are a lot of Chinese takeaways. The girls must have had plenty of free time."

It didn't warrant debate.

"OK, what about Lewis' computers, home and office?"

"Davy's working on those."

Craig walked his chair back to the EMO and waited for Davy to raise his brown eyes from his work. When thirty seconds had passed the detective gave a prompt.

"Veronica Lewis' computers?"

The analyst glanced up as if he didn't know who Craig was but he regrouped quickly.

"S...Sorry, chief, I was miles away."

"Something you've found?"

Davy's wrinkled nose said possibly.

"It's...maybe..." He set down the pen he was holding and sat back. "You'll think I've gone mad."

Liam's voice boomed across the floor. "He's one to judge."

Craig ignored him and shifted to the edge of his seat, sensing that something significant was about to come out.

"Why mad?"

Davy made another face. "W...Well, because if I didn't know better I'd say Lewis' emails were written in code. Take a look."

Craig moved to read over his shoulder. The email on the screen seemed innocuous. Just Veronica Lewis contacting someone called Elizabeth, arranging an appointment for a facial.

"Where's the code in that?"

"Well, the appointment's at a weekend. That's possible, I suppose, for a beauty place, but the email address doesn't exist. Well, it exists, but it doesn't belong to a real person. It's a s...sock puppet, a false account. Every time I try to trace it, it dead-ends in Korea."

Both Liam and Ash perked up. "North Korea?" Visions of nuclear holocausts over Belfast Lough filled Liam's mind, while Ash's thoughts flew to Barat Dudaev selling the satellite codes to Kim Jong Un.

"South, thankfully."

While Ash looked almost disappointed that the Belfast madam hadn't been about to rain Armageddon on their heads Liam's thoughts diverted immediately to lunch. Meanwhile Craig focused on what they had.

"OK, so Elizabeth and her facial were fake."

"And the email bounced off several different s...servers on the way between wherever and here."

"That's what's making you think it's written in code?"

Davy shook his head. "No. Lewis seems to have had a few stock phrases she used, like booking a facial, booking a massage, etcetera. Although I s...suppose they're common enough things for women to have." He rolled his eyes. "Judging by what Maggie spends anyway-"

Maggie was Davy's fiancée.

Craig cut him off. "Or you think they could be euphemisms for different sex acts."

Liam overheard and snorted. "And we can all guess what a facial is-"

He was silenced by Nicky stuffing a biscuit from her secret stash in his mouth. She kept a tin filled with all things sweet and carbohydrate that she relocated every day to prevent Liam pilfering the lot.

Craig was still talking. "But you don't think it's that simple, do you?"

The analyst shook his head. "No. I mean if someone is just booking time with a beautician or one of Lewis' escorts, why use a fake email address?"

"Unless it's not Elizabeth booking a facial and it's really a powerful man who wants their privacy maintained."

Davy shook his head again, surprising the detective. "I can't see it, chief. Men that powerful w...wouldn't write anything down at all." He gestured at Ash. "They're probably Ash's withheld phone numbers. But this." He tapped the screen. "This is way too elaborate. So elaborate, I don't think it's got anything to do with Lewis' sex or beauty businesses at all."

Craig had another thought. "Was the email listed under one business or the other?"

"Neither. There's no reference attached to say which business each email applies to, although the content, facial etc. could refer to either I guess."

"Do the appointment times coincide with anything else you've found?"

"Well, they're all at weekends in the summer-"

Craig finished the sentence. "And weekday evenings in the winter months." He nodded to himself, realising what it meant. "The emails are to do with the parties Lewis was organising."

As he prepared to leave and give the analysts space to work, Davy shook his head.

"I hadn't finished, chief. The emails *might* be using some sort of simple code for the s...services, but." He moved his cursor onto an ornate looking figure four at the bottom of the frame.

"What's that? Lewis' business logo?"

"It's only on emails going to Lewis so I don't think it belongs to her."

It was too much for Liam's curiosity and he wandered across to join them. Meanwhile the analyst had answered Craig's question by clicking twice on the figure, and as they watched a series of screens flashed by, until the final one appeared containing nothing but numbers.

Ash leapt up, unable to contain his excitement.

"It's a gateway! Let me at it!"

Davy fended him off with an outstretched hand. "Wait." He opened a second email to Lewis on his left-hand screen and clicked on the logo again, watching the sequence repeat.

"OK, what we've got is steganography. Concealing a file, message, image, or video within another. S...Someone's embedded information in bland emails arranging beauty appointments, and no-one would have known to click on that symbol but the recipient-"

"Or you."

He brushed off the compliment. "It takes us through a series of pages until it lands on that." He gestured at the numbered screen then turned to his junior. "Have a go at that one if you fancy, but I don't think you'll get anywhere. They aren't algorithms. My guess is it's a simple Ottendorf Cipher."

"What's that?"

"A book code." To prove the point, he highlighted a section. "The numbers are in groups of four; probably referring to the page, line, word and letter. But the question is from which book? It could be anything from the Huckleberry Finn to the Bible, but both sender and recipient must be working to the same text for the code to make sense. Or... it could lead to a file that only party attendees are given, and by using the numbers they can w...work out where the parties are and when." He nodded admiringly. "These guys do *not* want to get caught."

Liam hadn't finished. He prodded the figure four that Craig had queried as a logo.

"Does that squiggle on its back mean anything?"

Davy shrugged. "Maybe. It looks occult to me." He pre-empted the next question with a shake of his head. "Give me time."

Liam gave a tut of disgust. "I just hope it's not some sort of witchy coven crap. I couldn't cope with a Hammer Horror movie playing out in some country house."

He noticed that Craig had said nothing for a while.

"A quid for them, boss?"

"You tell me."

It was the sound of a gauntlet being thrown down. Liam

was bright but lazy and if he was ever going to make superintendent Craig knew he had to use his brain far more. The D.C.I. took the challenge in the spirit it was intended and perched on a nearby desk, rubbing his hands together as he thought.

"OK. So, you're thinking that no matter how kinky the sex is no-one bothers with this level of secrecy just for that. After all, what are they likely to get if they're caught? If the girls are all over eighteen, nobody's trespassing or hurting anyone, the worst penalty would be a caution. OK, so they're well known and probably married and they don't want anything getting out, but their minders would stop things leaking to the press, so *that's* not the reason either." He nodded decisively. "Nope, the reason they're going to all this trouble to hide the parties is because there's something more important going on at them than sex."

Craig smiled. "And it's the same thing that got Veronica Lewis disappeared and the C.C. called in." His smile became a frown. "So, what the hell is it? Drugs? Arms? Smuggling-"

The sound of Liam's stomach rumbling cut his speculation short and made Craig spring to his feet.

"It'll have to wait for the briefing. OK, Davy, get on that after lunch, please. Liam, give Ash those queries about Regent's bank account and the fire escape, and everyone over to The James for lunch?"

Carried along in the stampede, Craig was at the exit before he noticed that Nicky was still sitting at her desk, her lips pursed primly as she typed. He walked back wearing a look of contrition.

"I'm sorry, Nicky. You had something that you wanted to tell me when I arrived."

She tossed her head huffily. "You're too late. You'll just have to wait for Kyle now."

He wheedled his way to her side. "I'll buy you some of that Devil's Food cake you love."

If it was a choice between taking offence and taking chocolate, Nicky was easily bought. She grabbed her handbag and was past Craig in a flash, and during the trip down in the lift she informed her boss that Billy Regent had had a seven-year-old daughter that he'd apparently doted on, making the case for the ex-soldier committing suicide look increasingly thin.

# Chapter Six

### Whitehall, London. 1 p.m.

The air inside the club's dark library, stale even in winter, was so stagnant that the dust particles suspended in it had barely moved in the hour that they'd talked, making the visitor wonder if the same molecules had been circulating since the club's grand opening in eighteen-eighty-eight. His elderly host had the same stagnant appearance, the sheen of his dark wool suit and the patina of his black brogues shouting money, but only of the old sort.

The Fox ran a hand over his own close-cropped hair, suddenly embarrassed by his lack of locks. In England, long hair on men seemed to be a sign of breeding, and a voluntary lack of it seemed somehow déclassé. He'd been given a pass because he was a foreigner, but only just.

The foreigner opened his mouth to speak, only to close it again immediately when his host shook his head and a waiter he hadn't noticed lifted two tumblers from a tray and set them on their table, before melting away again.

His shiny companion waved him on.

"The woman will give no more trouble. Any qualms she had have been subdued."

The older man wobbled his Churchillian jowls from side to side. "You should have replaced her completely."

The Fox demurred. "She holds all the contacts. And besides, the police might have started snooping if she'd disappeared for good."

A loud tut made him jerk back in his seat.

"*Might have?* They already are! Bloody plods. That idiot Flanagan gave it to one of his Rottweilers to deal with and now he's starting to dig. If he links the woman to McManus we're done."

His companion rushed to reassure him. "They won't. The whore's terrified of us now and she's been warned to keep the police off our backs. And as far as McManus is concerned, we've already got a fall guy for that. A disillusioned ex-soldier with PTSD and surviving on benefits finally cracks, kills the First Minister and then kills himself. It's all sewn up."

The host lurched forward, surprising his guest with his vigour. "You'd better be sure, because if it hits the fan we're not going down with you! And if you're arrested you won't be given the chance to spill your guts."

The Fox swallowed hard, knowing exactly what that meant.

\*\*\*\*

## Maghera, County Londonderry.

The wood was sparse, and thankfully, after dragging her aching frame for what felt like miles, Veronica Lewis found herself staggering onto a narrow road. Its smooth, tarmacked surface gave her hope: governments rarely maintained roads unless some nearby community needed the access, and where there was a community there were always cars. Within an hour she'd been proved right, the appearance of a small pickup truck with mud-splashed wheels saying that there was a farm somewhere nearby. Thankfully the driver was meandering rather than belting down the rural thoroughfare, and Lewis' calculated risk of stepping into its centre resulted in him slowing down.

The man yanked on his handbrake and stuck his head out the window, his dark scowl heralding a yell.

"What the hell are you doing? I could have killed you..."

The words tailed off as he took in her bare feet and bloodied face.

He leapt from the truck and rushed towards her.

"My God! Who did this to you?"

The exhausted madam shook her head as the experiences of the previous few days finally caught up.

Dropping to her knees on her way to unconsciousness, all she could think about was that she was safe.

\*\*\*\*

## The C.C.U. 3 p.m.

"OK, grab a coffee and let's start. John, Des, thanks for joining us."

Des Marsham smiled cheerfully through a mouthful of cake that had deposited a coating of crumbs on his shaggy beard. While Nicky winced at the sight, thinking that his facial hair needed a good trim, John answered for them both.

"Nice to get out of the lab for a while." The pathologist gazed around until his eyes alighted on Annette. "I left your other half with Mrs Regent. She was in a bad way."

Before Annette could answer Kyle did, bristling from the new-found emotions that were still giving him pain.

"Not as bad a way as the seven-year-old she left alone in her flat! I'd have called social services if a neighbour hadn't appeared."

John frowned. "Whose child was it?"

"Billy Regent's. Eileen Regent is her gran."

Craig had allowed the exchange to run while the room settled, but now they really needed to start.

"We'll get back to that in a moment. First, Nicky?"

Sated by chocolate cake the PA honoured him with a smile, then rotated the white board by her desk to reveal the words Craig had written there ten minutes before. The detective tapped them with a marker as he spoke.

"Right. We have two cases now. Number one, a personal request from the C.C; the kidnapping of Mrs Veronica Lewis, fifty-one. A fashion designer, beauty consultant and, we believe, a high-level madam, Mrs Lewis hasn't been seen since Friday. It's kidnapping because the office where she was thought to have been at the time of her disappearance was turned over, but I'll come back to that. Our second case is the assassination-"

Liam gave a "Whoa" at the word.

"You object to my description?"

The D.C.I. screwed up his face. "Well...no, I suppose not. It's accurate enough, but it's just not a word you hear used every day."

He was right. Despite the fractious nature of Northern Irish politics, no-one had taken a pot-shot at a local politician since The Troubles had ended with the Good Friday Agreement in nineteen-ninety-eight. The last shooting that bore any similarities to McManus' had been at Laganside Courts in twenty-fifteen. That had been a professional hit carried out by a hired gunman, Stevan Mitic, a man that they'd last heard was in the Middle-East being pursued by Interpol.

Craig shrugged off Liam's objection and continued.

"OK, so, as I was saying, our second case is the assassination of Peter McManus, First Minister of this fair land and a member of the Independent Britain Party-"

Kyle snorted. "Whatever the hell that means."

Jake smiled. "I think isolationist would be the word."

Craig shook his head. "I want personal political beliefs kept out of this, is that understood? Whether you voted for McManus or not the man is dead."

Jake had the grace to look embarrassed, although Craig doubted the expression's sincerity, but an indifferent shrug said that Kyle's new-found sensitivity was well and truly buried again. Craig was tempted to pull him on the gesture but they didn't have the time and continuing his door-to-door duties would subdue the D.I. soon enough.

"OK. Veronica Lewis first. Aidan, what have you found out on her activities?"

The three months out of Vice, although they doubted that Vice was completely out of him, D.C.I. gave an open-mouthed yawn and opened a buff file headed 'Sex Crimes' that was resting on his knee. Liam was too far away to stick his finger in Hughes' mouth so he decided to spoil his run-up in another way.

"We keeping you awake, Wensley?"

It got him the chorus of laughter that he'd craved. Wensleydale had been Hughes' occasional nick-name since the summer he'd come back from Turkey the colour of honey-roasted peanuts, which with his yellow-blond hair and lanky frame had made him resemble a stick of the cheese.

While Liam mouthed an explanation to the newer members of the team, Hughes gave the comment the contempt it deserved and carried on.

"Right. Veronica Lewis, one son, divorced from Harry Rand, a garage owner she was married to for ten months twenty years ago. Variously known as Veronica Lee, Ronnie Lee-"

"Gypsy Rose Lee."

It earned Davy a bow from John and a snapped putdown from Craig.

"Everyone's a bloody wit today! Shut up, all of you, and stop interrupting. You're not in the pub."

Hughes moved things along hastily. "OK, anyway, Ronnie Lee started out young. At sixteen she was picked up for soliciting, but let off with a caution. That was the last time she was found out on the streets. She must have gone into a house or a massage parlour after that, because the next time she came to our attention she was thirty-one with a four-year-old son."

Andy roused himself. "We met him. Rupert."

Craig nodded. "We'll come back to that. Go on, Aidan."

"That time she was picked up working at that brothel out near the airport. Lilith's, I think it was called. It closed down last year."

A crimson blush lit up Liam's pale cheeks. He'd been set up at Lilith's by his mates during a case once; they'd paid two dominatrices to lock him in a room and taken snaps. Thankfully no-one seemed to have remembered except

Craig, but his raised eyebrow said it might only stay private for as long as Liam behaved. Aidan was still reporting.

"Again, Lewis was cautioned, this time under the name Veronica Lee. After that she stayed pretty much off our radar. We knew she was still at it, but it turned out she also had a talent for the rag trade. Put herself through college with her ill-gotten gains and opened a legitimate front: Veronica Lewis Design and Beauty." He closed the file. "The rest isn't on paper. I asked around and several of the Vice lads said they'd heard rumours about high-level parties being held out in the sticks. Big name clients, lots of coke and some kinky stuff-"

Craig interrupted. "How kinky?"

Hughes shook his head. "Nothing hard core. Just S&M, Furries, and lots of naked pensioners running through the trees."

Liam mouthed, "Furries?", making Craig shake his head.

"Look it up. I don't have the time to educate you. Aidan, any of those big names known?"

"Not so you'd swear on a stack of bibles, but I did hear that there was a well-known hotelier and a banker on the list. Nigel McArdle and Joseph Bell. Some local politicians as well apparently, but I don't have their names."

"Probably because their Stormont advisors had them erased."

Annette made a face. "Mike and I had dinner at one of McArdle's hotels a few weeks ago. I'll never be able to eat there again."

Craig turned his chair towards Andy and Jake, who were sniggering at something that Andy had just drawn.

"Care to share that with us, Leonardo?"

Before Andy could hide the page, Liam had swooped, seizing a caricature of an overweight banker contorted into a dubious sexual position and waving it around the room. John nodded approvingly.

"You can really draw, Andy."

The artistic D.C.I. didn't have the wit not to say

"Thanks".

Craig rolled his eyes, confiscated the art and moved on. "When you pair have finished behaving like adolescents, what did you make of Lewis' son? Jake?"

Jake stifled the remnants of his grin. "Rupert Lewis, every bit as elegant and privileged as his name might suggest but he seemed like a genuinely nice guy. Twenty-four, private school, now at Queen's studying drama, and appeared to have absolutely no idea about the seedier side of his mother's life."

Annette cut in. "I hope you didn't tell him?"

Jake shot her a scowl. "Give us some credit, for goodness sake."

Andy joined him in his offence, continuing the report. "The lad seemed to have no idea that his mum was even missing. He said that she often goes away on jaunts for a few days, usually local or down south, but occasionally abroad. Weekends in summer and weekdays in the winter months."

Aidan nodded. "Which would suit the members of our loyal assembly. During summer recess the MLAs all go back to their constituencies, mostly out in the sticks. In winter, they normally stay in Belfast while the Assembly's sitting, so midweek parties would suit them better, as long as they were local."

Andy smirked.

"That's what we thought. Anyway, we also spoke to two of Lewis' girls and one of them, Jenny Wasson, gave us more detail. She said the parties are run at different locations across the country, north and south. Pretty grand places as well. The girls never know where they are because they're blindfolded and driven there, but she described one as having acres of grounds and a marble statue and being about two hours' drive from east Belfast. Davy was chasing up the description for us."

As all eyes swivelled towards the analyst he tapped his smart-pad to project an image onto the screen by Nicky's desk. It was of a huge, broad-fronted Georgian mansion set in what looked like extensive grounds. Another tap and an aerial view of the property was displayed, confirming its acreage, while a third photograph showed a marble 'rider on horseback' statue set on a stone veranda that led down a grass slope to a small wood beyond.

Liam's slow whistle said it for all of them but John added more detail.

"That's the country seat of the Williamson family! They're one of the oldest Anglo-Irish families in the country."

Craig kept his eyes on the screen as he asked Davy more. "Where is it?"

"County Louth. Just over the border in the Republic."

"And how sure are you that it's the place Jenny Wasson saw?"

Davy screwed up his face. "I'd like her to look at the photos, but pretty s...sure. There are very few places within that driving distance that have any statues at all, and none with acres of ground except this one."

He tapped again and the image of a grey-haired man appeared. "Garrett Williamson. Tenth Earl of Louth, and until he lost his seat in February's election, a TD in the Dáil Éireann."

TD was the abbreviation for Teachta Dála, the Irish equivalent to an MP, just as the Dáil was Ireland's Houses of Parliament.

Annette said what everyone was thinking. "So, the politicians involved aren't just from the north."

Craig poured himself a fresh coffee before commenting. "OK, so we have wealthy and influential clients indulging in a spot of God knows what in private homes. But as Liam pointed out previously, none of the girls were underage or being coerced, so why the need to disappear Veronica Lewis unless something else has gone on? Ideas, anyone?"

"Drugs." "Illegal arms deals." "Antique smuggling" and "Murder being concealed" hit the air almost simultaneously. Craig allowed the group to speculate for a moment longer then he raised a hand to silence the room.

"Apart from dark political machinations not being mentioned, I can't disagree with any of those. Lewis knew something incriminating that she shouldn't have about powerful people, so she had to be taken out."

He turned the board to its clean side and wrote up the four suggestions plus 'political deals' before turning back to the group.

"Right. Aidan, you and Annette follow up on the possibility of someone having been murdered recently and no body being found. Investigate every potentially relevant disappearance: runaways, under-age prostitutes of both sexes, known associates of Veronica Lewis, anyone who could have suffered an accident at one of these parties and disappeared. Go back and speak to Jenny Wasson, and whoever else she can give you, and get anything more that you can, including dates. Take Davy's photos with you so she can identify the house. Davy and Ash, do a bit more digging on our Earl, and on McArdle and Bell. The Earl must have given permission for his home to be used. Also, check customs and excise and the UK Border Force for possible smuggling."

Annette shook her head. "Sir, wouldn't it be better if Jake went with Aidan considering that he's already met Wasson?"

"Fair point, but you go as well, please. She may tell you something she doesn't want to tell a man."

He turned to look for Liam. He was behind Nicky's desk searching for more cake.

"Liam, you take illegal arms deals with Andy, and pick up on some of the contacts you made on that bomb case in Smithfield in twenty-fourteen to ask about antiques smuggling as well."

He was referring to a book shop that had been deliberately destroyed in an explosion, to cover the theft of an original Crusader text by Islamic terrorists.

Liam sat down again, palming a muffin he'd managed to

free from Nicky's stash without her noticing.

"Tommy might know about both of those as well, boss. Remember he was the middle man for the sale of that old book."

John shook his head at the description of the ancient text as an 'old book' but Craig nodded.

"Good thinking. Take Rhonda with you as well." He scanned the group. "Where is she by the way?"

Rhonda O'Neil was the squad's detective constable. Seconded from Australia for two years, her striking dark-haired, ice-skinned looks and romance with the edgy Sergeant Karl Rimmins of the drugs squad made her recent makeover as a Goth seem like a natural choice.

"Dentist."

"OK. Well, when she gets back can you brief her, please, Annette. She's friendly with Karl Rimmins in Drugs, so I'd like her to ask around about that possibility too."

He turned back to the whiteboard. "Which just leaves us with political machinations and Kyle and I will take that one. OK. That leads us on to our second case." He rapped his knuckles against their shooting victim's name. "Nicky, pull up a photo of Peter McManus, please."

A considerably healthier looking politician than the one they'd seen the day before appeared on the LED screen.

Craig leant against a desk and faced the group. "Peter McManus, forty-years-old, married, father of three. His wife Emily is a barrister, usually working with the Public Prosecution Service. Some of you may know her as Emily Rickert, she mostly works on fraud."

It didn't ring any bells.

"OK, well, McManus had been a member of the Independent Britain Party since twenty-ten, previously serving as an independent unionist MLA. He was elected as the IBP MLA for North Antrim in twenty-eleven, became deputy leader in twenty-fourteen, and earlier this year he took over as leader of the party and First Minister when his predecessor stepped down due to ill health-"

John Winter cut in. "Internal party election?"

"Probably. Ash, check that out please. What's your point, John?"

"Was anyone's nose put out of joint by such a young politician getting the leadership?"

Craig's navy eyes widened; it hadn't even crossed his mind that the killing could have been down to simple jealousy.

"Good call. Kyle, ask around your contacts and see what the situation was. Any internal resentment against McManus, party dissent, etcetera."

The Intelligence Officer looked thoughtful for a moment. "Will do, but my guess is that his rivals across the floor of the Assembly probably hated him a lot more. It isn't a secret that there was no love lost between him and Gloria O'Rawe."

"I thought the Whole Ireland Party welcomed McManus' appointment, on the grounds that some of his more unpopular views were likely to drive votes their way."

Kyle's face said he wasn't so sure. "I'll check."

John interjected again. "Actually, Marc, that's a point. What *were* McManus' political views? The only two I can think of were that he wanted Northern Ireland to remain in the UK, but he was anti-leaving the EU while some of his party were pro."

Liam concurred. "He had that in common with gorgeous Gloria then."

The European Union referendum scheduled in nine days' time was driving a coach and horses through UK politics, and turning even party colleagues against each other, obliterating the traditional ideological lines. Both the Leave and Remain camps had their fanatics, and the glitterati of the media, celebrities and wealthy were leaping on board as well, with even pop singers and reality TV 'stars' spouting off like someone really gave a damn what they thought.

Suddenly an Australian voice piped up from across the floor. "McManus wanted rid of me."

Liam swung round to face the newly dentisted constable. *"You in particular, Rhonda?* Why? What did you do to him?"

Rhonda O'Neil took a seat, shooting him a sceptical look. "Immigrants in general, I mean. Wasn't that one of McManus' election promises? Northern Ireland for the Northern Irish, or something equally catchy."

Craig tried to imagine anyone telling his Italian mother that she'd have to leave her County Down home after forty-odd years. She would have shot Peter McManus herself.

"OK, that's enough speculating, everyone. Ash, find out exactly what Peter McManus' public promises were, and dig out what he said in private as well if you can." He turned back to the board. "McManus was shot around three p.m. yesterday with a sniper rifle. Des, have you managed to confirm the ballistics on that?"

The forensic scientist nodded. "The bullet found at the McManus scene matched the rifle found with William Regent."

John tagged on "And his fatal injury was definitely caused by the bullet found. One through and through shot to the forehead. Death would have been instant."

"OK, good. What about the guns' makes and models?"

Des made a face. "That might take a bit longer. They're not anything that I recognise and every distinguishing mark has been filed off."

Liam shook his head. "Someone didn't want to be traced, boss."

"Regent?"

"Only if he'd thought he was leaving that roof. If not him then maybe our second man?"

"If one exists." Craig considered for a moment. "If someone really doesn't want to be traced then they don't leave two guns behind."

"So, what are you thinking?"

"They removed the markings to slow us down?" It was a question, and one that couldn't be answered right away so

Craig moved on.

"OK. What about the trajectory, Des?"

Des nodded Davy to tap his smart-pad again. A diagram and map appeared, showing the arched trajectory of the bullet from the top of Carson Tower on the Travis Estate, through a small grove of trees between there and Hillsborough Castle and straight over its wall, impacting at the exact position on the forecourt where Peter McManus had died.

"It was a beautiful shot." Realising how admiringly he'd said it the scientist back-pedalled hastily. "That's if it hadn't killed anyone, of course."

Craig nodded. "Don't worry, Des. There's no need to observe the niceties in here."

Nicky sniffed loudly. "I beg to differ."

But Craig had already moved on.

"OK, so an expert marksman *could* have made that shot, in those weather conditions."

Des nodded. "He could and he did. There was virtually no wind yesterday and it was perfectly clear. Conditions were perfect." He glanced apologetically at the PA as he went on. "Regent found a small break in the trees and lined his shot up perfectly. The events that followed led Armed Response officers to the Travis Estate, marked with the letter A on the map, and there to Carson Tower, marked with a B. After clearing the fifteen floors of the building they reached the roof, marked C, where they found the body of William Regent." He turned to the pathologist. "John, can you take it from there."

The pathologist rose to stand beside the screen, gesturing Davy to show the next slide. It was a picture of Billy Regent lying bloodied and dead on the ground, and was the cue for Nicky to busy herself making fresh drinks. John shone his light pen at the screen.

"OK. As you can see, *this*..." He drew a circle with red light "...found lying on the ground beside him half-packed in a bag, is the rifle that Billy Regent used to shoot Peter

McManus. The ballistics is a match, as we've said, and GSR was found on Regent's hands."

Craig opened his mouth to interrupt, but John shook his head, moving on. He tapped the screen with a finger.

"And *this*... is the handgun that was actually found *in* Regent's right hand. It's a semi-automatic pistol and we found a bullet that matched it in Regent's skull, lodged against his left temporal bone, which means that the shot *had* to have entered from the right-hand side. Close inspection revealed stippling and charring typical of a contact wound on Regent's right temple."

He leant against Nicky's desk, sighing. "Our first impression was that Regent placed the pistol against his right temple and fired, killing himself, but unfortunately it's impossible to say whether the GSR on his hands came from it or the rifle." He saw Craig's face fall and moved on hurriedly. "However... initial swabs have revealed traces of latex on both of Regent's hands."

Craig frowned. "Gloves?"

Liam chimed in. "There were no gloves at the scene."

Aidan shrugged. "Maybe someone else got rid of them."

Liam wasn't having it. "Between when Regent shot himself and us getting there? I don't think so. Boss?"

Craig shook his head. "Unlikely. One, Aidan and Armed Response were already on the estate when the suicide shot occurred, and Carson Tower had been locked down, so no-one could have got on or off that roof, or at least not in through the cordon. And two, why the heck would anyone have bothered to remove Regent's gloves, *if* he was wearing them? Come to think of it, why would Regent have been wearing gloves at all if he'd planned on remaining at the scene to shoot himself?"

John waved him down. "You didn't let me finish. If Regent had been wearing latex gloves to avoid leaving prints on the rifle, which he wasn't because prints from both his hands were all over it, that would surely have signalled his intention not to be IDed and therefore his intention to escape, so why *then* commit suicide? Or, if he'd been planning suicide all along, he wouldn't have bothered with gloves at any point, so where did the latex come from?"

Des jumped in, eager to play Devil's Advocate. "Let's say Regent had his rifle half-packed and was about to leave the roof, when someone else, wearing latex gloves, appeared. They forced the handgun to Regent's temple, transferring the latex trace to his hands somehow, shot him and then left the roof. Couldn't they have hidden in some flat inside the tower until your lot left?"

Craig's expression was equivocal. "It's a long shot."

"But not impossible. The only other alternative is that Regent put on gloves to kill himself and someone removed them afterwards, and who would do that? Who would have tidied up after him?"

Liam put forward a theory. "Someone who loved him and didn't want anyone to know it was suicide? His mother maybe? We can check her alibi for the time of his death."

Aidan jumped in. "It might have been done to ensure his life insurance paid out?"

Annette looked sad. "Maybe someone tried to stop him but they were too late, and they didn't want Regent's daughter growing up knowing that he'd killed himself."

Craig shook his head. "All of those are possible, but I think John's right. Why would Regent have put on gloves at all if he'd planned suicide? Although... if he *was* wearing gloves when he shot himself, the GSR you found must have come from the rifle." He wrinkled his forehead, trying to make sense of the scenario. "No... none of those ideas work." That left only one reasonable conclusion. "Someone else must have killed Billy Regent."

John nodded excitedly, his imagination racing ahead. "To tie up loose ends."

Liam objected before Craig could. "Whoa. Not so fast, Doc. You're implying Regent killed with or for someone else, and we can't say that till we know a lot more."

Andy had been quiet during the discussion but now he

raised a finger to make a point.

"Something to suggest, Andy?"

The spiky-haired D.C.I. looked puzzled. "More something to clear up, chief. We're positive that Billy Regent pulled the trigger on McManus, are we?"

There was a series of nods, except for Craig.

"No. Andy's right, we can't be one hundred percent that Regent made that shot. The GSR on his hands could be from the handgun and his prints could have been planted on the rifle deliberately, after he was dead. Also, I'm pretty sure now that someone else was on that roof, for whatever reason. But just for the moment let's *say* that Billy Regent shot the rifle and killed Peter McManus. What's your point, Andy?"

"Well, I've two, but one's a question really. *Why* would Regent have agreed to kill McManus? He was on McManus' side of the political fence; Loyalist, ex-British Army, plus he had a young kid to live for. So, what would have made him risk everything to kill Peter McManus? Secondly, if there *was* someone else on that roof, then the person most likely to have been able to slip away when the tower was on lockdown would have been either a Carson resident or someone in uniform."

There was silence for a moment and then Liam slapped his fellow D.C.I. so hard on the back that Andy almost brought up his lunch.

"Bloody brilliant! There *is* a brain in that gelled up head of yours after all!"

Craig was equally impressed but drew the line at physical assault.

"Excellent thinking, Andy. It's clear we need to know a lot more about Billy Regent. You and Liam take that together; we learned a little about Billy from Tommy Hill earlier, but there's bound to be more."

Liam shifted to the edge of his chair. "And the idea that someone in police uniform might have done for Regent, boss?"

Craig answered by turning to the analysts. "CCTV?"

Davy nodded. "There's bound to be some on the estate."

"We'll need images from both inside and outside the tower, and it was a long way up to that roof, so they may have used the lift. Also, we need to continue door-to-door-" There was a loud groan which he ignored. "-enquiries. Liam, bring Reggie up to speed with our thinking."

He glanced at his watch. "OK, let's wind it up. Everyone knows what they have to do. We'll pick it up same time tomorrow."

John shook his head, halting him. "There was something else, Marc. Regent had skin under the nails of his left hand. I think he got a piece of his attacker."

Craig's hopes rose. "DNA?"

"Preliminary only. It's not a match for anyone in the system but we're running deeper analysis."

"Good. Keep me informed, please."

Just as the group was about to disperse, the phone on Nicky's desk rang. Her responses made Craig stop in his tracks.

"Where? How long ago?"

As she scribbled down the replies Liam read over her shoulder, and before the phone went down he and Craig were heading for the door. John watched balefully as his chance of a pint and some banter exited with them.

"What's happening, Nicky? Who was that?"

"The front desk. Apparently, some sergeant near Maghera called through half-an-hour ago, but they transferred him to the wrong squad. He said Veronica Lewis has been found alive."

# Chapter Seven

The forty-five-mile trip to Drumnaph Wood near Maghera was punctuated by Liam losing his way several times and swearing, and Craig falling deep into thought, the mystery of Billy Regent's demise preoccupying him. He wasn't sure why a killer's death should bother him so much except perhaps that he hated loose ends, particularly when that loose end might implicate a uniformed officer or imply that Regent hadn't been acting on some vengeful motive of his own.

But the more the detective thought about it the more doubtful he was that Billy Regent *had* been pursuing a personal vendetta. Or could he possibly have blamed the First Minister for his war experiences; as a symbol of the British government if nothing else? Craig shook his head, rejecting the idea almost as soon as it occurred to him. No, unless Billy Regent had been driven insane by his PTSD, which was highly unlikely, he was moving closer to believing that either the squaddie had been paid to kill the First Minister and then disposed of by his paymasters, or that he had been completely set up.

As Liam swore at the GPS that he'd just reluctantly switched on, his mistrust of computers of all sorts extending to anything that even beeped or clicked, Craig resorted to his far less technical notebook, scribbling down: Peter McManus, any military connections? And, Get Billy Regent's psychiatric history and check payments to his bank account. He added a P.S.: Check the Regent family's accounts as well, and then signed off with, arrange a meeting with the Armed Response commander who was working yesterday.

To the backing track of Liam thumping the dashboard Craig pulled out his phone and called Nicky to allocate the tasks.

"Liam already asked Ash to check Regent's bank

account, sir, but I'll add in his family's, shall I? and would you like me to contact Ken Smith about Regent's and McManus' military records?"

Ken Smith was an Army Captain stationed at the nearby Craigantlet Barracks and the partner of Craig's younger sister, Lucia. He was also about to leave the military to start a career in the police.

"Good idea. Ken's not leaving the army for a few more days. Ask him to call Liam when he gets a minute as well, please. He had something to ask him too. About Billy's mental health."

Liam's instantly raised eyebrow said he'd completely forgotten the task he'd left Tommy Hill's with earlier that day.

"Fine. I'll get Doctor Winter onto the psychiatric history as well if that suits, and I'll set up that meeting with the AR Commander for tomorrow afternoon."

As Craig ended the call, the elusive police station finally appeared in front of them. Liam gave a smug smile that implied he'd never been lost at all.

"There you go now. We're here. Easy." He pulled into a nearby parking space, one of eight left empty in a row of ten. There obviously wasn't a crime wave. "Although why the hell they built the place up this cow-rucked lane beats me. I'd have thought the middle of some town square would have been a better idea."

Craig was out of the car before the engine was turned off. "Maybe because this is a farming community and they were trying to accommodate that." He slammed the door shut. "Anyway, it gave you a chance to practice using the GPS, so taking an hour longer than we should have done wasn't a total dead loss."

He'd walked too far ahead to hear Liam's response, which was probably just as well, and as he pushed at the low door of the cottage-like station, he wondered what would greet them inside. He had visited a station in Fermanagh once where the desk sergeant had kept chickens, but this was sheep country so maybe a lamb or two might come gambolling out.

Thankfully there was no livestock to be seen, but the station's small, warm waiting area, strewn as it was with quilted cushions and low-slung rattan chairs, was a far cry from the no-frills, hard-seated ambience that Jack Harris maintained at High Street. That station reception seemed designed to dissuade wrong doers, whereas this one seemed to welcome them in.

Craig walked up to the reception desk and rang a brass hand-bell that definitely wasn't standard issue, its musical ding bringing a round woman in less than formal uniform hurtling from the back room. As she was doing up her top button and straightening her belt Liam appeared, and the W.P.C. scanned his six-foot-six enormity so slowly it was as if she never expected to reach the top of his head.

When she'd come back down to earth she turned to the marginally less outsized Craig with a smile.

"Can I help you?"

Her voice was a low, soft burr that reminded Craig how attractive some country accents could be. He was so used to the harder tones of Belfast he'd almost forgotten.

He nodded at the woman greeting. "We're from the Murder Squad in Belfast. We received a call about a woman who'd been found."

The constable's smile froze on 'Murder' and she nodded them, rictus-like, to the rattan seats and disappeared swiftly whence she'd come, only to return a moment later with a man whose three stripes and well-polished shoes said he was her boss. Her earlier dishevelled appearance suggested that he might have been something else as well.

The sergeant took charge immediately, beckoning the detectives across again and reaching out a hand to shake theirs in turn.

"Murder Squad, eh. And why might you lads be interested in a missing person?"

Liam showed his warrant card automatically, watching

amused as the man twitched into an on-guard position at the sight of his rank.

"It's a long story, Sergeant...."

"McCausland. Sir."

"Well, Sergeant McCausland, myself and the chief superintendent here..."

McCausland gave a gulp.

"...have been tasked by the Chief Constable to deal with this, so we would be grateful if you could show us to your guest."

The woman shrank into the background, the trauma of dealing with two senior officers apparently too much for her. McCausland shook his head apologetically.

"You can't see her, sir, because she isn't here. She was picked up on the road by a local farmer and brought here around two o'clock, but she'd been wandering in the woods for a while so she was in a bad way. We managed to get her name, Veronica Lewis, but that's all. Just enough to see she'd been listed as missing and contact the Crime Unit. An ambulance took her to the local hospital an hour ago. One of my lads is with her there."

It was all Liam could do not to swear. Craig shot him a warning look and asked the million-dollar question.

"And where would the hospital be?"

McCausland lifted the desk flap and moved past them to the front door, pointing the men back the way they came.

"Fifteen miles that way. You can't miss it. There's a big purple sign."

As Liam stormed past the pleased looking sergeant and got into the car, Craig thanked the rural lovers with a smile.

\*\*\*\*

## Annadale Embankment, Belfast. 6 p.m.

John had hung around the lab for as long as was feasible, but even he had to admit there was only so long you could watch a DNA analysis running without turning to stone. Mike Augustus had finished Billy Regent's P.M. earlier and confirmed what he'd already known, that the squaddie had died from a bullet to the brain via his right temple. The summary on Peter McManus held the same diagnosis, referencing his forehead, albeit fired from a much larger gun. Both reports had been written and filed, Regent's body already identified by his mother, and McManus just lay waiting for his wife, returning from holidaying with their kids in Scotland, to give him the inevitable nod.

But that would have to wait until tomorrow, and in the absence of his anticipated post-briefing pint at The James the pathologist had finally run out of excuses not to go home, and was standing now with his key extended, about to insert it reluctantly into his front door lock.

It wasn't as if he didn't like his home. He and Natalie had spent the nearly two years since they'd got married turning it into a Scandinavian hygge dream that was the envy of all their friends. And it wasn't that he didn't love his wife: she was a dynamo who'd added an adventure to his life that he'd grown up as the only child of elderly parents never expecting to have. It was just... well, nowadays he never knew how she would greet him.

She'd always been tempestuous but now she was moody and cranky as well, flying off the handle at him for the slightest thing. The rest of the time she was locking herself in the study, and when he listened at the door he often heard her arguing with herself. As her parents were fine and they hadn't had a fight about anything in particular, he'd assumed that her self-flagellation was something to do with work; the life of a general surgeon wasn't easy.

So up till now he'd let things lie, in the hope that they would settle on their own, but as his key turned in the lock and the door opened to the sounds of crockery being slammed hard into the sink, John Winter, the most easy-going man imaginable, decided that he had finally had enough.

He stormed into the kitchen and grabbed the Le Creuset pan that was about to follow the crockery, wresting the orange object from his tiny wife's hand and holding it above his own head. Natalie's glare said that it had been the wrong move.

"What do you think you're doing? I was using that!"

John set the pan down hurriedly, well out of reach, and perched on a stool at the breakfast bar.

"For what? An assault on the dishes?" He warmed to his theme. "What's been wrong with you lately, Nat? You're either shouting and banging things, or locking yourself in the study and not speaking to me at all. Is it something that I've done?"

He reached for her hand, only to have it snatched away.

"It's nothing!"

She made to leave the room but he blocked her exit, glaring down at his red-faced wife.

"Speak to me, Nat, *please*. Tell me what's wrong."

When she tried to duck past him, he blocked again.

"Move, John."

"No. Tell me what's wrong."

She glared up at him. "There's nothing wrong. I'm just tired."

"No, you're not. You slept for hours last night and you haven't been on-call all week." He drew her to him. "Just tell me if it's something that I've done."

She wriggled away. "It's nothing you can help me with."

"That's not an answer."

When she tried to duck past him this time, John moved out of the way, and he thought that he read surprise on her face. When he spoke next the pathologist's voice was flat.

"I'm your husband, Natalie, and I love you. But if you won't let me help you then perhaps you need to speak to someone else."

His last word was drowned out by the slam of the kitchen door.

\*\*\*\*

## Woodgrange Hospital. Tobermore, County Londonderry.

Veronica Lewis' thin face was turned away from them on her pillow, just as it had been since they'd entered the ward. After ten minutes in which she'd given them nothing but her name, address and date of birth Craig left his deputy to it, beckoning the young P.C. who'd accompanied Lewis there out into the corridor.

"Did Mrs Lewis say anything at all to you on the way here?"

John Ryan narrowed his eyes as if it was a trick question, but Craig soon realised the look wasn't one of suspicion but the fear of saying something wrong. After a long moment, the constable nodded.

"After she gave me her name and details, she asked had her disappearance been mentioned on the News, sir."

Craig was taken aback. Either Lewis had the wrong idea about how they dealt with people who had only been missing five days, or she thought she was more famous than she was. He corrected himself immediately; Veronica Lewis didn't think that *she* was famous but that someone she was linked with was, and that the police might inadvertently have leaked something to the press.

It might be something they could use to make her talk.

"Did she say anything else at all? Mention her son, or say where she'd been?"

As Ryan shook his head his hair flopped over his eyes; it was black and curly and rambling down towards his neck. It was on the tip of Craig's tongue to tell him to get it cut but he changed his mind: rural policing probably required more relaxed rules and those curls were undoubtedly a big hit at the local weekly dance.

"Only that she'd been in the woods, sir, and that she'd been hooded and brought there in a car boot by two men.

*Damn.* That meant she couldn't have seen its registration or her assailants' faces, not that she'd have given them either if her current behaviour was any guide. Still, the news angle might be leverage. Craig nodded the P.C. to return to her bedside and send Liam out.

He joined his boss in leaning against the corridor's eau-de-Nil painted wall.

"What do you think, Liam?"

The D.C.I. inhaled deeply before speaking. "She's been battered fairly hard, boss. Bruises on her face, back and legs, and restraint marks on her ankles and wrists."

Craig nodded. "We need John to look at her. He'll be able to say if they came from a beating, or just restraint followed by rough handling when she was dumped. Give me a minute."

He took out his phone and made the call, saving John from spending another evening alone in front of the box.

"I can be down there in an hour, Marc. It's a straight run on the M2."

"Don't tell Liam that. It took him twice that long."

He turned back to see an offended expression on the D.C.I.'s face.

"If we'd just been heading for the hospital I'd have found it, no problem! It was going to that backside of nowhere station that got me lost."

"Yeh, yeh, and nothing's ever your fault. Anyway, Constable Ryan's just told me something that could prove useful."

He repeated what Lewis had said about the News. Liam's response was to rub his hands gleefully.

"We've got her! If we say a politician's just appeared on the six o'clock news, appealing for a friend of his to be returned-"

Craig shook his head. "She'd have to have been mentioned by name. And it'll have to be a newspaper. She could check the TV and find out that we'd lied."

"It'll have to be a paper that isn't online then. She could

ask to see it on the ward computer."

Craig's face fell.

"We're done then. They're all online."

It was Liam's turn to take out his phone. "Oh, ye of little faith." Craig was saved from asking who he was calling by his next words. "Davy boy, are you with your delectable lady by any chance?"

Craig smiled. Maggie Clarke, Davy's fiancée, was News Editor of The Belfast Chronicle, one of the country's biggest tabloids, and not averse to helping him with his work.

After a five-minute call, Liam hung up with a smirk.

"You heard all that. They're mocking up a page saying that the Earl has appealed for help finding Veronica Lewis, a dear friend of his wife's, who designed her dresses for the Dublin Horse Show last year. He'll text me with the web link in a minute."

Ten minutes later they were looking at a mocked-up Chronicle front page that no-one but them would ever see.

"OK. You thought of it so you should show it to her, Liam. Just let me do the build-up first."

"Lead on."

Lewis was lying in the same position as they'd left her, so Craig told Ryan to take a break and then perched on the edge of her starched counterpane.

"It seems that you're a famous lady, Mrs Lewis. Friends in very high places. I'd wondered why the Chief Constable had asked us to find you when you'd only been missing for a few days."

Despite her efforts to ignore him, Craig thought he detected a tiny thaw. He nodded Liam to show her the link.

"This is the cover of this evening's late edition Belfast Chronicle. It's coming out at nine o'clock, so if there's anyone who you think should be warned before they see it, I suggest that you give them a call."

As Liam held out his phone Lewis jerked upright, grabbing it from his hand. The detectives watched as her already pale face paled even further and then as she jabbed frantically at its keys to make a call.

Craig motioned his deputy to move away.

"We'll leave you in peace for a few minutes, Mrs Lewis." Adding beneath his breath. "And after that resounding confirmation that the Earl is involved, once John has checked you over we'll be taking you straight to High Street."

\*\*\*\*

### The Demesne Estate Police Station. 9 p.m.

Reggie Boyd blew out an exasperated puff of air that lifted his lengthy eyebrow hairs half-an-inch, then he shook his head and continued reading the witness statements in front of him, beginning to despair of humanity. Criminal cases were like jigsaw puzzles and the police relied on the public to help them find the missing pieces, but canvassing the residents of the Travis Estate had been even less use than he'd hoped; a mixture of unanswered doors, silent stares, and, his particular favourites, the mouthy ones who told his P.C.s to 'piss off', calling them the names of various farmyard animals and imbuing the words with a venom usually only heard from rioting yobs.

The Travis was supposed to be Loyalist estate and they'd been asked to help solve the killing of one of their own MLAs, and yet his uniforms hadn't elicited a single useful statement amongst the forest of felled trees on his desk.

The veteran sergeant corrected himself. *Maybe they had one*. He lifted the single page that he'd set aside and read it through again. Kelly Atkins, number three Brookeborough Tower. She'd been hanging up her washing in the small back yard of her ground floor flat when she'd noticed Billy Regent rushing past just before half-past-two the afternoon before. Reggie read the verbatim statement aloud, hoping it might make the words develop more weight.

'I've knowed Billy since we wus both young, and he was

in a hell of a hurry to be somewhere, I knowed that much.'

'Which way was he heading, Mrs Atkins?'

The interviewing officer had helpfully recorded his own words verbatim as well. It was a technique that Reggie hadn't seen employed much but he'd soon be telling his own staff to do the same.

'Fer Carson Tower. I thought it was weird 'cos he lived in Faulkner with his mum and we'an. Molly she's called. Lovely wee thing.'

'Was Mister Regent carrying anything, did you notice?'

'Nah. He wusn't.' Reggie could picture her inserting a pause for effect before delivering her next words. 'Mind ye, the bloke he were with wus.'

The sergeant scribbled down a reminder to visit Kelly Atkins and get more detail about the second man; if he'd been privy to the debate that Craig and John had had earlier that day then he'd have jumped in his car right away. However, he wasn't, so instead he continued reading.

'What was it that the other man was carrying, Mrs Atkins?'

'A gym bag, it looked like. You know, one of them sort wi' a logo on the side. Ye can get just as good stuff down Primark fer a fiver, so why they pays hundreds just fer a stupid badge beats the life out of me.'

Reggie could picture her arms folding as she'd discussed the financial idiocy, and remaining folded as she'd carried on.

'He needed the gym, mind. The other man, nat Billy. Ar Billy always had a lovely build.'

'Why do you say the man needed the gym, Mrs Atkins?'

A curled lip was bound to have preceded her next words.

'Well, he wus tall enuf, but a reel scrawny article. Hardly a man at all beside Billy. Mind ye, when ye see all the cut af sum of them pop stars nowadays...'

The ... was Reggie's own addition. If there had been any onward discussion about modern music the constable had had the good sense to leave it out, and the statement had ended with Kelly Atkins leaving to collect her children from school.

Reggie set down the piece of paper and glanced at his watch. Eight-thirty. His wife would have dinner on the table in an hour and she'd be expecting him home long before that. He was just about to lock up the station and head there when some instinct born of decades of experience made the Donegal man think again. He'd met the Kelly Atkins of this world, and despite the danger they lived amongst they were usually decent, truthful sorts. She'd taken a risk telling them what she'd seen so the least that he could do was follow it up properly.

So, instead of turning left out of the main gate of the Demesne, towards the Knock Dual Carriageway, home and food, Sergeant Reginald Boyd turned right, towards Belfast City Centre, the M1 south and the Travis Estate. He had no way of knowing it but he was about to uncover one of the jigsaw's most important bits.

\*\*\*\*

Kyle Spence knew he should be at the Travis interviewing Eileen Regent, but he loathed contact with relatives, especially ones who might cry on his suit. Besides, the woman had just viewed her son's dead body so she'd need some time alone, and with any luck another day would change Craig's mind about him interviewing her and he'd give the task to someone more sympathetic like Annette.

It was enough rationalisation to justify the ex-spook making the call that he'd wanted to make all day, and ten minutes later he was parking up a Cathedral Quarter alley to walk the remaining few yards to his destination on the less favoured side of the street. The venue was one of the quarter's lesser known pubs, as yet undiscovered by the local hipsters and yuppies, although he conceded mournfully that it was bound to happen soon. Then it would be all poncey micro-brewery ales, and cocktails with curly straws. But for now it was just the sort of pub that Spence liked: dark, almost empty, and with whatever punters that were there of the borderline criminal sort. This was the sort of place where secrets dropped, from the mouths of people who got paid by the word.

A moment's sojourn by the bar was ended by a quick scan of the space and a nod, then the detective lifted his pint and moved soundlessly to a back table, where the expensively suited man who was waiting for him sat with his back to the room. Spence was slightly surprised; not by his guest's stance but by his outfit; he'd only ever seen Trevor Rudkin wearing jeans before. Rudkin's stylish suit was a marker of his recently elevated status as special advisor and his new and very useful proximity to power; it was also a reminder of the genius that had made the Intelligence Officer spot the civil servant's potential years before when Rudkin was a lowly admin officer and recruit him as his snout.

The D.I. pulled up a stool and sat opposite his floppy-haired informant. Nothing was said for a moment, both men sipping their drinks in the tense, silent romance of a detective and his source. Occasionally Spence would snatch a glance at the man facing him, taking in first Rudkin's hands, both visible and unarmed, and then his expression, a man with something to impart but something that was making him afraid. Good. Informants were only useful when they were nervous, the rest of the time he just wanted them to fade back into their mire.

Halfway down his pint the ex-spy broke the silence.

"You've got something for me."

It wasn't a question.

"Spill."

Trevor Rudkin shook his head. "I need a guarantee first."

"Of what? You'll get paid, don't worry about that."

Rudkin's face contorted angrily, taking the detective aback. Weak, faux-liberal and gruesomely ambitious had been Spence's assessment of the civil servant, but aggressive hadn't been anywhere on the list. Rudkin spat out his next words.

"Fuck your money! You couldn't pay me what this is worth. I want my back watched until you've locked them all up."

Spence leant forward, his interest piqued. "All who? I need names."

"Guarantee my safety first."

The D.I. narrowed his eyes in disbelief. Who did the man think he was? The bloody FBI? Organising witness protection was a near impossible task on an island as small as this one, but after a qualm of conscience that died in its infancy Spence nodded the lie that said he could.

Appeased, Rudkin started to spill.

"I've only got one name, but I'm on the road to getting more."

"Who's the one?"

The informant glanced around the room, for what Spence had no idea. The nearest table was twenty feet away and a directional mike would have stood out like a nudist in a church.

Rudkin dropped his quiet voice even further. "Joshua Loughrey. He's the IBP's member in the European Parliament."

An MEP. Spence knew that it meant something more than the obvious, but what he didn't have a clue.

"What about him?"

"He was involved in the hit on McManus."

As Spence felt the familiar dart of excitement that made his life worthwhile, Rudkin sat back and folded both arms across his Armani.

"I don't know anything else."

The ex-spook wasn't having it, he needed as much information as possible right now. Not to solve the case or for brownie points from Craig, he didn't give a monkey's about either of those, but for his own, almost pathological his father had said, need to be the smartest kid in the room.

His next question emerged in a hiss.

*"Involved how?* You can't just say that and not elaborate. Was Loughrey there?"

*Damn*. As soon as the words were out Spence knew he'd given something away.

Rudkin frowned. "I'd heard it was a lone gunman on a roof."

The D.I. back-pedalled swiftly. "It was. I meant was Loughrey in on the planning? Is that what you mean by involved?"

The confusion in the civil servant's eyes said that he might just have got away with his gaff. After a moment Rudkin unfolded his arms and leaned forward again.

"Not the logistics of it, but definitely the decision. That was what I heard anyway. I'll know more in a few days. I'm accompanying him to Brussels for a trade meeting tomorrow, until Thursday night."

Long enough for Spence to do some digging around.

"I want details of your itinerary."

A tightening of the advisor's lips said no. He didn't want Spence asking the Belgian plods to follow them around.

"OK, then, a blow by blow of what happens over there as it does."

A shake of the head indicated that the detective would have to wait.

"When I get back. I can't take the risk of being caught on the phone to you. I'm on trial. It's my first big trip with him."

Spence nodded; it was fair enough. He had a lead that he could run with now, so he would get on with that. He decided to change tack.

"Tell me what you know about Veronica Lewis."

The immediate upward flash of the civil-servant's eyebrows said any denial that he knew the madam would be a lie. Rudkin realised instantly that he'd blown it so he tried for obfuscation, answering the question in a vague tone.

"I may have heard the name somewhere. Who is she?"

"Don't kid a kidder, Trevor. You know her all right.

How?"

A heavy sigh signalled the advisor's surrender.

"She hosted a party that senior IBP members attended a few months back."

The D.I. didn't attempt to conceal his sneer. "Kid's birthday party?"

Rudkin snorted, sending a fountain of white wine down his silk tie. He dabbed furiously at it as he spoke.

"Only if the kids were grown men wearing nappies."

Spence nodded slowly. "Ah... *that* sort of party." He asked another question that he already knew the answer to. "Was it the first or just the most recent party?"

The government servant called his bluff. "You obviously already know the answer to that."

"OK, then. Here's another. Where are they held?"

Rudkin shrugged. "Beats me. I've been too low down the food chain to get invited until now -"

The detective cut him off. *"Until now?"*

The smug expression that appeared on Rudkin's face nearly made him puke.

"Loughrey said the Brussels trip would just be the first of my perks."

Spence smiled to himself. He could tolerate a bit of smugness if it gave him an inside man. Rudkin was still talking.

"I do know that they're mostly held in Ireland, both parts, but last year there were rumours of one being held near Bruges."

Kyle felt the dart again.

"Same people, or would there have been more MEPs at that one, by any chance?"

Rudkin joined in his smile. "There was at least one."

Spence drained his pint before asking his next question. "So, this party you've been invited to, when is it?"

"I didn't say..."

The denial faded away as Rudkin conceded with a shrug. He'd never admitted to having a definite invitation, but

Spence was clever, so there was no point withholding the date now.

"This Saturday night. I don't know where yet. I'll let you know if or when I do."

The D.I. nodded, his pulse speeding up. He would be at that party as well, even if he had to hide in Rudkin's car boot to get there. It would be the perfect opportunity to find out what was happening inside the IBP.

As he rose to leave, his mind was racing with everything he'd just discovered. Joshua Loughrey had attended at least one of Veronica Lewis' parties, and there'd been no love lost between him and the dead First Minister for some reason, despite both of them being in the IBP. Internal political strife, assassination plots and sex scandals; the week was beginning to look up.

\*\*\*\*

## High Street Station. 10 p.m.

Veronica Lewis' pallor had subsided by the time they'd reached High Street, and it subsided further there, courtesy of her make-up bag. By the time she was judged fit for interview the madam was back in control, and Craig cursed the decency he'd been burdened with by his parents for not pushing her harder when she'd been more likely to break.

Liam shook his head from side to side in an 'I told you so' and switched on the interview room recorder, while Jack Harris settled down in the viewing room with his tea. Craig cut straight to the chase.

"Why did you react so strongly to the Earl's plea for your safety, Mrs Lewis? So strongly that you felt the need to call your son and tell him that you were safe and not to speak to the press?"

Veronica Lewis pursed her lips and said nothing so Craig moved forward in his seat.

"Let me tell you what *we* know then. You were

kidnapped from your office last Friday, held hooded and restrained somewhere for five days, and then driven from there in a car-boot to be dumped in Drumnaph Wood. But not before you were roughed up. Comments?"

The answer was silence and a narrowing of her brown eyes.

"OK. There's more. You have a record for soliciting and prostitution, and as well as your apparently respectable design and beauty business you now run a lucrative sideline. Sex parties for wealthy and powerful men."

As her jaw dropped Craig raised a hand. "Please don't bother to deny it. We've already spoken to two of your girls and we know one of the locations you use is the estate of that Earl of Louth, a former TD in the Dáil."

He leant further forward, closing the distance between them.

"Personally, I don't care if these men want to dress up as dogs and be taken for walkies every night of the week."

Liam stifled a grin as he continued.

"But if that's all it was, even if they do have famous faces, I very much doubt that you'd have been treated the way you were." He sat back decisively. "So what else is going on, Mrs Lewis? Drug smuggling? Arms? Trafficking of girls?"

They were the magic words. Suddenly Veronica Lewis disappeared and in her place sat Ronnie Lewis, a vulnerable but fiery sixteen-year-old, left to fend for herself in the world. She snarled at him, her lipsticked lips peeling back to reveal slightly protruding teeth.

"Trafficking? My girls? No bloody way! Do you think I'd ever let those bastards touch underage girls? I'd knife them in the heart before I'd let them do something like that!"

Craig seized on her outrage, lurching forward again. "*Then help us.* Tell us what they're really up to. Tell us *why* they tried to silence you. And they must think that they've succeeded or you'd never have seen daylight again!"

He watched the madam begin to form some words but then think better of it, pushing her chair back and folding her arms tight across her chest. As Lewis shook her dark head Liam thought he caught a look of sadness in her eyes.

"I can't."

"Then just tell us what it isn't. If not girls, is it drugs?"

"Some" was muttered beneath her breath but the way it was said made Craig think they weren't talking about bulk.

"Arms?" and "Antiques smuggling?" were greeted by blank stares that said that both were unlikely, or just as likely that she wasn't privy to everything that went on.

Liam asked the final question of the night. "What else might it be?"

It brought a renewed tightening of her gaze, and Ronnie Lewis, the tough street-fighter, reappeared.

"Nothing else I can tell you, boys. Sorry. And you can't hold me. I'm the victim of an abduction, not under arrest."

They couldn't argue with that, and if they'd been inclined to then Jack's sharp rap on the window would have stopped them in their tracks. But as Veronica Lewis was escorted out to be driven home in a car, Craig wasn't looking half as depressed as Liam's head-in-hands pose suggested he should be.

They decanted to the staff room where Jack had coffee already perking, so Craig filled three mugs before sitting down.

"Well, we've learnt something anyway."

Liam snorted derisively. "What? That Lewis won't tell us a bloody thing?"

"But she did. *Didn't she, Jack?*" Craig turned to see the sergeant nodding his head. "She didn't deny that she was a madam, *or* running the parties, and she told us that whatever the reason was they wanted her silenced, it definitely wasn't because they were trafficking girls."

Liam was unimpressed. "We knew all that already"

"No. We didn't know, we speculated. We also know now that there are drugs in play, *possibly* just for recreational use but we need to get the Drugs Squad on that to make sure. And if there *are* arms or antiques involved then they're a very secondary thing-"

Liam cut him off. "She didn't say that, she just said nothing."

Craig shook his head. "There *might* be some smuggling happening and she mightn't have been told about it, but if it was anything major she would have noticed something, and her reaction would have been hard to disguise. No. If there's smuggling going on it's very small beer. We also have the Earl's estate confirmed by both Lewis and Jenny Morris now. Plus, it was definitely the sight of his name on that webpage that had shocked Lewis, as well as the idea that the press might know more. Which means something else, but I'm not sure what yet."

A frown appeared on Liam's face. "I've a question. Why didn't you ask her about political shenanigans? Like you mentioned at the briefing."

"It was a deliberate omission. I'm not sure that I trust Mrs Lewis not to barter information for her own safety, and until I'm sure of my thinking on that I don't want her party guests alerted in any way." He turned back to the desk sergeant. "So, OK, Jack. What does all that tell you?"

The sergeant shoved Liam's feet off a chair and sat down. "You're right. Recreational drugs when they've never been raided, and legal, if kinky sex, wouldn't force anyone to shut her up. It must be something more. She says there's no trafficking and I believe her, but there could be some dealing and smuggling worth investigating, although my guess is they'd all be pretty low key."

Liam opened his mouth to say something but Jack sped up.

"But there's something really big being discussed at those parties, and Mrs Lewis has either overheard or been part of the talk." He dunked a biscuit in his coffee and took a bite, speaking as he chewed. "So, what's important enough to warrant kidnapping her, and why didn't they finish the job? They need her alive for some reason, that's why, so they put the fear of God into her and let her go."

Liam shrugged. "They need her 'cos she supplies the girls. No girls, no parties."

He was answered by a tut. "Ach, get away with you, Liam. Girls are easy to find."

"You didn't say that when we were on the pull thirty years ago."

Craig smiled at the thought of a twenty-something Liam and Jack lining the walls of some dark club, trying to screw up the courage to speak to girls.

"Jack's right, Liam. There are plenty of brothels around, and if there aren't any local that they fancy then this lot have enough money to fly girls in. Veronica Lewis wasn't kept alive just for her girls."

The D.C.I. frowned. "Maybe she holds the contact list for the parties, then. And before you say it, yes, I know that could be collated again but it would take time. Or maybe they're afraid she'll release the names."

Craig nodded. Both good points. But Liam hadn't finished.

"Or...maybe whatever's going on is time sensitive in some way, and that's why Lewis can't be replaced. They just don't have the time. It would fit with the gun markings being removed."

He didn't see Craig's congratulatory push of the arm coming, and neither did his coffee-filled mug. The brown liquid splashed all over his legs and the floor, eliciting a groan.

"Aw hell! What was that for? These trousers are only new!"

Craig's attempt at a contrite look lost out to his grin.

"I'll buy you a new pair for being a genius. Forget Lewis blackmailing them with the names; unless she'd covered herself with a solicitor releasing her list if she was killed they wouldn't have been afraid of that." He thought again. "Although, let's check that, Liam, just to be sure. But it's your idea that something's time sensitive that's important. If you're right, then working out what that schedule is should tell us exactly what it's for."

\*\*\*\*

**The Demesne Estate. Midnight.**

Tommy Hill had always done his best work at night. Romantically; chasing girls at late night parties and seducing them in the dark. Dealing; drugs and arms, or whatever illegal commodity was in vogue that week. And terrorism; sneaking through Belfast's poorly lit back streets in search of men to assault and kill, or boarding the last bus to gun them down. In fact, he'd been so well known for the preference in his youth that 'Late Night Tommy' had been his onetime moniker.

Nowadays his nights were spent bouncing his granddaughter on his least arthritic knee, or settling down with a whisky to watch Game of Thrones. But every so often, when someone like the cops opened the door, he got the opportunity to remind himself and others of the man that he'd once been.

Tonight was one such occasion, and as he clambered out of his bashed-up Vauxhall and sniffed the danger in the city air, the ex-paramilitary, if such a thing was even possible, felt testosterone surging through his body again. His age-shortened stride lengthened and his knock on the battered front door he'd approached was sharp, the shock on the face of the man who answered it saying that the old Loyalist's reawakened virility wasn't just in his own still-clear mind.

Tommy pushed past his host into the living room, immediately claiming the most luxurious chair in the place.

"Whada ye huv tee drink, McCrae? I've a thirst wud make a python choke."

Rory McCrae had been gawping since he'd opened his front door. Tommy had been the boss of all of them for almost forty years, but he'd gone out to pasture in the sticks three years back and all his old gang, him amongst them, had thought him well out of the way.

Years back or not the old pecking order reinstated itself within seconds and McCrae did as he was bid, retrieving a bottle of Bushmills from a low cupboard and setting two Perspex tumblers on the table, filling them halfway to the top.

Tommy kept talking as he did so.

"Yeer wunderin' wat I'm deein' here."

It was too dangerous to speculate.

"Billy Regent. Wat dee ye knaw abyte him? An' dun't haul anythin' back."

Nervous that it was a test of some sort, McCrae stammered out his reply.

"B...Billy's deed. Shot hisself after he shot McManus, they seed."

Hill snatched a tumbler and swigged down half its contents. "Who seed?"

McCrae took a hard seat opposite, risking a small shrug. Any bigger and Tommy might batter him for disrespect.

"The pigs, I suppose, but nye it's the word on the street. Billy did hisself in wi' a handgun. Right in the heed."

Tommy fell silent for a moment, gazing down at the honey-coloured liquid and swirling it this way and that in the light of a small, fringed lamp. When he spoke again it was in a way he liked to think of as investigative, picturing Jeremy Paxman giving him the nod.

"*Ye think?* Do ye believe everythin' that yeer taul?"

The question's ambiguity made his erstwhile follower freeze. Rory McCrae had been tricked by Tommy asking questions like that before, and one wrong response had landed him with a bullet in the leg. Thankfully Tommy's role-playing didn't require any comeback and he carried on as if McCrae had already filled in the gap.

"Tell me abyte Billy. Word is he wus a right heed-case afer he gat demobbed."

That one McCrae could answer with authority.

"Aye. He wus. Under some army doctor he wus. Used to

take hisself up there twice a week."

"Up where?"

"Craigantlet Barracks. That's where they dee awl that therapy shite. Billy seed all they did wus talk abyte things that'd happened. He seed it wus jest making him wurse."

Tommy would leave it to Craig to pull the medical records, what he needed to know now was who, if anyone, Billy Regent had blamed for his trauma. He asked the question, but the answer wasn't what he'd hoped.

"The A-rabs. That's who he blamed. Billy said we shud never huv gone back there in oh-three. Said it wus the wurst days work the guverment ever did."

That sounded more positive.

"Ar guverment? So Billy blamed *awl* politicians? Fer starting the war, like."

Hatred for politicians could explain why the First Minister had bitten the dirt. McCrae's emphatically shaken head dashed Tommy's hopes again.

"Nah, only the yank ones. Billy said once America'd started it we had to go along. Ar lat had no say wun way ar another, no matter wat they thought. Mind ye, he hated that English primeminster twat."

Damn. Without Billy blaming *all* UK politicians his shooting of McManus made no sense, and the only thing he could do was point Craig towards the army shrinks. As Tommy was about to leave he thought of another question that made his hopes rise one last time.

"McManus wus definitely ar man, wusn't he?"

McCrae nodded warily, wondering where the question might lead. "Aye, aye, he wus."

"So he was well in with UKUF and awl the gangs, like?"

McCrae had inherited UKUF from Tommy and been running it in his image for years, so he could answer the question with certainty.

"No doubt. McManus even drapped down to see me in the affice nye and then, just to be sure we wus getting ar dues from guverment, like. Like the valuble community wurkers we ar."

Milking the system more like.

Tommy sat forward slowly, his rasping tones becoming more intense.

"Wus he welcum?"

The question made McCrae furrow his brow in confusion, then his face cleared again as he realised what Tommy meant.

"Aye, well, the big boys awl welcummed him, like, but there wus a few wee shites who'd thought he'd sold out. On account of his Europe love, like. We kicked them back intee line if we heered. McManus wus ar lad."

So not all Loyalists had agreed with Peter McManus' Pro-EU stance, but the usual suspects who might have killed him, the paramilitary gangs, the MLA had had the sense to keep sweet.

The information was enough for Tommy. It would earn him some more dosh from the Ghost. He twisted his thin lips into a smile, slammed down his glass and jumped to his feet, his new-found testosterone administering a cheerful slap around the head to his old deputy as he marched past him to the door.

# Chapter Eight

**Wednesday. 9.30 a.m.**

Jennifer Wasson was surprised when she answered her front door to find three police officers standing there impassively, instead of the one predictably eager customer that she'd expected to greet, but not as surprised as Jake was when he saw the glamorous, perfectly-coiffed beauty who'd replaced the soccer mom they'd interviewed two days before. The transformative effects of make-up and creative upholstery always left him in awe, but the effort it took to apply them always made him grateful he was a man.

Annette gave the escort an apologetic look and slipped past her into the apartment's hall.

"We won't keep you long, Ms Wasson. I can see that you're expecting company."

The fact that it was only nine-thirty in the morning confirmed all Annette's suspicions about men.

Jenny Wasson squinted suspiciously at the D.I.'s words, but despite searching hard for some judgment in them there was none to be found. Annette never condemned people who sold themselves, only those who sold and bought them, and her moral judgements were never for anyone who'd experienced poverty. She had no idea what she would have done if she'd had no partner, no job and kids to feed, and her government benefits had barely made ends meet, but selling her body would probably have been on the list.

The escort gave a heavy sigh and waved the group through to the living room, glancing pointedly at her watch.

"You've ten minutes. What do you want to know?"

Aidan Hughes produced the photograph Davy had given him. "Can you confirm that this was the venue you visited in May?"

The young woman gazed hard at the photograph, then admitted defeat and produced a pair of glasses from behind the clock, donning them with an embarrassed explanation.

"They don't fit the image. Men don't make passes at girls who wear glasses, and all that."

Aidan smiled at her. "I like specs myself."

Wasson looked at the photograph again and then nodded. "That's the place. How did you find it so quickly?"

"The statue you described, and we have a good analyst."

She handed the print back with a question. "Who owns it, then?"

Hughes shook his head and nodded towards a chair. "Mind if we sit down?"

"Sorry. Forgot my manners." She turned back to Annette. "Something else to ask? Only time's moving on."

Annette had split the next part into two, nodding Jake to start.

"Jake."

He'd been so busy analysing the ingredients of the housewife's transformation that the prompt caught him on the hop.

"Sorry. Yes." He produced a list from his pocket. "Ms Wasson, do any of these things ring a bell, in your experience of the Lewis parties. Trafficking of girls?"

She shook her head hard.

"Drugs?"

"Weed, Blow and Viagra. Nothing else that I saw."

"Large or small quantities?"

"Medium. Recreational. Vero supplied it for the punters."

Drug dealing; Veronica Lewis had conveniently omitted to say that the drugs had come from her. He moved down the list.

"Antiques or gun smuggling?"

The escort's on-fleek eyebrows shot up.

"Who do you think we are? The Mafia? There's nothing like that going on. It's just a bunch of sad old men living it large."

The D.S. folded up the page and put it away. "That brings

us onto the next question. Can you think of anyone who might have been injured, or perhaps disappeared suddenly from a party? One of the regular party goers perhaps? Girls or punters?"

This time her gaze was sceptical. "You think they'd get so excited they'd kill a girl?"

"Would they?"

Her emerald eyes widened in alarm. "NO! It's not that kind of sex. There's no hard-core S&M, just a bit of light bondage and a lot of idiots who want to clean the lav with a toothbrush. The strongest stuff I've ever seen was one of the girls locking a man in a cupboard because he'd enjoyed it so much at his posh boarding school."

Jake pressed the point. "Anyone ever injured?"

She frowned. "One fat man had a heart attack and they carted him off in an ambulance."

"When was this?"

Her reply was to produce a diary from beneath the kitchen sink. When Aidan saw a list of dates he had to stop himself making a grab for the book.

Jenny Wasson rifled through the pages until she stopped at a red asterisk.

"January twentieth; it was a Wednesday. Don't ask me where it happened though, 'cos I've no idea. They took him away in an ambulance."

Jake had an idea. "Did it have an area logo?"

"Nope. Just Northern Ireland Ambulance and that green and yellow chequerboard down the side."

"Did you take down the number plate, by any chance?"

Wasson's eyebrows did an amused dance. "And where would I have kept my pen and paper? I wasn't wearing a lot of clothes at the time!"

As they'd been talking Annette had gently eased the diary from the young woman's hands, reassuring her when she'd finally noticed with. "It's just so I can make a note of the party dates."

The escort considered for a moment and then shrugged,

knowing that the dates wouldn't give them places or names.

"They're the ones marked in red."

Jake returned to his theme.

"Any of the punters ever disappear?"

"Like I said, not so I noticed, but I didn't keep a list of who was there." She glanced at her watch again, becoming exasperated. "Look, if I give you a couple of other girls' names so you can check with them, will you please stop coming here?"

The sergeant took out his phone, his finger poised to type.

"OK. Grainne Masters and Izzy Watson will speak to you. I've checked." She gestured towards Aidan. "Your mate here will know how to find them. Now, you really need to go. *Please.*"

She was answered by a final question from Annette. "Do you recognise any of these men as attending the parties?"

Unnoticed by their hostess the D.I. had been carrying a smart-pad, and it was now displaying images of every male MLA, MEP, MP and Irish TD. They watched as Wasson's eyes widened.

"I'm not telling you! Do you want *me* disappeared like Vero? No-one's seen her for days."

Annette's reply was quiet. "Mrs Lewis is well and back at home."

The young woman's relief was palpable, but her pink lips pursed tightly, accompanied by a determined shaking of her head.

"I've two kids to think of. I'm saying nothing more."

"We can protect you."

Wasson gave the snort that she felt the words deserved. "Don't make me laugh! Belfast's graveyards are full of people the police protected."

She walked past Jake and into the hall, opening the front door pointedly. As they filed out past her the young mother repeated her warning of two days before.

"You'd best be careful yourselves. These people are

seriously connected, and they won't hesitate to get rid of anyone who threatens them, even the police."

Then they were back on the landing with the door closed behind them, trying hard to ignore the red-faced man lurking by the lift.

\*\*\*\*

## The C.C.U. 11 a.m.

Kyle Spence was hovering. Not literally, he'd have had to have been a superhero or a Harrier jet to manage that, but irritatingly, so irritatingly that Ash wanted to swat him like a fly. After ten minutes of not being able to hit the detective and being unable to pretend that he wasn't there, the analyst sighed with the theatricality of an Elizabethan actor and turned his colourful head towards the stalker.

"Yes?"

It was all the prompt Spence needed. He pulled up a chair and leant his elbows on the computer expert's desk.

"Peter McManus."

"I'll need more than that. If you'd just wanted his bio you could have googled it yourself."

Spence sat back, folding his arms. "I have. I've also accessed his Police Intelligence file. It's in your inbox now."

Ash checked immediately, surprised to find that it was true. He didn't trust Kyle Spence; he was the kind of man that would make him want to count his fingers after they'd shaken hands, and if he was giving him information now he had to have an ulterior motive.

He decided to call the D.I.'s bluff.

"So? What do you want from me?"

The cheekiness of the question brought a guffaw from the jaded spy. He liked people who took no shit; in his experience, they were the type you could rely on when there was devious stuff to be done.

"The American spooks. You're working with them. Yes?"

Ash pointed to his hair. "What do you think?"

Spence sat forward again. "Well, OK then. We're in business. See, the bio on McManus released by the Assembly, the one from his party website, and even his Intelligence file all say the same thing. Forty-year-old family man. Some weed smoked when he was a kid, a bit of medium-core porn watching when he thought the wife isn't looking, but basically the most radical things about the man were his political views."

Ash had been typing as Spence spoke, now he turned his screen around for the detective to see. It said what Kyle Spence already knew. Peter McManus had been the youngest ever leader of the Independent Britain Party, formed in two thousand and six. The party had had an almost meteoric rise since its inception, now holding forty percent of the popular vote. Its policies were simple: unionist, anti-immigration, tax breaks for the indigenous population and no health or social security benefits for residents of less than five years, but it had traditionally stopped short of saying that it wanted out of the EU.

Ash was surprised. "The IBP's Pro-EU? I didn't expect that. Did you?"

It was a hard one to answer but Spence tried. "Pro might be a bit strong. Publicly, it's not *against* remaining in the EU, but my guess is that most IBP members wouldn't exactly cry if we left. But presumably that Pro-EU public stance was why McManus could act as IBP leader. He'd been very vocal about not wanting to leave because he thought it would be bad for the UK, although he *had* wanted the EUs' powers radically limited here."

"Sounds like he was trying to appease the party hardliners with that. It's unlikely to happen anyway; you're either in or out, and in means following all the EU's rules. David Cameron learnt all about that inflexibility when he tried to negotiate a better deal with Brussels."

Kyle nodded.

"And privately that's what a lot of the IBP's members

think as well. The party's hard right-wing definitely wants out, and they'll be given a free vote in the referendum. No-one's being forced to vote along party lines this time."

Ash scratched his head. "So...what? You're saying McManus was unpopular within his own party, even though they'd voted him leader?"

"A substantial proportion of it." Spence chose his next words carefully, in light of what he'd learnt the evening before. "But I honestly can't see the *party* killing McManus, not weeks before the referendum vote. It risks too much confusion amongst their grass roots voters."

Which didn't rule out a plot by a lone wolf like Josh Loughrey, or even a small group.

"Even though McManus is succeeded by his deputy, Roger Burke, who everyone knows is to the right of Attila the Hun?"

The D.I. shook his head immediately. "Nope. Too obvious. Assassinating McManus risked bringing public sympathy for his family *and* his Pro-EU political opinions, and a seasoned politician like Burke would never have taken that risk."

Ash nodded. "OK. But you think there might be something else in McManus' background that could give a reason for his death, so you want me to find out if there's a CIA file on him."

Spence shook his head, surprising the analyst again. "I already know that there's a file. What I want *you* to do is get me a copy of it. And while you're at it, check out Joshua Loughrey MEP as well."

\*\*\*\*

## The Labs. Saintfield Road, Belfast.

John stared at the computer readout through bleary eyes, the product of a night of insomnia from worrying. Natalie had slept on the pull-out bed in the study instead of beside him the night before, and as well as worrying about her unhappiness it had made him afraid for himself.

He'd decided very quickly after saying 'I do' that he liked being married. Even with all the petty arguments about chores, the colour scheme debates when they'd been decorating that had continued into the wee small hours, and the way that his beloved bachelor solitude, often spent seemingly doing nothing but staring at a wall, although in reality he was of course thinking great thoughts, was invaded now by Natalie's less than quiet hurling of her shoes at her wardrobe rack, in an attempt to best her own record for accuracy as if she was playing some bespoke version of crazy darts. Even *with* all those irritations he enjoyed the institution of marriage, and he would prefer that his endured longer than a mere two years.

Tiredness made his mind career wildly to a scenario where Natalie suddenly hurled her shoes at him instead of into the wardrobe, and followed by pointing her finger towards the door and muttering the word *"divorce"* in an ominous tone. The image made him shudder and lift the phone. Ten minutes later he'd enlisted help with his domestic dilemma and was able to return to his computer with a clearer mind.

The DNA profile that he was looking at was, however, even less clear than it had been the day before. Given that the profile had matched no-one on the UK database, or even those criminals one hundred miles south of where he stood, he had passed it on to Davy to run it through Europe's databanks and perhaps even further afield.

However, somehow he'd still expected that when the deeper analysis yielded the perpetrator's ethnicity, it would have been mainly Celt, Anglo-Saxon, or perhaps, at a stretch, possess Spanish or Viking remnants, reflecting the times when those races had either been shipwrecked off or had invaded Irish shores, but the profile in front of him held none of those things.

It was distinct, almost one hundred percent pure and a

profile rarely found in Northern Ireland, and as it printed out in front of him John made a second call. This time to Craig.

\*\*\*\*

## The C.C.U. 11.30 a.m.

Craig stared hard at the biography in front of him, hoping that its content would miraculously morph into a clue, or even better, a reason for a man to die. Almost forty-eight hours had passed since the death of the First Minister and still nothing made sense.

He scanned Peter McManus' file again. The pages held everything that the IBP, Assembly and Police Intelligence held on him, the latter given to Ash by Kyle, in his opinion rather too eagerly. His old flatmate was up to something, but then, wasn't he always? It was a trait that irritated the buggery out of him as a police officer, and yet he couldn't deny that Kyle's subterfuge yielded results, which was the only reason that he tolerated him at all.

It was ironic. He was the Head of Intelligence now as well as Head of Murder, but the information that came to him through legitimate channels via Roy Barrett was never half as juicy as what Kyle pulled out of his hat. The moment that hat was empty he'd shunt him back to where he belonged.

He turned back to the biography. On the face of it Peter McManus had had an uneventful life until his death. A local boy from East Belfast he'd been an average student at grammar school, until A Level when he'd suddenly excelled at politics. It was an excellence that had sent him via Cambridge University to the incubator of Washington, and then back to Northern Ireland's turbulent political microclimate for maturation and an accelerated rise to the top.

Craig squinted at the description of their dead man's

party-political views: 'Unionist. Middle of the road, albeit with a firm line on immigration, but no Loyalist paramilitary links and a quasi-liberal, Pro-EU stance'. It made McManus sound like the political equivalent of white bread, but no-one shoots a sliced loaf, not even a Belfast one.

The detective shook his head in frustration. There *had* to be something more in McManus' past, something that had made someone hate him; not even a dissident Republican would have been so offended by the views in front of him that it would have made them raise a finger against the man, never mind a gun.

So convinced was Craig that they were missing something that he opened his office door and yelled, "Ash. Can you come in here? Liam, you too."

As they approached something else occurred to him.

"Actually...why are you here, Liam? I thought you'd decided to go and see Ken instead of talking over the phone."

Liam continued walking into the office, taking a seat before he replied.

"Two o'clock. Andy's coming too. Soldier boy couldn't see us till then. Something to do with the paperwork for his leaving thing."

"Resigning his commission. That makes sense. There must be red tape."

Craig closed the door, then lifted the file on his desk and waved it in the air.

"Is this really all there is on McManus, Ash?"

The analyst was hovering beside the percolator so the detective took the hint, pouring three coffees before sitting down. Ash took a sip of his before answering.

"That's practically what Kyle said. He's asked me to check if McManus has a CIA file as well."

Craig raised an eyebrow. "Anything else Kyle asked for?"

Ash smiled, setting down his mug. "Everything I can find on the IBP MEP, Joshua Loughrey. He didn't say why."

Liam grunted cynically. "Because Spooky's up to his old tricks, that's why!"

As the analyst gave him a quizzical glance, Craig answered for them both.

"You have limited experience of our newest inspector, Ash, but Liam and I know Kyle of old. If he's asking about Joshua Loughrey it means that he already knows something."

Liam nodded. "Something he's keeping to himself until it's the right time to score him points." He took a gulp of coffee and then returned to an earlier point. "McManus will have a CIA file, for sure. So will Loughrey. They all have once they're elected. The yanks like to keep tabs on things."

Craig concurred. "Not that it will say much more than you already know. There might be a few more details on McManus smoking behind the bike shed at school and whatnot, and they'll have listed any suspicions they had about him, however unfounded, but anything really juicy they'd have been obliged to share with MI5 and six. Joshua Loughrey's much more interesting. His name hasn't come up before."

Ash took out his smart-pad and tapped. "That's what I thought, so I checked." When a government page bearing a photograph of the MEP appeared, the analyst read aloud. "Joshua Clem Loughrey, thirty-five, single, studied law at Queen's and was called to the Bar in two thousand and nine as a barrister specialising in European law."

He set down the pad, continuing from memory. "He only practiced for two years before joining the IBP and getting elected as one of their MEPs in twenty-fourteen. He seems to spend most of his time in Brussels, in fact he's off there again today. Back on Friday."

Craig considered for a moment before speaking. "Anything up in his private life? Women? Men? Robots?"

The question made Ash smile and the smile's slowness perked Liam up.

"Aye, aye, I know that look. It's the one tabloid

journalists get when some celeb's been caught with their trousers down. Smurf?"

The analyst obliged his curiosity with a grin.

"The internet's a wonderful thing, you know. It can hold social media accounts for decades. Even ones that people have forgotten all about."

He tapped his pad again several times, pulling up a FaceChat page which showed a younger looking Joshua Loughrey in bed with three women, each of them wearing nothing but a winning smile.

Liam gawped at the images, gesturing Ash to scroll for more. When he reached the bottom of the page everybody laughed.

"Where were they taken?" and "Who were the girls?", was followed by Craig's slightly more relevant "The white powder on that table didn't look like chalk."

Liam got back to the point.

"OK... so our Joshua, the Joshua that Kyle's investigating for some reason, was a naughty boy in his youth. But that was years back-"

Ash cut in, shaking his head. "Only six. The photos were posted in two thousand and ten."

Craig's eyebrows rose; the MEP had looked much younger than twenty-nine in the images. Power must have had an aging effect on him, or the chalk.

Liam continued, put out at being interrupted. "OK, but they weren't taken nowadays, that's my point. Loughrey wasn't an MEP in those photos, so where's the relevance to our case?" He added a caveat, realising the naiveté of his assumption. "That's always supposing it still *is* our case that Kyle's working on, and not some bloody hobby horse of his own?"

It wasn't as farfetched as it sounded, Kyle undoubtedly marched to his own drum, but Craig thought that the fact that Loughrey was in the IBP made it unlikely this time. He answered Liam's first question in fits and starts, leaning back in his chair.

"OK...We have Peter McManus, leader of the IBP and First Minister, murdered for reason or reasons unknown. We also have Kyle curious about Joshua Loughrey, also member of the IBP, but on the MEP side..." His forehead furrowed as he thought. "MEP...MEP..."

Before he could say it a third time Ash cut in.

"The IBP is a nominally Pro-EU party, but Kyle hinted that might just be its public face, with plenty inside the party bound to vote leave in the referendum, including McManus' deputy Roger Burke."

Craig nodded, still frowning. "Pro-EU, and Loughrey's an MEP, which means if the referendum results in a vote to leave the EU Loughrey will be out of a job in two years."

He sat forward suddenly. "Park that thought. It might mean something but that's not what's on my mind. Just bear with me for a minute while I think this through. OK. So, Josh Loughrey aged twenty-nine was a naughty boy. There were women and booze in those photos, and probably drugs. So, he was living it up generally."

Liam nodded. "And without the wit God gave him not to put it all online. How the heck he avoided being arrested for possession beats me. And disbarred. He was a first-year barrister in those snaps."

Craig shook his head. "Check the location on the images. Loughrey was in the Caribbean at the time. Even if the police here *had* speculated that the powder in those photos was coke, there would have been no way of proving it. But it's not what Loughrey did then that interests me. What interests me is how often, in your experience, does a sexually adventurous, hard drinking, drug user stop doing those things?"

Liam grinned. "I did, when I got married."

Craig laughed so hard he almost choked. "In your dreams! The hardest thing you've ever taken is an aspirin, and as for being sexually adventurous, three women in twenty years really doesn't count."

While Ash did the sums on his own love life, Craig

carried on.

"But even if you're right, Liam, Ash said Loughrey was still single, so even if he's acquired the sense not to post about it nowadays, I very much doubt that his liking for the high life has changed. Which begs the question; how come it's never hit the tabloids here? First chance they'd got The Chronicle's journalists would have plastered it across the front page."

He lifted the phone suddenly. "Davy. Can you check something for me...Yes, now, please. Joshua Loughrey; he's a European member of parliament for the IBP. See if he's been mentioned in the press or media here or in Europe in the past..." He covered the receiver quickly. "Ash, when did Loughrey join the IBP?... OK, Davy, since two thousand and eleven. Quickly, please. And bring in whatever you find."

As he dropped the receiver, Liam nodded. "You think Loughrey's still drugging and wenching-"

"Wenching? What is this? Medieval times?"

"Ach, you know what I mean. Girls! But you think he's just doing it privately now."

"If Davy doesn't find anything, I'd say that he has to be."

Liam shrugged. "OK, but so what? Who's to say he hasn't just been doing it at home?"

Craig was sceptical. "With girls he's picked up in bars or clubs? Or even escorts he's hired over the phone? You honestly think that he'd risk one of them selling an 'MEP in a threesome' story to a local tabloid?" The detective shook his head. "No. Loughrey's doing it much more discreetly than that. He's one of-"

Just then the office door opened and Davy appeared. Craig waved him in.

"That was fast. What have you got?"

Davy shook his head. "I haven't finished yet. I've left the s...searches running. But I'll tell you what I *have* found." He set a printout on the desk. "This."

Craig read aloud. "This person has requested that all information on them since two thousand and six be removed from the internet.' Loughrey's taken advantage of the Right to Be Forgotten ruling."

Ash sniggered. "Well, they obviously missed FaceChat." At Davy's curious glance he added. "I'll show you later."

Davy crossed his arms and leant against the door frame. "I *can* tell you that the only mentions of Loughrey in the Irish or UK press are reports on IBP functions and events at the European Parliament. I'd already created a s...search algorithm to target the press here. There's nothing on the main media channels' web caches either. The rest are running now so I'll let you know about those soon."

Craig gave a satisfied nod. "Thanks, Davy. I don't think you'll find anything there either but keep looking."

The senior analyst straightened up to leave. "Just before I go, chief. Ash dug into McArdle and Bell, so I'll send their bios through to your computer."

"Anything exciting?"

Both analysts answered "no", then Davy backtracked.

"OK. So...if you believe what you read they're both solid family men."

Craig heard the unspoken caveat.

"But?"

"Well, apart from the fact that even attending Lewis' parties s...says different, both are also substantial donors to the IBP."

Liam turned, surprised. "How did you find that out? Political donations don't have to be made public here."

Unlike in the rest of the UK, but then Northern Ireland had always made up its own rules.

Davy tapped his nose. "I have my sources."

Craig shook his head. "I don't want to know."

Ash did, but it would have to wait.

"OK, good work, Davy. Check Bell and McArdle out on social media as well, just in case something slipped through like with Loughrey. Let me know what you get."

As the analyst closed the door behind him, Craig turned to gaze at the river, thinking aloud as he did.

"Three men: Loughrey, McArdle and Bell. Two of them we're certain attend Veronica Lewis' parties, yet all three look squeaky-clean online -"

Liam cut in. "Except for FaceBat."

Ash rolled his eyes but let the error pass.

Craig turned back to face them. "Luckily Loughrey missed that, so we now know what his hobbies are. Hobbies that he's unlikely to have given up. But he can't risk exposure now that he's an elected official, so he has to be certain that the girls he sees won't talk and that his drug use doesn't get him arrested, and where better to do that than Veronica Lewis' parties." He banged a hand on the desk suddenly, making the others jump. "We need to find out when the next party is, and we *need* to get a man inside."

Liam puffed out his cheeks, expelling the air slowly. "Nice idea, boss, and we might stand a chance on the first if Annette and Aidan dig up something from Lewis' girls, but we haven't a hope in hell of getting someone in undercover. It would take months of work to get Lewis to trust us now that she's been got at, and anyway, a cop would stick out like a sore thumb, not to mention what the C.C. would say if he got wind of it."

Craig sighed, knowing that he was right. Even if they found out the date of the next party and where it was being held, they hadn't a hope in hell of getting someone inside fast enough to be of use to their investigation. But as the detective thought through the possibilities further he perked up, his lips lifting in a smile.

"We might not be able to get someone new inside, but we could lean on someone who already is."

# Chapter Nine

**The Cathedral Quarter, Belfast City Centre.**

The Fox wasn't happy, and the troughs that frowning had left in his normally smooth forehead were testament to that fact, as was the number of cigarettes he'd sucked his way through that morning, first in the air-conditioned bathroom of his city centre hotel room, and then as he wandered the Cathedral Quarter's streets in search of a bar where he could smoke inside.

He wasn't sure why he was less happy than the day before, but he was. As far as he knew the investigation into the First Minister's killing was nearing an end, a dead one from what he'd heard from his sources in the force, and the madam's discovery and interview had given the cops nothing, just as she had promised it would. So why could he feel a beast with sharp claws gnawing at his guts?

Even if he would never admit it out loud he already knew the answer. The situation had too many moving parts. A madam whose promise of silence relied only upon fear and her desire to protect her kid, normally a solid bet with a mother but you could never tell with a promiscuous slag like that. And his shooter, who was so convinced they'd covered their tracks on the rooftop that it was verging on arrogance. OK, setting up a disillusioned soldier who felt the State had let him down to take the fall had been genius, but it still made him nervous; there were too many people who might care that Billy Regent had died. Yes, they were the poor and powerless and the powerless were usually voiceless too, so he could hope that any queries they raised would be ignored or squashed by the stature of the man that Regent had killed; but hoping always made him nervous, he much preferred certainty. Billy Regent's family had better let the sleeping squaddie lie or they would find themselves joining him in the grave, even if he had to pull the trigger himself.

The Fox glanced up suddenly to find himself outside an entry whose cobbles and cosy ambience, palpable even from where he stood, said there would be a bar there that would exactly fit his bill. As he turned to walk down the narrow thoroughfare in search of comfort he failed to spot the man following behind, a man whose presence would only ever be made known to him if the operation was about to fail.

\*\*\*\*

**12 p.m.**

Liam had it all nicely planned. Lunch at The James then out to see Tommy after one, returning to the ranch via his two o'clock meeting at Craigantlet Army Base, just in time for the briefing Craig had called. The D.C.I. was rubbing his stomach in anticipation on his way to the lift when he found Andy and Craig suddenly walking by his side.

"Liam, you're with us."

His automatic "Aw, boss" was cut off by Craig's brisk shake of the head.

"I don't want to hear it. We're off to the Travis to meet Kyle and then John wants to see us at the lab." As the lift doors opened he added. "As Andy's tagging along for your later meetings, you can take him in your car."

There was no more conversation until they arrived at the estate, parking at the makeshift headquarters Reggie Boyd had established in a van and clambering up its steps to get inside. Craig got to the point immediately.

"Where's Kyle? He was supposed to be meeting us here."

Reggie had been sitting with his head down, writing in a log book, forming each of his letters with a care that Craig hadn't taken since he was five. He responded without looking up.

"Good day to you too, sir."

Craig knew when he was being told off.

"Sorry, Reggie. Hello. But I'm in a bit of a hurry, so could you tell me where to find D.I. Spence, please?"

The Donegal man set down his pen and turned to face the group, his soft tones less chastising than before but considerably more bitter.

"You may well ask where Inspector Spence is, sir. I would very much like to know the same. He was supposed to return today to interview Mrs Regent, but I haven't seen hide nor hair of him." He tutted as loudly as Craig thought his good manners would probably allow. "I had to take a W.P.C. up and do it myself, and that's really not on."

Craig sighed and shook his head, while Liam pictured himself roasting the D.I.'s nuts over a barbeque and revelled in the joy that it aroused.

"I'm very sorry, Reggie. It's not good enough. Think of the worst task you can for D.I. Spence, please, and I'll make sure he does it." He gestured to Andy. "Call Nicky and find out where Kyle is. Liam, give Intelligence a call and find out if he's there."

While they did he pulled out a chair and sat down.

"Did the interview with Eileen Regent yield anything?"

The screwing up of the sergeant's face said it might have.

"She was adamant that Billy wouldn't have hurt a fly."

"Despite evidence to the contrary."

Reggie shook his head.

"I believed her, sir. She said he was just starting to get on his feet again after a rough patch when he first came home from Iraq. Apparently, he'd got a new job, starting next week."

Craig's dark brows shoot up. "Working at what?"

"On the new wind farm components at Belfast Docks. He'd worked in the shipyards for a while when he was young. Apprenticed as a welder." He shook his head sadly. "She also said he would never have topped himself because of his wee girl, Molly. Her mum died five years ago, so she really needed her dad."

Craig rushed to shut the image of a crying seven-year-old from his mind. It was a pitiful situation, but he'd have time to feel sad when they'd worked out who'd killed her dad. The thought shocked him; it meant that he'd definitely accepted someone else had pulled the trigger on Billy Regent, and if they *had* done, then who was to say that Billy had shot Peter McManus at all? Or if he had, under his own volition? Billy Regent had had a daughter he loved and a new job starting in a week, so why would he have taken that risk?

An image of someone driving the young man up to Carson's roof by threatening him with death, a death they'd given him ten minutes later anyway, was becoming more and more clear in Craig's mind.

He tuned back into the sergeant's words, asking another question.

"You know that Doctor Winter thinks there was a second man on the roof? Someone who killed Regent and made it look like suicide."

Reggie nodded. "I'd heard something like that. You think he slipped away and mingled with the cops."

Craig corrected him hastily. "Or the residents. He could have been disguised to look like either. I'm checking with the Armed Response Commander later, but even the slightest possibility that he mingled with the residents makes it important that you keep your ears to the ground. OK? But no-one's to say a word about our theory. As far as the killer is concerned they need to believe they've got away with things."

As Reggie responded with a nod, Liam came off the phone.

"You'll never believe where that git Spence is! He's only up at Stormont digging around!"

"From that look, I take it you don't mean in the flower beds."

"In the Executive Office, no less! He's questioning their private office staff."

The Executive Office, so named following the Fresh Start Agreement one month before, was the kingdom of the First and Deputy First Ministers and their advisors, with all the intrigue that implied.

Craig rolled his eyes, picturing the damage their resident spy could do in that setting. He wouldn't put it past Kyle to elicit information by threatening the civil servants with unearthing murky deeds from their pasts.

The detective thought quickly. He needed to get to the lab, John had been insistent that he needed to see him, and Liam had all the diplomacy of a breeze block, so he couldn't let him near the Executive Office on his own. That just left their renaissance man.

"Andy. Get up to Stormont and stop Kyle doing whatever he's doing. If I want personnel up there interviewed, which I may well do in the future." He had to hand it to Kyle; he anticipated some of his moves. "Then we'll do it in an orderly way, not let loose Belfast's answer to Jack Bauer."

Liam snorted. "He wishes."

"I meant *verbal* force in Kyle's case."

Craig turned for the door. "Reggie, sorry, but we need to go. Have a squad car take Andy to Stormont, please, and do what you can on what I mentioned. Also, can you send that transcript of Eileen Regent's interview through in full."

As the sergeant followed him out the door, wondering whether he should mention his conversation with Kelly Atkins the night before, Craig reached his car and then turned back.

"Liam, I'll go to the lab on my own. You've got to meet with Tommy. Andy, once you've subdued Kyle, and use a taser on him if you need to, bring him straight back to the ranch. I need to see him, and tell him that *isn't* a choice."

Reggie decided Kelly Atkins would have to wait.

\*\*\*\*

**St Mary's Hospital, Belfast.**

It had been a happy few months since she and Craig had

reconciled, after her near-death episode at the hands of one of his murderers and her subsequent terror of a repeat event. The experience had made her pray to stop loving the detective and try hard to make it true, but the effort had failed abysmally so Katy Stevens, a sensible physician to her patients and colleagues but a blob of romantic putty in Craig's lean, tanned hands, had had to accept that her love for the policeman wasn't something that either she or a psychopath could kill.

They'd been back together for six months now and, fingers crossed, things were going well, so well that since the subject of Craig redecorating his shabby, bachelor-who-was-only-ever-there-to-sleep, apartment had arisen, he'd been dragging his size ten feet. Of course, that *could* just be because his idea of interior design was a wholesale lift from the pages of 'bland home monthly', where the only sign of anything vaguely stylish was a wafer-thin TV on which he and John could watch sport, and he was secretly psyching himself up for a trip to the grey paint aisle of the nearest DIY store. Or...it *might* mean that he was beginning to view his whole single lifestyle with something less than glee, and was considering a makeover of his place to rent it out to students, and a move into the cushion filled, cosy haven that she liked to call home.

Katy was just topping up her coffee and doodling a romantic looking rose in the corner of her notebook, when her pleasant daydream was interrupted by a thud and clatter at her side. She knew who it was without looking; only one person would ever dare disturb the church-like peace of the Doctors' Sitting Room in such a way. The physician sighed inwardly and set down her pen, preparing to greet her friend and already bracing herself for the next in the series of rants that had so far punctuated Natalie Winter's week.

When her heavy "Hello, Natalie" was answered by silence, Katy finally dragged her eyes away from her flower. The sight that greeted her ranked up there with alien invasion on the list of things that she'd least expected to see.

Natalie's small round face was red and contorted, in a way that in any other human being would have said she was about to cry. Not such an unusual sight you might think, except that the tiny surgeon prided herself on not having shed a tear since she'd cut her knee so badly that it had needed stitches at the age of five. Katy leaned towards her friend anxiously, peering into her rapidly shrinking blue eyes and watching as they brightened, grew even bluer and then filled with fluid, before some rebellious tears broke ranks to trickle down Natalie's cheek.

John had been right. Something was seriously wrong with his wife. When he'd called her the night before to say that he was worried about Natalie she'd half dismissed it, and even when he'd called again that morning she'd just made soothing noises about surgeons' heavy workloads. After all, Natalie was the least likely person in the world to have a problem that she couldn't solve.

Now she felt thoroughly ashamed for having dismissed his worries, and immediately determined to make things right. But for that they needed privacy to talk, so, oblivious to the small herd of doctors now roaming the room in search of coffee, Katy took her friend's hand firmly in hers and led her assertively out the door.

\*\*\*\*

**Templepatrick.**

As Craig reached the Pathology Labs Liam was pulling into Tommy's cul-de-sac, and as John Winter was pouring his friend a coffee, Liam was being forced to make his own cup of tea and one for his host as well. The D.C.I. set the drink in front of his old enemy and took the most comfortable chair that he could find, cutting to the chase.

"So, what have you got on Billy Regent?"

Tommy shook his head mysteriously, implying that he'd

unearthed incredible things. If he said straight out that all he'd discovered was that Billy had been, as McCrae had said, 'a heed case', and pointed the detective towards his shrink, then he'd be diminished in both their eyes. No, the way to keep his power was to imply that there was much more to the matter but throw Liam the psychiatrist as a bone that they could chew.

Tommy's misfortune was that Liam Cullen had a master's degree in bullshit, both the speaking and the understanding of such, so he recognised the aging loyalist's obfuscation as meaning that he had bugger all useful to give him and was draining his cup and halfway out the door before Tommy had barely opened his mouth.

"Here! Where dee ye think yer goin', Ghost?"

Hill's overplayed indignation crushed any residual nanoparticle of doubt that Liam might still have had.

"I'm leaving, because you're about to try and bullshit me. You got nothing on Regent from your contacts, so just admit it."

"I *didn't* get nuthin'."

Double negative aside Liam knew that he was right. That didn't stop Tommy following him out to his car, shouting the odds.

"Billy wus nuts, that's what I got. He wus under the shrink in Craigantlet."

Liam stopped dead in his tracks and turned.

"OK. And?"

The move took Tommy aback, but he knew that any retreat would be perceived as weakness and the ancient art of bullshitting would forever be betrayed. To underline his firm stance, the old warrior folded his arms across his chest, moved one foot back slightly and rested defiantly on his hip. One touch from Liam and he'd have toppled over, but it made for a good display.

"An, an Billy hated politicians. Blamed them fer the Iraq War."

Tommy judged that some economy with the truth about

exactly which politicians Billy had hated was necessary now, to save face.

Liam narrowed his eyes, still unconvinced, but he had to give the old lag a B for Baloney, so he reached inside his jacket and withdrew fifty quid, holding it out.

"Keep digging. I want you to ask around about antique and arms smuggling as well. And don't tell me you don't have contacts there. I remember you dealing that Crusader book. If you get anything useful then there'll be more cash."

Then he turned his back on the delicately balanced statue now teetering in the driveway, and got straight onto Craigantlet Barracks on his phone.

\*\*\*\*

**St Mary's Hospital.**

"Natalie, tell me what's wrong. *Please.*"

The two doctors were leaning against the shiny-fronted cupboards in the theatre equipment room; the fourth room that they had entered in search of privacy and the only one that hadn't been filled with students. Natalie had managed to limit her lacrimation until they'd found the private space, but as Katy had closed the door firmly behind them and wedged a chair beneath the handle to keep it shut, the flood gates had opened, and now five minutes later the surgeon was a mess of watery sobs.

Katy took her life in her hands and gave her friend an awkward hug, Natalie not being partial to physical contact of any sort, except from John.

"Is it your job?"

Natalie shook her small blonde head.

"Your mum and dad?"

Another shake and a wet, "they're both well."

Katy's heart sank like a stone. That only left her marriage to John and she'd *really* been hoping that it wasn't that. She still couldn't see it; Natalie and John had been an unusual but inspired match. It was as if the powers that be had looked at them and said, 'you each have needs that only the other can fulfil', and then waved a magic wand to make them fall in love.

John's social awkwardness with Natalie's gregariousness, John's reticent-to-the-point-of-muteness -at-times with Natalie's rash tendency to put her foot in her mouth; together they made one big-brained, amazing unit, and she and Craig had spent many a conversation speculating what their kids would be like and then laughing about it like drains.

Suddenly Katy froze. The floods of tears, the recent moods, which even for Natalie had been spectacular. That was it! She stared down at her friend with widening eyes.

"You're pregnant!"

It was the cue for another flood. When it had abated slightly Katy added with a grin.

"But that's wonderful. What did John say?"

Natalie sniffed inelegantly, grabbing for some theatre roll to wipe her face.

"It's not wonderful, it wasn't planned. Anyway, he doesn't know."

Katy didn't understand. "But why not? Are you waiting until you're sure? Have you done the tests? I can do an ultrasound for you if you want me to check."

She watched as Natalie's face creased up to cry again and then as the surgeon changed her mind, muttering "catch a grip, woman" to herself as she searched around for a chair. When she found one she dragged it to the centre of the room and thudded down on to it, continuing to mutter and sigh before finally raising her eyes to Katy's own.

"I can't have it."

Katy fell back against the cupboard, feeling for its solidness to convince herself this was real.

"But why not? You have a wonderful husband, a great job... John will be an amazing dad... You can't-"

She cut herself short, swallowing her next judgmental

words, but it was hard. She would have given anything to have been in Natalie's position with Craig, and deep down she felt a visceral revulsion at abortion. But this wasn't about her, and her friend needed her support.

She hunkered down in front of Natalie's chair.

"Are you afraid it will hold back your career, Nat? Is that it? I know surgery isn't the most female friend-"

Natalie shook her head vigorously. "No! That's not it. Anna McRandal's a mum, and so is Delia Legge. Work's got nothing to do with it." She lapsed into silence again for a moment, shaking her head repeatedly, as if she was trying to shake something away. When she spoke again it was in a factual tone.

"You know I'm adopted."

Katy immediately tightened her jaw to prevent it dropping in surprise. It was the first she'd heard of Natalie's parents not being hers biologically! And she'd lost count of how many times she'd said how like her mother the surgeon was, never to be contradicted. But if Natalie believed that she'd already told her she was adopted now wasn't the time to contradict, so as Katy's mind raced, searching for clues that she might have missed, she nodded her friend to carry on.

"When I was eighteen I decided to trace my birth mother. Don't ask me why because I honestly don't know. I love my parents, I couldn't have wished for better, but something inside me just had to find out who she was-"

Katy jumped in, trying to offer a comfort that Natalie's expression said she needed.

"Being adopted doesn't mean you won't be a great mum yourself. You know that."

Natalie shook her head in a way that said the search hadn't yielded good news.

"That's not it. It's just..." She gave a sigh that Katy felt in her bones. "Oh, I don't know what I expected her to be like. Like me probably. Clever and energetic..." Natalie had never considered modesty a useful trait. "But she was..."

The sentence tailed away, leaving them sitting in silence, until eventually the surgeon pulled herself together briskly and carried on in a distinctly unsentimental voice.

"She was sixteen when she had me and she couldn't tell me much about my father. He'd been a one week stand apparently, a maths teacher at her school. It happened just after her O Levels. One thing led to another and..." She shuddered at the image of a man abusing his in loco parental trust before going on. "But there was something she did tell me." Her eyes dropped to the floor. "She has a family history of a severe form of Haemophilia, a strong history. She told me that she was a carrier of the condition, which means there's a one in two chance that I am as well." She swallowed hard before going on. "That means any son that John and I might have has a fifty percent chance of being born with it."

Katy's mouth dried like parchment. Haemophilia. One of the most serious blood clotting disorders there was. Carried on the X Chromosome it was passed from carrier mothers to some of their sons, with some of their daughters possibly also becoming carriers.

Her heart broke for the decisions that Natalie had in front of her, then it broke again at what it might first mean for her life with John.

\*\*\*\*

## The Executive Office, Stormont Estate.

The short, square, one year from retirement government official, pressed his back so hard against the office wall it was as if he was trying to push through to the room next door. Six inches in front of him stood a pale-eyed, pale-haired ex-Intelligence Officer with all the skills and tricks that title implied, apparently doing nothing to cause the retreat except stare.

But what a stare. Kyle Spence's eyes were unblinking, his

pupils dilated to discs, and his jaw was set so hard it looked as though it might crack. Although strictly speaking the detective was wearing no expression, the older man could detect menace in his every pore. It emanated from the spy like a heavily spiced cologne, filling the room with the possibility of violence if he didn't get what he'd come there for.

"Information."

The short man seemed uncertain which of them had said it, so Kyle repeated the word to remove any doubt.

"Information. *That's* what I need from you, Mister Iveston. Tell me what you know of the First Minister's private and public views."

Norris Iveston reached out for support, missing his desk by six inches, but his direction had been clear so Kyle immediately seized the papers lying there.

"*These?* You were reaching for these?"

He glanced down to see a printed manifesto leaflet from the last election. It said nothing but that Peter McManus stood for 'An Independent Britain in Europe. Working in cooperation but controlling our own destiny.'

*Catchy?* Kyle didn't think so. He hurled the leaflet at the bin and turned back to the man with a scowl.

"If I'd just wanted propaganda I wouldn't have bothered coming all this way! That's the rubbish you feed Joe Public, Mister Iveston, but I need the full S.P. The *real* stuff. What McManus said to you behind closed doors."

He could see the private secretary's legs beginning to buckle, so he pulled out a chair and pushed Iveston to sit as the civil servant blurted out his defence.

"Minister McManus" Obsequious even in death. "Was a decent man. What he said in public he said in private."

*Not like some of them* was muttered beneath the official's breath.

Spence perched on the desk and glared down at him. "Let's just say I believe you. Let's just say Mister McManus *was* Pro-EU, like he said, but wanted the UK to have controlled immigration and free trade with the rest of the world-"

Iveston nodded furiously. "He did. He really did."

The D.I. jumped back in. "*So, who didn't?* Who in the IBP wanted McManus gone?"

The advisor's eyes widened as if he'd been shot as well. "No-one enough to kill him!"

Spence didn't give the official time to breathe before he thrust the man's chair back against the wall.

"But someone enough to want him out?"

"I..."

"Who?"

"I can't-"

"What? Can't say? Can't tell me? *Who was it?"* The D.I. loomed over the man. "*Who, Mister Iveston?* Who wanted shot of your boss?"

He could see Iveston's flush darkening and spreading down his neck. Any minute now the man would break, he was certain of it. As the civil servant's lips formed a word and "Burke" emerged, the office door was flung open and Andy Angel entered the room.

"This interview's over! NOW, Detective Inspector."

His glance took in Iveston's head-in-hands relief and then his sigh, loud enough to fill the room, but Andy failed to spot the smirk on Kyle's face before his expression altered to faux chagrin and shame. And as the two detectives left the office, Kyle in front and Andy behind barking him on, the former Intelligence Officer, well pleased with the results of his interrogation, was already planning his next move.

\*\*\*\*

**The Labs.**

Craig swung his long legs up on to John Winter's desk and sipped at the coffee the pathologist had thoughtfully poured, before speaking.

"You had something for me, John. What was it?"

The pathologist shuffled the papers in front of him, reluctant to impart his DNA find immediately. If he did that Craig would jump up and leave, and, without confiding in him directly about his marital strife, he hoped that by prevaricating for long enough the detective might work out that something was wrong with him all by himself.

In fact, all the prevarication managed to do was irritate Craig, and after five minutes of John's hemming and hawing the policeman drained his cup and sprang to his feet.

"If you don't have anything, I really need to go."

Winter hurriedly removed a page from the bottom of his pile, floating it across the desk. Craig scanned it, his eyes narrowing, and when he glanced up again his voice was incredulous.

"German! You're *sure*?"

"DNA doesn't lie."

*"Pure German?"*

"Ninety-eight percent. The rest was Nordic DNA. I compared the whole thing with some profiles of ethnic Germans and it fits the bill."

Craig frowned, puzzled.

"How many German's live here?"

"Almost four thousand according the twenty-eleven census."

The detective was surprised it was that many. He considered for a moment and then asked another question. "Male or female DNA? I mean it was probably a man, to subdue Regent, but I'd still like to cross the Ts. Unless they had a gun of their own, of course..."

John shook his head tiredly. "The processing's still got a way to go. I should know more tomorrow."

The flat tone in which he said it made Craig straighten up. An unexpected result like this would normally have had John doing cartwheels; something was wrong with his friend. His humanity said he should ask what, but his curiosity got in first.

"OK, so a German...a tourist?"

"A tourist who came here just to kill McManus? Unlikely. Oh, I think I'll just go to Belfast for the weekend to see a concert, and I might just bump off the First Minister while I'm there!"

The sarcasm added to Craig's concern so he allowed his humanity to come to the fore.

"Something wrong, John?"

The pathologist batted it back. "Who? *Me?* What could possibly be wrong in my perfect life?"

The sarcasm was tinged with huff this time at Craig not asking the caring question before, and, in the ancient Irish tradition of cutting off your nose to spite your face, John deflected the concerned look on Craig's face by returning to the DNA.

"You should get Davy to check out German nationals living here."

"Could that DNA be found in any other group?"

"You mean a Polish or Eastern European immigrant?"

There were plenty of those in Northern Ireland, but John shook his mouse-brown head.

"It's unlikely, unless they were Germans who'd been living there. I'd say this person had both parents and all four grandparents German, which is unlikely unless they actually came from there. First generation German immigrants here and *maybe* tourists would be Davy's best bet."

Craig frowned. Why the hell would a German want to kill Peter McManus? Unless they'd been hired to do so. He reached for the desk phone.

"Mind if I make a call? My battery's running low."

Within seconds Davy was on the line and John was pouring Craig a second coffee hopeful that it might make him stay.

"Davy, the DNA found under Billy Regent's fingernails indicates an ethnic German. Check for German nationals living or working here, and get passport control to check for anyone who travelled here in the past two weeks. Boat and plane. Get onto Interpol and see how their DNA matching's going, and give the German Federal Police in Berlin a call. There's a Chief Inspector Vala Raske there. I met her on a secondment she did at The Met and we've kept in touch. Mention my name and ask for her assistance, please."

As he dropped the call, his mobile rang, displaying Andy Angel's name.

"Andy. Did you find Kyle?"

"I did...Interrogating McManus' private secretary at close range... We're heading back to the ranch now."

Craig rolled his eyes, knowing that his pauses indicated bad news. He didn't want to hear the detail until he had to but he was already wondering whose ass he would have to kiss to calm the situation down.

"Keep him there. He's not to leave until he's seen me. Understand?"

"Loud and clear."

He cut the call and took the cup John was proffering, but instead of sipping the coffee he set it on the desk and sat forward, staring hard at his friend.

"Huff, sarcasm, and I've never seen you so unexcited about a DNA result. There's something wrong with you, John, so tell me what it is. Please."

It was as if he'd said Open Sesame. John Winter's floodgates opened and all his marital woes came rushing out.

\*\*\*\*

## Craigantlet Army Base, The Craigantlet Hills, County Down. 2 p.m.

Liam was on his second meeting within an hour and he was far more impressed by the Officers' Mess coffee than he'd been with Tommy's tea. There were biscuits as well this time, and decent ones at that, all served by some sort of batman who reversed away. It seemed a high old life being an officer and the D.C.I. was just wondering whether he should have joined the military at eighteen instead of the police, when Ken Smith appeared beside him dressed in battle greens. The biliousness of the colour was enough to confirm to Liam that he'd made the right career choice; he could never have spent thirty years wearing that.

Ken fell into the armchair opposite and poured himself a drink, seeing Liam's envious glance around the high-ceilinged sitting room, with its carved wood and portraits of old generals, and allowing himself a small smirk.

"Impressed?"

Liam gestured at the embossed ceiling with its heavy crystal chandelier.

"You've got to admit it's better than neon lighting." He indicated the tray in front of them. "We have a drinks machine and you have a silver tray." He added a loud guffaw that drew glances from a group in one corner. "Oops. Do you have a noise policy here?"

The soldier smiled, shaking his head. "It wouldn't take us to. Mess nights can be pretty rowdy occasions." He set down his cup and relaxed back in his chair. "But I won't miss it you know. Fifteen years is long enough to move from country to country. It's time to settle down."

The twinkle in his eyes said that he didn't plan to settle alone.

"Anyway. How can I help you, Detective Chief Inspector?"

"Ach, get away with you. It's Liam to you."

Ken shook his head firmly. "Not during working hours. I'm starting basic training next week and I'll be a P.C. for quite a while to come, so I'd better start getting used to the rank system in the police."

It was a fair point, although Liam had a hunch the captain wouldn't be a constable for long, not with his experience.

"OK, then, P.C. Smith. There are two things. One, what do you know about arms smuggling?"

Ken looked surprised. "Generally, or in the army?"

"Whichever. I'd like you to do a bit of digging on it if you could."

"I'm only here for another few days, so it'll be a push."

"Do what you can. We've customs and excise and the border force digging as well."

Ken made a note. "And the second thing?"

"Corporal William Regent of the Mercette Regiment. You were finding stuff out on him for me."

A slim blue file appeared from inside Ken's tunic, finally explaining to Liam why soldier's top halves always looked so puffy. They could probably carry a small child, an encyclopaedia and a year's supply of nuts in there without anything showing up on the outside. Ken opened the document and started to read.

"This is Regent's service record. The big things were two tours of Iraq in two thousand and three and seven. He received several commendations for bravery and when he left in twenty-fourteen he got an honourable discharge."

Liam snorted. "Don't give me that old flannel. He had PTSD."

The captain nodded. "He did, but there's no dishonour in that, and it wasn't why he left. He cited his young daughter as the reason."

Liam gestured at the document, itching to get his hands on it. "I don't suppose you'd let me look?"

"You don't suppose correctly, but if you ask me specific questions I won't lie."

Liam took a swig of coffee before going on.

"OK. Regent's medical records. Are they in there?"

Ken loosened a single page and held it up. "I can't give it to you, but if you put in a written request the base doctor will most likely release it." As Liam opened his mouth to object he carried on. "I can tell you that there was no indication that Regent was violent. Quite the opposite in fact. He was a gentle lad overall, and so depressed at the end that it had rendered him almost catatonic. The report says that before he left it was an effort for him even to get out of bed at times."

Liam frowned. How the hell could Regent have got motivated to shoot a man?

"Anything about him hating politicians? We've been tipped the wink."

Ken scanned the page, stopping halfway down. After a moment's indecision, he began to read aloud.

"Corporal Regent resents the American political regime that entered Iraq in two thousand and three, but on questioning does not appear to harbour the same resentment towards the UK, with the exception of the British Prime Minister and his cabinet at that time."

Liam's eyebrows shot up. "It says that?"

Ken nodded. "They asked the question specifically, in case Regent was a threat to the politicians here on discharge. He was an expert sniper, after all. The base doctor was convinced he wasn't, although in light of what's happened-"

He was cut short by Liam shaking his head and standing up. "The more I learn the more I think that your doc was right. Billy Regent would never have killed Peter McManus if he hadn't been being used by someone else."

\*\*\*\*

**The Travis Estate.**

Reggie Boyd took off his uniform cap and wiped a hankie over his thinning hair. It was hard work questioning people who didn't want to speak to you, especially when it was scores of them a day, but he'd felt guilty sending the youngsters to do all the leg work so he'd taken a floor of Faulkner Tower himself. Between the slammed doors when they realised he wasn't the bloke from the housing executive there to fix their windows, and the woman in number forty who'd answered hers wearing nothing but a pair of leggings and an inviting smile that had had him picturing Mrs Boyd's ire if she'd ever found out, he reckoned he'd got off lightly if all he'd done was sweat.

He blamed his urge to get down in the trenches on his interview with Kelly Atkins the night before. She hadn't added much to her written statement, other than that Billy Regent's companion had been wearing a pulled down baseball cap so she hadn't seen his face, but if she had done she was certain that 'he wudn't have been as good looking as Billy wus, specially in his uniform.' But he *had* managed to get her to draw the logo that she'd seen on the sports bag and passed it on to Davy Walsh. It might produce something, or not.

The sergeant's meditation on urban life was interrupted suddenly by a sharp tug on his jacket, and he glanced down expecting to see a child from the estate, only to be taken aback at the sight of a W.P.C. so youthful looking that if she'd asked him for fifty pence for a bar of chocolate he wouldn't have been at all surprised.

The Donegal man closed his increasingly myopic eyes and counted to five for strength. When he reopened them, the constable was standing in exactly the same place, completely failing to foresee her impending chastisement, just as she'd failed to comprehend that tugging your sergeant's jacket as if he was your dad wasn't the way to go.

Reggie tried for world-weary tolerance in his words.

"W.P.C. Prentiss, since when do you attract the attention of a senior officer by tugging on their coat?"

The girl's blank look said that she needed more instruction in life than he had the time to give so after a brief pause Reggie carried on.

"What can I help you with?"

Her face brightened. "There's a woman, sir."

"There are many women in this world, Prentiss." Too many at that moment for him. "To which particular lady are you referring?"

She walked to the edge of the balcony they were standing

on and pointed left, towards a block of apartments that he hadn't asked anyone to check. Reggie counted from six to ten before speaking again.

"Is that Andrews Tower?"

The estate was arranged in two clusters of three blocks, Carson, Brookeborough and Faulkner Towers together, and then a distance away, across a courtyard, Andrews, Chichester and O'Neill. He'd deemed the second cluster too far away from the scene of the shooting to be worth investigation.

She nodded energetically. "Yes, sir."

"And did I *ask* you to check Andrews Tower?"

"No, sir."

He waited for the penny to drop. Unsurprised when it didn't he carried on.

"Leaving aside that I didn't, why would this lady interest me, Prentiss?"

"Because I found these, sir. In the bins at the back of her flat."

With a flourish, she whipped an evidence bag from inside her stab vest. Reggie leaned down to peer at it and made out the shape of two plastic gloves inside. The effect on him was electric and Prentiss instantly sensed his change in mood, her speech accelerating in step.

"You see, sir. I heard a CSI talking about latex being found on the dead man, so, I thought gloves. Don't ask me why, but I decided to have a rummage in all the bins around the estate, and I found these in the bin belonging to number fifty-two in Andrews. A Mrs Sally Johnston lives there. She's the lady."

Even being pedantic the sergeant couldn't have faulted her process, so he ushered her ahead of him into the lift, radioing for a criminal records' check on Sally Johnston on the way. By the time they'd reached her apartment he knew that the worst thing Sally Johnston had ever been chastised for had been smoking in the toilets at her local church hall, and her warm smile when she answered her front door told the experienced policeman that if Sally *had* disposed of the latex gloves in her bin then she'd probably only worn them to clean the fridge. It didn't negate the find, and when the housewife denied ever dumping the gloves, following up with "My bins are emptied on Tuesday evenings" meaning the gloves had been dumped after that, and "I've a latex allergy" both things that could easily be checked, Reggie Boyd's hopes soared again.

The gloves would go to forensics who would, he hoped, match them with Billy Regent's trace evidence, and even more hopefully find a print or DNA that belonged to his killer, confirming that they had stripped off their gloves as they'd escaped from Carson's roof and dumped them a distance away in Sally Johnston's bin.

If *that* happened he would buy Emily Prentiss a chocolate bar himself.

\*\*\*\*

**The C.C.U. 3 p.m.**

"Davy, come and look at this."

The dark-eyed analyst glanced up from his computer screen, calculating swiftly whether he had the time for Ash's request. He had searches running on McArdle, Bell, Loughrey and Peter McManus, not to mention checking Veronica Lewis' email and trying to crack the book code. Thankfully Craig had given him Rhonda to help scan the Travis Estate CCTV and Ash was checking the DNA and the smuggling, otherwise he would never get out of there that evening and he and Maggie had a booking to check out a wedding venue.

He'd been engaged to the newspaper editor for six months now, and so far it was going well, except that their families kept dropping hints about setting a date so the occasional visit to a wedding venue or an appointment to taste cake was proving necessary to keep them quiet.

Tonight's booking was just the latest smokescreen. They would get married when *they* were ready, and they'd already decided that when they tied the knot they would do it literally with a druidic hand-fasting ceremony where their wrists were tied together with silk rope. They'd do it at one of Ireland's many mystical sites, followed by a short honeymoon on the remote Clare Island, spent in its totally unique Lighthouse Hotel.

They would do the traditional church thing as well to keep the old folks happy, but only after they'd already been husband and wife for a while. The secrecy had been Maggie's idea and the hand-fasting his, the idea of someone literally binding them together feeling more meaningful to both of them than any wedding ring.

The analyst's daydream was interrupted by Ash repeating his request, this time with an added shove that almost knocked Davy off his chair. He glared at his junior, wondering how to make him treat him like his boss and show him the respect that everyone accorded Craig, although he grudgingly acknowledged that might have been because the detective had a gun.

He rose from his seat to loom over his colourful workmate.

"What do you want, Ash? I'm busy."

The words had been meant to sound threatening, but Ash grinned at his PC screen, clearly unintimidated.

"Check this out. It's Veronica Lewis' phone calls; in and out."

As he scrolled down a list of asterisks Davy wondered what he was supposed to be seeing.

"Big deal. So those ones are w...withheld."

Ash hit enter with a flourish, and the asterisks disappeared leaving a list of numbers in their wake.

"The phone companies have just unmasked them for me."

Davy pulled over a chair and sat down. "Which one's got you so excited?"

Another tap and one number was highlighted in green, so many times that the screen looked like a golf course.

"How many calls?"

"Eighteen times since the beginning of May. All of them lasted between five and thirty seconds, silent calls would be my bet. Guess who owns the number?"

"Some pervy bloke who didn't have the bottle to speak to a real live woman?"

Ash shook his head, looking pleased with himself. "Wrong. It's a woman." He switched to a second screen. "This one. Mrs Annabel Montgomery."

Davy frowned. The middle-aged woman whose image he was looking at looked normal, even pleasant, but her name seemed familiar and he couldn't say why. Ash saved him from having to ask.

"Or, if you were being retro, Mrs Leonard Montgomery."

The fashion for naming women as extensions of their husbands thankfully having become outdated decades before.

Davy gawped at the screen. "Minister of Finance Leonard Montgomery?"

"The very man." Ash lounged back in his chair with a smug look on his face. "It looks like Loughrey and the Earl aren't the only naughty politicians around. My bet is that Annabel sussed out that old Leonard was phoning someone a bit too often and did some phone stalking to find out who it was. She probably called Lewis' office the first time just trying to find out who the number belonged to and then realised hubbie was having dealings with ladies of the night."

The phrase made an eavesdropping Rhonda giggle like a schoolgirl; with her Goth tendencies ladies of the night always made her think of vampires.

"So... Annabel kept phoning Veronica Lewis's office just to wind her up."

Davy shook his head, puzzled. He'd never understood what people got out of silent calling.

"This is dynamite, Ash. W...Well done." He gestured at the screen. "Are any of the other withhelds significant?"

"Yes, actually. Quite a few came from Parliament Buildings, but there's no way of tracing which extensions they came from. But either politicians or their civil servants have been phoning Veronica Lewis, so it looks like the chief was right about these parties."

\*\*\*\*

Craig had a lot of respect for Bill McEwan, but not a lot of time, the reason being that when James Murray had defined the word monosyllabic for the Oxford English Dictionary in eighteen-seventy-nine he must have had the Armed Response Commander in mind. A meeting with the man was an interesting study on the value of small talk, and more precisely how much of even the most basic business meeting was comprised of words that had nothing to do with work. 'Would you like a coffee', 'dreadful weather' etcetera; phrases that until you tried to converse without them seemed trivial, but after a meeting with McEwan carried the import of a diplomatic treaty.

Nevertheless, Craig attempted to oil the wheels by opening their encounter with a courteous "Haven't seen you for a while, Bill, how's the family?" providing the "Good. Fine." answers himself before getting to his reason for being there.

"I'm going to cut to the chase, Bill."

A slight twitch of the commander's heavy eyebrows acknowledged the words.

"So...forensics and pathology have shown that Billy Regent didn't kill himself and there was someone else at the scene, someone wearing latex gloves. They shot Regent and made it look like suicide."

Craig was aware that he hadn't paused for acknowledgment or comment. It sounded strange to his ears, but preferable to deafening silence.

It was what it was so he hurried on.

"There was DNA under Regent's nails, and we're following up on that, but, given that the shot that killed him was fired while your men and mine were at the estate, and there was no-one but Regent on the roof when we checked, that means the killer must have escaped while we were there."

He was surprised when McEwan both shook his head and spoke. "You can't say that."

"What? That the shot was fired or that they got away?"

"That the shot that killed Regent was fired when we were there."

It was the longest sentence he'd ever heard the man utter, and it didn't make sense.

Unless...

"You're saying Regent might have already been dead when police arrived."

The commander gave a curt nod.

"As a possibility you might be correct, but what then would have been the point of someone firing another shot when you were there? It only attracted attention and made D.C.I. Hughes lock down the tower. Plus, the pistol was only one bullet short, not two."

McEwan acknowledged the logic with a shrug that was as close to saying he was wrong as Craig knew he would get. But his point, while wrong, had been useful; it was making Craig think things through again.

"Unless they actually *wanted* our attention..." He shook his head; he would consider that option another time. "OK, for now let's just say that they didn't. So, the shot happened while police were there, the tower was already cordoned off, and yet the shooter still got away. That means the shooter was either disguised as, or actually was, a resident who slipped down from Carson's roof and into an apartment, *or* they were wearing uniform and mingled with your men."

McEwan's response was dry. "Or a suit and mingled with yours."

His logic was impeccable, except for one thing. Only three detectives had been there during the lockdown: Aidan, Liam and him, and they'd have noticed a fourth man in a suit. Craig continued in an even tone, refusing to let the commander's defensiveness get to him.

"Uniform is more likely. We're interviewing all of the residents, so I'd like you to interview your men and ask if they saw any uniformed officers they didn't recognise."

"They all know each other."

This time Craig barely suppressed a tut. The strong silent act was starting to piss him off.

"I meant someone *else* in police uniform, yours or ours. Someone they might have assumed had arrived with us. OK?"

A grunt was all he got to say that McEwan agreed, and as Craig left, glancing pointedly at the commander's wedding ring and thinking that his wife must be an angel, he prayed that the man's verbal economy at work meant that he stored up most of his words for romance.

# Chapter Ten

**The C.C.U.**

Nicky stared at her PC screen slack-jawed, scarcely able to believe what was playing in front of her eyes. She'd been checking the local news bulletins, part of her routine every few hours just in case something new happened in the world that might affect a case, when the video had just started to play. This was the second time that she'd watched the one-minute clip, in the hope that she might have been delusional the first, but sadly there could be no doubt. There, as large as life and wearing an expression of grief so fake that not even a soap actor would have been proud of it, stood Roger Burke, IBP MLA, and now, by dint of his inherited leader position in the party, the new First Minister of the land, holding a public press conference!

Quite apart from the fact that the man had been sequestered by the Chief Constable, Burke was expounding on events that might affect their case. Nicky listened until the end of the clip and then beckoned frantically for Liam to join her as she watched it a third time, knowing that by doing so she was neatly passing the responsibility for informing Craig and taking any subsequent fall-out to the D.C.I.

\*\*\*\*

Interviewing Jenny Wasson's two comrades in arms had yielded about as much information as Annette had expected it to. The women described the same blindfolded journeys as Wasson, but whereas she had been aware enough to take note of her surroundings, they had apparently been out of their heads on drugs. The only venues they could describe sounded like they'd been painted by Jackson Pollock.

By lunchtime the three cops had had enough of walking

on the wild side and moved on to the suburban half of their task, interviewing Peter McManus' grieving wife. A call from Nicky said that she'd secured them passage past the Stormont Mafia and close protection team to arrange a meeting with Emily McManus at her well-appointed Helens Bay home, probably with IBP advisors censuring every word that she said.

The detectives made a pact before they left Annette's small car; while one of them elicited answers from the widow, the others would head her censors off at the pass. So it was that Annette found herself leaning in close to the First Minister's widow asking the difficult questions, while Aidan and Jake distracted the men placed there to ensure that she toed the Independent Britain Party line.

"Can you think of any reason someone might have wanted your husband dead, Mrs McManus?"

"Emily."

Annette smiled again. The first time she'd smiled was when she'd entered the warm family sitting room and seen a jeans clad Emily McManus playing on the floor with her toddler son. The boy was sitting on the lawyer's knee now, less as a barrier and more as a bond between the women. Annette suspected that he was a comfort blanket for his mother as well.

"Emily. Can you?"

The younger woman rolled her tired blue eyes, red rimmed and shrunken from hours of crying.

"Opponents across the floor, perhaps. Or rather, not them but their hard-line supporters-"

Annette cut in gently. "Dissident Republicans? I can understand your reasoning; Republican versus Unionist, but why now? Had your husband had threats from them?"

The widow set her wriggling toddler at her feet, shaking her head. "No more than usual. Well, not that Peter had told me anyway."

She waved a hand vaguely through the French windows towards a small rock garden, where a three-man protection detail was hovering, grudgingly giving them some space. "They would know more about it than me." She wrinkled her smooth forehead. "But if you're referring to more recent reasons for Peter being threatened...he had ambitious party rivals."

"Such as?"

A name emerged without hesitation. "Roger Burke, Peter's deputy. He's always wanted the leadership." She glanced around the room distractedly. "But could I see him killing Peter to get it?" She fell silent for a moment and then reluctantly shook her head. "No...not that Burke wouldn't have wanted to, you understand, but I honestly don't think he'd have the balls."

The last few words were clipped and dismissive making Annette see the prosecuting barrister that Craig had described. The widow went on.

"The only other reason I can think of is the EU Referendum."

She glanced quickly at the party advisors, who were halfway across the large room straining to hear their conversation through the wall of sound being caused by Aidan Hughes' strident voice, deliberately asking them things about government that the D.C.I. didn't care if he never knew.

Emily McManus dropped her voice and leaned in. "Peter was genuinely Pro-EU, you probably know that, but there are many in the IBP that aren't. But whether they'd kill him..." As her voice tailed away her gaze skittered around the walls. "To kill someone for what they believed in...I can't..."

Annette spotted her impending meltdown and knew that she only had time for one more question.

"The man we believe killed your husband was an ex-soldier, a Loyalist and Unionist as far as we can tell. Can you think of any reason why such a man -"

The young mother cut her off. "Traitor. That's why."

"The killer was a traitor to your husband, you mean."

She was surprised by the violent shaking of McManus' head.

"Not him. Peter. Plenty in the Loyalist community saw him that way. They thought Peter was a traitor to the UK for wanting to stay in Europe."

Her gaze dropped to her son, who even at his young age already looked like his dad.

As Annette caught the others' eyes and signalled that it was time to leave, Emily McManus murmured "He wasn't a traitor, he wasn't" and started crying fresh tears.

\*\*\*\*

"SHUT UP!"

The words emerged with a force so strong that the listener felt them like a blow, even down the phone line.

"Just do as you're fucking well told! Your ticket will be at the airport, so get ready to go on my call. Until then, keep your head down, and if anyone starts asking questions, you stick to the cover we agreed."

The Fox's words didn't require an answer, his silent *'or else'* loud and clear. When the silence between them continued a full minute they both knew he'd made his point and the call ended without niceties.

It didn't matter. All the goodbyes in the world couldn't change their shared history, or alter which one of them really held the power.

\*\*\*\*

## The C.C.U. 4 p.m.

Much as Craig enjoyed peace and quiet, after spending time with the world's most recalcitrant man he welcomed the cacophony that greeted him when the lift arrived on the tenth floor. The noise was loud even in the hallway, but when he entered the squad-room it hit him like a wave, making him stop dead in his tracks and search around for its source.

There was the usual tapping and clicking of computer activity, and the gathering roar of a kettle coming to the boil, but that was just everyday squad-room white noise, nothing to make him want to tell people to shut up. He focused harder, landing on Liam, the usual culprit when his quiet was disturbed, but the deputy was simply sitting, large feet up on his desk, with the only noise he was generating the sound of a pen being tapped against his teeth.

Craig did however notice that Liam tensed when he saw him standing there, and how tensely he rose to said large feet and started to approach, but he was still engrossed in finding the source of the row, so his gaze moved on to the next suspect on his list; Aidan Hughes, whose Belfast accent was so strong that it could strip the varnish off wood. And OK, yes, Aidan *was* talking, to Nicky, but not at the top of his flat-vowelled, town-crier's voice. That only left one corner of the open-plan office unchecked, and as the thing you're looking for is always in the last place that you look for it, Craig discovered the source of his impending headache straight away.

As the detective homed in on the sound he wasn't sure which shocked him more: its angry, shouted volume or the fact that Andy Angel, easy going man that he was, a man who couldn't muster the energy to put himself out if he was on fire, was the person making the noise. The fact that everyone else was ignoring it led Craig to the added conclusion that the din had been continuing for some time, and as he approached the corner, preparing to tell Andy to put a sock in it, he was halted by Liam suddenly blocking his way.

"Shift, Liam."

"Can't, boss. There's something you need to see right away."

As if to underline the point the D.C.I. pointed to Nicky, their agreed signal for her calling up a video to play. Craig watched in silence as the short clip ran to its end and then he nodded the PA to play it again, his initial surprise at Roger Burke appearing in public having altered to shock when he'd heard what the man had had to say.

*'Peter McManus was killed by an ex-soldier and Loyalist who thought that the First Minister was a traitor to his own people, that his desire to remain in the EU ignored how anti-British that sentiment might be viewed as by some in our community.'*

Cue hard swallow to choke back tears.

*'And whilst we at the Independent Britain Party unequivocally condemn this heinous act of violence, it will make us reconsider our stance. Our grassroots followers have supported us through thick and thin, and if this is how the Loyalist community is really feeling then we must consult widely, and if necessary think again about our party's approach to membership of the EU.'*

Craig said nothing, but the turmoil and disgust Liam read in his eyes said that when his next words eventually came they would be angry. Liam didn't believe in reticence so he said exactly what was on his mind.

"That bastard Burke's using the deaths for political advantage." When Craig didn't respond he added something more. "In fact, I wouldn't put it past the IBP to have organised McManus' hit for just this end."

Craig's slow stare was as close to agreement as Liam was going to get at that moment, then the D.C.S. entered his glass-walled office to think. Unfortunately, just as he did so, Craig spotted what Andy had been yelling at.

In the corner, behind an artificial dividing wall created from filing cabinets and cardboard boxes by Nicky a month before, to give some privacy to officers viewing CCTV, sat the source of Andy's ire, leaning back in his chair insouciantly and cavalierly examining his nails. Kyle Spence.

Craig's eyes widened and he raced back on to the floor, but instead of chastising Andy for shouting he rested a hand on his shoulder, silencing him, and then turned towards his arrogant D.I.

"Why am I not even slightly surprised that you're the cause of this aggro, Spence?"

Before Kyle could open his mouth to answer what had clearly been a rhetorical question, Craig followed on, his tone hardening.

"STAND UP WHEN I'M TALKING TO YOU!"

It made everyone turn to see what was happening and Liam count to ten beneath his breath, as Kyle rose slowly, so slowly that his pace verged on insubordination and if he'd been Craig he would have grabbed the Emory Board from the cheeky bugger's hand and shoved it where the sun didn't shine.

But Craig was made of stronger stuff. He'd heard the last sentence that Andy had been shouting and the words had made his blood, already red-hot from Roger Burke's press conference, start to boil. He moved to stand just inches from Spence's face, his deep voice cool but restrained.

"You went to the Office of the First Minister."

As Craig spoke he kept moving forward, giving the D.I. no other choice but to retreat.

"Where, from what I just overheard, you harangued his private secretary and practically assaulted him. In fact, you had the man backed against a wall when Andy arrived, and it will be a miracle if he doesn't sue."

As the delinquent D.I.'s back was quite literally against the artificial wall now, nobody could miss the parallel in Craig's words.

"What did you intend to do next, Inspector? Shoot him?"

Liam said a silent prayer that Craig would take out his Glock to make the point. He lived for things like that. In the event, they would never know whether Craig would have drawn his gun or not, because as he took another step towards the most challenging member of his team Kyle Spence jerked backwards, demolishing the carefully constructed but inherently unstable partition that it had taken Nicky a day to make and scattering boxes and filing cabinets all over the floor. As the clatter reverberated around the office the ex-spook teetered for a lengthy moment, his arms flailing wildly in the air, before finally he lost his balance and landed hard on top of them.

There was complete silence until Liam gave a roar that was picked up by Aidan Hughes. By the time Jake, Andy and the two analysts had joined in it had become a derisory cheer. Craig stood his ground, saying nothing. Not offering his subordinate a hand up, and with a glance forbidding the others to do the same.

When he'd viewed Kyle's furious, red-faced embarrassment for long enough the detective turned on his heel and strode away, his mind raging with a combination of Roger Burke and what to do with the Intelligence Officer next. Kick Kyle back to Intelligence where his cowboy tendencies had been an advantage, allocate him a full-time minder, except that he didn't have the spare men, or learn to live with him and find a way to turn his behaviour to good use? Although somehow he doubted that the latter option would prove good for his own mental health.

"Andy. Write up the events at Stormont, please. It will be going in Inspector Spence's file."

Then it was over. Kyle was suddenly vertical again, Jake began rebuilding the wall, and Craig pushed back the briefing for an hour to contemplate the Lagan and the future from his chair.

\*\*\*\*

**St Mary's Hospital.**

The two women had been standing in the theatre equipment room for hours, although neither could have guessed the time. Both had been silent for the greater part of it; one wrestling with a decision that would change her life and the other still stunned by what she'd heard. Finally, Katy broke the quiet, realising that it was up to her to offer practical advice. She risked Natalie's discomfort again by pulling her into another hug as she spoke.

"You'll find a way through this, Natalie, and I'm going to help."

The surgeon's renewed sobbing was welcome; it was far better than the coldness she all too often used as a shield. Katy kept talking.

"The first thing we have to do is get you tested."

She felt Natalie try to tear herself from her arms but she held on tight, forcing her friend to hear.

"If you don't then you may do something you'll regret. You might end this pregnancy *in case* the baby has the condition, when it could have been free of it all along."

This time Natalie was too strong to hold. She wrestled free and took a step back.

"I don't want to know if I have it! I don't want to live the rest of my life knowing that I'm a carrier! Can't you understand that?"

Katy's instinct was to shout 'NO', but she managed to stay calm.

"You need to find out, Natalie. For the baby-"

Natalie shook her head furiously. "IT'S NOT A BABY YET! Stop saying that."

Katy thought that it was, but them arguing opposite sides of an ethics debate that had divided countries wasn't going to help anyone right now.

"I understand how you feel, but surely you need to know if you're even a carrier before you make any decisions? If you're *not* a carrier then your baby *can't* have the condition in any form. Don't you want to know that before you even *think* about termination? Otherwise you're ruling out ever having *any* child. Is that what you really want?"

It stopped the surgeon in her tracks, and as Katy watched her friend's expression change, she realised that in her fear of the future the normally ultra-rational Natalie hadn't thought things through. It was a mark of how upset she really was.

Katy gazed down at the tiny surgeon kindly, choosing her next words carefully.

"You should get tested, Natalie, and then at least you'd know what you're dealing with."

The absence of an immediate "NO!" gave her hope, so she said nothing more for a full minute, watching as Natalie wrestled with herself, every move playing out on her face.

Finally, the surgeon gave a weak nod. It was something, but it wasn't the real decision. That would come after the test, if it was positive, and if Natalie wouldn't discuss things with John then at least she could make sure that she wasn't dealing with things alone.

# Chapter Eleven

**5 p.m.**

The briefing, when it finally happened, was business-like. There was no discussion of what had happened an hour earlier, and the report of Kyle's exploits at Stormont was given by Andy, censured heavily, so that all the group learnt was that Norris Iveston had, under duress, given Roger Burke, the newly succeeded First Minister, as someone who'd wanted Peter McManus gone.

Craig turned to Annette.

"You met with McManus' wife, Annette. Did she say anything?"

Annette took out her notebook and then decided against it, reporting from memory instead.

"She was genuinely cut up, sir. Very distressed. But she wouldn't say much initially, with the IBP's advisors around." She glanced at Jake, smiling. "When Aidan and Jake distracted them, she said a bit more. Initially she said her husband had opponents across the floor, or rather not them but their hard-line supporters-"

Craig interrupted in a doubtful tone. "Dissidents?"

Annette made a face. "I wasn't convinced and neither was she, said her husband hadn't told her of any such threats, although that didn't mean he hadn't had them. But then she moved on to more recent reasons for him being in danger and said ambitious opponents within the party, namely Roger Burke, might have been behind his death."

Burke again. That was two people saying it, but Craig still wasn't sold. Burke was an IBP loyalist and killing McManus so close to a vote could have disrupted the party's plans. Annette was still reporting.

"Then she mentioned the EU Referendum. She said McManus was very Pro-EU, but there were many in the IBP that weren't. She also said that a lot of people in the Loyalist community viewed McManus as a traitor."

Craig's eyebrows rose. "Traitor? She used that actual word?"

It echoed what Burke had said in the clip.

Annette nodded. "Vehemently. The fact the killer was a Loyalist didn't seem a huge surprise to her."

Craig frowned, muttering. "If Billy Regent actually fired the shot."

It made everyone sit up, so he thought that he'd better elaborate.

"I met with Doctor Winter earlier, and it seems the DNA beneath Regent's fingernails was almost pure ethnic German in origin."

Liam's astonishment spoke for everyone.

"What the hell's that about?"

"We don't know yet, but given the evidence it seems likely that it was this German wearing latex gloves who held the gun to Regent's head and killed him, making it look like suicide. That scenario has to raise the question of whether Regent even made the kill shot on McManus."

Liam made a rewind motion. "Go back a bit. Regent had GSR on his hands, and if he didn't shoot himself he *must* have got it from firing the rifle. But now you're saying he mightn't actually have made McManus' kill shot either? Sorry, but I can't see it, boss. No-one else could have done it, and Regent *was* an expert sniper. And if they hadn't needed Regent to make the shot why the heck was he even there?"

Nicky piped up. "Regent could have been set-up to suggest that Loyalism was fed up with McManus. Burke looked pretty pleased in that clip, behind his crocodile tears."

Craig nodded. "You're both right. Regent *may* have fired the shot but not wanted to. He could easily have been set-up."

"He was forced by this German?"

"It's looking likely, but we can't say how yet."

Liam nodded knowingly. "That pretty much fits with what Ken said. The army doc said Regent was so depressed he could barely get out of bed, much less muster the energy to kill someone."

"Have you got the report?"

"Nope. Ken couldn't give it to me but he read some of it out. It basically said Billy Regent was like a limp rag."

Craig nodded. "And Eileen Regent said that her son could never, and more importantly *would* never have done it. He was just starting to look forward to life, with his daughter and his new job. OK, anything else on the door-to-door?"

Jake nodded. "Reggie interviewed some woman last night who said she'd seen Billy with another man the day of the shooting."

Craig sat forward eagerly. "Time? Description?"

"Around two-thirty that afternoon. He was the same height as Billy and skinny, but she didn't see his face; he was wearing a pulled down baseball cap. But he was carrying a gym bag with some sort of logo, so Reggie got her to sketch it."

Davy raised his pen. "I've got it, chief. It's running through the databases now."

Craig turned to his deputy. "Liam, did the rifle bag have a logo?"

"Nothing. Just plain black-"

Jake cut in. "She said Regent wasn't carrying anything, chief. Reggie specifically asked her."

Liam nodded. "The rifle bag must have been inside the logoed one carried by the other man. They were definitely working together."

Craig shook his head. "I'm still not convinced on that. OK, so the logo must have been on the second man's bag and he must have taken it with him. Let me know when you I.D. it, Davy. Go on, Jake. Anything else on the door-to-door?"

When the D.S. nodded Craig's hopes rose again.

"Nothing more from the interviews, but they found some latex gloves dumped in a woman's bin. Her name's Sally Johnston. No record and Reggie doesn't think she's involved in anything. The gloves have gone to forensics and Reggie's taken her to High Street for a DNA sample to rule her out, but he's pretty sure the gloves aren't hers. She's allergic to latex. The other thing is her bins were emptied on Tuesday at ten p.m."

"That's late."

"Blame the Council. The thing is, that means the gloves must have been left there after that."

Craig shook his head automatically. Sally Johnston wasn't their killer. Whoever had killed Billy Regent was too slick to dump evidence in the bin outside their own flat. In fact, why dump the gloves locally at all, except as a false trail? He would wait for the forensics on them but he wasn't holding out much hope of their use. The only interesting thing was that it meant their killer had remained local until Tuesday night.

Suddenly something occurred to him.

"Liam, where did the guns come from?"

Liam shrugged. "Don't know yet. They're still with Des for checking." Then it dawned on him what Craig meant. "Ah, you're thinking maybe Billy nicked them from his army base before he left. He wouldn't be the first squaddie to demob with more than a short haircut."

Craig nodded. "Chase their origins. They might lead somewhere." He moved across to the whiteboard. "OK. So, we're starting to form a picture of Billy Regent. He had PTSD with passive depression, and was a good soldier with an honourable discharge who wanted out of the army to get back to his little girl." He turned to Davy. "Davy, find out what his GP has to say about his state of mind *since* he demobbed."

"Already done. He saw him last week and said Regent was tearful but definitely not dangerous. He had him on anti-depressants designed to give him a lift."

"That fits with the lethargy Ken described."

He lifted a marker and drew a circle around Regent's name with radiating lines ending in question marks, tapping on the first.

"OK, the guns. Liam's on that. Next, Billy Regent's most recent state of mind, Davy's got that. Friends. Did Billy Regent have any friends that he confided in? Jake and Aidan, chase that please. Go back and speak to Tommy Hill if you get stuck; he might know. And check if Regent was based in Germany at any point; he may have made his killer's acquaintance there."

Liam nodded admiringly. It was a good point and one he hadn't thought of; the British Army had training camps all over the place.

Craig tapped the fifth question mark.

"Annette, find out how Peter McManus was *really* viewed in the loyalist community. Was it actually as bad as his wife says and Roger Burke implied at that press conference?"

She made a face. "What press conference, sir?"

He realised that only three of them had seen the clip.

"Nicky, play the clip for everyone after the briefing, please. OK, back to the way McManus was viewed. Even if he *was* viewed as a traitor, would anyone in the local Loyalist community really have carried it through to killing him? Reggie can help with that by finding out the thinking on the Travis and Demesne. My view is no, and if they *had* been going to, they'd have chosen a much simpler way. Bomb most likely."

He paused, running through anything he might have missed. When he couldn't find anything else he wanted to cover right that moment he turned back to Davy again.

"Davy, update us on Veronica Lewis' calls and computers, please, then we'll take Ash on the CCTV."

He fell into his chair as Davy handed around some printouts, but before the analyst could start reporting, Liam began shaking his head. Craig signalled Davy to wait for a moment.

"OK, either your shampoo's giving you problems, Liam, or there's something you're burning to say."

The shake became a nod. "Not say, ask."

"Which is?"

"Are we treating Madam Lewis' disappearance and the McManus shooting as two parts of the same case now? 'Cos it sounds a lot like it to me."

It did, but Craig didn't nod as the D.C.I. had expected, instead his forehead creased, not in a frown but in thought. When it had ironed out again Craig was equivocal.

"Look at it like this... The deeper we dig into McManus' death, the more we're led back to the IBP, some of whose members-"

Ash interjected.

"Several, chief. Loughrey, two substantial donors to the party, McArdle and Bell, and now possibly Leonard Montgomery."

The last name made Craig's eyes widen, but he carried on.

"OK, *several* people linked with the IBP seem to have habits that might lead them to, or we already know them to be frequenting, Veronica Lewis' parties."

Craig hadn't missed Kyle twitching and shooting Ash a hostile glance at the mention of Loughrey's name; as if the analyst had betrayed him in some way. He deliberately didn't dig into the details; if Kyle wanted to know what Ash had found out on Loughrey then he'd have to ask him himself.

He waved Davy on again.

"OK. On page one you'll see the outgoing calls from Lewis' office. There's very little interesting there...so far, but we're only a third of the way through. It's mostly Chinese takeaways-"

Annette interrupted. "What about supplies? Creams, makeup, materials? She's supposed to be running a beauty and design business from that office."

It was a good point. Davy shook his head.

"None of the calls fit. We'll be dumping Lewis' home phone next, s...so we may find them being ordered from there." He turned over the page. "The incoming calls were more interesting, once Ash got the phone providers to uncover them. Check out the ones marked in green. That number belongs to Annabel Montgomery, wife of the Finance Minister."

Liam gave a throaty laugh that said it all. "Who's been a naughty boy then?"

"More than likely. We think his wife found out and has been making s...silent calls." Davy smirked. "But we thought we'd leave the pleasure of asking to you."

Craig sat forward hastily, picturing the complaint Liam's tactlessness might cause. "By you he means me, Liam. Nicky, make an appointment for me, please."

Her eyes widened incredulously. "*With Mrs Montgomery*?"

Craig rolled his eyes. "With her husband. Let's hear what the Minister has to say for himself first. If he *has* been using Lewis' escorts then he may have been at her parties as well, and that could prove useful. Well done, Davy. Keep going."

The analyst covered his next point from memory. "So far, we've found nothing Europe wide on the DNA, but Interpol can take a while."

"John says he'll give you the complete profile once it's finished running. Tomorrow sometime."

"OK. Knowing it's German will help narrow things down anyway." The analyst turned to his junior. "Ash has been checking out McArdle, Bell and our Earl."

"Before you get to them, what about that email code. Any joy?"

Davy shook his head. "It's almost definitely a book code, but without knowing the book it will be impossible to decode. I'll keep my s...searches running just in case. Ash?"

As Ash opened his mouth to speak, Liam cut in again.

"Hang on. Boss, what did Bill McEwan say about his men

being suspects?"

Craig scoffed. "What do you think? Very little, and all of it defensive. He said he'd ask if they saw anyone they didn't recognise in any sort of police uniform, *even a detective's suit,* and let me know, but I'm not holding my breath. He did raise one interesting point though; what if the shot we heard at the Travis when we arrived wasn't actually the one that killed Regent?"

Liam looked sceptical. "What, so Regent was already dead but they thought they'd just fire off another to draw attention to themselves? Why the hell would they?"

Hearing it put so succinctly convinced Craig that they'd been right all along.

"I suppose they *could* have done it to confuse us, but no, you're right. The killer-"

Davy interjected. "Henceforth known as the German."

"When I can remember. OK then, the German killed Billy Regent just as we arrived and then disguised themselves as a resident or one of us."

Liam shook his head. "Not just us, boss."

"What do you mean?"

"He could have hidden for a while till the CSI's arrived, and then put on a white jumpsuit and left with them."

*Damn. He'd completely missed that possibility.*

He turned back to Davy. "Davy, give Des a call and find out who attended the scene from his office, then Nicky can arrange for them to be interviewed."

*More bloody work and too few of them to go around.*

"Enlist Jack Harris' help with those interviews, please. OK. Ash. On you go, please. McArdle etcetera."

Ash went to shrug, but at the sight of Craig's frown converted it to a twitch and a contrite look.

"Only basic bio stuff, chief. Sorry. It looks like their businesses are all above board and none of them have as much as a parking ticket."

Craig had to admit that he was surprised. The men's sexual predilections must have been the only bit of naughtiness in their lives. He pressed the point.

"Never? Not even as youngsters?"

Ash shook his head. "Nothing. I went right back to schooldays."

Liam gave a knowing nod. "Sure sign of guilt."

Annette had been thinking quietly, now she sat up straight. "Since when has a *lack* of criminal activity proved someone's guilt, Einstein?"

"Since three middle-aged men haven't even been done for drinking underage."

He grinned, remembering his own misspent youth, then frowned as he recalled the thick ear he'd got from his dad when the cops had brought him home one night and swiftly diverted attention to the other men in the room.

"OK, which of you lot wasn't dragged to the copshop at least once when you were a kid?"

Annette was just about to dismiss the question as nonsense, and follow up with an objection to him excluding the women in the team, when she noticed Jake start to blush. It was followed by some of the other men shuffling their feet and averting their gazes, and in Craig's case his chin hitting his chest in shame as he recalled the time he'd almost beaten a man to a pulp when he'd attempted to abduct a six-year-old Lucia from their front garden.

Annette quickly changed what she's been about to say. "So, Bell, McArdle and the Earl have been keeping themselves squeaky clean because-"

Not one to have his thunder stolen Liam cut in.

"They're up to something bigger. But the point is, what?"

Annette shook her head. "Someone might just have wiped any early offences they had."

Nicky groaned. "Oh God, not another crooked cop."

Craig straightened up again, glad to be off the topic of youthful crimes. "That'll be something to consider if Liam's idea doesn't lead anywhere, but for now, good catch, Liam. Davy, pull up any occasions when the men might have connected with each other in the past. If you find anything bring it straight to me."

Annette stared at him curiously. "You think they knew each other before the parties, sir?"

"I don't know what I'm thinking yet, Annette, but Liam's right, they're too damn clean." He turned back to his senior analyst. "CCTV, Davy. What have you got?"

Davy's response was to gesture to Rhonda. "Ash and Rhonda checked it."

"OK. Rhonda?"

The Snow-White look alike nodded, and as a video clip appeared on the LED screen she turned to Aidan Hughes.

"This clip runs from before the gunshot you heard, forward to when the chief and Liam arrived on the estate. It was taken from the cameras outside Carson Tower."

She pressed start and the group watched as the shabby tower block, of which they could only see the lowest six floors, went from being a community playground, with young girls playing handball against its walls and a group of teenagers lounging on a balcony planning God only knows what, to a hive of activity as the police land rovers screeched in, making the kids all stop what they were doing and turn to look.

They kept viewing as the Armed Response Officers disembarked from their vehicles, raised the cordon around Carson and started scoping out the estate. One minute further on there was a sudden crack, that sent the kids scattering and made the officers eyes jerk up. The video rolled on as the cops disappeared into the tower and then as Craig and Liam appeared on the screen.

Liam pointed at the grainy images. "That's just before we went up to the roof to take a look."

Craig didn't comment, just turned back to the DC. "Isn't there any CCTV that shows the roof? Or even a shot from inside the block?"

Ash made a face. "We checked and there are no cameras on any of the roofs, chief. We'd been hoping a camera on an adjacent block's roof might have caught what was happening on Carson's." He brightened up slightly. "There was a camera inside Carson's lift though." He switched to another media file and this time they saw Billy Regent entering the block's lift carrying a black bag.

Liam nodded. "Rifle."

He was followed into the lift by a narrower figure wearing a baseball cap.

"That's the bloke Reggie's witness must have seen. The German."

Craig nodded Ash to pause the video and crossed to the screen, pointing. "There's your logo, Davy. On the bag Billy's carrying. His rifle bag must be inside that one."

Davy nodded. The logo was exactly as Kelly Atkins had drawn.

"But Reggie's witness said Baseball Cap w...was carrying the logoed bag."

Craig gave a shrug. "They must have passed it between them, so Billy was going along with whatever was happening." Before Liam could say something smug he added. "But he still might have done so under duress."

Craig peered at the narrower figure, as if staring at it hard enough would remove the man's cap and allow them to see his face. After a moment, he shook his head and sat back down.

"Keep going."

As the lift travelled the fifteen floors from the lobby to Carson's roof, Billy Regent kept staring straight ahead, while the other man, now standing behind him, didn't lift his head at all.

"He's hiding his face, boss."

Craig nodded. "The question is, why isn't Regent? He must have known that he would be IDed. Lifts in those towers always have cameras. It's how the council detects vandalism."

Liam shrugged. "Maybe he thought it was broken."

"Or maybe he *wanted* us to see his face, and why would he do that if he intended to kill McManus of his own volition?"

Liam sat forward in his chair, marginally less disbelieving than he had been.

"You really think Regent was being forced to do it under duress and wanted the cops to know that?"

"Yes. Which means he didn't expect to die on that roof."

"OK, but where's the duress? They walked in together. Even if the German had a gun in Billy's back-"

Suddenly Liam rushed over to the screen and tapped on the point where the two men's torsos were closest.

"Ash, can you enlarge that?"

One second later they were looking at an unquestionable dent in the back of Billy Regent's coat.

Ash tutted to himself. He'd missed it completely. "If we'd had the facility to rotate the image we could have seen the gun and typed it."

He was vindicating himself unnecessarily, Craig had already moved on.

"Good catch, Liam. The model of handgun's irrelevant, Ash, it was probably the one left at the scene. What's important is that we now have proof that Billy Regent shot McManus under duress and not because he or Loyalism had targeted the man. My guess is that if we could see more clearly, his killer would have been wearing gloves."

Ash nodded energetically, reversing the tape. "He was. Look."

The German had entered the lift wearing black gloves on a summer's day.

"And beneath those, he was wearing the latex ones John found in trace."

Craig fell silent, thinking things through. Billy Regent had had a gun in his back coercing him, yet the squaddie had still believed he was coming back alive and had wanted them to see his face to prove his innocence. Something still didn't fit and he and Liam asked the question simultaneously.

"Why didn't he fight?"

Liam's added "boss" hit the air a second later.

Jake was confused. "What?"

Craig turned to the sergeant, repeating the question. "Why didn't Regent fight? He was bigger than the German and trained in combat. He could have overpowered him in the lift."

Annette's eyes widened. "Because he was protecting someone else! The German must have told him that he had to comply or they would kill his daughter or his mum."

Liam screwed up his face, puzzled. "Eileen Regent didn't mention anything when she was interviewed."

He turned to Kyle, breaking the team's hour long unofficial shunning of the D.I.

"You saw Regent's daughter. Did she mention anything?"

"Not a word. She just wanted her gran."

"Right then. We need to interview them both again. Boss?"

Craig was sitting with his head in his hands, deep in thought. A threat *would* have ensured Billy Regent's compliance, yet neither his mother nor daughter had mentioned it. He roused himself, looking up.

"Ask them again, just for certainty, but I don't think either of them knew that they were under threat." He sat up straight. "Which doesn't mean to say that it wasn't real. They could have had someone watching them from a distance, or the German could have threatened Billy that he would kill them afterwards if he refused to make the shot. Either way he was obviously convincing enough to make Billy comply."

As the group debated for a moment he turned to Ash.

"Was he inside the cordon after the shooting?"

"What?"

Craig's response was to walk to the screen and point to Billy Regent's killer.

"Did you or Rhonda see him amongst the people held inside the cordon?"

Ash glanced quickly at the constable, and then both of them shook their heads.

"We can check again, chief."

Craig nodded, already doubting that they'd find the German there.

"Check all police and CSIs, as well as the residents. We don't have a face, so you'll have to work on his height and weight alone." He turned to Annette, moving on.

"OK, Annette, what did the other escorts Jennifer Wasson gave you have to say about the parties?"

"The same as her, but with even less detail. Recreational drugs, but nothing else that they knew of, and they were blindfolded so they'd no idea of the venues. They were both stoned at the time so I think Wasson's our best bet. She gave us the Earl's estate and we've got the dates of the parties now. The next one is this Saturday."

This time Craig *did* comment on Kyle's twitch.

"But then you already knew that, *didn't you, Inspector Spence?*"

Kyle was tempted to say 'oh, so you're speaking to me now, are you?', except that he knew it would make him sound like a ten-year-old. Instead he shrugged so arrogantly that nobody but him was shocked by the speed at which Craig blew.

He bellowed across the group, almost deafening Liam who was sitting beside him.

"IF YOU SHRUG AT ME ONCE MORE, INSPECTOR, YOU'LL BE WALKING A SODDING BEAT ON THE DEMESNE! *Did* you already know about this weekend's party? Yes or no, and don't bloody lie to me!"

No-one moved. Some because they'd seen Craig's temper blow before (what had happened earlier with the boxes didn't compare) and didn't want to get caught in the backdraught, and others because they hadn't and weren't quite sure what would happen next. Kyle Spence fell into the first category.

Just as Craig's university experience of sharing a flat

with Spence had taught him how slippery the ex-spook was, so had Kyle's taught him about his flatmate's personality. To the world Craig was easy going and well mannered, and so he was, until he wasn't, and that happened when someone severely and repeatedly pissed him off. When that occurred Craig's façade of civilisation collapsed, and in the past, windows, bouncers in bars and men who'd been rude to his girlfriends had all felt the end of his fist.

Nowadays Kyle imagined the fist had probably been replaced by invective, although if he'd been present at John Winter's Christmas party two years before to see Craig punch through a window he would have known he was being optimistic, but even the thought of lacerating invective was sufficient to make the ex-spook decide to blurt out the truth.

"Trevor Rudkin."

It was a name that none of them knew. Craig's frown deepened and changed quality, from fury to curiosity.

*"And he is?"*

"A snout that I've cultivated for years."

Seeing that was insufficient the D.I. carried on.

"He's a snivel pervert."

Liam translated. "He means civil servant. It's not exactly a pet name."

Craig had heard the pejorative term before.

"A civil servant where?"

"Department of Trade."

"And?"

Kyle swallowed hard to clear his throat; he felt like he was choking and it was no longer from fear of Craig. He hated the idea of sharing even the existence of his snouts with anyone else. They were his. He'd cultivated them as diligently as if they were plants and he was a gardener, spotting their potential in some social setting that he'd attended just for that purpose and then approaching them stealthily and slowly drawing them in. Setting the scene with how they could help the police and their country by passing along information they might come across, then sweetening the pot with tales of excitement and promises of financial remuneration if they did.

He'd grown Trevor Rudkin from a tiny seed. A lowly entrance-level official, Rudkin had clambered up through the civil service's Dantean circles to the position that he currently held. And now, just as Rudkin was about to prove useful for the first time in ten years, he had to share his creature with someone else. It made Kyle want to spit as well as choke.

Craig had watched as the intelligence operator's emotions played out on his face, his own countenance set hard. Now he spoke again.

"Trevor Rudkin told you about this weekend's party. How did he know?"

Kyle's sigh could have been heard all the way to Stormont.

"Joshua Loughrey is his boss."

*Ah*. That explained his curiosity about the MEP.

Craig added what he knew.

"And Loughrey is a member of the IBP. He also has sexual preferences that might link him to Veronica Lewis."

Kyle turned to Ash, furious at being out of the loop.

"What did you find?"

"Loughrey was on FaceChat six years ago, playing four in a bed."

Kyle swung back to Craig. "And you extrapolated to Lewis' parties."

"Correct. The next of which is this Saturday. Is Rudkin going?"

"He might be."

*"Is he?"*

Kyle smirked knowingly, then dropped the expression hastily in case it brought more wrath.

"He said he might be, that's all I know. Described it a possible perk of accompanying Loughrey to Brussels this week."

Craig knew there was more. "What else did Rudkin tell you? There has to be more than a trip and possible party."

Kyle averted his gaze, wondering if Craig had read the existence of another secret there. His next words said that he had.

"There's no point hiding, Kyle. I know there's something else, so what is it?"

Craig's voice had returned to its earlier 'don't fuck with me' tone, so, with a sigh, Spence reluctantly met his eyes.

"He said that he'd heard something. Just a rumour, mind you."

Liam wanted to hit the D.I. now, and he would if he dragged things out any longer. Low blood sugar was making him irritable: it was definitely snack o'clock.

"Spit it out."

Kyle squeezed out a reply.

"Loughrey...might, just might...have been involved in planning..."

Even Annette wanted to scream 'HURRY UP!'

"Peter McManus' hit."

The words were greeted by stunned looks all round. Then, without another word, Craig beckoned the spy, both analysts and Liam into his office and closed the door.

\*\*\*\*

## Dublin Airport.

The German gazed up at the departure board, eyes falling on Hamburg and running along the line that said the flight had been delayed an hour. It didn't matter. The escape from Belfast had been the important part. This leg of the trip was just a formality.

The sliding doors to the outside world and a longed-for cigarette coincided with a vibrating mobile and a hidden numbered call. It was answered as the first hit of nicotine hit the killer's lungs and their sigh of pleasure was heard at the other end.

It made The Fox long for a cigarette of his own, but he deferred that pleasure till he was sure things had been sewn up.

"You left the gloves where they will find them?"

His tone was brisk and focused on business. No-one listening could have guessed what his subtext was.

The German took another slow drag of their Gitanes, exhaling the smoke in an elegant stream before answering.

"Of course. In the rubbish behind some pleb's apartment. The DNA will confuse them perfectly."

The response was snapped out.

"Don't get cocky! They're not stupid over here."

The silver-haired man reined in his anger by taking a deep breath. He still wanted to shout at the assassin, but as always, his fury was tempered by other considerations.

"You have your orders. We'll meet on Monday in the usual place."

Hearing him about to sign off Billy Regent's killer rushed to respond. "Wait. Why Monday? I thought the plan was to meet on the twenty-fourth?"

"It's not necessary to wait that long. The party this weekend should swing it. Now that McManus has gone the others will fall in line. The British are sheep, after all."

It prompted a shared laugh that shifted gradually into murmured words that would have surprised many.

"Bis Montag, meine Liebe." *Until Monday, my love.*

His sign off was still efficient. "Right. I'm losing this phone so don't try to call it. I'll contact you when we need to talk again."

\*\*\*\*

**Craig's Office. 6.30 p.m.**

"Davy. Tell me what you got from D.C.I. Sheridan's images. We need possible venues for this party before the weekend."

"Which night, chief? Are we sure it's S...Saturday?"

The question made Craig turn to Ash.

"You've got Jenny Wasson's list of party dates. Which nights do they happen on?"

A moment of squinting later the answer came back. "Saturdays. Always, by the look of it. The summer ones anyway. The winter ones are mid-week."

Satisfied, Davy set his smart-pad on the desk and pulled up a series of maps. The first was of Northern Ireland, with a handful of blue crosses dotted across the counties.

"These are the only locations D.C.I. Sheridan sent through that fit the bill. High security, heavy personnel numbers, and infrastructure like towers and fences, plus hefty power bills for providing electricity. I also s...searched domestic alarm companies, but none of the properties they served could provide the isolation a party would need."

Craig gazed at the crosses and nodded, before asking another question. "Any south of the border?"

Davy made a face. "That's proving a bit more difficult. I've been on to the equivalent team in the Gardaí but they won't s...send us what they have. Said they have to run it up their chain first."

Before Craig could ask, Liam leant forward. "I'll take that, boss. If I need the C.C. to chip in I'll let you know."

"Good. Thanks, Liam. Make sure you tell them it's unlikely the party will be at one of their venues, too far from Belfast, but we may need some of their men to stake them out."

Kyle had been shaking his head since the word 'unlikely', so Craig reluctantly took the bait.

"OK. Tell me why I'm wrong, Kyle."

The D.I. resisted the temptation to give him a list and instead answered with one word. "Bruges."

Liam knew Craig needed more and a punch in the arm ensured that he got it. The D.I. continued, moaning and rubbing his bicep.

"Loughrey went to a sex-party in Bruges. If they have

parties there then the Republic would be easy, and we already know the Earl's place in Louth was a venue in the past."

It was a fair point and one Craig nodded Liam to pursue.

"OK. Davy, tell us about the properties Theo Sheridan sent through."

As the analyst ran through the list of a National Trust property, a museum, a private home and two health clinics, Craig's mind raced ahead.

"No to the clinics, too many patients. No to the Trust property and museum, they'll both have guards. Tell me about the private residence."

Davy homed in on the relevant cross in County Down, and as they watched a magnificent modern house appeared, set in a vast expanse of ground.

"Darrian House, six hundred acres near Ballywalter. Home of Emmett Darrian, billionaire heir to the whisky empire. His personal wealth is around eighty million pounds, expected to increase to over a billion s...soon, when the business expands into the US."

"Tell me more about him."

Davy tapped twice and the image of a fifty-something man appeared.

"Strictly speaking he's Emmett Darrian the Fourth. His great-grandfather established the business in eighteen-eighty, and it's been handed down through the eldest sons. Next in line is his son, called, yes, you've guessed it, Emmett Darrian the Fifth. He's only five-years-old, so the business will be with the fourth for a while yet-"

Liam cut in. "Wife?"

"Three. The latest is half his age and the mother of his two youngest kids. She was s...some sort of model before she married him."

Liam gave a knowing snort that exposed his prejudices. Craig gave it a pass; he was too busy this week to worry about Liam not being politically correct.

"Tell me about Darrian's political leanings, Davy, that's

if he has any."

"He does. Right of centre. He's donated to the IBP."

The answer made Craig lean back in his chair. "The IBP...again. Kyle, remind us what you know about the IBP."

"Nominally Pro-EU, but with a *very* strong right-wing who are against staying in the EU."

"OK, so...the Pro-EU First Minister Peter McManus has been removed in favour of Roger Burke, who we know is anti-EU, and so far, we have the following IBP supporters' names in the ring: The Earl, McArdle, Bell and Loughrey, definitely attending the parties. But Loughrey's an MEP so if we leave the EU he'll be out of a job."

"He'll be out of *that* job, but if he's a party faithful the IBP will soon find them something else."

"Fair point." Craig turned to the analysts. "What do we know about the Earl's political leanings?"

Ash answered eagerly. "Liberal TD but very Republican. He wants a United Ireland and doesn't mind how it's achieved."

Liam was puzzled. "But the Republic's in the EU, so how could the UK leaving the EU help him with Irish unification?"

Davy and Kyle said it at once. "The economy."

Davy waved the D.I. on.

"OK. If, as predicted by all the big banks, leaving the EU damages the UK economy, then the thinking is that even the staunchest UK Loyalists in Northern Ireland will get fed up. People's political opinions change when they're hit in their pockets. If that happens then linking Northern Ireland up with the Republic in a United Ireland and us re-entering in the EU might make financial sense to a lot of people."

Craig had been nodding since they'd said economy. "OK, I can see that. The Earl's motivation for supporting the Leave campaign is a United Ireland, and we know the others want out for ideological Pro-Independent Britain reasons. Now we have Emmett Darrian, a businessman who presumably thinks with his wallet. All keen for the UK to vote out of the EU, and all attending or hosting Veronica Lewis' parties." His eyes widened suddenly. "These parties are nothing to do with sex!"

Liam gave him a knowing look. "I wouldn't say *nothing*."

But Craig was adamant. "I would. OK, so they may have sex at them and maybe they take incriminating photos to blackmail people into supporting them, but essentially the girls are just a front."

Liam shook his head. "Now, hang on, boss. You're talking like there's only the IBP attending the parties. As far as I recall Jennifer Wasson mentioned there being up to twenty men at each one, and so far, we've only named four or five linked to the IBP."

It made Craig pause, but only for a moment. "Perfect."

"Huh?"

"A party within a party. It's the perfect cover. Think about it. While the usual antics are happening all over the house, the inner group can slip away, or maybe *not* even slip away, they may be discussing things openly, certain that everyone else is too drunk or stoned to hear."

"So, the sex and drugs are covers?"

"Not for the other men there, but for the IBP, yes. Yes, I'd say that they probably are. If they've been using the parties to plot, that could be why they needed to ensure Veronica Lewis toed the line. Maybe she was planning on stopping the parties, or maybe they thought she was about to talk, but whichever it was they had to subdue her to keep their cover."

"Which they did. She's so terrified she won't even speak to us now. OK, so what about the arms and antiques smuggling? Have we given up on those and the drugs?"

"Keep asking the questions but my guess is they'll turn out to be a dead end. Although I want Karl Rimmins at tomorrow's briefing. The Drugs Squad could still have a part to play."

The group was silent for a full minute until Davy broke the quiet.

"Chief..." He swallowed hard before going on. "Why is the Chief Con involved? Is he an IBP supporter?"

The question took Craig aback and by the time he went to answer Liam had leapt in.

"There's no way! He's not supposed to have any political links, but I've seen him at a few GAA matches so if he did I'd say they'd be for Gorgeous Gloria's side."

Surprisingly Kyle agreed. Surprising because he rarely agreed with anyone, on principle.

"I had Flanagan checked out. He's clean. Even the GAA matches he attended were for charity. He's as politically neutral as someone can be, and he's faithful to his wife, so there's no sign that he's been going to Lewis' parties himself."

Craig could have hugged the ex-spy, despite himself. He'd convinced himself that it wouldn't matter to him if Sean Flanagan turned out to be a coke-snorting, womanising, right-wing acolyte, he would still like him, but he was bloody relieved that the man wasn't and that he'd been right about him all along.

Liam conceded the point. "OK, so this bunch of fascists-"

Ash's eyebrows shot up. "That's a bit strong."

"Matter of opinion, but OK. This *little clique* is using Lewis' fun parties as a cover to meet and discuss politics, in an environment where they can be positive they're not bugged, there'll be no reliable witnesses, and any that there are can be blackmailed to keep quiet." Something occurred to him. "Here. Where are the politician's security details while all this is going on?"

Davy shrugged. "Once they've checked out the host and swept the venue for weapons, my guess is they'll be parked up s...somewhere in the grounds."

Craig rose and opened the office door. "Aidan, can you join us, please. And grab a clean white board on your way." He pressed the percolator on his way back to his chair and five minutes later they were staring at a newly marked-up board with coffees in their hands.

"OK. We know there's a party this Saturday night, because Kyle's snout is attending with Joshua Loughrey. We also know the most likely venue is here." He tapped the position of Darrian's estate. "If not there, then Liam will find us another venue down south. OK, Liam?"

He was answered by a nod.

"That means we'll need at least one and perhaps more teams if we find other venues in the Republic, and three of them will need Gardaí members on Board." He glanced at his watch. "This is Wednesday. That only gives us two days to locate all the venues, scope them and prep this operation-"

He was cut off by Aidan's pen shooting up. "Which is?"

Liam was about to say, "bloody obvious" when Craig shook his head.

"Aidan's right. We need to define exactly what the purpose of the operation is. It's not purely information gathering, because all of you are doing that already, and it's certainly not a Vice raid, or any type of raid. It's..."

Davy clarified his thoughts. "It's a confirmation exercise. To make sure that what w...we think is happening actually is."

Craig nodded energetically. "Yes, but more than that. We're the Murder Squad and we may find information on McManus' and Regent's killings, but I've a feeling that this is part of something far bigger and I'm hoping that we'll find out what that is."

Kyle looked puzzled but he would never ask for clarity. Liam had no such pride.

"Why? We've already decided they're meeting to discuss voting out of the EU."

Craig laughed. "If that's all they wanted to talk about they could just go on TV. Even popstars are spouting off about Leave and Remain on the evening news." He shook his head. "Yes, they want out, but it's *why* that I'm interested in, and whether they're planning to corrupt the public vote."

This time Kyle spoke. "By exerting influence."

"And by threatening IBP voters who might vote Remain. I think that's why McManus had to go. Remember the IBP's official slogan is 'An Independent Britain *in* Europe'. McManus was a figurehead for IBP voters who wanted to stay in the EU, and that's a big percentage vote. Possibly enough to swing the whole election here. With him gone and Roger Burke in place now, they have less than two weeks to swing IBP supporters towards a coherent anti-EU vote."

Both Liam and Davy shook their heads.

"What if that doesn't make a big enough difference?"

"For all we know killing McManus isn't the only thing they've been doing, and we *won't* know unless we can hear what's being said. Meanwhile they could be pulling strings in other directions. All we know about is what they're up to in Northern Ireland, but who knows what they're up to in England, Scotland and Wales."

Kyle found himself agreeing with Craig again. "The polls are all saying the referendum vote will be close. A few percent here and there could make all the difference."

Craig wasn't listening; he was too busy watching the analysts exchange a look.

"Penny for your thoughts, you two."

Davy waved his friend on.

"Well, it's just...we both agree that's probably what's going on, chief, though you're right, we do need to get proof. But the question is, why? *Why* so hell bent on leaving the EU? I'm not saying leaving's wrong, but right or wrong, is this just a bunch of people who hold an opinion and want to impose it on everyone else, in which case they must be pretty bloody minded about it to kill two men, or is it something *bigger* than that?"

No-one had an answer for him.

## Chapter Twelve

Annette was struggling. Not physically, after all the baby in her arms only weighed twenty pounds and even with her energetic wriggling she could easily cope, but emotionally she was all at sea, and she wasn't quite sure why. Carina, or Carrie as she called her, wasn't her first baby; her son and daughter with her ex-husband were in their late teens, and she'd held down a full-time job and run a house when they were young, so why did everything feel so different this time?

She was tempted to say it was because she was older, but that would only explain fatigue and she felt as fit as she always had. So, why was leaving her baby every day for work ripping her apart this time? And making the idea of being a stay-at-home mum seem attractive?

Mike was a great dad, and apart from her having to concede and name the baby Carina, pretty, but an anatomical term to describe part of the lungs, a true pathologist's choice, he would have given her anything under the sun. The thought brought Annette up short. Could *that* be it? With Pete, she'd never had the option of staying at home, both of their salaries desperately needed, but Mike had enough money for both of them so now she had the freedom to choose, and in ways that freedom was screwing her up. If she didn't have to work but *chose* to, did that make her selfish, a bad mum?

She stared into her daughter's bright eyes as she thought, replaying all the arguments about being a good role model for her versus fourth-wave feminism giving women *real* freedom to choose. Telling a woman that they were letting down the side by staying at home was now considered every bit as dictatorial as telling them that they couldn't or shouldn't work.

As her baby snuggled into her and Annette started to count the lashes resting on her cheeks, the detective knew that whichever decision she made she'd be damned in someone's eyes. So, she did what she always did when she didn't know the answer to something, she deferred it to another day.

\*\*\*\*

**The Labs. 7.30 p.m.**

Craig had been summoned. Not by a barked order but by a strangulated gurgling on his phone twenty minutes earlier, a sound that always indicated John had something exciting to impart. He was unsurprised then to see his friend waiting at the carpark entrance to the labs, mentally hopping from foot to foot.

"Couldn't this have waited, John? I was supposed to collect Katy from work."

The question went unanswered, the pathologist already halfway down the corridor. Craig was surprised when, instead of entering his lab, John began the three-flight ascent that led them to Des Marsham's office. He was equally surprised to find the Head of Forensics still inside, his experience of the man saying that, short of a national disaster, Des logged off his computer at five p.m. and was in his car by ten past.

"Hello, Des. John shanghaied you as well, I see."

The scientist shook his hairy head. "Didn't have to. I wanted to see you as well."

Craig knew this was something good. He reached for a stool and sat down.

"Fire away."

"Very apropos."

To prove the point Des tapped on his computer and the image of a gun that Craig recognised appeared on the screen.

"The sniper rifle Billy Regent used to kill the First Minister...allegedly."

To Des' dismay Craig seemed only mildly surprised.

"So, you either don't think he made the shot, or you think that he made it under duress."

Craig knew he should probably have feigned ignorance of the possibility but he wanted to get home. He felt a forensic scientist's huff coming on.

"Well, if you put it like that..."

The detective relented. "Sorry, Des. Why don't you take me through it?"

*Just don't take all night.*

Des perked up again.

"OK, well, the GSR on Regent's hands definitely came from the rifle and his prints are all over it, although some have been smeared but I'll come to that. Also, it was a hell of a tricky shot, so I doubt there'd be many men capable of making it, and few of them in Belfast, so on balance I'd say that Billy Regent *did* make the shot that killed Peter McManus."

"But?"

"Well, that's the thing. This is where it gets confusing. There's no GSR from the handgun on Regent's hands."

Craig sat forward. "Hang on. I thought you couldn't tell the difference."

Des hemmed and hawed. "Well... you can and you can't, sort of. But even on quantity alone there was only enough GSR for one shot-"

Craig cut him off. "So why was it definitely the shot from the rifle?"

"Because it was smeared."

Now Craig *was* confused. The scientists saw it and cheered up immediately, then Des lifted a rifle that Craig hadn't noticed and began to demonstrate.

"OK, here's where Regent's hands would have been when he was firing the rifle. Inches away from the working parts. Any residue on his hands from the shot should have been minimal, but it *isn't*. There's far too much of the stuff!" Before Craig could interrupt again he produced Regent's handgun. "OK, now this is the pistol that killed Regent. See how close to the working parts his right hand would have been if he'd committed suicide. Lots of GSR from the pistol you'd think, and you'd be correct, except that there's too much GSR on Regent's hands for the rifle shot, but not enough for if he'd fired *both* guns."

"You're saying he fired the rifle but not the handgun. But we already know that. Someone else fired the pistol to make it look like suicide and they wore latex gloves."

Des shook his head. "Not so fast. You *think* you know what happened, but you really don't. *We* didn't until Reggie found those gloves in the bin."

"The ones worn by the second man."

John's eyebrows shot up but he said nothing, whereas Des' "NO" was very clear.

"What do you mean, no?"

"I mean those gloves weren't worn by your second man, they were worn by Billy Regent. His DNA was all over their insides."

As Craig struggled to keep up, Des woke his computer and started a simulation. It showed two men appearing on Carson Tower's roof, each carrying a bag. As they watched, the Billy Regent avatar opened his bag, withdrew a rifle and donned a pair of gloves, positioning himself to take the kill shot.

Craig nodded, realising what he'd missed.

"Regent was wearing gloves when he took the rifle shot because he'd expected to leave that roof alive. But he wasn't sure what *would* happen, hence showing his face to the lift CCTV, to prove his coercion even after his death."

John glanced at him, surprised. "I didn't know you'd got CCTV."

"Ash found it. I'll have him send it across. Regent was forced to kill McManus. A second man held him at gun point in the lift up to the roof."

He missed John's small smile as Des called their attention back to the screen.

"OK, but at this point Regent still thought that he was getting off that roof, which is why he wore latex gloves to cover his prints when he took the rifle shot."

"So how did he get the rifle's GSR on his hands?"

"Keep watching."

As he did Craig saw Regent's avatar make the McManus kill shot and then start packing up his rifle, only to be stopped by a handgun pressed to the side of his head, causing first a struggle and then forcing Regent to lie down.

"This is where Billy Regent dies."

The second avatar, also wearing latex gloves, shot Regent's in the right temple. Craig nodded.

"OK, so you've explained the latex traces on Regent's hands, and I understand the lack of two lots of GSR. But if Regent wore gloves and only took the rifle shot, where did the GSR he *did* have on his hands come from? He shouldn't have had any at all. And explain the quantities to me again."

Des fast forwarded to where the German avatar carefully removed Billy Regent's latex gloves right side out and smeared the GSR from their exteriors onto Regent's palms. They then placed the sniper rifle in the dead man's hands, holding it there for a moment before returning it half-packed to its plain black bag. Craig's mouth fell open in realisation.

"Ah...Hence Regent's smeared prints on the rifle."

"Exactly. Also..."

Des forwarded the sim and Craig watched as the German avatar removed its own gloves, again right side out, and smeared the GSR from the handgun onto Billy Regent's palms.

"Not all of the GSR will have transferred from the two sets of gloves-"

Craig cut in. "So, they left too much GSR for one shot but not enough for two."

John nodded. "I've found some epithelial cells that match the German's DNA amongst the GSR on Regent's hands. They had to have come from the gloves they wore."

Craig followed the logic through.

"And I'm presuming that somewhere along the line, long before they reached the roof, Billy got a piece of his killer's DNA under his nails."

"That's the only thing explains it."

John chipped in. "So, then the killer took Billy's latex gloves and dumped them on the estate sometime later, just to delay or confuse us, I presume. But they must have taken their own gloves away."

"Probably burned them somewhere else." Craig shook his head. "Very clever, and they might have fooled us but for your hard work."

As Des preened himself John added excitedly. "Don't forget we've got the DNA under Billy's nails as well. The killer mustn't have known about it, or my guess is they would have chopped off his hands and taken them away."

Craig nodded and stood up. "The only thing missing in your sim is that there were two bags, and the killer took the outer one with them. It had a logo that Davy's checking." As Des opened his mouth to ask, Craig explained. "Someone from a neighbouring block saw Billy with another man on the way there. OK, the important thing is this clears Billy Regent completely, so his family will get his benefits. The poor sod was chosen for his shooting ability and threatened to make him do what he did. We think they probably told him they'd kill his mother and daughter if he didn't go along with things." He turned to go. "Thanks for this. Hopefully the German's DNA will soon get a hit."

He couldn't miss John's smile this time.

*"You've already got a name?"*

The pathologist demurred hastily. "No, sorry, it's not that. It's something else on the DNA. Something that I suppose *shouldn't* surprise me in these days of kick-ass, warrior-"

Craig finished the sentence for him.

"Princesses...The German is a woman!"

"You might have let me say it!"

The pathologist's lips clamped together in what Craig knew was going to be a sulk. He calculated quickly. Katy had gone on home after he'd called to cancel her lift, and he'd said he'd come by later with a takeaway. But that could wait for an hour, so with a contrite smile he suggested they all go for a pint, and John's sulk faded like hot snow.

\*\*\*\*

**Whitehall.**

"You're certain they found the gloves?"

The Fox sipped at his just poured rum. He was a whisky man but had decided that as someone else was paying he would try it just for a change. The red-brown liquid slid down his throat more smoothly than even the best whisky, but it was its instant warming effect that surprised him most. He was just adding it mentally to his list of regular tipples when the older man spoke again.

"*Well?* Are you?"

Irritated at his drinking being interrupted, the silver-haired man answered more abruptly than he'd meant.

"For God's sake, yes! How many times do I have to say it?"

His host's sudden lurch forward from his wing-backed armchair and the wrinkled hand gripping his throat said the words had been a mistake.

"*You may speak to your superiors at home like that, but never make the mistake of confusing me with them. This is a gentleman's club and you will behave like one. Do. You. Understand?*"

A nodded yes and The Fox's throat was released to cough and splutter into his glass, then the elderly man continued as if nothing had occurred.

"They may busy themselves postulating about why McManus was killed. That doesn't concern me at all. Just as long as the evidence leads them in the direction we wish."

"It will. I assure you."

The words were accompanied by a red-faced nod and then the older man gestured at the door.

"Leave then. We have no further need of you."

As being dismissed went it was unequivocal, but The Fox remained where he was, taking his life in his hands with his next utterance and pushing his chair back to a safe distance before he spoke.

"I disagree. I must remain in Northern Ireland for the party. It is to be the final one there before the vote."

The host's face went first pale and then red at being contradicted, fading slowly to pink as he considered the validity of the words. He was also considering a second grab of his companion's carotid, but decided that would have to wait for another day. He liked to practise his wet-work skills occasionally but it seemed that now wasn't the time.

"Very well. Attend the event, but do not take part. Observe and report to me. I will let Darrian know that you are coming and he will take you to the group."

A second, sharper indication of the exit persuaded The Fox not to push his luck again. He would go straight to Heathrow and return to Belfast, back to his obligingly smoke friendly bar to think.

\*\*\*\*

## 9 p.m.

Craig was still shaking his head on his third pint. *A woman.* Half of him still disbelieved it even as the other half was thinking *'of course'*. In many ways, it made sense.

An unknown woman could have got closer to Billy Regent than an unknown man. More quickly as well. Men were susceptible to a pretty face. The thought brought the detective up short. Who said the German was pretty? And yet the more that he thought about it the more that it made sense.

Both sexes could be influenced by good looks; it wasn't just men's weakness, no matter what the tabloids implied. And if approached by an attractive stranger, both sexes would be more likely to engage them in conversation than not. It told him something else; the German was probably Regent's age or a few years either side; he doubted that a grandmother figure would have engaged the young man in quite the same way.

So, if it was a woman, why was she German? It wasn't a nationality with a large population living in the province. Polish, Lithuanian, Indian, all those groups had substantial communities in Northern Ireland, but a German was still more likely to be a tourist or a student than anything else. A tourist on a killing spree? A narrowly targeted one.

His mind turned back to the figure on the CCTV. It could easily have been a woman; tall and slim, with her hair concealed under a baseball hat. The detective gave a snort of disgust. Tall and slim, the description was ubiquitous. They needed to look at the tapes again, see if there were other clues: hair colour from a wayward strand perhaps or a distinctive walk, something, *anything* that could help identify the killer in the crowd caged within the cordon when they'd arrived on the estate.

He was making a note for Davy to distribute the CCTV to Bill McEwan, Des, Aidan, Reggie and anyone else who might be able to help when he had another thought; everyone within the cordon who wasn't in uniform would have given their name and address. In their killer's case, it would be false of course, but it meant someone might have spoken to them at least once. He scribbled down 'talk to the interviewing officers' and finally looked up from his notebook just in time to see John rise to his feet.

"You leaving, John?"

A glance said the pathologist had been thinking of it, but he slumped back down again.

"What for? All I'm going home to is an argument."

Des took it as his cue to leave. Craig was John's best

friend and he could give him better advice than he ever could, besides which, he had two small children to kiss goodnight. As the forensic expert left the pub Craig ordered another round and prepared himself for a tale of marital woe, with half of his mind still on a killer from a thousand miles away.

\*\*\*\*

## The Demesne Estate, East Belfast. Thursday. 9 a.m.

Liam's morning was being ruined by Craig. The D.C.I. had had the hours from nine to twelve all planned: chase up on the guns' serial numbers to see if he could trace their origins and then follow up with Ken and Davy on Regent's mental health; after that it would be off to The James at twelve o'clock to see what was on for lunch. But the call he'd received from Craig at eleven the night before had put paid to all that. He'd had to delegate the gun and psychiatric stuff and get himself down to the Demesne, where Reggie Boyd was now back in permanent residence, just how permanent was being indicated by the way the sergeant had his feet up on his desk.

He didn't move when Liam arrived, not even to offer him tea, preferring instead to point the D.C.I. to the kettle with "Make one for me as well."

"What did your last servant die of, Reg?"

"Gratitude. There're some biscuits in the tin, just underneath there, so you can bring those across as well."

Several Jaffa Cakes later Liam was feeling better so he announced what he'd driven there for.

"You've seen the CCTV, I suppose?"

Reggie nodded, dropping his feet to the floor with a thud and switching on his computer. As the aging P.C. booted up the sergeant elaborated.

"The lift shots mainly, but there's another clip your lads found and sent across about twenty minutes ago."

He tapped 'enter' and they watched as a grainy video flickered to life. Liam said what they were both thinking.

"I wish to God they'd improve the quality of those things. It's impossible to tell who's who."

As it happened it wasn't an issue; there were only two figures on the screen. Two tall, straight figures that looked like youngish men. They were walking across the optimistically named 'Travis Square' between the tower blocks, the man wearing a baseball cap also carrying a logoed bag.

Reggie pressed pause and tapped the screen. "That one's your killer?"

"Aye. They pressured Billy to take the shot on McManus and then they blew him away. See the black gloves? There are latex ones under those, but they're not the ones your Mrs Johnston found."

"Who did those belong to then?"

"Billy was wearing latex gloves himself. Even though Baseball Cap was pressuring him to kill he still had the wit to cover his prints. It all says he believed he was getting off that roof alive."

Reggie shook his head sadly. "There's none so blind as those who will not see."

"Thank you, Confucius." Liam gestured at the screen. "Play that clip back from the start and just watch Baseball Cap."

Both men watched for a moment as the slimmer figure crossed the square close behind Billy Regent and then Liam signalled stop.

"OK. What did you notice?"

Reggie screwed up his face. "Tall enough, but scrawny. Billy could have taken him in a fight."

"What's your impression of colouring? Quick. First thing that comes into your head."

"Fair skinned. Although I don't know why I'm saying that. You can't see his hands or face."

"Aye, you can. There, just the tip of the chin. It's

definitely pale. OK, anything else?"

Reggie sat back and folded his arms determinedly. "I know you, Cullen. This is where you pretend you've worked something out all by yourself when really somebody else told you, and you try to make me look thick. Well forget it, I'm not playing. Tell me what you know."

Liam gave a fake sigh. "Ach, you're no fun anymore, Reg. Time was when you'd have gone along with me."

"Time was when I'd nothing better to do. Spill."

Liam gestured at the computer. "Oh, OK. Baseball Cap's a woman."

Another thing that Craig had told him in his late-night call.

The revelation made Reggie sit forward again to peer at the screen. "No way."

"Yep. The DNA says there's no doubt. Billy's killer was a German woman."

Reggie looked shocked. "*German?* That's rare over here." He turned to the screen again. "But now you say that it's a woman, I can see it. It's the pointed chin that gives it away."

"Whatever it is, someone spoke to her. Everyone inside that cordon had to give their name and address, so some copper interviewed a tall, slim, youngish woman."

The sergeant's response was to reach into his desk drawer and pull out a sheaf of pages. He split the pile and pushed half across the desk.

"Start looking."

Thirty minutes and two more biscuits later, Liam looked up from his papers, shaking his head.

"I've only got youngsters under eighteen, and a couple of old dears."

Reggie was similarly perplexed. "I've got nothing but men here, and there's no way a woman would be mistaken for a man if they were interviewed face to face. Your girl wasn't inside the cordon. She must have slipped out before it went up."

Liam shook his head emphatically. "Aidan had that cordon up before the shot that killed Regent. He went to the Travis as soon as trajectory analysis said McManus had been shot from there. And I had Ash check and there were no unknown CSIs or police on scene."

"Well, no-one spoke to her so she *must* have slipped out."

Liam's jaw dropped in realisation. "No, she bloody didn't. She was still hiding inside the block!" He jumped to his feet and headed for the door, beckoning the sergeant to follow him. "I'm going to kill Bill McEwan. His trigger-happy bunch of Rambos did an incomplete search!"

\*\*\*\*

As the two policemen left to murder the Armed Response Commander, something that was unlikely to be achieved unless every gun but their own was removed from the room, Liam got a call. He pressed answer, expecting the withheld number to be Craig calling from the office, only to hear Davy's voice on the line.

"Have you seen the chief?"

Liam suppressed his reflex quip about feeling unwanted because of the stress in the analyst's voice.

"No. Have you tried his mobile?"

"It's cutting to voicemail. He must be in a dead zone. He went to interview Leonard Montgomery about thirty minutes ago, but-"

"Whatever you've got can't wait. Reggie's with me, but say what you have to say."

Davy swallowed hard, knowing that what he had was basically gossip, but gossip from a very reliable source, Maggie, who knew everything there was to know about Northern Ireland's journalistic world.

"Ray Mercer."

The name made Liam feel sick and the sudden sour taste in his mouth said that he just might be. Ray Mercer had been News Editor at The Belfast Chronicle two years before, and the bane of their lives for much longer than that, with his distorted and biased reporting. One transgression too far had seen him reported to the newspaper's Executive Board and cost him his job. He blamed Craig for it and they'd almost come to blows last time they'd met.

The last Liam had heard of the reporter was that he'd been working as a freelancer in Dublin, and Mercer reappearing and disturbing their peace now, especially during such a sensitive case, was something that they could all do without.

Davy was still speaking.

"He's back in Belfast, w...working for The Belfast Journal."

The *real* gutter press.

"And he's got something on McManus' killing."

Liam found his voice. "When you say something, do you mean fact or fiction?"

"Maggie doesn't know. All she knows is that Mercer's been dropping hints about some big scoop he's got, on a s...secret club being involved in McManus' death."

A secret club? Did he mean the group who met at Lewis' parties? Could the newshound possibly have found out something that they'd missed?

Liam thought fast, pulling his car into a U-Turn as he did. Leonard Montgomery lived on the Malone Road somewhere and Craig needed this information fast.

"Davy, what's Montgomery's address?"

"The chief's meeting him at his office on the Upper Lisburn Road."

"OK, send me the address. We're heading there now. You get back to Maggie and see what else you can find out, and I want to know where Mercer is. We may need to pick him up."

And chuck him in a deep, dark hole if he had any say in it. As Davy ended the call, Liam made another one, this time to Aidan Hughes. He dispensed with the niceties.

"I need you to do something for me."

Aidan Hughes put his mobile on speaker and continued doing his sit-ups, hidden behind Nicky's now repaired wall. It had proved a valuable construction. Not just for yesterday's spectacle, but for the fact that he could do some keep fit while he worked and no-one could see to gawp.

"OK. What?"

Liam stared at the hands free, listening to the D.C.I. pant and grunt. It dawned on Reggie what was going on and he mouthed 'sit-ups', making Liam roll his eyes.

"Are you exercising in the office, Wensley?"

"Yep. It helps my bad back. Five minutes an hour makes for nearly an hour a day."

Liam was torn between asking him what exercises he was doing, he had a bad back himself, and telling him to stop immediately. In the end he did neither, continuing on.

"I need you to contact Bill McEwan."

"Armed Response?"

"Ach, how many other Bill McEwans do you know?" He didn't wait for a reply. "Anyway, go and see him about the sweep his men did of Carson Tower on the day of the shootings."

Aidan jerked upright and grabbed the phone. "Why? I was on site. It was all done by the book."

"Well then, you're as stupid as McEwan is, because his men missed something huge. It turns out Billy Regent's killer was a woman. The DNA beneath his nails was conclusive." He heard Hughes inhale sharply. "But Reggie and I just checked the interviews held within the cordon and no-one fits the bill. I think Regent's killer hid in the tower until everyone had gone, and she could only have managed that if one of McEwan's muppets didn't do their job."

"Shit!" It was followed by an even more astonished "Bloody hell, Liam", as Aidan Hughes realised exactly what he was asking him to do. "You *seriously* expect me to tell Bill McEwan that his men let a killer escape! There's no way! Do it yourself."

This was where seniority proved useful and Liam felt his chest swell as he realised he had the power to compel the more junior D.C.I. This must be what the Chief Constable felt like every day.

"D.C.I. Hughes, you *will* visit Commander McEwan, and tactfully, or not, and actually I couldn't give a monkey's which, you *will* find out how this happened. Meanwhile, I want you to get some uniforms down to that tower, checking every flat to find where our woman might have concealed herself. I suggest they start with the empty gaffs. Go down there yourself after you've seen McEwan and take a C.S.I. team along. Reggie will be joining you as well."

Aidan wasn't so awed by Liam's authority that he couldn't manage a question. "And where will *you* be all this time? Swanning around, I suppose."

That *had* been the plan, until the idea of Ray Mercer at large had begun to gnaw at him and he'd turned the car back towards the Demesne, deciding to leave Reggie back to his car and lift Mercer himself.

He wanted to interview the reporter before telling Craig what Maggie had heard, but the idea that listening to Ray Mercer spouting off could be categorised as swanning gave Liam his best laugh of the day so far.

\*\*\*\*

**The C.C.U.**

Davy had just finished a follow-up call to Maggie when his one hundred and eighty IQ kicked in. They'd already deduced that a group might be using Veronica Lewis' parties as a place to meet, their secrecy ensured by the other party-goers having too much to lose if things came out, but what if Ray Mercer, with all the time and contacts that only an investigative reporter had, really *had* managed to discover something more? And what if what they'd called a clique and Mercer had called a secret club, was actually more of a cabal? A political faction powerful and sinister enough to influence world affairs.

The more the analyst thought about it the more that it made sense. The group seemed to have a political agenda, didn't balk at killing if it was necessary, and the members that they were aware of had, between them, wealth, influence and interests worldwide. The book code that he was still unable to crack fitted with the secrecy they craved, and perhaps more than that, the use of encryption was well known to every government that used clandestine agencies.

The question was how and when had the group formed? And was it a onetime deal of people drawn together by a common interest, quitting the EU, only to disperse once their goal had been attained, or did it have deeper and more extensive roots than that? With powerful, permanent members that brought issues they needed resolved to a group of the equally powerful, in a dangerous arrangement of 'you scratch my back and I'll scratch yours'?

One thing was certain; these people stood to gain from whatever they were doing, which meant that with Peter McManus out of the way things were likely to speed up. It prompted Davy to draw up a table and begin populating it, hoping fervently that a common thread would appear.

\*\*\*\*

**The Upper Lisburn Road, South Belfast.**

Leonard Montgomery, MBE, MLA had folded like clean laundry as soon as Craig had mentioned the word escort. It marked him out not as one of the hard core they needed to break but as a man that they could use.

Craig sat across the impressive maple desk in the Finance Minister's constituency office, considering the politician. He looked like every second middle-aged businessman in Belfast: a decade-out-of-fashion-cut grey or navy suit, plain white cotton-mix shirt and not too colourful silk tie; plump, thinning on top and with skin that was either toasted brown from too much sun or fish-white from never having glimpsed its rays. He'd often wondered how the lean-hipped students of Northern Ireland morphed into these rotund, characterless men, whose only attempts at individuality seemed confined to the buckles on their belts or their socks. It was as if there was some factory that made them out of heat-moulded plastic comprised of their long dead hopes and dreams. If he woke up like one of them one morning it would be time to give up the ghost.

While Craig's thoughts meandered through his mind, Leonard Montgomery's were racing across his face, and they all amounted to one thing; the politician was well and truly screwed. Knowing that 'Screwed and panicking official' wasn't a good look, before Craig had time to ask the questions about escorts that he already knew would break the MLA, Leonard Montgomery obliged all by himself.

He lurched forward, blurting out his words in clumps as if someone was punching the air out of him.

"It was...only a few times!... My wife and I... We've been having... problems." The official coloured. "Of the marital sort... She doesn't like..."

Craig's heart sank. There was nothing he hated more than people whining excuses, especially if he had to listen to them crying about their lack of sex. He raised a hand to stem the politician's diatribe on his wife's frigidity and moved forward to the edge of his chair.

"Parties, Mister Montgomery."

"What?"

"Have you ever attended a party hosted by Mrs Veronica Lewis?"

The MLA's averted eyes told him that the answer was yes.

"When?"

Montgomery's brown eyes widened beneath their concertinaed lids.

"I didn't say that I-"

"Not in words, no. So, *when* did you attend?"

The answer came slowly and in a mutter.

"Say that again, please, Minister. This time so I can hear."

Craig heard this time all right.

"In January! OK?"

The detective's reaction was to raise an eyebrow.

"Perfectly OK, I suppose, if you're into that kind of thing. Now... Was Peter McManus present?"

A nod. Craig slipped a folded page from his pocket, spreading it out on the impressive desk.

"And these men?"

Montgomery scanned the page slowly, muttering to himself as he did.

"Louder please."

"THEY ALL WERE! Happy now?"

"Ecstatic. I enjoy nothing better than spending my day like this."

While the Minister tried to work out if it was the truth or sarcasm, Craig ran his gaze down the list. Montgomery had just confirmed Loughrey, Burke, the Earl, McArdle, Bell and McManus. It was time to play a hunch.

"Did they absent themselves from the party at any point? As a group?"

When Montgomery gave up all show of reluctance Craig knew that the MLA had computed his odds; if he cooperated with the police now there was just a chance they wouldn't tell anyone he'd been using escorts. Craig had never intended to tell anyone, but if Leonard Montgomery thought that meant his wife would never find out then he was heading for a fall. But he'd drop that bombshell at the very end, right now he had information to extract.

"So? Did they?"

Montgomery nodded.

"All of them. Although McManus returned to the party pretty quickly."

It was interesting. Was it in January that the group had

realised McManus' Pro-EU stance was genuine? If they'd argued about it seriously enough then it might have triggered the planning for the First Minister's subsequent demise.

"Did you attend any other parties?"

The politician shook his head.

"I was invited, but the dates always seemed to clash with work or home."

The MLA stopped speaking suddenly and Craig could see him calculating again: do I tell this cop more and hope that it saves my ass, or just say nothing and hope the same? Montgomery opted for the former.

"There's a party this weekend. Saturday."

"You're invited?"

"Yes."

"You're going."

"No, I'm not. It's my son's sixteenth."

Craig shook his head slowly. "That wasn't a question, Minister. *You're going*. And if you do as we need you to do then your past behaviour will remain between us."

Apart from your wife, whose anonymous phone calls say that she already knows.

\*\*\*\*

## The Labs. 12 p.m.

"Any progress on the guns or logo, Des?"

John Winter received a vague grunt, that in his experience of the Head of Forensics meant good news.

"Will they lead anywhere useful?"

The grunt had a higher pitch this time, saying maybe no, maybe yes. It gave him hope. Des wasn't a teaser, not at work at least.

"OK. Can you give me any details yet?"

This time he received a full-on snort. Translated it meant 'Bugger off, John. I'll call you when I'm done'.

Six miles away Davy was having much the same conversation with Ash, and about one of the same things. Clarity on the logo was going to take some time while the FBI's Logo Comparison Programme ran, so both analysts had turned their attention to other things. In Ash's case, it was the DNA profile that John had sent through. He was just about to chase it up with Interpol, with the added benefit now of knowing that it belonged to a woman, when his desk telephone rang.

Even on "Hello" he knew that the caller was foreign, and by "May I speak to" he'd narrowed their accent to Europe. Not being a great believer in coincidence he knew that fate had just saved him making a call.

"Speaking. How can I help you?"

His exaggerated politeness made Davy turn and stare. Either Ash was speaking to his mum or his Hindu guru, because no-one else ever warranted such a deferential tone. The addition of "Monsieur Moreau" said that he was wrong, so Davy lifted his own receiver and quietly pressed two buttons so he could listen in on the call.

"I am calling from Interpol in Lyons regarding a specimen that your police sent through. We have a match that I will send by secure email."

A moment later the phone went down and after another the analysts were staring at a profile on their screens. Beatrix Hass, aged forty-three, although her photograph showed that she looked two decades younger. In fact, if Ash had seen her in a club he would have chatted her up. But however well the woman in front of them was aging, she had a rap sheet as long as Davy's gangly arm. The most interesting information lay in a section named Politische Straftaten or Political Offences.

Hass had been a member of the National Offensive from nineteen-ninety to ninety-two, then dabbled in various Reichsbürger groups and Der Autonome Nationalisten (The Independent Nationalists), essentially Neo-Nazis, before moving on to join an even more extreme group earlier that year. The fine print on the groups' constitutions probably differed, but all their ideologies were right-wing nationalism, some of which was imposed through anarchy and violence.

Ash recovered from his shock enough to ask, "What's a Reichsbürger?"

Davy's response was to pull up a search engine so they could both read that Reichsbürgers in general subscribed to the theory that the Federal Republic of Germany, founded in nineteen-forty-nine, had *never* been a legitimate state, because Germany hadn't signed a peace agreement with the Allies, and that German 'Basic Law' required a public referendum for it to be voted a legitimate constitution.

The senior analyst gave a slow whistle then said what they were both thinking. "What the heck is a right-wing German activist doing killing people over here?" He went in search of the answer, starting to type. They couldn't give Craig this information without some context, but what that would turn out to be he had no idea.

\*\*\*\*

### University Street, South Belfast.

Journalists can be tricky creatures. Not just because they can bias reports that the public is likely to be influenced by, but because the skills that enable them to sense a story, sniff out sources and persuade those sources to spill their guts, are the very same ones that can make some of them as slippery as hell.

They also had a nasty tendency to turn questions back on the questioner, bleat 'freedom of the press' at anyone who might listen, and refuse to keep things off the record, and Liam had no desire to see his name and face splashed across a front page.

While Ray Mercer had been a discredited freelancer it had been easy to ignore him, but now he had a soap box, albeit one as disgusting as The Belfast Journal, which meant that some well-paid inhouse legal team was willing to defend what the reporter wrote, and that way lay uncensored verbosity. Liam knew he needed to be careful what he said to the wee scrote now, which irked him enormously, when what he really wanted to do was smack Mercer around the head hard enough to make him cough up whatever he knew.

It was with those frustrations in mind that the D.C.I. parked outside the Journal's satisfyingly dingy looking offices in University Street, hoping against hope that their aged façade was a mark of the paper's lack of success. The glossy reception area Liam discovered once he'd pushed through the street door said that it wasn't, and that the outward decay was more likely some sort of urban street-cred, shabby chic kind of thing. He hated that fake front shit. Businesses should be like Ronseal and be exactly what they said on the tin.

The sleek receptionist that greeted him made Liam's heart sink even further, and when he said, "I need to see Ray Mercer" her immediate flutter told him the reporter was high up the newspaper's food chain. He thrust out his warrant card petulantly, only to find that it didn't have the same aphrodisiac effect.

There was no justice in the world. Mercer had contravened all the ethics that journalism possessed two years before, by feeding a story he couldn't write himself to a teenage blogger, so that when it eventually became visible he could pick it up and reap the accolades. And yet here he was, insufficient penance time later in Liam's opinion, back in the game in the big smoke.

It made the detective long for a lunch and a pint. He was on his second beer mentally when Ray Mercer appeared, and strangely the journalist's appearance gave Liam a frisson of pleasure. Not because he liked the man, there was no ambiguity about that, but because the weasel faced, scrawny little ratbag looked like crap. A holiday in a gulag would have had a better effect on his looks.

Liam didn't rise in greeting, his top-to-toe sneer easier

to demonstrate from where he sat. The look got to Mercer even though he'd expected it as soon as he'd known who was waiting, and he snapped out the opening words.

"If it isn't the big bastard himself!" He cast a look over his shoulder. "Don't bother making coffee, Darlene, this definitely isn't a VIP."

Liam rose slowly to tower over them both. It was in moments like this that he loved being tall.

"No, don't bother making coffee, Darlene, because Mister Mercer is coming with me."

Mercer's sharp eyes narrowed. "On what charge?"

"To help with our enquiries, like the good little citizen that you are."

A hand beneath his elbow told the reporter not to disagree, and as Mercer was propelled towards the front door Liam waved with his free hand.

"Toodle Pip, Darlene. Don't wait up."

*Mister Mercer is likely to be late.*

# Chapter Thirteen

Veronica Lewis felt nervous and she wasn't certain why. All she had to do was the job that she'd been given and both she and Rupert would be safe, she knew that. But still, there was something in the air that was making her very afraid. She was still unsettled by her ordeal in the wood, of course, and no-one liked living under threat, but the unease the madam was feeling wasn't to do with either of those things and she couldn't give it a name.

She shook her head sharply to clear it and smiled at the young woman across the desk.

"It's a really flash party this time, Jenny, so wear your glad rags. The host has said no expense is being spared."

Jenny Wasson knew better than to ask who that host was, or where the event was going to be held. It would be the same routine as usual: blindfolds and a limo, with the same on the journey back. Yet she felt nervous as well, although *her* nervousness was tinged with excitement; she'd known when she'd given the list of party dates to the police that they'd do something with them, and this weekend's party would be her first chance to see what that was.

She secretly hoped that they'd follow her, burst through the door at just the right moment, and catch all the dirty old buggers with their trousers around their feet. OK, it would mean no more parties and her losing money, but she'd been for an interview that week for a teaching post so she hoped that her escort days were numbered anyway.

It was time. Her kids were starting to ask why she had so many glittery dresses in her wardrobe, when her social life with them consisted of nothing but PTA meetings and visits to the flicks.

She suddenly realised that Lewis had asked her a question and brought her attention back to the here and now.

"Sorry, Vero, I missed that."

Lewis smiled. Jenny was her favourite girl by far. Apart from really liking her she was always punctual and polite, and, as comfortable at the opera as the art gallery, she was the one her best clients asked for again and again.

"I said there'll be a bonus for you for this one. Five thousand."

Jenny gawped. "That's my fee?"

"That's on top of your fee. The host's paying it, for what he said will be some very special guests." Her tone changed to a warning. "But just be careful, Jen. There'll be a lot of blow around, and God knows what else. One of the customers is bringing it this time. So just watch that no-one spikes your drink. I've heard one of them likes it a bit rough."

It made up Jennifer Wasson's mind. She would stick to water this time, from a bottle, and this party would definitely be her last.

\*\*\*\*

**1.30 p.m.**

The call when it came was unwelcome. Craig had planned to drive to the Travis and see what was what with the search for their assassin's hiding place and then on to headquarters to bring the C.C. up to date, so when Liam's name appeared on his mobile his instinct was to ignore the call. They'd be catching up later at the office anyway and there was nothing that couldn't wait. By the third missed call Craig was exasperated so he called the D.C.I. back.

"What do you want?"

Liam was so pissed off after an hour with Ray Mercer that he missed the terseness in his boss' voice.

"Ah, good. You got my messages."

Craig hadn't, having deliberately chosen not to listen to them. There was a reason for that. Liam's telephone messages always fell into one of two categories: a single word, usually 'shit' because he'd had to use the answerphone, which he hated doing; or rambling opinion pieces woven around the facts he needed to impart, that often made Craig think the D.C.I. should write a column for the Daily Blah.

He decided not to lie about it, bluntness being the mark of a true friend.

"Didn't listen to them. So, what do you want? I'm on my way to the Travis."

"I wouldn't if I were you, boss."

"Why not?"

"Let Wensley take the grief from McEwan and tidy things up afterwards. It'll be easier all round."

Craig knew he was right, although he felt a bit guilty leaving Aidan Hughes to take all the flak.

"OK. Then I'm off to headquarters to update the C.C."

"Nope. That can wait too. You need to get to High Street. I've someone for you to see."

Highhanded though the statement was it made Craig curious.

"Who?"

"An old -" Liam stopped mid-sentence. He *had* been going to say 'friend' because the saying required it, but he couldn't stomach using that word in relation to Ray Mercer.

Craig tutted impatiently.

"Old what, Liam? Man? Woman?... Enemy?"

Liam's sigh said that he'd got it in three. Craig's pulled onto the M1 cityward and continued speculating into his hands free.

"Enemy then. So, OK, who? Harrison, Susan Richie...?"

D.C.S. Terry (Teflon) Harrison was Craig's erstwhile boss and now oversaw both Drugs and Vice. The fifty-six-year-old was a lecherous, ambitious snob whose trail of mistresses, often younger than his daughter, had recently resulted in his divorce. The two men had clashed on many occasions, whereas with Susan Richie it had just been once. When Craig had been given oversight of the Intelligence

Section she'd been its ruthless Director, protecting killers just to get their information and score career points. He'd kicked her out to work in Staff Training. It was safe to say that neither officer would be sending him a Christmas card.

Craig was onto enemy number five when it occurred to him just how many people he'd pissed off through the years, and that as Liam hadn't halted him he hadn't even reached the end of the list.

"OK. No more guessing. Who is it?"

Liam swallowed hard. "Mercer."

Craig was incredulous. "*Ray* Mercer?"

Liam's sarcastic 'how many Mercers do you know?' remained unsaid.

"Yep. He's back in Belfast working at the Journal."

Craig didn't know whether to be disgusted or furious. He still had the scar where he'd punched a window instead of Mercer's head, at a Christmas party two years' before. It still hurt when it was cold which in Northern Ireland meant that the journalist was never out of his thoughts for long.

Finally, he opted for jaded.

"Why do I care?"

Surprised at how lightly he'd got off, Liam went on enthusiastically. "Because Maggie says he's about to publish a piece about some secret club."

Silence.

"A club linked with McManus' death."

Still silence, but this time only because Craig's jaw had dropped. *A headline two days before they got to the party and hopefully exposed the whole plot! No bloody way.*

"Lift him."

Liam smiled the smug smile of the clever boy.

"Already done. That's why you need to come to High Street. I had a quick go at him but he gave me nothing but crap, so I thought that you might fancy a try."

Anticipation brought a cold smile to Craig's lips. "I definitely do. Well done. But let's leave him to stew until after this afternoon's briefing. I want to see what everyone's got first.

****

**Craigantlet Army Base.**

Ken Smith gazed at the equipment spread out on his bed, ticking each piece methodically off his clip-boarded list and memories along with it. His dress uniform, worn at summer and winter balls where he kissed many pretty dates. His service dress and combat dress, just two of the many uniforms that he'd worn around the world. The list went on, but no matter how long it was it didn't seem much of an epitaph for a fifteen-year career, even if they did all have pips. The soon to be ex-captain lifted a pair of black boots and sat down in a chair, polishing them absent-mindedly for five minutes before returning to his count of the berets, caps, belts and tunics that sketched out a soldier's career.

But even through the wave of nostalgia he was surfing Ken couldn't deny the bubble of excitement in his chest. He paused his inventory for another moment, trying to identify the feeling's origin. It couldn't be excitement at not having to wear a uniform any more, he'd just be wearing a different one in the PSNI; and it couldn't be excitement at not having to obey orders, there would still be plenty of those. Then it came to him, and if Lucia Craig had been able to read her boyfriend's thoughts at that moment he'd have found himself kicked into touch for at least a week. Ken Smith was excited by several things but the most exciting one of all didn't bear her name.

It was the promise of physical freedom. No more having to move to a new country at a day's notice, with no option but to comply, and no more being confined to base for any number of reasons, most of which they never knew. The only place he'd be confined to in future would be a home of his own with a wide screen TV, and then only ever by his own choice.

The soldier smiled to himself as the more feminine reason for his excitement came back into view. And when he was in that home with its super-king bed and luxurious bathroom his companions wouldn't be a bunch of hairy great soldiers, but the woman he loved and the Red Setter pup that they were going to buy.

\*\*\*\*

## German Federal Police (The Bundespolizei/BPOL). Berlin, Germany.

At first Erster Polizeihauptkommissar (Chief Inspector) Vala Raske had been surprised to hear the name, and then her surprise had given way to a smile. Marc Craig, old Mister Heartthrob himself, although to be fair he'd probably never known that had been his nickname at The Met. She dragged her gaze away from the view from her office window to the photo of London that she kept on her desk, casting her mind back to the years that she'd been seconded there.

She'd learnt a lot from The Metropolitan Police and hopefully taught them something too, that was what exchange visits were about. But her strongest memories were of Covent Garden and summer nights spent drinking there with her new friends. Now here was one of them popping up again; not, as she'd expected him to be, still at The Met but back in his home town of Belfast, and it made her wonder about Camille.

Camille Kennedy had been Craig's long-term girlfriend and she'd never liked the bitch. She'd been one of those women who'd thought the world revolved around her and had used her pretty face and body to get her way. As if she was speaking to someone else, the BPOL chief inspector rushed to defend herself. It wasn't envy that had made her hate the girl, she was attractive herself in a dark, slim way and very happy in her personal life, but she'd seen women like Camille ruin men with their wiles and she found herself hoping that Craig hadn't met the same fate. For all his slick suits and charm he had been a nice guy, and perhaps even slightly naïve in ways. He'd loved Camille for years, genuinely loved her, and unfortunately it had made him blind to her tricks.

Vala Raske smiled to herself, an old expression springing to mind. *It takes a woman to know a woman*; sometimes far too true. She feared that Craig had got the rough end of his relationship with Camille and that might explain why he was no longer at The Met. Or perhaps he had simply decided to return to his roots. She couldn't argue with that when she'd done the same thing herself.

The chief inspector shook the past away with a single movement and turned her chair towards the glass wall that separated her from her team, lifting the criminal file that lay on her desk. Beatrix Hass: thief, fraudster, political terrorist, but never until now an assassin. Yet you couldn't argue with DNA, especially not with a perfect match. Beatrix had gone on a hunting vacation to Northern Ireland and her old friend Marc Craig needed her help to find out why.

\*\*\*\*

### The C.C.U. 3 p.m.

As Vala Raske was gearing up to phone the UK, Craig was gearing up for a briefing. He stood by Nicky's desk surveying his troops, pleased to find everyone present and correct, although displaying varying signs of fatigue.

"OK, let's get to this."

The most fatigued looking amongst them nodded his head and Craig waved Aidan Hughes on.

"Swear if you like, Aidan. You deserve a bit of leeway after what you've been through."

For the benefit of the unknowing, Liam set the background, both of Bill McEwan's character and the reason Hughes had visited his lair hours before.

Aidan's words were heartfelt. "I have never..." He paused, casting a look around for sympathy. Craig obliged him with a knowing nod. "Never, *ever* been bollocked so loudly in my life-"

Liam interrupted incredulously. "McEwan communicated using words?"

Just what Craig had been about to ask.

Aidan's nod was pained. "Trust me, no-one was more shocked than me. I'd never heard more than two syllables from the man before, but as soon as I said that we believed the killer had been hiding in a building that his men had vouched for as cleared, I didn't get a chance to add, *which means they missed her,* before he started to rant." He shook his head, grudgingly impressed. "That man can *really* swear. In several languages too; I had to look some of the words up when I got back."

Liam patted him on the head. "Aw, diddums. Is oo traumatised den?"

The hand was batted away as Craig asked a question.

"OK. So, who's there now searching for the hiding place?"

Liam jumped in. "I told Wensley to do it."

Hughes rolled his eyes at him. "And I delegated it like a good chief inspector should." He turned back to Craig. "Reggie volunteered some men. They're at it now."

Craig nodded, ignoring Liam's scowl. He knew he'd been enjoying picturing Hughes going door-to-door asking people if he could rummage through their things.

Aidan Hughes was still speaking.

"There are ten empty flats in Carson, so they started with those. As soon as they find anything they'll call in the C.S.I.s."

"OK, good. Anything else, Aidan?"

"Aye. Billy Regent was a no-mates. You asked about his friends but it seems he hadn't made many since he'd left the army, so Tommy Hill's info on him is probably as good as we'll get."

Craig nodded and was just about to move on when he realised that he hadn't welcomed their guest. He turned to the skinny, raven-haired visitor, wondering if leather jackets and skinny jeans had now become uniform in the Drugs Squad.

"For those of you who don't know this refugee from a cologne advert, this is Detective Sergeant Karl Rimmins from the Drugs Squad."

It was clear from the blush on Rhonda's cheeks that she knew Rimmins far too well and Craig remembered that they'd been dating. The others seemed to know the narc as well, as the series of "Hi, Karl"s and casual nods underlined.

"OK, good. Thanks for coming, Karl. I've asked you because this case involves some high-end sex parties where there are apparently drugs in use-"

As Rimmins cut him off with a knowing nod Liam sniffed resentfully, noticing that The D.S.' dark quiff didn't budge at all when he moved; he'd had to rely on Brylcreem to elevate his when he was young, and it had wilted if he'd danced too hard. He wondered if even an explosion would make Karl's shift; ex-RUC officers tending to think of things in those terms, such had been the experiences of their youth.

"I'd heard of the parties, sir."

"From someone here, Karl?"

"Nope. One of our snouts mentioned them in passing on another case, around two months ago."

"Exactly what did they say?"

"That the prostitution scene here wasn't limited to the scuzzy end, and some big names were getting their freak on out in the sticks." He turned to Aidan Hughes pointedly. "I passed the info on to Vice."

Hughes shook his head vehemently. "Not to me you didn't!"

It made Rimmins think for a moment. "OK, no, you're right. It wasn't you I told. But it was someone downstairs,

I'm sure of that. I'll dig back through my records and check who."

Craig glanced sharply at Liam; if a police officer was involved in covering things up it could fit with the killer's escape from the Travis.

He returned to the issue in hand.

"Did you look at the parties from the drugs aspect, Karl?"

"I did a bit of digging. There seemed to be mostly coke and Viagra, but not in industrial quantities and we were busy with a big smuggling case at the time." He looked shamefaced. "So it got shunted to the bottom of the pile. Sorry. I'll take another look."

"If you would. I'd like you to get back to me on both those things by tomorrow."

It was already almost four so Rimmins went to stand up.

"I'd better get on with it then, unless you need me to stay?"

"Five more minutes, please." Craig turned to Kyle who was staring at Karl's quiff as well. "Kyle, what else do you have on the Intelligence side?"

"I'm still waiting for Ash to get me the CIA files on those politicians."

The small analyst jerked upright in his seat. "It takes time!"

The ex-spook shrugged and went on. "When I have those, I'll know more. Otherwise I've another meeting with my snout this evening."

"He's back from Brussels?"

"On the eight-ten Heathrow flight. He should give me more about the party this weekend-"

Karl cut in.

"You're expecting drugs there?"

Liam nodded. "A real snow storm."

The sergeant's face lit up. "Do you want us to raid them? We can if you like."

Craig shook his head. "Trust me, narcotics are the least of this bunch's transgressions. You'd go blind if you saw the rest. But the proximity of the party's why I need those answers quickly, Karl. And anything else you can find would be great."

Rimmins nodded. "One question, sir. When you say high-end parties, were you referring to the punters or the girls?"

"Both of those, plus the venue. We know that at least one party was held on an Earl's estate, and the possible host of this one is a billionaire."

It spawned a chorus of impressed whistles.

"So... the punters are media stars, or-"

Liam shook his head. "More the political kind. The sort of people with a lot to lose from an in flagrante appearance in the tabloids, not the sort it would earn big bucks."

Craig chuckled. "Well put, Liam. Yes, *those* punters, Karl, so we're interested in the drugs aspect as background mainly and perhaps for leverage later, rather than nicking them for it right now."

"Fine." The sergeant went to rise again, completing the action this time on Craig's nod. "I'll get on it immediately."

"None of this goes beyond this room, please, Karl."

"Understood."

Then, with a soft-eyed smile at Rhonda that completely trashed his street-cred, the skinny drugs sergeant was gone. Craig turned back to the group briskly.

"Right, I need to update you all on a few developments. First, the DNA found under Billy Regent's fingernails belongs to a German woman."

He'd expected questions but he mostly got blank looks, not least from Annette, whose stunned expression made Craig realise that he hadn't informed anyone but Liam and the analysts about the last bit.

"*A woman?* When were you going-"

Craig's apologetic wince cut her off. "Sorry, John and Des only told me last night and with all the stuff about Mercer I forgot."

Annette looked shocked again. "Ray Mercer who you

almost punched?"

"That's the one."

"But I thought he was gone. Working freelance for some car magazine down south."

"He's back and working at The Belfast Journal."

The importance of Mercer's mention didn't miss her. "He knows something about our case!"

Craig's gave a grimace. "Not about our actual investigation, but it seems he's been working on an article about a secret club that might be linked to McManus' death."

"Oh God."

Her expression of horror was shared by the group, but Liam nodded cheerfully.

"That's what I thought, so he's sitting in a cell at High Street."

Jake shook his head. "What about freedom of the press? You can't just lock him up."

"Too late."

The sergeant turned to Craig for support. "Chief?"

"Sorry, but I'm with Liam on this one, Jake. You don't know Ray Mercer like we do. He could and will blow our whole case if he gets out. So..." He turned to Ash. "Find me something to charge him with. Anything trivial will do: jaywalking, parking fines, disturbing the peace. I just need something to hold him on for questioning."

Ash screwed up his face. "What's the PACE maximum?"

"Twenty-four hours without charging, but I can authorise an extension."

The analyst nodded cheerfully. "OK, leave it with me."

Craig ignored Jake's 'you're violating Mercer's Human Rights' glare and moved on.

"So, we have a female German assassin-"

Ash cut in. "We have a name for her now, chief. Beatrix Hass. Interpol came through a few hours ago."

Craig perked up. "What else do you have on her?"

Ash lifted his smart-pad and read aloud. "Beatrix Hass.

Forty-three."

Too old to fit the theory of Billy Regent being influenced by a woman his own age. Ash saw what Craig was thinking and shook his head.

"She looks twenty something."

As he projected the woman's image onto Nicky's screen to demonstrate, Craig concurred. The youthful looking blonde looked like she should be at university, not a thousand miles from home killing two men. Billy Regent had probably thought Hass was chatting him up when she'd first made contact.

"You're right, she does. OK, what else do you have?"

As Ash read out the litany of Beatrix Hass' crimes against the German State Liam's jaw dropped.

"She looks like butter wouldn't melt!"

Ash kept on reading. "She's wanted by BPOL, the Federal Police in Germany, and on a European Arrest Warrant. And if GSG9 get their hands on her, she might disappear into a deep dark hole."

Liam never liked to show his ignorance so he nodded Jake on to ask the question.

"GSG9?"

"Germany's Elite Federal Commandos. They're the counter-terrorism side of BPOL, a bit like our SAS. Anyway, they've been after Hass since an explosion at a compound for Syrian Refugees in Dresden earlier this year. Several immigrants were killed."

Craig had been nodding the whole time the junior analyst spoke, although if anyone had asked him why he couldn't have explained. The seed of an idea was germinating but he wouldn't know what it would turn into for quite a while.

"OK, good work, Ash. Davy, anything further on the calls and emails?"

Davy had been fixating on Beatrix Hass' image and jumped at the sound of Craig's voice.

"Nothing more yet on the incoming calls to Lewis, but

w...we're still digging. The email text only makes sense if facials and massages etcetera relate to sex, but as far as the hidden information goes I'm still having trouble finding the reference book. My machines have been running word s...searches for hours, utilising the British Library's database, but I've nothing yet except a long list of books they've ruled out."

Craig had heard a 'but' since the analyst's first word.

"You've got something else, haven't you?"

The analyst screwed up his slim face. "The beginning of something, maybe. OK, so far we have the names Joshua Loughrey, Roger Burke, Nigel McArdle, Joseph Bell, Peter McManus-"

Liam shook his head. "He's dead."

"No shit, Sherlock. He's still relevant. And now we have Leonard Montgomery."

Liam's jaw had been hanging open since Sherlock, the analyst's cheekiness saying that he'd have to rethink his tolerant dad approach. Davy had progressed to adult back chat so the gloves were off. Henceforth he would feel the full force of his acerbic wit.

Craig tipped his deputy's mouth shut before going on.

"I'm not sure about Montgomery. Yes, he goes to the parties, but how much he's involved is-"

Davy shook his head firmly, cutting Craig off.

"Humour me, chief. All the men I just mentioned plus the Earl, and now Montgomery and Emmett Darrian, are either IBP members or donors, or sex-party hosts." The analyst woke-up his smart-pad and projected a table onto Nicky's screen.

"OK, I've been looking for commonalities between them, and I think I've finally found one." He highlighted a row in red. "All of them, except for the Earl, went to Edinburgh University." He lit up a second row. "Where they all studied Classics. The Earl also studied Classics, but at Oxford."

Craig felt the seed begin to grow.

Liam was confused. "What's Classics? Doesn't sound like

something you could do as a job."

It was so practical that Craig had to smile.

Davy elaborated.

"Classics or Classical Studies is the study of classical antiquity. It's the study of the Greco-Roman world, languages and literature, also its philosophy, history, and archaeology."

Liam was unimpressed. "So they can all read Plato while they're claiming the dole."

Aidan Hughes snorted. "That's something this lot will never have to worry about."

Craig let the jokes flow for a minute before moving Davy on with a question. "You're saying that they knew each other at Uni? But surely their age range precludes that."

The analyst was undaunted. "That's what I thought at first. But what if there's an alumni association?"

Craig nodded as realisation dawned. "Not for the specific university, but maybe for the degree. A worldwide Classics club that they're all members of!" Before he got too carried away he asked the question. "Is there such a thing?"

Davy looked glum. "Not that I've found yet. But I haven't given up. There's s...something here, chief. I know it."

Craig did as well. "Keep going, Davy. It's just a thought, but maybe the sex-worker killings you found elsewhere could give you a clue."

The analyst didn't get the chance to answer because Nicky's phone rang. She beckoned Craig over after the first few words.

"Who is it?"

"Some woman called Vala Raske, sir. She says she knows you well."

Craig's response was drowned out by a chorus of ribaldry, so he nodded Nicky to transfer the call to his room, answering his phone cheerfully.

"Vala! How are you?"

The sound of Craig's voice made the chief inspector smile, despite the serious topic she'd called about.

"Better for hearing your voice, Marc. It's been a while."

Craig tried to remember just how long, but she told him before he could.

"It's been eighteen years since my secondment to The Met. I must admit I was surprised when Yemi told me you'd gone home. I'd always pictured you as Met Commissioner by now."

His sceptical laugh made her join in.

"Oh, OK then, a deputy at least. What made you leave London? You're not married, are you? With five kids running around your feet."

Craig chuckled. "Hardly. And before you ask, Camille's not here with me. We split up back in oh-seven."

The Berliner didn't even try to hide her glee. "Good. You were far too nice for her."

Before Craig could defend his ex-fiancée's indefensible behaviour, Raske had already moved on.

"Beatrix Hass. Her DNA came across my desk."

"Tell me about her."

"Your analysts already have, I'm sure. Interpol has been onto them."

"Tell me again, anyway."

She smiled, remembering how he'd always liked to dot his Is and cross his Ts.

"Hass is a fraudster and far right political terrorist. We've been having real problems with them here since immigration increased. She cut her teeth in a few nationalist groups, and now she's wanted for the bombing of a refugee hostel in Dresden in March. GSG9 have her on their watch list."

"So, what the hell was she doing over here?" He corrected himself immediately. "We know the reason she was here, ostensibly to kill our First Minister, but what we don't know is why."

Raske frowned at the other end of the line. It didn't make sense to her either.

"McManus' party is right-wing, yes?"

"Not far right, but yes."

"But they're pro staying in the EU."

"Well..."

She knew what that meant. "You mean their public face is, but behind the scenes..."

"Exactly. We think McManus was genuinely Pro-EU, but his party has a hard-right core."

There was silence for a moment while Raske thought. When she broke it, it was with a statement.

"The IBP killed their own man to get their way in the referendum?"

Craig was about to agree, then he surprised himself.

"Not the party."

She heard the missing word. "You mean not the party *alone*. Left to its own devices the IBP wouldn't have assassinated its own man, not unless someone more powerful had wanted him gone."

The seed had just had a growth spurt, but Craig couldn't commit to it just yet.

"Maybe, maybe not. We're pursuing all options."

The 'we' unambiguously placed her on the outside. Raske shrugged. There was no point taking offense when they weren't even on the same force any more.

"OK. So how can I help?"

"You already have, by giving us her background. A list of her known associates across Europe would help as well."

"Done. But there must be more I can do than that." She paused for a moment, glancing at the personnel chart on her wall. "I can help you find her. GSG9 already have some leads we can chase."

Craig frowned, knowing what that meant. If the Commandos got wind of where Beatrix Hass was hiding they would lift her, then she'd disappear to an interrogation site and he might never find out how far this conspiracy went.

Raske heard his frown.

"Don't frown, Marc. You'll get wrinkles."

Her perceptiveness made him laugh out loud. The chief inspector carried on speaking.

"Look, here's what I'll do. I've had a man looking for Hass since I saw your DNA request. If she's back in

Germany we'll find her, but we won't lift her unless you give me a go. That way we might just find out who she's working with."

Craig's next sound was a sigh of thanks.

"That's brilliant, Vala. I owe you for this. You'll keep me informed?"

"Of course, and you can buy me a glass of your best Chianti if we ever meet again."

Craig had an idea that might happen sooner than she thought.

\*\*\*\*

## Demmin, North Germany.

"How did you get this number, Beatrix?"

"Solokov."

It gave The Fox a chilling reminder of who he was dealing with.

"So why are you calling me? I told you, no more contact until I called you."

Beatrix Hass might have been intimidated by his stern tone, but he was several countries miles away and right now she had something far scarier nearby.

"I'm being followed."

The words conjured up more possible names that she knew and The Fox raced through the list in his head, ranking them in terms of likelihood and danger before Hass could repeat her sentence again.

"Did you hear me? I'm-"

"I heard you. You're sure?"

"Would I have called you if I wasn't?"

She pushed back a lock of newly dyed red hair from her face. She hated having to dye her natural blonde but it was an occupational hazard, one that would take ten hours at the hairdressers and a year of conditioning treatments to redress.

"He was at the train station when I arrived, and I've just seen him again at the store. He was watching me, I'm certain of it."

The Fox had no time for sympathy. "You stupid bitch! He's probably just some commuter who lives locally! I knew we should never have used you. You're paranoid."

She barked back at him. "Fuck you, you communist throwback! If it wasn't for me McManus would still be in place and your plan would be nowhere. All you have to do is wine and dine your precious politicians now to smooth the way, *I'm* the one who made things happen and don't you forget it!"

He went to snap back but then bit his tongue. The truth was Beatrix was connected in the one way that he couldn't compete with. They might have been occasional lovers but she only really belonged to one man, Gleb Solokov, and if anyone harmed a hair on her head Solokov would cleave his off the next day.

The Fox swallowed hard, forming his next sentence carefully.

"OK. Be cautious, but there's no need to be paranoid. All you need to do is behave normally for another few days, then it will all be over and Solokov will send someone for you. *Can you manage that?*"

She gave a grunt that said yes, but he still had to have the last word.

"But if you phone me again, then Solokov or no Solokov I'll hunt you down and kill you, Beatrix."

Her expletive laden response fell on a dead line.

\*\*\*\*

Craig wound up the briefing soon after Vala Raske's call, nodding Liam to join him at the lift. Before they got inside he gave his deputy a warning.

"Keep your fists to yourself with Mercer, Liam. That's an order."

The D.C.I. couldn't let it pass. "Aye, I'll just punch a window instead, will I?"

Craig's attempt at severity died a death as he failed to suppress a laugh. "Fair enough. I deserved that one."

Liam pressed the point home with a glance at his boss' hand. "I bet that scar nips you in the cold weather."

"Not as much as it'll nip you if it hits your head."

It was the signal for a banter filled journey that ended at High Street's staff room fifteen minutes later. Craig perched on an under-stuffed settee that had seen far too many coppers' behinds, speaking in a serious tone.

"OK, here's how I want to play it. There's no point me trying to play good cop when Mercer already knows that I want to hit him." He indicated his deputy. "And Liam here kicked a chair from beneath him within living memory, so that won't work either. Jack, I'm afraid that means you're it."

Jack Harris levelled the teapot mid-pour, narrowing his eyes suspiciously. "It what?"

Liam tutted primly. "That's not good grammar."

"It still made sense though!" The sergeant set down the pot and folded his arms in a way that didn't bode well. "You want *me* to interview Mercer?"

Craig nodded hopefully. "I'll be in there as well. But I think if he sees the two of us." He gestured at Liam. "He'll be so busy worrying about being thumped that he'll just clam up."

Liam snorted sceptically. "If he hasn't already."

Craig ignored the comment, carrying on. "Whereas if he sees you, Jack. Caring custody sergeant..."

Jack rolled his eyes. "Friend of the oppressed, yada, yada. OK, you can stop sucking up, sir. I'll do it. Not because I want to but because I must. You're the boss, after all."

Craig gave him an offended look. "I won't order you, Jack. You *can* say no."

The sergeant's response was to finish pouring his mug of tea and then glance at Liam. "And risk Finn McCool here leaving a bruise on my charge. I have to account for any injuries in custody, you know." It prompted him to ask another question. "Oh, aye, and while we're at it, what the hell do you mean by having your analyst tell me to charge Mercer with outraging public decency?"

The detectives exchanged a look. Was that the best charge Ash could manage to come up with? Then Liam smiled, remembering something.

"That'll be 'cos Mercer swore as I put him in my car and

there were kids around. Ash must have found out."

Craig nodded approvingly. "Good man. Now we can hold him legitimately."

Jack went to object but he cut him off.

"You never know what other lewd acts he might have performed, Jack, and it's our civic duty to find out."

The sergeant's eyes narrowed again. "Then you'd better make sure to ask him during the interview." He headed for the door. "And the sooner we start the sooner I can kick you two out."

Liam lifted his coffee and headed for the viewing room, settling in while Craig appeared on the other side of the glass and Harris retrieved Ray Mercer from his cell. The sight of the normally dapper journalist looking bedraggled without his tie, and his lack of belt making him hold up his trousers with one hand, made Craig smile, but as far as revenge went it would have to do for today.

Craig swallowed the history between them and waved Mercer to a seat, allowing him five minutes to vent his ire before switching on the tape just in time to catch the journalist's last few obscene words.

"Mister Mercer, you have been charged with outraging public decency, in that you did..."

As Jack recited the charge Craig ordered his thoughts, then he started the interview with an open-ended question to which he knew Ray Mercer was bound to lie.

"Mister Mercer, have you at any time committed other acts of lewdness or obscenity?"

The reporter's response was to laugh. "What's this *really* about, Craig?"

"Answer the question please."

"I'm damned if I do and damned if I don't. If I say yes, then you'll double the charges, if I say no, you'll produce someone who'll say that I fucking well did. So why don't I save us all some time and *I'll* tell you why I think I'm here."

As Craig knocked off the tape Mercer snorted.

"Ah, *now* we're getting to it." He turned towards the two-way mirror with a malicious smile. "I suppose fat-head Cullen's behind there?" He gave a wave just in case. "OK, then. I'll bite. What's this all about?"

Craig leaned forward. "Cover your ears, Jack."

The sergeant obliged hastily.

"You're investigating Peter McManus' death."

Mercer shrugged. "So's every journalist in the country. Tell me something new."

"In your digging, you uncovered something about a secret club. I need to know what you've found out."

Mercer had started shaking his head on the word 'club'. "No way, Craig. This is *my* story."

Craig's voice became a hiss. "*And by the time you get out of here it'll be old news.* Every newspaper in the country will already have had it on their front page and relegated it to their editorials! I'll make damn sure of it unless you cooperate!"

He sat back, smiling coolly. "So, what will it be, Ray? Two days stuck here remembering every time you swore in public, or you tell us what you know."

The journalist bared his teeth in fury. "Door number three. I call my solicitor and he has me out in an hour."

Jack's fingers had been out of his ears long enough for him to scoff.

"And if you'd wanted to do that you would have asked me to get him here hours ago. The reason you didn't is because you're curious, Mister Mercer."

Craig smiled admiringly. Jack was right and Mercer's snort of bravado couldn't disguise it. The detective picked up the theme.

"Sergeant Harris is right. You knew our agenda as soon as we lifted you, but you wanted to see what you could find out from *us*, just like any investigative journalist would."

His bluff called, Mercer relaxed back in his seat. "OK, so... what do you have for me?"

It killed Craig to be dancing with the Devil but they needed whatever the reporter had.

"An exclusive interview when it's all over."

"With you?"

Craig shrugged a yes, surprised when the hack shook his head.

"No. I want the big fucker on the other side of the mirror."

He made a two-fingered gesture at the glass, making all three cops want to swing for him.

It made sense. Craig had only *really* pissed him off once, whereas Liam had a season ticket for the sport. Craig glanced apologetically at the mirror and then nodded his head, trying to ignore the heartfelt groan that vibrated the common wall.

But Mercer hadn't finished.

"And both of you apologise for everything you've done to me in the past."

It was too much. Craig was on his feet in seconds and Jack moved towards the journalist to escort him back to his cell.

"I'd like your help but it's not essential, Mister Mercer. We can get what we need all by ourselves."

Mercer spat out his next words. "Then I want my solicitor, Craig!"

"No solicitor."

Before Jack could object Craig reached inside his jacket, producing a page.

"I've an order from a Judge for you to be sequestered on the grounds of National Security."

The shooting of a First Minister ticked the box.

The journalist's small eyes widened. "You can't do that!"

"I already have."

"For how long?"

"As long as I deem necessary. So get comfortable."

Mercer backtracked hastily. "OK, OK. The interview with fat-head will do then."

Craig knew that he should bite his lip and accept it, sit back down and press record, but a sudden rush of blood to his head said no. Screw Mercer. He'd spin the wheel until just before the party, and if they hadn't cracked the club by themselves then he'd come back. Meanwhile, Ray Mercer could stew.

He headed for the door to the sound of Liam's cheer and the journalist's yells. It was only when they were at the car that Liam reluctantly asked the question that he knew might make Craig turn back.

"You're sure, boss? I'll do his bloody interview if it'll help the case."

Craig shook his head. "I'm sure. The party's not until Saturday so we have time."

As he opened the driver's door and climbed in Liam asked his next question.

"Do you really have a court order?"

Craig smiled. "Got it as soon as you informed me Mercer had been lifted, courtesy of Judge Eugene Standish, the last and possibly only reasonable man on Northern Ireland's bench."

\*\*\*\*

## The C.C.U. 4.30 p.m.

Aidan Hughes had received two phone calls at once, leading to him having both his mobile and desk phone in his hands. As, contrary to Liam's jibes, the Vice cop only had one face, and one mouth along with it, he opted to answer the loudest voice first.

"D.C.I. Hughes. What can I do for you?"

"It's Des Marsham in Forensics."

"Sorry, Doctor Marsham, but the chief's not here right now."

Des' answer was typically cheerful. "Out flying his kite, eh? Not to worry, it was you I needed anyway. It's about the forensics on that flat."

Aidan knew then that he should have taken the other call first and he hurried to repair his mistake.

"Sorry, could you hang on a minute, please?"

He covered his mobile and spoke into the other line.

"D.C.I. Hughes here."

A young voice that he didn't know rattled out its words breathlessly. "We've found it, sir, or at least we think we have. Flat fifteen, Carson Tower. Forensics have been and gone."

'It' could only mean Beatrix Hass' hiding place.

"What's your name, son?"

"P.C. Galvin, sir."

"OK, Constable Galvin. Wait there for me and I'll be

down as soon as I can."

He wanted to see exactly what Bill McEwan's men had missed.

"Before I get there, who found it?"

"I did, sir."

"And Commander McEwan's men had been searching as well?"

"Yes, sir. Ten of them were here."

Hughes tried hard not to laugh. McEwan would rip each of them a new one for embarrassing him yet again.

"Right, I'll see you soon, Galvin. And well done."

He swallowed his laugh and woke up the line to Des.

"Sorry about that, Des. I had another call. What were you saying?"

"I've had a quick check of the forensics on the Carson Tower flat, and the DNA from the hairs found there definitely matches your girl's."

Bingo. Beatrix Hass had avoided capture because she'd slipped down off Carson Tower's roof straight into a safe house, and there was no way she could have known that a flat in a foreign city was safe unless someone had tipped her off.

The D.C.I.'s reverie was cut short by Des' next words.

"When you see Liam, tell him I've got something interesting on his guns if he'd like to call in. I'll be here until seven tonight."

Thirty minutes later Aidan Hughes' suspicions were confirmed. He and a surprising hairy, given his youthful voice, Constable Galvin, were staring at a pull-down wall bed that would have provided the least comfortable night's sleep ever, missing as it was a mattress. The detective hunkered down to look at it sideways on. Without a mattress, there was an eighteen-inch gap between the bed's frame and the top of its slim headboard, not enough to hold a grown man but a woman might just fit.

He donned a pair of gloves and levered the bed into its vertical recess, smiling in admiration at the way it aligned perfectly with the fake bricks mounted on its wall surround. The fact that the same polystyrene cladding had been used to cover the bed's underside made the join seamless. To an observer it would have appeared like a smooth, fake-brick wall, a dubious design feature perhaps, but not something that would normally have aroused police suspicion.

Hughes turned to the P.C. in admiration. "How the heck did you spot that join, Galvin? It's nigh on invisible!"

The constable looked embarrassed. "I had a bed just like it when I was a student, sir. You'd never have known that it was there."

"Well, thank God for your landlord's dodgy décor then. We'd never have found it otherwise." He pulled the bed down again and pointed at the springs. "That's where forensics found the hairs?"

"Yes, sir." The P.C. pointed eagerly. "There was a clump caught in that spring at the top. It must have been torn out by the roots."

Facilitating the fast DNA lift.

"Excellent." Hughes had a thought. "Who's your boss?"

An immediate look of fear crossed the constable's face. "Sergeant Maguire at Stranmillis. Did I do something wrong, sir?"

The D.C.I. slapped him on the back. "You did something very right, Galvin, and I'm going to make sure credit's given where it's due."

\*\*\*\*

And blame as well. No sooner had Aidan Hughes returned to the squad-room when the phone on his desk rang again. He answered it absentmindedly, his thoughts on other things.

"Mmm..."

"Is that what passes for a hello up there?"

The D.C.I. stared at the phone. "Who's that?"

"Karl Rimmins. I'm getting back with the information the chief asked for, and I thought, as you used to be Vice..."

It sounded strange but Hughes knew what he meant. People were often identified by where they'd worked, so just as Rimmins was Drugs he was Vice, which he supposed made Craig Murder. They should form a band called the Seven Deadly Sins.

"Is this about the name of the officer you told about the sex parties?"

"Plus the names of a few politicians who we've warned over drugs. Do you want it over the phone or-"

Hughes cut him off. "I'll come down to you. It's safer."

Five minutes later he was returning in the lift, with a list of naughty MLAs in one hand and the name of a bent copper in the other. It was a name that made his heart sink.

\*\*\*\*

Hughes' call caught Craig and Liam just as they were leaving High Street, and Craig answered it while opening his car door with his other hand. When Hughes told them where Beatrix Hass had hidden the two detectives decided to look for themselves, so Craig passed his keys over to Liam and continued the call from the passenger seat.

"Good work, Aidan. We'll take a look, then I want to have a quick word with Eileen Regent. Tell Nicky we'll be back in about an hour."

The silence that answered him said that there was something more. Hughes gave up the easy information first.

"Des says he's got something on the guns if Liam's got time to drop in before six. He says he's not staying any later."

"We'll both go."

Craig knew the guns had just been an offering before the main event. "And? There's obviously something else, Aidan."

The D.C.I. swallowed hard before speaking and when he did he stumbled over his words.

"There's...someone..."

"You're trying to say that someone told Beatrix Hass where to find safe haven."

"Well yes, that, and...well, also, Karl phoned. He's given me a list of MLAs who've been busted for drugs. Cautioned mostly. I've got it when you want it. I didn't want to leave it lying on your desk."

"Anyone we don't know?"

"A couple of junior Ministers, but otherwise it's the

names that we've been talking about."

"Good. Thanks." After a brief pause Craig went on. "Karl also gave you the name of the officer he tipped-off in Vice, didn't he?"

Hughes' response was uncharacteristically subdued. "I've worked with the man, chief, and he's a good officer. I honestly can't believe-"

Craig cut in briskly. "I trust your judgment, Aidan. Go and speak to him. If it was him who buried Karl's tip-off I want the truth, but if you believe that it wasn't then find me the name of who did."

It was the best answer that Hughes could have hoped for.

After he'd hung up, Craig passed the info about the guns to Liam and then slumped down in his seat, puzzled. Who the hell would have known about a hiding place on a Loyalist housing estate and tipped off Beatrix Hass? It had to be someone local, someone who knew the territory, but what would they have in common with a German terrorist?

Ten minutes later, staring at the pull-down bed, he knew that it was an answer they might never find. The bed had been fingerprinted and if the heavens were on their side one of those prints would yield a hit, but it was just as likely that whoever was behind this whole messy business had paid some low-level local thug to arrange things, someone who may not have known or cared that Beatrix Hass was a criminal, much less what she'd done. The name of the thug was less important than the fact that the mastermind behind all of this had a very long reach.

\*\*\*\*

**St Mary's Hospital Genetics Clinic.**

"Nat, please call John and tell him you're having the blood test."

Katy Stevens was staring hard at her friend, hoping that somehow she could hypnotise her. Perhaps if she gazed at Natalie hard enough and long enough, she would eventually nod obediently and summon her husband to the hospital.

When Natalie's small mouth began to set tight Katy

knew that she had better back off. Any more pressure and the surgeon was likely to walk out of the geneticist's fern-filled waiting room, never to return.

She supposed that she should consider it progress to have even got this far; it had taken several phone-calls and two tickets to Deacon Blue at the Waterfront Hall in November, for her to persuade the consultant geneticist to see them privately at all. At least Natalie would be the one paying his bill.

Katy's thoughts were interrupted by an inner door marked 'advanced practitioner' opening, and an elderly woman in a pristine lab coat appearing at Natalie's side.

"Ms Ingrams?"

Natalie jumped up, braced for what was coming next. It wasn't what she thought.

"I'm Mrs Matthews, the clinic's counsellor, would you like to come in?"

Natalie scowled at the woman. "I don't have time for stuff like counselling, I'm here for a blood test! I'm on call tonight and I've got to be back in theatre for five o'clock."

The counsellor smiled tolerantly. "I'm afraid we need to talk through all of the possible outcomes before we do any tests. To prepare you for the full range of results."

She could have saved her breath after the second 'we', because Natalie was already out the door.

\*\*\*\*

### The C.C.U. 5 p.m.

Davy had started scratching his chin at the briefing, and two hours later Nicky was beginning to wonder if he was trying to drill a hole. She said as much in her loud, husky voice.

"Unless you're trying to reach Australia I'd scratch on the other side for a while, Davy. Otherwise you'll grow an uneven beard."

The analyst's lack of reaction made Ash glance up from his work, his vantage point, slightly behind Davy and to the left, giving him a good view of his three computer screens. On one a programme was running, flashing through pages of books at a rate of knots, but it was the other two screens that were more interesting; the central one was displaying a table of names, and the left hand one a map of the British mainland scattered with red stars.

He and Nicky reached Davy's desk simultaneously and stood gazing down at the computers. It was the PA who spoke first, gesturing at the map.

"Aren't those three stars marking places where you said prostitutes were killed?"

Davy pointed to the stars she'd indicated, in Manchester, Dover and Edinburgh.

"Yes. The rest I've just discovered."

Ash's "Wow!" said it all. There were fifteen stars on the map, each corresponding to a city, and against the matching locations in the table were women's names.

Nicky gasped. "Fifteen women have disappeared now?"

Ash's question was more practical. "What's the timeline?"

Davy answered without looking up, although thankfully he'd stopped scratching his chin.

"Just under two months. The police investigations have found nothing."

Nicky tapped the table on a row highlighted in purple. "Why's this name coloured?"

Davy's voice was flat. "She reappeared, but w...wouldn't give any explanation for why she'd been gone."

Her eyes widened. "That means the other fourteen are dead!"

Ash cut in. "You're thinking the purple one's another Veronica Lewis."

Davy turned to look at him.

"Yes. Running parties where all sorts were happening, until she decided that she wouldn't."

The junior analyst nodded.

"She must have changed her mind again and decided to cooperate, just like the boss thinks Lewis did. That's why they let her go. And the others?"

"Eleven found dead and three never reappeared." Davy shook his head glumly. "Their bodies will probably never be found."

It prompted Nicky to pull over a chair and sit down. She liked her job as a secretary and she knew that she was good at it, and if she'd wanted to be a cop, which she didn't, W.P.C.s' flat shoes definitely not being her style, she would have joined the force. But that didn't mean that she hadn't picked up the detecting bug, and being around a squad as good as Craig's had hopefully taught her a few skills. With that in mind, she stared at Davy's screens, screwing up her face in thought. They all did. To an outside observer they would have looked like a trio in pain.

After a couple of minutes Nicky smiled, not at the subject matter but at what all of them had missed. Before Davy could ask why she looked so cheerful the PA had jabbed at his central screen.

"There!"

"What?"

"The timeline."

He still didn't get it.

"It's obvious." She rolled her eyes and tutted. "And I thought you were the ones with the big brains. April the thirteenth. It was the date that Vote Leave was named as the official campaign for leaving the EU. The date everyone realised that both sides were serious."

"So? The first woman disappeared on the twenty-second."

"Exactly. Just long enough for her to be approached and say no to helping with the parties."

Ash snorted. "It's a bit of a stretch, Nicky."

Her gimlet glance said that he was dicing with death so the analyst backtracked hastily.

"Which isn't to say that you're wrong, of course."

He focused on the computer screens again, wondering if she *could* possibly be right.

"Davy, any sex-workers dead or missing in the two months preceding then?"

Davy shook his head.

"But fifteen, sixteen if you count Veronica Lewis, in the eight weeks since." Ash nodded to himself. "Nicky could be right. This all started, OK, so not to the day, but to the week of the leave campaign getting serious."

Davy wasn't so sure. "But why none in the w...week beforehand? Insiders would have known then that it was coming."

It was Nicky who shrugged first. "Maybe they didn't expect both sides of the campaign to come out so strong, and when it became obvious they were it was time to fix things for their side."

Davy thought through the evidence they had so far; the only thing that pointed to one side or the other of the referendum was the IBP core's support of leaving and the killing of the Pro-EU First Minister. He restarted his chin scratching, still unconvinced.

"So...Nicky, you're saying that all across the UK, someone who wants to leave the EU has been coercing sex-workers to... what? Blackmail or influence their customers' votes?"

As she nodded he went on.

"I *suppose* it might work, but it's still only a few hundred votes at most-"

Ash cut across him. "Unless the men that they're influencing are themselves influencers, or can in some way rig the vote."

"Gerrymandering?" Davy's headshake was emphatic. "No way. Voters I.D.s are checked, and the vote counters picked very carefully. No, *if* there's a chance of the vote being swung either way then it'll be through influential people in the campaign."

Nicky nodded smugly. "That's what I just said."

Sort of.

Davy shook his head again, but with less conviction this time. "It's still a gamble. Even if you get the political influencers on board, they can't *guarantee* delivering their s...supporters votes."

"Guarantee no, but it will definitely improve the odds, and that matters if it's a close race."

Ash was already convinced. "OK, let's just say we're right and someone's been using sex-workers to influence, or maybe even blackmail politicians. *However* they're trying to control them, it still leaves two questions. One, what else are they doing? They can't just be relying on this tactic to swing the vote their way; it's too unpredictable. And two, who but the pro-Britain right-wingers would give a shit *what* way the vote came out?"

The first point Davy agreed with. "We might find out what else they're up to if I crack the book code. But as far as your other question goes...there are a lot of people who want to remain in the EU."

"You think they'd kill to make it happen?"

Davy shrugged. "I wouldn't, but who knows. And you can't say the Remain lobby *wouldn't* kill any more than that the Leave bunch *might*. Just because someone has left-wing political leanings it doesn't mean they're a s...saint. That sort of judgemental thinking's the way that communism gets a grip."

The debate could run and run, but the real question was why would the referendum incite *anyone* to kill? When Davy couldn't think of an answer he knew it was time to seek outside help.

\*\*\*\*

Ten minutes after Craig had stood staring at the wall-bed, he and Liam were in Faulkner Tower knocking on Eileen Regent's door, and after thirty minutes of tea, sympathy and a few diplomatically worded enquiries they made their way back to the car.

"Let's head to the lab, Liam."

"OK. Do you want to drive?"

Craig shook his head absentmindedly, still thinking about what he'd just heard. Eileen Regent had been adamant that her son had had no reason to kill Peter McManus, even if the First Minister was, as she'd confirmed, thought of as a traitor by some in their community. And neither she nor her granddaughter had ever been under threat. That they knew of, was the obvious rebuttal; Beatrix Hass could have *told* Billy Regent that his mother and daughter would be killed if he didn't cooperate with her, and that they were being watched around the clock and it was so hard to prove a negative that the mentally exhausted soldier had probably just complied.

Craig's thoughts returned to the statements taken on the estate. No-one but Kelly Atkins had reported even noticing a stranger, and follow up enquiries had yielded no-one who had seen the gloves being dumped in Sally Johnston's bin. But what information they had said that Beatrix Hass must have gone into hiding in the bed immediately after the shooting on Monday afternoon and remained there until sometime between ten p.m. on Tuesday night, after when Sally Johnston's bins were emptied, and Wednesday afternoon when the gloves were found by a W.P.C. That meant Hass had stayed in her hidey hole for somewhere between thirty and forty-five hours.

A sudden tut from Craig made Liam turn his head.

"Bad dream, boss?"

A finger pointing straight ahead said 'keep your eyes on the road' and Craig returned to his thoughts.

OK. Scenario one: Beatrix Hass had scared or threatened Billy Regent into killing McManus, but Billy had still believed that he was getting off Carson Tower's roof alive, which explained why he'd worn latex gloves to conceal his prints as he took the shot. But Hass had subsequently killed the ex-squaddie, stripped off his gloves and planted his finger prints all over the rifle. Fine, so Billy *had* made the kill shot, but most likely under duress, although they had no proof of that yet as his mum had never felt under threat.

Scenario two: If Des proved that the guns had come from a British Army Base then logically Billy *could* have smuggled them into the country, which most likely meant that he'd been in on the plan to assassinate McManus all along. Also, if he'd been stationed in Germany, he might have known Beatrix Hass for years.

It didn't feel right and Craig was still convinced of the soldier's innocence, but they had to be certain before they made a wrong turn.

His abruptly barked-out question almost made Liam swerve. "Was Regent in Germany?"

Liam hit the brake and pulled over to the side of the road, turning to gawp at his boss.

"You nearly made me crash!"

When Craig showed no sign of contrition Liam sighed

and answered his question.

"No. I checked with Ken. Billy Regent was never on a base in Germany, not even for training."

"Positive?"

"Ken was."

OK, so Billy was unlikely to have known Beatrix Hass beforehand, but that still didn't rule out that he'd stolen the guns from elsewhere. Either way they would soon know.

Craig glanced up to see where they were. Ten minutes from the lab. He decided to use the time to catch up with Davy and pulled out his phone.

The analyst's own confusion came flooding down the line, and Craig was treated to the whole discussion that Nicky had had with him thirty minutes before. By the time Davy had finished updating him Craig had a headache.

"You're saying for the past two months there have been women being kidnapped and killed all over the UK. And they're all sex-workers."

"Yes."

"So what's to rule out a serial killer?"

Davy was prepared for the question. "I can't yet, but one of them reappeared alive, and just like Lewis she wouldn't explain where she'd been. I'm digging into their Vice records now to see if there's anything about high-level parties. They might be centrally organised."

Craig gave a groan. Liam's Orgies Incorporated suggestion mightn't have been that farfetched. The analyst was still speaking.

"Ash came up with two questions. *If* someone's trying to influence the referendum vote, aren't they likely to be doing s...something else as well? They couldn't just rely on compromising politicians to carry the vote."

"Like what?"

"No idea yet. His other question w...was, who besides the Pro-Britain bunch would go to this extreme?"

It echoed Vala's comment that the IBP couldn't be in this alone.

The conversation was cut short by Liam parking outside the labs.

"OK, Davy. Keep going on all that, and ask Nicky to set a

briefing for eleven tomorrow morning, please."

He cut the call and they entered the building, collecting a moping John from his office before heading upstairs to see Des. While Liam snuffled around the scientist's office for food and drink, Craig cut straight to the chase.

"Guns."

Des answered with one eye on Liam who was rummaging through his fridge for milk, getting ready to intervene quickly if the D.C.I. looked like finding the chocolate cake he kept for especially stressful days.

"Both Russian."

Craig stared at the Head of Forensics, his already fragile theories starting to crumble.

"Do you mean they're Russian makes, or that they actually *are* from Russia?"

His fingers were crossed that the former applied. Billy Regent had been posted to Afghanistan after Iraq, and there were still Russian armaments available on the black market there from when they'd lost the conflict in nineteen-eighty-eight.

"Both."

As the milk emerged and the fridge door closed, Des thought it was safe to turn around.

"We have a KSVK Large Calibre Kovrov Sniper Rifle and an MP-443 Grach semi-automatic pistol. Both manufactured in Moscow in 2013 and both registered in St Petersburg last year."

Craig felt his grip on the whole case slipping. He slumped onto a stool so heavily that John shot the forensic scientist a reproving look.

"Could you not have been a bit subtler?"

Des shook his head firmly. "Facts are facts. I can't just change them to suit the mood."

He poured a coffee from the percolator and placed the cup in Craig's hand, staring at the detective for a moment before he spoke again.

"Don't you want the good news then?"

Craig's head jerked up. "There is some?"

"Well, I think the name of the guns' purchaser might count. Gleb Solokov. I've sent it over to Ash to check out, but my preliminary checks say he's a member of the Russian Mafia."

Liam's groan was heartfelt. "Not those buggers again! We had enough of them in twenty-twelve."

Des' headshake was immediate.

"It's not the Vory V Zakone, which is a pity because at least they have a code. This is a whole new bunch. *Real* crooks. When the Soviet Union collapsed in ninety-one the free market created a lot of millionaires, and an equal number of people who coveted wealth but couldn't get it through legitimate means. Criminality was and is rife there. Not to mention the gangs in the former Russian territories: Chechnya, Georgia and Armenia are the worst-"

Craig interrupted. "This Solokov. Any record of him passing the guns on or selling them?"

"Legal selling, no, but they could easily have passed through underground trades. I found something else interesting just before you arrived." He woke up his computer and began to type. "Oh, by the way, there were lots of prints on the wall bed but none in our system."

Craig nodded. It was what he'd been expecting to hear. Des stopped typing and beckoned them all to look.

"What should we be seeing?"

"Last known sightings of Solokov. He was in Berlin four weeks ago."

Liam asked the question. "Business or pleasure?"

"Not sure. That's for you lot to find out. But I do know that there are several branches of the Russian mafia very active in Germany, especially in Dusseldorf and Berlin. The Tambov gang is a biggy, as is the Eugenov. Solokov is one of their top men. Money laundering, organised prostitution and extortion seem to be their activities of choice."

A Russian gangster whose guns had been found at Peter McManus' shooting had connections with Germany, as did Beatrix Hass. It was a tenuous link but right now Craig would take anything he could get.

As they finished their coffee and got ready to leave, Davy's question kept echoing in his mind. Who besides the Pro-Britain lobby would go to this extreme to influence the referendum vote?

## Belfast City Centre. 9 p.m.

Trevor Rudkin had on a new suit, even flashier than the one he'd worn at their last encounter, and Kyle Spence's quick feel of his sleeve implied that it was booty Rudkin wouldn't want the taxman told about. The D.I. shook his head.

"I don't bung you enough to afford this."

Rudkin jerked his arm away, bridling at the implication. "I do earn a salary you know!"

The detective scoffed.

"A civil servant's pay could never cover that! It must be three grands worth at-."

He frowned as something suddenly dawned on him.

"If you're not getting it from me or work then someone else is greasing your palm." He lurched forward, pushing his face close to his informant's. "If Loughrey's bought you, I'll-"

To his shock Rudkin laughed in his face.

"You'll do what, Inspector? *Arrest me?* For accepting a gift from my new boss?"

Kyle's mind raced at the speed that things had slipped from his grip. Two days before the civil servant had been his bitch: timid, controlled by the odd envelope full of cash, and feeding him information that could help crack the murder of the First Minister. Access to the sex-party this weekend depended on Rudkin as well, but if Loughrey had got to him then all that would be off.

Now the little scumbag was defying him and with a smugness that said someone far scarier than him was watching his back. Someone capable of murder perhaps, if not alone then as part of an elite group.

The Intelligence officer thought quickly. One of the things he'd excelled at as a spy had been thinking on his feet. Watching a situation suddenly get dumped into the toilet and yet still preventing it from being flushed. Kyle dug deep for that quality now, and came up with something more frightening to some men than death.

His voice dropped to a murmur, forcing the civil servant

to come close to him to hear.

"You didn't just come here tonight to tell me to fuck off, Trevor. You could have done *that* over the phone. But before you *do* try it, and make the worst mistake of your life, just remember what will happen to you if you choose the wrong side. Loughrey might have been involved in planning Peter McManus' death, and the penalty for aiding a murderer is substantial."

Trevor Rudkin's slanted eyes widened and he pushed his floppy hair back from his face with a trembling hand. As he did so Kyle watched the man work his way through his limited emotional range from smugness to surprise and then shock, as the possibility that he might have got something wrong started to sink in.

As it did, panic took shock's place, joined quickly by back-pedalling obsequiousness as Rudkin realised he might have just burnt his bridges with the detective without being certain what lay on his side of the river bank. The result was a swift readjustment of the civil servant's posture to humble and a half-smile appearing on his thin lips.

"You didn't think I was serious, Kyle, did you? I was only pulling your leg."

At the use of his first name Spence grinned inwardly, knowing that he had the little bugger on the run.

He kept his voice low and adopted a hurt expression.

"What else was I to think, Trevor, given your words? If Loughrey's buying your loyalty with flash suits, how-"

The sentence didn't need to be finished. Rudkin was on the back foot now so he signalled the barman for more drinks, a generosity that he hoped would reinstate him in the detective's good books. While they waited for their fresh pints the civil servant shook his head vigorously.

"It wasn't a bribe, honestly. Loughrey doesn't have any idea that I meet with you, so he couldn't be trying to buy my silence."

It was a lightbulb moment for Kyle. That was exactly what Joshua Loughrey was doing. Why else would he give a lowly advisor a three-thousand-pound suit? Loughrey might not know that the police were onto Rudkin or that he was a paid snout, or maybe he did in which case they'd have a whole new level of shit to contend with, but he was ensuring Rudkin's loyalty anyway. It was probably his standard operating practice for new staff who might get close enough to hear unfortunate things.

The civil servant was still talking.

"He said I needed to look smart, given the meetings I'd be accompanying him to. Sorry, I didn't-"

Kyle seized on the man's new-found guilt. "Tell me about the party."

Relieved that they were changing the subject Rudkin spilled his guts. "We're meeting Saturday six p.m., at Loughrey's place in Bangor. Then we're being taken by car to someone's house. I don't know where."

Bangor was only ten miles from Emmett Darrian's mansion. The venue was starting to firm up.

"What else did Loughrey tell you?"

Rudkin snatched his cold pint from the approaching barman, gulping half of it down in one swallow before he carried on. His nervousness made Kyle smile and he mentally retrieved the situation from the toilet bowl and firmly closed the lid.

"He said there'd be girls and drugs and did I have a problem with that?"

"Which you said you didn't, of course."

Rudkin gave his first wholehearted smile of the evening. "I definitely don't with the girls, but I'll give the drugs a miss."

Like hell.

"Whatever. Did Loughrey say he was meeting anyone there?"

The advisor shook his head. "Sorry, no. But he might be and just didn't tell me. Maybe he doesn't trust me completely yet." His eyes widened. "Maybe he's on to me?"

Kyle had dismissed that possibility at the mention of drugs. Loughrey had already told his aide far too much for a man that he didn't trust. Rudkin's cover was intact.

"No. He's not on to you, but telling you who he's meeting requires more than just loyalty."

He lifted his pint from the small round table and sipped at it as he thought. Rudkin was going to the party and he would definitely report back, now that he owned him again. But that wouldn't be as much use as hearing everything live. They needed someone else inside that party. Him.

The D.I. stared hard at his informant. "I need you to get me in there."

Rudkin scraped back his chair in alarm. "No way! Anyway, it's impossible now. Everyone there has to be vetted beforehand."

"How do you know that?"

The civil servant stumbled over his next words. "It's…that's…what I-"

Kyle's eyes narrowed into a glare. "You know something more. What? *What do you know?*"

The advisor shook his head frantically. "I don't know anything. Honestly. It's just…well…" His next words were blurted out. "Loughrey took my passport when we landed back! He said he needed it and he'd give it back to me on Saturday night."

Kyle slumped back in his chair, nodding his head in grudging admiration. Loughrey was having the aide security vetted more deeply than the usual civil service access checks, and probably cloning his passport at the same time, just in case he ever needed to frame Rudkin for something if he stepped out of line.

The Intelligence Officer frowned as he thought. Guests were being advance vetted and Rudkin didn't know where the party was being held. He could make the advisor wear a wire, except that the likelihood was that all guests would be searched before entry and if it was found the shit, and probably Rudkin, would hit the wall.

He wondered if Ray Barrett had had any new recording gadgets made recently, making up his mind to find out. If not, that only left one play. They'd have to tail Loughrey to the venue. If they had troops already at Darrian's mansion as well and they were right about it being the place then they could record everything on directional mikes. Kyle nodded to himself. Even if it wasn't at Darrian's place the tail might still get photos and recordings of a few guests.

Rudkin had been watching the detective intently, certain that he wasn't going to like what came next. When Kyle tutted suddenly, the aide's anxiety levels spiked.

"What? What have I done?"

Kyle shook his head. "You? Nothing, *yet,* although if any part of you is thinking of tipping Loughrey off remember those years in jail."

Kyle continued thinking. His plans only took them so far. They needed to get inside that party, and better still inside the clique if it met. He was starting to run through other options when he suddenly realised that he didn't need the civil servant there, so he handed the snout a new burn phone and with a wave towards the door Trevor Rudkin found himself dismissed.

"Keep that with you, and I'll call if we need to meet again before the party. Otherwise, any change of plans you contact me immediately. Understand?"

The fear of God way in which Trevor Rudkin nodded said that he most definitely did.

\*\*\*\*

## Katy Steven's Apartment, Laganbank. 11 p.m.

Craig was on the third button of Katy's cardigan, his progress punctuated by slow kisses, when a wave of guilt overcame the physician suddenly and she placed a delaying hand over his. The detective widened his dark eyes quizzically.

"Something wrong, pet?"

The way Katy smiled back said that he'd done everything right, but the shake of her blonde waves that followed and the way she rose from the sofa said that something else was going on. She lifted the wine bottle and held it over his glass, topping it up.

"I need to talk to you about something."

*This was it.* The big talk. The, why don't you rent out your apartment and move in here, talk. The next step up the ladder of commitment. Craig knew what was coming and yet for some reason his heart didn't sink; it had to be a good sign.

But when his petite girlfriend sat down again, this time

out of his reach, signifying the seriousness of her intentions, he was surprised when her first words weren't "I think that it's time, Marc", but rather "John and Natalie are in trouble."

It caught him unawares, but rather than say anything he nodded her on, listening for ten minutes without interrupting but with growing dismay, as he realised that what John had thought was just Natalie being difficult was far more serious than that.

\*\*\*\*

**Friday. 2 a.m.**

Ray Barrett was fast asleep when his phone rang, sleeping the sleep of a well-fed baby, which would have surprised many people given that he was the Director of Police Intelligence and must therefore have had a myriad of reasons to pace the floor all night. But then Barrett had always been a good sleeper; the only time he could recall a broken night was during the birth of his first son, who unlike his more obliging siblings had chosen the wee small hours to announce his entrance into the world. The transgression had been referred to many times during the boy's adolescence when guilt as a weapon of chastisement had been required.

Such a good sleeper was Barrett that it took three alarm clocks to wake him in the morning, and even then his wife had to slam down his customary mug of coffee by the bed. So it was with not a little surprise that he found himself awake now, and he felt for the reality of the bedside table, just to make sure.

How he'd been woken by the phone's ringing was a puzzle that could wait to be solved, but why it had rung was something he intended to find out right away. He snatched up the offending handset and snapped out a "Yes!" adding "Who in God's name is calling me at this unearthly hour?"

Kyle Spence was shocked by the question and then even more shocked as he realised what he'd just done. He'd worked for Ray Barrett for years and everyone knew about his sleeping habits, so why he'd chosen to call him at two in the morning could only be explained by him losing track of time. Explanation made to himself, now he had to decide what to do: hang up and thank the stars that his number was withheld, or plough on regardless and make the request that he'd intended to when he'd made the call.

Not being a coward or a kid playing 'knock door run fast' Spence decided to speak, preparing himself for the barrage of abuse that he knew he would get from his old boss.

"It's me, Director. I just wondered if research had come up with any undetectable recording or filming devices since I'd left. It's urgent. We need them for an Obo asap."

He moved the phone to arms' length and waited for Barratt's yell, but to his surprise the only reply was. "Call round tomorrow at one o'clock."

As the phone went down both men were left wondering if they'd just had a dream.

\*\*\*\*

## The Merchant Hotel, Belfast.

The Fox was satisfied. The final party was set for the next evening, just as the others elsewhere in the UK were as well. One last push and they would be savouring victory. He was convinced that they'd done enough. McManus was gone and Roger Burke, one of their true believers, was in his place. He would lead the final week of campaigning with zeal, and their men dotted around the housing estates would do the same on the ground, using violence, bribery and whatever else they needed to get out the vote.

He glanced around his ornate hotel room as he thought. It was a beautiful place, and one of the few things about the UK that he would be sorry to leave. The whole country made him uncomfortable with its weak self-indulgence, but at least it would soon be out of the back-slapping, corrupt entity that was the EU. Its fat eurocrats with their expense accounts made him sick. They needed to be taught a lesson and the outcome of this referendum would soon give them that.

As he walked to the high swashed windows and stared out at Waring Street the old warrior smiled at the thought; sex, subterfuge and threats of exposure worked on corrupt men everywhere, whether they were left or right wing.

Within a week the outcome would be definite and he would be back in his own country planning the next steps.

\*\*\*\*

## Police Headquarters. Malone Road. 11 a.m.

As Craig left Headquarters after giving Sean Flanagan an update, he was still reeling from what Katy had told him the night before. He had however managed to park his shock long enough to notice how grey the normally robust Chief Constable had looked, and to register Flanagan's response when he'd inquired if he was all right. The C.C. had just gazed at him unblinkingly for a moment and then opened his mouth as if he had something to confide. Then the moment had passed, his mouth had closed again and whatever stress was afflicting the man had drawn the pall further over his face.

What Craig had really wanted to ask the man was 'I know you're not going to the sex parties so what's your involvement with this stuff?', 'Why were you tasked with finding Veronica Lewis?' And 'If you're *not* corrupt then why are you allowing corrupt men to pull your strings?'

But he hadn't asked any of those questions, not from any fear of the man or deference for his rank, and not because he believed Flanagan was dirty, but because of some tiny particle of doubt that must still have existed inside him and the knowledge that if Flanagan *did* say something to disappoint him before he had all the answers it might knock him off his stride in the case.

The thing that gave him most hope was that Flanagan wasn't telling him to bury the investigation. All he'd asked was for them to investigate Veronica Lewis' disappearance, so he could easily have called a halt when she'd reappeared, yet he'd been quietly encouraging of the things they were starting to reveal.

Craig's thoughts returned to the bombshell that Katy had dropped on him twelve hours before. What the hell did he tell John? If he even had the right to tell him anything. Although part of him wondered if Natalie hadn't told her best friend *hoping* that it would get back to her husband, precisely to save her from having to tell John everything herself. The detective was halfway through town, replaying the problem for a third time, when his car phone rang.

"Craig."

Aidan Hughes' unmistakable voice came down the line.

"Can I meet you, chief? Somewhere off site."

Curious, Craig glanced at his dashboard clock and answered. "Twelve at Lady Dixon Park."

"I'll see you there."

As Craig turned his car and headed back the way he'd just come, Liam was sitting in his Ford on wasteland by the river, wracking his brains. The guns were Russian. Not just in make but in origin, ownership and probably nefarious use. The thought made him take out his notebook and scribble down, 'match bullet with other shootings' before descending into thought again.

OK, so this Russian mafia bloke who'd owned them, Gleb Solokov, had been sighted in Berlin recently, and in Berlin the second biggest name in the Russian mafia was the Eugenov gang, who just happened to list organised prostitution amongst their hobbies. It prompted another scribble 'could the Russian Mafia own the English brothels Davy identified?"

It brought a satisfied smile to the D.C.I.'s pale face. It might be Orgies Inc. after all. So...if the mafia ran the brothels in England, were the women there being forced to cooperate, and cooperate on what? And was the same bunch involved with Veronica Lewis' parties?

The smile was followed by a frown. Why just England and here? What had happened to Scotland and Wales?

It prompted a shout of "DAMN, DAMN, DAMN!" and then a call to the office.

Why was it the further they got into this sodding case the less they understood?

\*\*\*\*

**Craigantlet Army Base.**

Whether it was the finality of handing over his rifle and sidearm, or the seemingly petulant clang of the base's gate behind him as he drove out, no longer dressed in the olive green of the tribe that he'd belonged to since he'd been twenty-two, but in a navy, too well cut to ever be called a demob, suit, but Ken Smith felt almost bereft. He'd left the military honourably so why the hell did he feel like he'd just been cashiered? And why had he wanted to smash his commanding officer's face in when the crusty old bugger had handed over his discharge documents with a hurt, chastising look.

"Look, you lot, I've given you fifteen years of my life and now it's time to do something else", is what he'd wanted to say, but instead, like the good, obedient soldier he still was, he'd merely saluted, nodded and then spun sharply on his heel.

Those were the angry thoughts racing through ex-Captain Smith's head as he drove over the hills as fast as he could without ending up in a field, but mixed in with them was the far less negative urge to yell 'YAHOO!' and drive straight to Lucia's work to drag her back to his new apartment and bed.

Except that he couldn't because, driven by duty as he still was, he'd promised to sort out their new passports for the holiday they had planned, the first one in years that he hadn't known could be cancelled an hour before and then see him shipped off to some foreign war.

As he raked through the gears of his old TR6 and put his boot to the floor, the not so old soldier smiled to himself at all the freedoms that lay ahead.

\*\*\*\*

**Sir Thomas and Lady Dixon Park, Upper Malone Road.**

Twelve o'clock had come and gone thirty minutes before, but Craig wasn't as annoyed as he would normally have been at having to wait. He needed time to think, and while he usually did it in the comfort of his office, a view of flowers and trees and the sound of birds would do easily as well. While his eyes ran over his colourful surroundings aimlessly his mind was on other things, namely what the hell a German assassin using Russian guns had wanted in their tiny country. The upshot was a list of questions that had he known it matched Liam's almost identically. Satisfied, the detective nodded them into his memory and finally began to care that Aidan Hughes was late. It was timely, as just then the D.C.I.'s odd gold-rust coloured Citroen pulled up on Craig's passenger side and a moment later the Vice cop was in his car.

Craig turned in his seat and looked at him expectantly, as Hughes struggled with how best to frame his words. Finally, he abandoned the fight with a shrug and muttered a name.

"Moorfield."

"Place or person?"

"Person. He's a sergeant down in Vice."

Craig nodded. "OK, so I take it he's the one Karl passed the info to about the parties."

Hughes gave an equivocal nod.

"What does that mean? Was he, or wasn't he?"

It felt like he was pulling teeth.

After a few seconds, the D.C.I. answered like he was conceding.

"OK, he is." Adding hastily. "But it wasn't him."

This was going to be good. In preparation for what was bound to be a convoluted story Craig moved back his seat and folded his arms.

"Go on."

As if an invisible barrier had been lifted a smile lit Aidan Hughes' lugubrious face and he sat forward eagerly.

"OK, so Tony Moorfield, one of the best Vice guys I know, and as decent as they come, so he gets the info from Karl and drafts a memo-"

Craig raised a hand, cutting him off.

"You've seen this memo?"

"Yes." He thought again. "Well no, not the actual paper

memo, but the file it was printed from. I've seen that. It's on Tony's computer, dated and all."

It could have been written that morning, but computer forensics could soon tell them the truth. He waved the D.C.I. on.

"OK, so Tony. I worked with him for years. Really honest bloke. Never took a quick snort or a freebie with one of the girls like most of the lads."

Craig's eyebrows shot up. He wasn't naïve about what went on undercover, but he'd rarely heard it admitted out loud.

"Were you one of that most?"

Hughes's face was the picture of innocence. "Me, boss? As if."

It wasn't an answer and they both knew it, so the conversation continued as if Craig hadn't asked.

"OK, so if Tony says he sent the memo then he definitely did."

"Sent to?"

It prompted Hughes to do a quick scan of the area and the car's rear seat. The latter earned him a snort.

"Do you think Liam's hiding back there?"

"I wouldn't put it past him." The D.C.I. leant forward earnestly, as if he thought it was how secrets were meant to be exchanged. "Tony sent it to Harrison."

Craig's jaw dropped with a crack. Of all the police officers who might have been involved in the sex parties Terry Harrison hadn't even crossed his mind, although, as his mouth closed again slowly, he didn't know why not. Harrison was a well-known lecher and an infamous social climber who would do anything to speed up the police ranks, and if he could manage to combine the two activities he imagined that the D.C.S. would be a very happy man.

They had a mutual hatred forged through years of combat and he loathed Harrison, so why wasn't he pleased that the man was implicated in such a mess? After a moment's self-analysis Craig gave a shrug; he'd work out why later, right now they had a case to solve.

"And I take it Tony Moorfield didn't hear anything further?"

"Only a call from Harrison telling him to forget it and destroy any trail."

"Which thankfully he didn't. Good man."

Craig fell silent again as what the whole thing meant sank in. Not only was Harrison implicated in concealing the sex parties for two months, but for all they knew he might have been involved in the plot to kill the First Minister and help Beatrix Hass to escape. He'd certainly have had local snouts who could have organised her safe house; like all detectives Harrison would have acquired them as he'd progressed through the ranks.

But most informants they had enough on to turn would have had their prints in the system, and Des had been adamant that there'd been no traceable prints on the bed. Perhaps searching a different database might shed more light.

He suddenly realised that Aidan was staring at him.

"You look like you're waiting for some words of wisdom, Aidan. Well, you're out of luck, sorry. I'm going to need time to think about this one."

He was answered by a smirk. "We could bug Harrison's phone."

It wasn't a bad idea, but there was a problem.

"We'd need a warrant."

"No problem. I can get one through Vice. We're investigating a sex ring after all."

"Except that Harrison oversees Vice and he'd need to sign it off."

The smirk became a grin.

"Not this week. He's on holiday. Geoff Hamill in Gang Crime is covering."

Happy days. Something was going their way at last. Craig thought through the ramifications and then nodded.

"OK. But I'd rather use a tail with a directional mike. That way we'll get Harrison's calls whichever phone he uses. Put Jake on him, but only till tomorrow night."

"Why?"

"Because that's the party, and when we find out the venue I'll need everyone there listening to what's being said in that house."

\*\*\*\*

## Berlin, Germany.

Vala Raske frowned as she stared at the video playing on her computer. Beatrix Hass at Demmin's street market, Beatrix Hass stopping at a florist to buy tulips, Beatrix Hass sitting at a pavement café as if she didn't have a care in the world. It worried her. No, correction, it *disturbed* her. Hass was making no attempt to hide herself, which either meant that she hadn't spotted their man following her, or she thought she was flameproof even if she had. It spawned a list of possible reasons for the behaviour, top of which was that Hass was connected with far scarier people than the police, either criminal or in government.

The BPOL officer drained her coffee to the dregs and went in search of more, returning just in time to see a memo drop on her desk and its delivery man walk away.

"What's that, Rudi?"

The young officer turned back and shrugged. "Read it and find out, boss."

Tutting at how cheeky the young were becoming Raske slid her glasses onto her nose, her heart sinking further with each word she read.

\*\*\*\*

## The C.C.U. 2 p.m.

"Everyone drop what you're doing. We need a catch up."

One minute later Craig was at the centre of a semicircle nodding Davy on. The analyst's response was to project his map and table from the day before on to Nicky's screen. By the time he'd talked them through his reasoning Liam was shaking his head.

"Scotland and Wales."

"What about them?"

"Did you check them for dead or disappeared girls like I asked?"

Davy shook his head, unperturbed. "Not yet. I do need

*some* sleep you know."

The retort made Craig smile. "Let us know what you find there, Davy. I take it the woman marked in purple isn't dead."

"Disappeared and reappeared, just like Veronica Lewis. I've the local police interviewing her now."

"Good." Craig gestured at the screen. "Explain your thinking on column one." The dates that the girls had disappeared.

"It was Nicky who spotted it, chief, so I think she should tell you."

Craig beckoned the PA from her typing. "Front and centre, please, Ma'am, and tell us about these dates."

Nicky didn't move from her desk. "I can tell you from here. Those women started disappearing just after the EU Referendum campaigning began. No-one had disappeared before then."

Liam spotted the same anomaly that Davy had. "Not that very day."

Nicky shook that day's high ponytail. "Because it took a few days to realise that both sides were going to make a fight of it. If one side hadn't been bothered then the result would have been a done deal and there'd have been no need to try to sway it."

It confirmed what Craig had been feeling for days but he decided to explore their reasoning.

"So, you believe this case is about swaying the EU Referendum vote?"

The PA nodded.

"OK..." He was thinking as he spoke, already knowing the answer to his next question. "Which way?"

Ash jumped in. "I reckoned it was towards leaving."

"Mmm...OK, I'm not saying you're wrong, but explain your logic."

The analyst rubbed his hands cheerfully. He loved a good debate.

"Well, McManus was Pro-EU and he was shot, so that leaves Roger Burke as head of the biggest party here and he's definitely for leaving, plus we already know about Loughrey-"

Davy cut him off. "You can't villainise people just because they want to leave. It could just as easily be the Pro-EU side who killed McManus. They might have w...wanted McManus dead because he wasn't Pro enough."

Craig made a face that said he wasn't convinced. "I think Nicky was definitely onto something about the dates being significant, Davy, so the EU Referendum part makes sense, but we need more evidence to say which side. I have to say though that I think it's unlikely to be the Pro-EU lobby."

Liam gave a slow tut. "Now don't *you* tell me you're falling for that old rubbish about Pro-Leave being the bad guys and the Pro-EU lot all being good. That Italian blood of yours must be rushing to your brain."

Craig chuckled at the image. "Thanks for that picture, Liam, but no, that's not why I'm saying it's more likely to be the Pro-Leave side. It's because we know that the IBP core are for leaving, and because Beatrix Hass, our assassin, is linked with her country's fast growing right-wing, and some of them didn't even agree with Germany uniting with the Allies post World War Two, never mind uniting with most of Europe since."

Ash nodded furiously. "So, if she's involved it's *bound* to be the right wing organising everything."

"Except that the two men she killed over here supported the most right-wing party we have." Liam went to interrupt but Craig didn't yield. "Albeit Peter McManus might not have been hard core enough for his own party, and Billy Regent was just a set-up to throw us off the trail."

Liam's face brightened as he remembered something. "I meant to tell you something on that, boss. Tommy gave me a bell this morning."

Craig smiled at the strange closeness between the two men. "What did he have to say for himself?"

Liam adopted a knowing look. "It seems our info about Loyalism viewing McManus as a traitor was bullshit. He'd been friendly with UKUF for years. Dropping in for tea in the office friendly."

The information made Craig frown, mainly because he wasn't certain how it fitted. Liam clarified.

"If the paramilitary *gangs* didn't want McManus dead, then they'd have vetoed any local hit on him that they'd heard about, and they hear *everything,* on all sides."

Which made it unlikely that anyone at street level in Northern Ireland had been involved in the First Minister's death. It backed up what they knew. They were dealing with purely upper echelon thugs.

"And Tommy got this-"

"From Rory McCrae, his heir apparent."

"You believe him?"

Liam nodded without hesitation. "I do. Mind you, I'm not sure what it means. We already knew Billy didn't kill McManus for any ideology, and he definitely wasn't hired. His bank account's showing no deposits and his mum barely has enough to get her to the end of the week. The poor bugger was coerced into taking the shot, and threats to his family seem the likeliest leverage."

Craig nodded and crossed to the LED screen. "OK, let's follow things through. Pro-Leave are trying to increase their vote by... what? Compromising senior figures across the UK?"

Nicky cut in. "Compromising men who can influence others to support the vote."

"And you really think that would be enough to swing it for Leave?"

It was Liam who answered. "It might be, boss, especially if they're whipping up grass roots support on the estates as well. The IBP has forty percent of the vote here, and their followers will pretty much do as they ask. Any stragglers could be picked up by intimidation on the day." He gestured at the map. "I bet the same picture's being played out in working class areas all over the mainland."

"It would have to be targeted at different political parties over there. The IBP doesn't have a mandate."

Nicky nodded. "Any party with right-wing supporters would do."

Liam had a thought. "Why don't we get Hughesy to ask his Vice buddies to see what's what at the English sex parties?"

Hughesy had had his head buried in his notepad, but

when his name was called it shot up. "What?"

"Get your Vice buddies to find out which politicians have been going to those naughty parties in England."

Annette rolled her eyes at the way Liam made smut sound like a playground game, but Craig nodded in agreement.

"Can you, Aidan?"

The D.C.I. thought about it for a moment before replying. "It might be a bit sensitive to organise over the phone, chief."

Craig waved a hand around the group. "Take your pick. Any one of these likely officers can take a trip."

Kyle shook his head. "Not me. I've got my snout going to the party."

Craig suddenly remembered he'd wanted Jake to tail Harrison. He changed it to Annette and Rhonda and offered up Jake for the England trip. The sergeant's smile said that he was fine with the jaunt so Craig moved swiftly on.

"OK, anything more on the computing side?"

Both analysts shook their heads. Davy was close to an answer on the Classics Club but there was no point even mentioning it until he was there. Craig turned back to Liam.

"Anything?"

The D.C.I. took out his notebook, turning to a page near the back. "Lots. Some questions, some answers. Nothing on antiques smuggling, even Tommy's come up cold on that. Arms smuggling's still a possibility so I'll keep you up to date. I've the Gardaí on board for tomorrow night's operation- they've offered us the teams that we need, so that's all sorted, and I asked Ash here to run the bed prints past them as well as Interpol."

He paused for breath, waving the junior analyst on as he did.

"OK, so one set on the bed belonged to a man from here who was arrested in Vienna of all places. For stealing handbags."

Liam chuckled. "Must've taken a holiday especially."

"He's a Mark Wilberforce, originally from the Demesne Estate. He still has an address there so I've asked Sergeant Boyd to keep an eye out for him."

Davy asked the question that Craig had been about to. "Does he have a record here?"

Ash frowned. "Strangely no."

It could only mean one thing. Once a thief always a thief, whether in Vienna or Belfast. Mark Wilberforce's misdemeanours had been expunged from their system locally because he was someone high level's snout.

Craig smiled a well-done. "That it, Liam?"

"Nope. I had a few thoughts earlier."

Aidan whispered. "That explains the burning smell."

Liam didn't even glance up as he thumped his insulter mid-thigh, continuing his report over the Vice cop's groans.

"So, I was thinking, what if the bullets in McManus and Regent matched other shootings across Europe and Russia?"

Annette's eyes widened. "Russia? What's that about?"

Craig waited patiently while Liam explained about the guns, before returning to his intended question.

"So, you've had Des send the markings through to Interpol and the FSB?"

Liam gave a smug smile. "I have indeed, because I'm a genius. We're waiting for a result now." He turned the page. "Also... do the Russian Mafia own the English Brothels Davy identified? And could they be involved with Lewis' set up as well?"

Craig nodded to the analyst. "Do what you can with that, Davy, although I'm pretty sure we'll only get some of these answers when the case is cracked. But good points, Liam."

He waited to hear if the D.C.I. had anything else and when he didn't he turned to Kyle.

"I need everything your informant gave you, Kyle."

His folded arms said to leave nothing out so Kyle reported sulkily on his latest encounter with Trevor Rudkin, finishing with his phone-call to Ray Barrett at two a.m.

Craig thought for a moment before speaking.

"It's looking more and more like Emmett Darrian's place *will* be used, but if we tail Rudkin and Loughrey from Bangor we'll know for certain."

Liam agreed. "Also, we should have people already set up at Darrian's for when they arrive. If it turns out not to be at his place they should still be able to get to the right venue quickly."

Craig smiled at the image of the Keystone Cops racing through the woods.

"OK, so we can progress the background stuff between now and then, but we really need to get a man inside that party. Kyle, Rudkin said they're all being security screened. Any idea to what level?"

"Rudkin will already have had a counter terrorism check for his job with Loughrey, and probably advanced security checking as well, but developed vetting, DV, takes longer, unless Loughrey has some way of speeding things up."

"Almost certainly." Craig scanned the group. "Who here has been advanced security checked?"

Every detective but Jake and Rhonda raised their hands.

"OK, who's been DVed?"

All but Liam's, his own and Kyle's hand fell, and most surprising of all Ash lifted his.

"When did you get DVed, Ash?"

"Sorry, I meant to raise my hand on advanced security, chief. I was DVed as well when I worked with GCHQ. I have STRAP too."

DV and STRAP was the highest possible level of security clearance. Some STRAP levels even authorised the bearer to receive details of NSA recorded telephone calls.

Liam gave the analyst an 'I'm not worthy' bow then laughed at Kyle's sour expression.

"What's the matter, Spooky? Pissed off that Ash can spy on someone you can't?"

It prompted a round of laughter that Craig let run for a moment before moving on.

"OK, so Liam, Kyle, Ash and I have DV, but we can't use Ash on the operation because he isn't a police officer so I can't authorise him to take any risks. That leaves the three of us, so the next question is, how do we get inside?"

Ash shot him an 'isn't it obvious' glance and followed up with a name.

"Veronica Lewis. She could bring someone in with her."

Annette shook her head. "A girl maybe, but why would she be bringing a man along?"

"Don't sex-workers have body guards sometimes? They do on TV."

Liam was taken aback at how spot on the suggestion was.

"That's not a bad idea, boss. One of us could go in with Lewis, and just have our DV show up under a different name." His hand shot up. "I bags it."

Craig shook his head. "It's not the last slice of pizza we're talking about here, Liam. Anyway, you would stick out like a sore thumb!" Before Liam got defensive he added. "As would I. We could be recognised by someone. We've both had dealings with MLAs in the past."

The growing smirk on Kyle's face made him want to smack it off, and if they hadn't needed the Intelligence Officer he might have.

Craig's next words were forced out.

"Unfortunately, of the four of us Spence is the only one who's not known and is a police officer." He turned to the D.I. "You'll be wired, and the first sign of you deviating from the script I give you and we'll be in on top of you." He glanced at the wall clock. "OK, anyone got anything else to share before we wrap this up?"

The way Ash glanced at him said that he had, but that it was too sensitive to share with the group.

"Right then. Aidan, bring Annette and Rhonda up to speed on that issue we discussed, please. They'll need to know everything for surveillance. Davy, can you brief Jake on the English brothels so that Nicky can get him organised to leave asap. Kyle, Liam, Ash, I need to speak to all of you, with Ash first. In my office, please."

Before the analyst moved he rubbed salt in Kyle's STRAP wound.

"Oh, by the way, Kyle, I got those CIA files you wanted,

but sorry, your clearance isn't high enough. I shouldn't worry, there was nothing very exciting in there."

His ill-concealed smirk as he entered Craig's office implied exactly the opposite.

As the detective closed the door he got straight to it.

"Right. What was that look about?"

Ash took a seat. "OK, so you know I get some NSA phone tap detail, chief."

"And?"

The analyst set his smart-pad on the desk. "Listen to this. The NSA picked it up on a random sweep yesterday."

Craig raised a hand hurriedly. "Whoa! Are you allowed to share it?"

"They said that I could with you."

Craig found out why as soon as the analyst pressed play. A man and a woman were speaking in German and it was clearly a heated exchange. By the end of the one-minute clip, three names had come across loud and clear: Beatrix, McManus and Solokov.

"That's Beatrix Hass?"

"Yes. We don't have a name for the man she's speaking to. The NSA's traced his number but unfortunately it was a burn phone. Anyway, this is the translation they gave me."

Another tap and the words were dubbed into English, clarifying the conversation's theme. They'd been spot on about Beatrix Hass' involvement in Peter McManus' killing, and that the right-wing was involved, but it was the communist comment that worried Craig most. German communism had all but collapsed when the Berlin wall had come down in eighty-nine, and it was that and the fact that the man speaking sounded too old to be part of any new wave that was making him twitch.

He parked his questions for the meantime and returned to the issue in hand. Beatrix Hass had obviously spotted one of Vala's team following her, but what was more worrying was the information that she was the girlfriend of one of the Eugenov Gang. He needed to pass this information on to

Vala as soon as he could.

Ash stopped the clip and shook his head. "They were careless speaking on the phone."

"The man realised. That's why he was angry." Craig frowned as something occurred to him. "Why did the NSA think to give this tape to you?" Suspicion tainted his next words. "*Have you been sharing information about our case?*"

Ash's immediate offence made him want to lash out, but instead he recalled the Hindu precepts that he'd been brought up with and bit his tongue until he could reply in a calm voice, albeit coloured with a definite huff.

"They watch the news so they know McManus was murdered, *sir,* and I *had* asked the CIA for sight of some files, but the real reason the NSA passed the tape on to me was because the man was calling from here."

Craig's eyes widened. "Here meaning the UK?"

The analyst shook his multi-coloured head. "Here meaning Belfast. Somewhere in the city centre, but they couldn't be more accurate than that. Hass was in Demmin, in the North of Germany."

Craig was still reeling from the information when he dismissed Ash a minute later, with a muttered apology for his earlier suspicion and instructions for the analyst to keep digging as far as he could. He beckoned Liam and Kyle into the room in a half-daze, and imparted the information on Harrison with far less discretion than he should have done.

He pushed past Liam's stunned expression and Kyle's nudge nudge, wink wink jokes.

"The issue at hand now is, does Harrison know you, Kyle? If he's at the party and makes you for a copper it could blow everything."

Kyle's shake of the head was so emphatic that for once Craig believed he was telling the truth.

"I've been in Intelligence since I left training college, and we tended to avoid plods, no matter how high their rank."

The dig didn't pass Liam by and he added it to his list of

things to avenge. He'd been keeping the catalogue since nineteen-ninety-five and every so often he tested his memory by reciting it from the beginning, only ever removing a perpetrator when they'd either retired or died.

Kyle was still spouting, oblivious to his possible future fate.

"The only time Harrison *could* possibly have seen me was when I transferred here, but I'm pretty sure we've never been in the squad-room at the same time, and you're the D.C.S. who handled my paperwork for the move."

Craig needed more reassuring. "Liam. What do you think?"

Liam shot the spy a dirty look before conceding that it was unlikely Harrison would recognise Kyle's smart-assed face.

"There *was* that time Teflon came down blasting off about Hughesy defecting from Vice, but if Spooky was here then he was probably up on the roof smoking a fag, as usual. But I still can't get over Teflon being involved, boss. Do you think he knows how murky this whole thing is, or is he just following his dick?"

Craig laughed out loud. "The second one for sure, but he's also social climbing. Harrison's an ambitious snob, so hobnobbing with politicians would be like manna from the gods."

"Women, social climbing and career advancement; his three favourite pastimes all in one place. He must be in hog heaven."

"We can speculate about that after the party." Craig turned back to the D.I. "OK, Kyle. Get whatever you need together and we'll chat again before the off. Now leave us, please. Liam and I need to talk."

About the female assassin who'd escaped to Germany and a man who was still in town.

## Chapter Fourteen

Craig was pleased when Vala called him again; it saved him having to remember to call her, yet another thing to do on his never-ending list. His pleasure changed to bemusement when he realised that she was whispering, so quietly that not only would she have been inaudible to whoever she was concealing her conversation from in Germany, but he could only make out every other word.

"I'm sorry, Vala, I can barely hear you."

"Scheisse, Marc! I'm whispering because I'm in trouble. Hang on."

As the line went dead Craig pictured the scenario at the other end. The chief inspector phoning from some stairwell at Berlin Police Headquarters to avoid being overheard by her team, only to find that casual traffic meant even more people could have heard her words. When Vala phoned back ten minutes later her voice was louder, but this time it was competing with the city's traffic noise.

"OK. I can talk now. Marc, this thing you're involved in has arms and legs everywhere."

"I know."

Her strong voice rose anxiously. "How? I only know because I had a summons to Headquarters and I was told in no uncertain terms to back off Beatrix Hass-"

Craig cut her off. "Do they know that you've been helping me?"

"No." The weak negative hadn't even convinced her so she said it again more emphatically. "NO. They definitely can't know about that or I would have been kept longer than ten minutes, but what I don't understand is why they want me to back off Hass."

"No explanation given?"

"None. Just 'pull the surveillance on Beatrix Hass stat'. When I asked why, I got nothing. Just *do it or else*. The thing is, I don't even know how they knew, never mind what's got them so twitchy."

Craig knew. His mind had flown from Hass' conversation with their mystery man, to the NSA and then onward to someone in the German Government or BPOL. The NSA had probably just passed on their record of the call in the spirit of international détente, but the decision to shut down Vala's surveillance said that their case had ramifications in Germany and who knew where else.

"I think I do, Vala." But telling her over the phone, knowing what he now knew about the NSA, was far too risky. "But I can't tell you right now. Look, you've done enough to help us, so don't take any more risks. I promise I'll tell you everything as soon as I can."

Before the phone went down Vala Raske had already made up her mind to ignore both her bosses and Craig.

\*\*\*\*

**The Demesne Estate, East Belfast.**

There were many things Reggie Boyd didn't like about his job: the standard issue tea-bags sent down from headquarters, which contained so few tealeaves that a cuppa was the colour of porridge even before he'd added milk; the high necked collars of his old-fashioned shirts that rubbed against his stubble giving him a permanent rash; OK, so he could have worn the new ones but he didn't think they looked as smart, and in his book trading off a professional appearance with a skin condition shouldn't have been an either or. But the one thing that he *really* hated about his job was rudeness.

He'd been brought up to say please, thank you, and sir or madam, and he stuck by that training even when faced with the roughest of the rough, so he really couldn't have it when a shaved-headed, tattoo covered yob like Mark Wilberforce polluted his station booking room with expletives and then spat in the face of the W.P.C. who was trying to help him out.

It brought out the beast in the quietly spoken Donegal giant and Reggie found his fist twitching into a ball, so it was just as well he'd had the foresight to call Liam when he'd arrested the little thug, and a miracle of timing that the D.C.I. appeared just as Reggie's twitching was on the verge of becoming a blow.

"Now then, now then, Sergeant Boyd. What's happening here? A tea dance?"

Liam had spotted the whitening fist by Reggie's side and decided to save his friend's pension with a joke.

"Tea dance, my aunt Aggie!" Reggie jerked his now unfurled hand in the direction of their guest. "This animal has just sworn and spat at my constable, and I'm not having it. No, I am not."

Liam's gaze jumped from the sergeant to the W.P.C. wiping her face with a wet cloth, and when it finally landed on the scrawny, pock-marked specimen of humanity responsible for the assault he knew exactly what to do. He hoisted Wilberforce to his feet by the neck of his T-shirt and trailed him out through the door to the cells, nodding Reggie to open the nearest one, where Liam threw the offender less than gently against its back wall.

"Stay there and shut up, Wilberforce! Understand?"

With the survival instinct possessed by even the lowest in the animal kingdom, Mark Wilberforce considered his chances against the six-foot-six Liam and decided to acquiesce. As the door slammed behind them and Liam and Reggie walked away, the sergeant gave Liam a wondering nod.

"How come he decided not to mess with you, when I'm as big?"

Liam smiled knowingly. "Because he knew that in the time you took to *think* about punching him and struggle with the decision, I would have laid him spark out. Now, make me a cup of tea and tell me what the wee bastard said when you lifted him."

Ten minutes later Liam had heard everything and he knew that Craig had been right. Terry Harrison was up to his neck in their case. Wilberforce had been Harrison's snout for years when he'd been a street detective, and when Teflon had offered him fifty quid to find him an empty flat on the Travis he'd practically bitten off his hand. No matter which way you looked at the situation, D.C.S. Terry 'Teflon' Harrison had organised Beatrix Hass' safe house, and that meant he was implicated in killing the First Minister.

\*\*\*\*

**The C.C.U. 4 p.m.**

Craig had been struggling with a decision since the previous evening, and for once it had nothing to do with work. Ever since Katy had blurted out what she knew about Natalie's situation he'd been torn about whether to tell John or not. The more he thought about it the more certain he was that's why Katy had told him, although she'd obviously needed his support as well. While a problem shared isn't really halved at least it puts two of you in the boat.

After another thirty minutes of will I, won't I, and several lifts and drops of the phone, Craig decided that he had to distract himself so he lifted the list of drug-taking MLAs that Karl Rimmins had sent through, scanning it with an increasingly elevated brow. He'd never thought that politicians were angels but he admitted to being surprised by the length of the list and by some of the names.

The usual suspects were there of course: Joshua Loughrey, Leonard Montgomery and even Roger Burke, but when he reached a Methodist local preacher and a member of a Rosary Group he had to set the paper down. It wasn't as if their drug use was minor either, every name on the list had used either Ketamine or Cocaine, although he supposed that might explain some of astoundingly stupid policy decisions emerging from Stormont nowadays.

But why the hell hadn't the MLAs been charged when they'd been lifted? It smacked of one law for the rich and another for the poor, and it was something that he intended to ask Karl about. Although, as Terry Harrison was the superintendent heading up both Drugs and Vice, they now had an obvious explanation to the blind eye being turned. The other question was, could the list be of use to them the following night? Was there anyone on it that they could squeeze to provide Kyle with cover inside the party, or was that a risk too far for even a hedonistic MLA to take?

He was still pondering when Liam's fist fell against his door and he entered the office before waiting for a yes. Craig was grateful for the distraction so he let the transgression pass.

"What can I do for you, Liam?"

The D.C.I. fell into the nearest chair and glanced pointedly at the percolator. As Craig obliged him with a mug he outlined what Mark Wilberforce had said.

Craig fell into his own chair with a whistle.

"Harrison's *really* involved in McManus' killing."

"You say that like you're surprised, boss."

"I am, actually. I honestly didn't think he was capable of this. Or that." He pushed the list of MLAs across the desk. "I need to ask Karl more about it, but my instinct is that this lot would have been lifted ages ago if Harrison hadn't intervened."

Liam read the list and shook his head. "This would've been blocked higher up the food chain than Harrison."

Craig immediately realised that he was right. Someone more senior in the force would have got the call from Stormont if a politician had been caught using drugs, and there was only one name that could fit.

"You mean Flanagan."

"Has to be, although I can't see him letting them off willingly. But if you get a call from Stormont saying the arrest of some MLA could bring down the executive he'd be between a rock and a hard place, wouldn't he? Especially if they'd nicked a bunch of them at once. It'd be a choice of arrest them all and risk the scandal collapsing the government, or wait till they lose their seats at the next election and charge them then. I know which I'd choose."

It made Craig wonder how many things a Chief Constable had to swallow just to keep the peace.

"Kyle can gather more evidence at the party, so when we arrest this bunch we can get them on fresh drugs charges as well."

Liam helped himself to some custard creams that Nicky had set out. "OK. So, what do we do about Harrison?"

"Nothing until after the party, but tell Reggie I want Wilberforce kept incommunicado. We can't have him tipping off Harrison that we're onto him before tomorrow night."

\*\*\*\*

While the two detectives in Craig's office were debating Terry Harrison's future, Davy was gathering up his things outside, an activity that didn't escape his office mother's beady gaze. Nicky waited until the analyst made a move towards the exit and then raced to the exit doors to block his way.

"Where are you going? It's only ten-past-four."

Davy gave her an old-fashioned look and went to move on past.

"You didn't answer my question, young man. You're not on a half-day."

"And you're not Cerberus."

She stared up at him. "Who?"

"I thought you knew everything, Nicky."

"I know when someone's being cheeky, that's what I know!"

"Cerberus. Guardian of the Underworld in Greek mythology. He stops the dead from leaving. It's a clue to my destination now."

In the seconds the PA dropped her guard to think about it, the analyst made good his escape. He could still hear her calling after him as he descended in the lift.

"You'll pay for that, Davy Walsh."

For eternity if the mythology was correct. Even longer if Nicky discovered that Cerberus was a three-headed hound. The thought amused him as he caught the bus to South Belfast, and was still making him smile when he arrived at Queen's University and tapped on the office door belonging to the Archaeology Professor that he'd come to see.

Niall Murphy answered the knock energetically and Davy was surprised to see that the academic wasn't much older than him. Why he was surprised he wasn't certain, except that he always pictured Professors as tweed-jacketed and round-shouldered, those in Archaeology and Ancient History with an added patina of dust, and the muscled, T-shirted Murphy didn't fit the mould.

"Hello, hello. You must be Mister Walsh."

Davy smiled, the cheerful greeting adding to his surprise. "Davy, please, Professor Murphy."

Murphy waved him to a seat. "Niall, please. OK. Now that we've the introductions dispensed with, tea or coffee?"

"I'm OK without, thanks." Davy set down his rucksack and withdrew his smart-pad, nodding towards the desk. "I thought it would make it easier if you could see the s...symbol I mentioned on the phone."

"Absolutely. Go ahead and set up."

Within seconds the ornate figure four appeared on Davy's screen and a smile covered Niall Murphy's face.

"Wow! That's an old one."

The 'wow' shattered another illusion Davy had long held; that academics communicated in long sentences devoid of contractions, and most definitely devoid of words like 'wow' or 'cool'.

"Old in the sense of an ancient language?"

Murphy shook his sandy head.

"Not any that I know. No, what you've got there is an

astrology symbol. The number four represents the Roman God Jupiter, and his Greek equivalent, Zeus. The bowing on the upright portion is said to represent the personality of the soul, and the vertical cross below represents matter. It's the sort of thing alchemists were fond of back in the day as well."

He took his seat, gazing at Davy intently. "Any of that make sense in the context of whatever you're investigating?"

Davy knew he was dying to hear about the case, but unfortunately he couldn't oblige.

"Might do. It depends on the answers to a few questions. Do all Classics courses cover both Ancient Rome and Greece?"

"They do."

"OK. Two more. Is there a s...standard textbook used to teach on courses? And do you know of any alumni clubs for Classics grads that cover the whole of the British Isles?"

The professor's response was to leap to his feet again and cross to a bookshelf that the analyst hadn't noticed. The academic scanned each shelf intently, finally seizing a leather bound, hard-backed volume and placing it in front of Davy on the desk.

"The Zeus Circle. It's the standard joint text for Ancient Greco-Roman studies, and every Classics graduate will know it inside out. You can borrow that copy as long as you return it." Murphy shook his head. "But as far as your second question's concerned, no, I'm sorry, I don't know of any clubs that cover the British Isles, just single university clubs. But that doesn't mean one doesn't exist."

Davy smiled slowly. He already knew that one did, and now he knew exactly what it was called.

# Chapter Fifteen

**Saturday. 9.30 a.m.**

Jake was glad of the change of scenery, and he could see from the aeroplane window that it was beautiful scenery too, with a shifting vista of moors, hills and quaint villages visible on their descent into Manchester Airport. By the time he'd disembarked and grabbed his bag, the D.S. had remembered that a change of scene was just what the doctor had ordered, literally. He hadn't told anyone at the squad but the addiction specialist he'd seen during his steroid rehab had been insistent that changing his work environment would help prevent a relapse.

He also hadn't told them that he'd been approached to work in the Hate Crimes Unit in central Belfast, a new team set up to deal with everything from homophobic abuse to race and sectarian crime. He hadn't considered the offer seriously because he liked Craig and had made friends on the Murder Squad, but the sudden head-clearing sensation he'd got on the flight at the thought of working with new people, even for a few days, made him wonder seriously whether it was time to make a change.

The appearance of an unfamiliar but indisputably police uniform by the airport's exit made Jake shelve the decision for another time, and he extended a hand to the constable who'd been sent to meet him and then sank into the passenger seat of his patrol car for their twenty-mile drive.

As soon as they arrived at the station in Wythenshawe Jake found himself swept into an office with white boards on every wall, and five minutes later an older detective was talking him through their case. When he'd finished Jake asked a question.

"The women who disappeared or were killed, were they working in brothels or alone?"

Inspector John Ellery sat on a desk to answer.

"They mostly worked through agencies, we think, although we can't be sure. Most were madams or long-term escorts, but none of them worked out of brothels, we do know that."

"Then did the ones who were escorts get work from the madams who died? Or perhaps even attend the same organised events?"

He didn't want to use the word party unless there was some sign that they were on the right trail.

Ellery gazed at him suspiciously. "How could you know that?"

"So they *were*. Working for the same madams that is?"

The inspector nodded. "And the events, we think. It's only rumour, but we think some of the madams organised parties for the rich and famous, and they always needed girls."

Party. It was the magic word and Jake's cue to take out his smart-pad, so that they could start comparing facts.

\*\*\*\*

## The C.C.U. 10 a.m.

The squad-room was buzzing. Kyle was behind his nemesis the wall with Andy, trying out the gadgets that Ray Barrett had supplied, amongst them a set of cufflinks, one of which carried a recording device and the other a camera so small that Liam had wondered aloud how the hell it could capture anything, until he saw a picture of his backside displayed in all its glory five-foot-wide on Nicky's screen.

Annette and Rhonda had watched Harrison until midnight, relieved by uniforms for the overnight shift, and as they entered the squad kitchen to fill their flasks with coffee before leaving for more hours in a cold car, Annette wondered idly what she'd be doing now if she was a stay-at-home mum. She would never admit it to anyone, but even hoovering was starting to look good as long as she could stay in the warm.

In the middle of all the hubbub the analysts were like an oasis of calm. Davy peering silently at each of his three screens in turn, while Ash sat with his eyes shut wearing giant headphones, listening to NSA phone transcripts as two programmes ran on his PC: one searching for deaths and disappearances of sex-workers in Scotland and Wales, and the other live-feeding Interpol and FSB searches for the bullets' match.

Craig stood behind them watching for five minutes, before the junior analyst realised the detective was there and slid his headphones off. "I'm not going to ask how you're accessing a live feed in Russia, Ash."

The analyst grinned mischievously. "A, I'm not really, it's just a mirage, but B, you really wouldn't want to know if I was."

Craig leaned in closer and pointed at the screen. "What's it doing, specifically? Bullet matching?"

"It's not the FSB's actual bullet matching programme, just a live feed of their forensic reporting on it. You don't need to keep watching it, chief. If there's a match it'll ping."

It was Ash splitting colourful hairs as far as Craig was concerned, but he didn't really care as long as they got results. With one caveat.

"They can't trace your hack, can they? I'd rather not have Cossacks kicking down our doors."

The analyst arched an eyebrow. "No-one can trace my hacks, chief. You must know that by now."

Craig smiled 'I believe you' and turned towards Davy. "What are you working on?"

Davy's vague grunt said that whatever it was he wasn't ready for the big reveal, so Craig left him to it and went in search of his deputy. He found Liam about to wrap his hands around Kyle's throat.

"Put him down, Liam. Annoying as he is we'll need him alive tonight. Come with me, we're going to High Street. I've had Wilberforce moved there and I want to see Ray Mercer again." He scanned the squad-room on his way to the lift and stopped by Nicky's desk. "Nicky, where's Aidan?"

"He went to see that madam." Her loud sniff made her opinion of Veronica Lewis clear. "He knew her when she was young, I think."

When she was Ronnie Lee.

"OK, we're heading to High Street. We should be back in an hour or so, but if we're not then take everyone to The James for lunch, please, and put it on my tab. I'll need a briefing called for two, and I want everyone here, including Rhonda and Annette."

They were almost at High Street when Liam asked something that had been on his mind.

"Leonard Montgomery. You saw him so he knows we're interested in Lewis. What's to stop him warning whoever's running tonight's shindig?"

Craig chuckled. "Shindig? That makes it sound like a ho-down and I can hardly see MLAs wearing denim dungarees."

"Ach, you know fine well what I mean. What's to stop Montgomery giving us up?"

Craig pulled into the station's carpark, turning off his car engine before he replied.

"OK, one, Montgomery doesn't know Kyle so he can't give him up, and two, I paid him a reminder visit last night to point out how fragile his position was and exactly what he's got to do this evening to stay out of jail. He's agreed to watch any clique members he knows of carefully, and tip Kyle the wink if they start to slope off."

Liam gawped at him.

"You went to his home at night? *At night?* When his *wife* could overhear!" The D.C.I. tutted primly. "That's dirty pool, boss."

Craig's response was unequivocal. "This isn't a bloody game, Liam! He needed to be reminded how easily his wife *could* find out, but as you seem so concerned for his marriage I'll tell you she was already in bed when I called and we talked outside."

Liam's gaze continued chastising. *"Still, boss."* Then he gave an incongruous snigger. "The poor bugger must have nearly had a coronary. Her upstairs already suspicious and you there to talk about a sex-party he's going to the next night. You're an evil sod, you know that."

Craig grinned and climbed out of the car. "Katy says it's my greatest charm."

He walked towards the station's rear door still talking.

"OK, let's take Mercer first. We've got Wilberforce on a possible accessory charge at the moment, but that might change when everything comes out. I managed to get a court order to prevent him having any contact with the outside."

Liam stopped in his tracks. "Don't tell me. Judge Standish again."

"National security trumps everything."

Liam rubbed his hands together eagerly. "Even the rights of the fourth estate."

\*\*\*\*

**The Malone Road.**

When Veronica Lewis eventually opened the door of her penthouse apartment it was by only a tiny crack, and even that access was limited by a chain. The slim brunette squinted suspiciously at Aidan Hughes, scenting police even before he'd flashed his warrant card.

Her squint tightened further as she perused the D.C.I.'s angular face. "I know you, don't I?"

The ex-Vice cop smiled, marvelling at her memory for faces. He hadn't seen her since twenty years before at Lilith's, and his murmured greeting told her just how long it had been.

"Hello, Ronnie."

The use of her younger name made the madam's eyes widen and Hughes pressed the advantage generated by her shock.

"Is your son here?"

Her head shake was automatic.

"Well then, let's have a chat."

They both knew that it wasn't a request, and Lewis slipped the chain from its mooring immediately, opening the door. The action was performed with a passivity that almost saddened the policeman; he remembered her as a sparky young adult when he had been the same, but Veronica Lewis' bowed head as she turned towards her sitting room told him that years of being used by men and life had finally ground her down.

The D.C.I. knew she probably viewed him as just another one and the idea disturbed him somehow. But could he really argue with it? He was a man and he wanted something from her, and although it was information not sex and he would never use violence or money to get his way, he *could* take away her freedom and that was just as bad.

It made Aidan Hughes want to turn on his heel and walk out the door, to knock and start again, to ask for her help instead of expecting or insisting on it. But he couldn't. They had a case to break that affected far more people than just her.

Instead he decided on a compromise. He took the chair that the madam nodded him to and perched on its velvet edge, waiting until she was seated before staring intently into her dark eyes.

"I want to say something, Mrs Lewis. You have a choice whether to help us, and if you say no I'll speak to my boss and ask if we can do this without you. But first I'd like you to hear me out. OK?"

She had only heard one word. "*This?* What's *this*? You mean you're *not* here to arrest me?" Her passivity was suddenly joined by anxiety. "Or to tell my Rupe how I paid for his school?"

Aidan Hughes shook his head firmly. "I promise you that

I'll do neither of those things, whatever you say."

Her response was to sit back, her eyes still fixed on his face. "What do you mean by *this,* then?"

Her change in body language gave him hope, so with as much background as he could give without blowing their operation, Hughes explained how, if she helped them by taking Kyle Spence along as her bodyguard that evening, they could free her from the men who were ruining her life for good.

\*\*\*\*

## Manchester.

"This is the list?"

Jake's eyes widened as he read the computer printout. Instead of the fifteen names of dead or disappeared women that Davy had collated there were at least as many more. Thirty-one sex-workers had either vanished or been killed in the space of eight weeks.

The tired looking inspector nodded, gesturing towards a map up on the wall.

"That's only in the North and Midlands. Norfolk, Kent and Devon and Cornwall forces have reported at least five more, and God knows how many London will have."

Jake did the sums quickly in his head. A possible forty-plus sex-workers had been affected in the last two months, and even allowing that a few might have been victims of random perpetrators the picture it painted was as scary as hell. If the majority were madams like Veronica Lewis then whoever was behind this had been targeting established escort organisations to get them to cooperate, and killing anyone who'd said no. He asked the question to be answered by a nod.

Ellery pressed a switch and the names on the computer separated into groups.

"OK, the names clustered together all worked for the

same escort agencies. The top name is the madam running it, and the others her partners or longest serving girls. You'll see from the dates of their disappearances that there's a gap of a few days between each name, as if someone was taking the time to pick them off one by one."

Or make each of them an offer in turn, which if they refused would lead to their death. Jake frowned, realising what it meant. It fitted Liam's theory that one group was taking over established escort agencies, offering the madam and her top girls the chance to run parties for their specific purposes, and if the women refused they were killed. The ruthlessness of their opponents was in no doubt.

Jake tapped on a name. "Zoe Donnat. She was reported disappeared and then reappeared, so what can you tell me about her?"

The inspector shook his head, puzzled. "That one's a mystery. She was the third to disappear from that area of Norfolk, and the team there had presumed her dead, then she reappeared suddenly on an abandoned airfield but wouldn't tell them where she'd been."

"Assaulted?"

"A few cuts and bruises, and there were restraint marks on her ankles and wrists, so it looked like she'd been held somewhere. I can get you her file if you like."

"And a car as well, please. I'm going to Norfolk."

\*\*\*\*

### High Street Station.

"Well, that was a whole lot of useless, boss."

Craig really couldn't argue with him. Their conversation with Ray Mercer had been punctuated with expletives, and threats of an exposé on police brutality as soon as the journalist was freed. Craig leant against the viewing room glass.

"What do you think, Jack?"

The sergeant dragged his eyes away from the man about to give him aggro when he returned him to his cell and gave Craig a jaundiced look.

"I think you'd better hurry up and let the old hack out."

"He'll be out tomorrow, but he'll still be gagged from writing his article until we've closed the case. The Journal too. Judge Standish issued me a belt and braces order. I don't want them slipping the news out through some loophole."

Jack folded his arms and sat back. "Well then, I'll just house and feed him till you give me the word tomorrow, then I'll kick him to the kerb. I take it you want Wilberforce now? He'll be easier. He was lippy to start off with but now he's crying for his mum."

Liam gave an evil smile. "Just the way I like them."

Craig nodded the sergeant out and took his chair, watching as an obscenity mouthing Ray Mercer was nudged from the interview room and one minute later a burly, sweaty faced man of around thirty was led in. Craig nodded Liam to move and within seconds Jack was back on his side of the glass.

Craig glared at Mark Wilberforce for a moment, until he judged that the man was about to cave, then he turned on the tape machine and sat back in his chair, nodding Liam on.

"Right now, Mister Wilberforce."

It was a step up in politeness from 'Right, you little scrote', Liam's normal affectionate greeting for those he deemed to belong to the criminal class.

"Why did we find your prints on the bottom of a wall bed on the Travis Estate when you live on the Demesne? And before you say you were visiting a friend, or even that you were *in* said bed, obliging some misguided female, let me remind you that we know that apartment to have been untenanted since two thousand and ten. So...?"

Despite the fact Wilberforce had already given them Harrison Craig had expected him to save face by obfuscating for a moment, or at least to defiantly shake his head, but there was none of that. Almost before Liam's mouth had closed the young man leaned in close to the tape and began shouting at a rate of knots.

"It wus a pig who asked me to git the place! Seed he needed a safe house for sum undercover cap working on a drugs bust. Seed they'd been infiltratin' sum gang and-"

Craig waved him down before he burst a blood vessel.

"Who was this pig?"

Much as it pained him to use the word it seemed like the quickest way through.

"Harrison. Slimy bastard." *He'd got that right.* "Had me wurkin' fer him since I wus a kid. Seed he'd slip me fifty if I dun OK."

Liam picked up the questioning. "And Harrison told you it was about drugs?"

Wilberforce nodded. "Seed it'd tuk them months to get intee the gang, an' their agent might huv tee lie low, so he'd need sumwhere."

He? Mark Wilberforce had never met Beatrix Hass!

Liam had an idea.

"When were you expecting them to use the place?"

The snout shrugged. "Dun't know. It's been ready since January. Cud huv been ony time."

*Damn.* Craig wanted to punch the wall, knowing exactly what it meant.

He switched off the tape and signalled Jack to return Wilberforce to his cell. When the snout had gone he turned to Liam, shaking his head.

"You know what this means."

"Harrison was planning well ahead? Maybe he set the flat up in January because he didn't know exactly when they'd take McManus out."

Craig scoffed at him. "He set up a safe-house six months in advance? I don't think so."

Liam's pale eyes widened. "You're saying Harrison wasn't involved in McManus' shooting?"

Craig thought quickly. "OK, let's think this through... What if Harrison really *did* set up the safe house for a drugs undercover agent? And then someone else found out about the place and decided to use it as part of the McManus plot? *They* could have tipped Hass the wink."

Liam was sceptical. "What are the odds Karl Rimmins wouldn't have told us if they'd been working a drugs undercover Op on the Travis?"

"He mightn't have known. Karl's only one of six sergeants on the Drugs Squad, and maybe the operation was kept at inspector level and above."

Liam spotted a massive hole. "OK, then, so why did Harrison then bury the stuff about the sex parties that Tony Moorfield passed to him?"

Craig frowned, wracking his brains. If there *had* been a drugs op going down on the Travis in January and Harrison's setting up of the safe house was legitimate, then *could* someone else have found out about the place? Either through there being another cop involved, or through Harrison opening his big mouth? Harrison being indiscreet wasn't a crime, but Liam was right, none of this explained his burying of the sex-party information two months before, unless... Harrison *had* been leaned on by the same people at Stormont who'd leant on Sean Flanagan. Perhaps Flanagan had even OKed it. Much as he hated to admit it, Terry Harrison might actually be innocent.

He voiced his thoughts reluctantly and to Liam's chagrin they made sense, then the D.C.I. spotted a glimmer of hope.

"If Teflon's at the party tonight then all bets are off, boss. He wouldn't be there unless he was up to his ears in the whole thing. Sex, drugs, intrigue, *and* the assassination plot."

Craig nodded, considerably less hopeful than his deputy. "Agreed. But it's a big if."

\*\*\*\*

**The C.C.U. 1.30 p.m.**

When Davy had answered Craig's query with a grunt the superintendent's assumption that he'd been on to something was right, and when the analyst resisted Nicky's coaxing to come for lunch, preferring to keep working, Ash also knew that something big was about to break.

The junior analyst wasn't what you would call competitive, or not what *he* would anyway, but deep beneath Ash Rahman's colourful haircut and strange taste in clothes lay far more ambition than his quirky image would allow him to admit, and at Davy's undoubtedly impending moment of greatness it started to rear its ugly head. The good thing was that Ash's ambition didn't manifest itself in doing his workmate down or trying to sabotage Davy's work, but by spurring him on to work harder and deny himself lunch as well.

By one-thirty when Craig and Liam reappeared and other well-fed staff members were lounging slug-like at their desks, the analysts' efforts had begun to bear fruit. But before they could bask in their genius in front of an audience Craig's office phone rang and he went to take the call.

"Craig."

Jake McClean's voice came down the line.

"I think I've got something, chief. I'm in Norwich in Norfolk, and I've just interviewed a woman called Zoe Donnat."

"The sex-worker who reappeared?"

"That's her. It's a long story, but she's finally admitted that she was kidnapped and threatened that unless she agreed to run kinky sex parties and invite a specific list of local politicians and businessmen, she would go the same way as her old boss. When she agreed they dumped her alive at an old airfield."

Like Veronica Lewis but substituting a wood.

"Who kidnapped her?"

"They never gave their names but she said they were

from Europe somewhere."

"OK, what exactly did they ask her to do?"

"The same as Lewis. Run parties at different anonymous venues, with drugs and kinks. The parties have been going on for two months, sir, stepping up in frequency in the past few weeks."

Craig considered for a moment. Hartnell was the only English survivor that they knew of, but it was likely that parties had been happening all over the country with the same aim. It was time for the sergeant to come home.

"OK, good work, Jake. Get the next plane back, but first I want you to call D.C.I. Andy White in Drugs on the North Coast and ask him to check something for me. Quietly, please, and let me know what you get."

When he'd finished the call, Craig walked back onto the floor, ordering the post-prandial dippers to wake up.

"OK, Jake's just confirmed a similar party scenario in Norfolk to the one we have here with Lewis and there are likely to be a lot more. Escort agencies across England have been high-jacked to run parties over the past few months, with any workers who didn't cooperate being disappeared or killed."

He scanned the group until his gaze fell on Aidan Hughes. "Speaking of that, what happened when you met with Veronica Lewis, Aidan?"

Hughes smiled. "She's agreed to cooperate, chief. She'll take Kyle along tonight as her body guard."

Liam sniffed. "A puny one."

The spy was unoffended. "Brains not brawn, Liam, that's what the ladies love."

Craig ended the inevitable war of words before it started. "That's enough, you two. Good news, Aidan. Well done."

Hughes shrugged. "She wants this over as much as we do. It was only fear that stopped her telling us before. They threatened to harm her son if she squealed, but I've promised that we'll keep him under watch."

"OK. Good. Put some uniforms on him. Discreetly,

please. Right now-"

He was cut short by Rhonda raising a hand.

"Yes, Rhonda? And everyone, can you stop raising your hands, please. This isn't school."

He nodded the D.C. on.

"Well, it's just one thing, sir. Why did so many of the girls in England refuse?"

"Refuse what?"

"To cooperate. If they were being threatened with death, surely they would just have agreed to run the parties? If they were only as we've been told." She frowned, wrinkling her pale forehead. "It doesn't make sense to me."

By the widening of eyes and the silent 'oh's being formed it appeared that it didn't make sense to many of the team, including Craig. Rhonda was right and he could have kicked himself for missing it. Liam saved him the effort.

"She's right, boss, you totally missed that."

"First prize for stating the obvious, Liam. But well spotted, Rhonda. There's obviously something more unsavoury going on at these parties than Veronica Lewis has chosen to admit."

Aidan shook his head. "Maybe not, chief. It might just apply to the ones on the mainland. Remember we haven't had any dead sex-workers turning up here, just a disappeared Lewis."

Craig thought for a moment and then nodded. "OK, well whatever it is we don't have the time right now to find out. It must be bad for so many women to refuse on pain of death, so my guess is we're looking at children, animals or snuff movies. Andy, ask Jake to liaise with England on that, once tonight's party's over. OK, before we move onto tonight, Liam will update you on our assassin's escape route and how we've handled the press."

As Liam reported Craig sat down beside Annette, whispering. "Anything on Harrison?"

A sharp shake of her head said no.

"So where is he now?"

"Playing golf up in Antrim with his mates. Some accountant and a GP. He spent last night in his apartment with a takeaway." She grimaced. "His life's almost as exciting as mine and Mike's."

Craig smiled. "Minus the new born." He rose again. "Thanks for that. Tonight should see an end to the surveillance, but it's important that we know where Harrison is while the party's on."

"No problem, sir. Amy's babysitting."

"Mike working?"

"No. He's taking Doctor Winter for a drink. He says he's pretty low for some reason."

Craig felt a sharp prick of guilt. He knew that he'd been neglecting John, but he would just have to wait for now. What they had to discuss couldn't be rushed.

He walked back to the whiteboard just as Liam was winding up.

"Thanks, Liam. Right, I'll get onto the logistics of this evening's operation in a moment, but first, Davy and Ash, what do you have for us?"

Instead of Davy speaking first he nodded his friend on. He knew Ash well, and he'd spotted the green-eyed monster rearing its head before lunch. The junior analyst jumped in eagerly.

"I've got lots actually."

OK, so there was eager and then there was showing off.

"The bullets. I've been searching the Interpol and FSB databases-"

Craig interjected. "For searching read hacking."

It earned him a nod.

"OK, so hacking, but I've got something. Not on the pistol but on the KSVK rifle. The same gun was used in a shooting in Minsk in twenty-fourteen and a second killing in Frankfurt last year."

Liam interrupted. "Any name on the shooters?"

"Not definitive, but the FSB report mentions the Diebe im Gesetz. They're a gang that was first founded in Stalin's labour camps with their own laws and a secret language. More recently they're thought to have been recruiting within German prisons. Apparently, the Russian mafia is very active in Germany."

Liam nodded. "Des told us." He turned to Craig. "They could be pool guns, boss."

"What do you think, Ash?"

"I don't know about the pool aspect, but the rest might link in with Germany's growing right-wing."

Craig made a face. "Fascism and communism. What a marriage."

Davy shook his head. "Communism was replaced by capitalism when the Soviet Union fell, chief, and fascism and capitalism have worked together for centuries."

"Fair point. OK, what else, Ash?"

The analyst tapped up a map of the British Isles on Nicky's screen.

"OK, so I was thinking about what else might be happening to increase the Leave vote, if that's what this is all about. The sex parties, blackmailing powerful influencers etcetera will only get them so far, so they would still be playing tight odds, plus I can't find any missing or dead sex-workers anywhere in Scotland or Wales-"

Aidan Hughes cut in. "You're saying the sex parties are confined to England and here?"

"Looks like it."

"What does that tell you about our politicians?"

No-one voiced their thoughts.

"It's on a far larger scale in England, obviously. Jake emailed to say he's got over forty women missing or dead now."

Liam gave a whistle. "I thought there were just fifteen?"

Davy answered him. "Some of the forces mustn't have recorded them centrally yet."

Annette was shocked. "Forty dead sex-workers! That's huge."

Ash shook his head. "That's only some of them. Jake said they haven't finalised the figures for London yet."

Images of women being abducted and killed on streets that he'd walked down for years filled Craig's mind. He shook them away hastily and moved on.

"I can't imagine they've left Scotland and Wales completely untouched."

A glance from Ash said he was right.

"You'd found something?"

"Two somethings." The analyst pointed at the screen. "Check this out."

As the group watched, a series of yellow dots appeared around Dundee and Glasgow, followed by more, until the whole of Scotland, as far up as Shetland, was scattered with them. A moment later a similar rash appeared over Wales.

Liam looked puzzled. "What are-"

He didn't get to finish as Ash clicked on a dot outside Aberdeen and a video file opened on the screen. The team watched as a news reporter reported on an attack at a local army cadet training facility. A second click and there was a clip from the following day where angry locals, acting on the story that the attack had been carried out by Eastern European immigrants, protested outside the immigrants' community club. More clicks across the country and they witnessed damage to a military base, a pipe bomb planted at an RAF club and a second at a war memorial, with angry residents protesting after each attack.

Ash moved his cursor to the dots in Wales, opening newspaper reports of sex attacks by 'Arabic looking men' and men with 'European accents', with similar reactions to Scotland and even a few revenge attacks.

By the end of the demonstration Craig was gawping at the analyst.

"You're saying that someone's been deliberately whipping up anti-immigrant feeling?"

Ash nodded. "It's been effective too. In areas where there *have* been attacks there's been a steady swing in the opinion polls against remaining in the EU, particularly against its Schengen free movement across countries policy. And this is the ordinary people in the street. Combine that shift in attitudes with their elected politicians influencing and you've got real momentum."

Craig shook his head. "Very clever, but what's the cabal's *reason* for wanting out of the EU? I understand that some people in the UK might want it, but why are Germans and the Russia Mafia getting involved?"

When no answers came back he shook his head. "OK, let's park that for now. Understanding the motive for everything isn't our job. We're here to solve Peter McManus' and Billy Regent's murders, and if that exposes a political plot, which right now we can still only speculate exists, then we'll deal with that when it comes. OK, thanks for that, Ash. It's good background."

He went to move on but Ash shook his head.

"One last thing, chief. That voice speaking to Beatrix Hass."

"Yes."

"I'll need to update you after this."

His position as International computing expert well and truly reinforced, Ash threw his line-manager a self-satisfied glance and sat back. He was less than amused when Davy showed zero sign of being put out. Craig knew exactly what Ash had been hoping for and smiled to himself; even if Davy *had* been jealous the Emo was so cool that no-one would ever know.

"Davy, what do you have for us?"

The senior analyst answered by tapping his keyboard and wiping Ash's map off the screen, to replace it with a symbol that only Craig and Liam had seen before. The group stared at the ornate figure four, each member wondering if the other would ask what it was. In the end Aidan Hughes did.

"What's with the squiggle? It looks like medieval stuff."

Davy smiled. "Much older than that. This is an astrological four, also the s...symbol for the Roman god Jupiter, God of Thunder, and his Greek equivalent Zeus. The reason I'm showing it to you is because it was on the bottom of some emails sent to Veronica Lewis' office, which led to an Ottendorf cipher. A book code, which unless you know which book you're using as reference would make no sense."

Craig smirked, knowing that such things drove Liam mad.

"You've cracked it, Davy?"

The analyst smiled.

"Yep. The clue was when I discovered everyone we knew from the clique so far had studied Classics, and I thought that maybe there was some sort of British Isles Classics club. I couldn't find one so I consulted a prof at Queen's who said there was none that he knew of, s...so it's pretty certain our little clique formed by itself. Not to study Classics but for another reason, probably political. The prof also said that the standard textbook for Classics undergraduates is called The Zeus Circle. It seemed like a great name for a clique to me and, with the symbol on the emails referencing Zeus, I wondered if the group had chosen that text for their Ottendorf cipher. Anyway... they had, and here's what I found when I broke the cipher."

With a quick tap, a page of text appeared on the screen, and as Craig scanned it his jaw dropped. The document had been drafted in the nineteen-seventies and marked embargoed until twenty-twenty-three. Its contents referred to years spent planning a strategy for leaving the EU, since long before Margaret Thatcher had been in power. Several groups were referenced, some of whose names he recognised as right-wing British establishment; none of them considered hard-line organisations but with links with others that were. There were supplementary groups that he recognised as well, from what Vala had told him.

When the detective found his voice again his first words were "This is a manifesto." He shook his head in astonishment before elaborating. "A manifesto for getting the UK out of the EU."

Davy nodded. "It looks like they've been planning this for decades. All in preparation for when the referendum they longed for might be called."

Liam was stunned. "But Britain only went into Europe in seventy-three! Are you saying people have been plotting how to get back out for nearly all that time?"

The analyst shrugged. "I've a lot more to decode, but it seems that way. But it also looks like they knew it would be w...wishful thinking unless they gathered allies, which takes us back to where Russia, Germany and who knows where else comes in."

Liam asked a question. "Formal or informal?"

"What?"

"Are there formal links with Russia and Germany, like with their governments, or just informal, e.g. with the mafia and other thugs? Boss?"

It was an excellent question but Craig didn't answer. His head was hurting trying to work everything out. A group of powerbrokers calling themselves The Zeus Circle, who may or may not have had links with Russia and Germany, had been blackmailed and pressuring local politicians, although... some politicians were also undoubtedly *part* of the Circle too. Whoever the members were, they were also attacking the military, inciting racial hatred and exploiting the subsequent bounce-back patriotism all for one end; to get the UK out of the EU? It seemed ludicrously farfetched and yet apparently it was all too true.

But he didn't have time for a sore head, they still had two murders to solve, so he motioned Davy to shut down his screen and used a fifteen-minute break to allow the debate that was raging burn itself out.

As soon as they reconvened Craig acknowledged the work of the analysts, and sketched out the added information Ash had imparted to him during the break; that the man heard conversing with Beatrix Hass from Belfast had also been voice-matched by NSA's linguists to a conversation recorded inside a private club in Whitehall five days before. They had no IDs on the speakers but the location made everyone pay attention. If members of the current British Government were involved, it gave the cabal's plot a completely new slant.

Craig perched on the nearest desk, fatigued by the thought of the night that lay ahead.

"OK. It looks as if we're dealing with a clique or cabal that is essentially a coalition of the willing, and it may well cross borders within and outside Europe, if Russia is involved. Tonight's party is our chance to see some but probably not all of this Zeus Circle in action, and it's imperative that everyone is on the ball." He turned to their resident spy. "Kyle, you'll be playing the main role so I want you with Veronica Lewis right after this briefing. Bring everything that you need and Aidan will drive you to her place."

He turned to look for Andy, who was sitting with his feet up on his desk.

"Good to see you're not stressed, Andy."

It earned him an over-enthusiastic laugh that betrayed everyone was still in shock at what they'd heard.

"OK, you and Jake, when he arrives back later, will be posted outside Joshua Loughrey's place, ready to tail him and Kyle's informant Trevor Rudkin wherever they go, which we *really* hope will be to Emmett Darrian's estate, where Liam and I will already be waiting. We'll have Armed Response backup in place as well, just in case we need them. We'll also have cameras set up along the estate's perimeter, and Liam and I will have cameras and directional mikes. Unfortunately, we can't actually enter the grounds because of the security Darrian has in place. The aerial photographs show that it's substantial."

He turned to Kyle. "That means you'll be on your own in there." His voice grew serious. "The closer you can get to the Circle the better, and you'll have Rudkin and Leonard Montgomery to help point the way, but *don't* take excessive risks. Dead is no use to me. *You understand*?"

He was answered by a shrug that angered him and Craig immediately spat back.

"There are no bloody points for bravado, Inspector! These people are killers and you're no good to me with a bullet between your eyes. Do you understand? Say yes or you're not going."

Kyle grunted a begrudging "OK" that earned him a shove from Liam.

"He asks you to say yes and you can't even give that, you stupid glipe!"

Before someone did something that drew blood, Craig shook his head at his deputy. Unfortunately, he needed Kyle or he would have sent him home then and there, but he knew he could rely on the D.I.'s insubordination continuing long into the future so he'd soon get another chance to kick him into touch.

Craig glanced at the clock. Almost four. "OK, let's call it. Everyone take a couple of hours break and be at your posts for six o'clock on the dot. Glocks and Kevlar, everyone, and no unnecessary risks."

It made Annette sigh. Kevlar was uncomfortable at the best of times, but she was still carrying baby weight. She thought she'd chance a request.

"Rhonda and I won't be at the scene, sir, so couldn't we do without our vests?"

Craig raised an eyebrow. "I admire your optimism, Annette, but you don't know *where* tonight's surveillance will take you, so the answer is definitely no."

He was still torn on whether he wanted Terry Harrison to head for the party or not, but it was good to be prepared.

# Chapter Sixteen

### Eglantine Avenue, South Belfast.

Ken Smith was dragging the last of the items he'd bought from Ikea up to his third-floor walk-up when his mobile began to ring, so he shouldered open his front door hastily, dropped his new duvet in the hall and rummaged for the phone, managing to answer before the call cut out.

"Yes?"

"Hi, Ken."

He was surprised to hear Craig's voice, although why he should be given that the man was almost his brother-in-law, he didn't know. When he checked the phone's screen his surprise gained more conviction; it was the weekend yet Craig was calling from an unknown number which meant that he was phoning from work, and the edginess in his voice said there was something up.

"Hello, Marc. Are you OK?"

Craig turned to gaze out of his office window at the river, smiling at how perceptive the soldier was.

"I'm fine..."

*For now,* went unsaid.

Ken entered his newly carpeted sitting room and perched on the arm of a chair.

"But you're not certain that you will be fine soon, and you wanted me to know, just in case."

When there was no reply he went on.

"And if anything happens to you while you do whatever you're doing later, then I'm to take care of everyone."

It was a short-hand conversation he'd held many times before with members of his regiment, usually before they patrolled some war zone.

A quiet sigh was his only confirmation before Craig changed the subject.

"How does it feel to be a civilian, then?"

It sparked five minutes of chat that to the casual listener would have been about mere pleasantries but to the two men having it was about anything but.

\*\*\*\*

## 6 p.m.

While Annette was sitting in south Belfast, scratching uncomfortably and trying to get comfortable in her car outside Terry Harrison's divorcee's pad, Andy and Jake were twenty miles away in Ballyholme in Bangor, in a state of high alert.

Thirty minutes earlier, a man that they'd IDed as Trevor Rudkin had knocked on the door of Joshua Loughrey's townhouse and disappeared inside. Now a limousine with darkened windows had pulled up, driven by a man whose bulk and ill-concealed handgun said that his passengers wouldn't be heading to the local pub.

Andy slid further down in his seat and motioned Jake to do the same.

"This is it. Any minute now Loughrey and Rudkin will appear and oft we jolly well go."

The last five words were said in an upper-crust English accent that made Jake want to laugh; it sounded nothing like the real ones he'd heard on trips to London and made him wonder why every Irish impersonator chose the aristocracy or cockneys to copy when they mimicked an Englishman.

His speculation was cut short by the predicted appearance of Loughrey and his advisor, and as the driver opened the car doors for them and scanned his surroundings in a very unfriendly way, the detectives held their crouched poses until the man was back in the car and its engine had started up.

Jake reached for his ignition key immediately but Andy shook his head to wait.

"This is a quiet street. If we pull out right after them they'll spot that we're a tail."

The D.S. watched anxiously as the limousine reached the end of the street and turned right.

"We're losing them!"

Andy rolled his eyes. "We're losing nothing. I've a spotter van on the main road and they'll tell us where the car is in two minutes time. Then we'll go."

Jake's eyes widened in panic. "But they could have turned left instead of right!"

"Calm down, would you. I've vans set up both ways."

While the sergeant champed at the bit Andy remained slouched in his seat, until two minutes to the second after the limo had left the radio began to buzz. Andy grabbed it before Jake could.

"Where is he?"

"Donaghadee Road Roundabout just heading onto the B21."

"Thanks." He dropped the handset. "OK, what's keeping you, Jake? Off you go. But stay two cars behind when you spot them, mind, and don't change lane even if they do or they'll make us."

That burst of activity over, the D.C.I. slid down in his seat again and took out his mobile to call Craig.

"Rudkin and Loughrey are in a blacked-out limo, chief. Registration DEZ 17B. One armed guard that we could see, driving, but there might have been others inside the car."

Craig drummed his fingers absentmindedly on his steering wheel as Andy reported, and when the D.C.I. had finished he nodded to himself.

"Where are they now?"

"Just pulling on to the A2. We'll be on them in a minute, especially since Jake's driving my car like a bat out of hell. It looks like the party's definitely at Darrian's place, so we should be with you in around fifteen."

"Good. If anything changes give me a call."

He cut the line and turned to see Liam leaning against the passenger door with his eyes tightly shut.

"I'd better not hear you snoring."

The deputy responded without opening his eyes. "I beg your pardon. I'm meditating."

"On what? Your dinner?"

Liam turned to him in surprise. "How'd you know that? Danni's got me a lovely steak for later."

Craig chuckled, his eyes still fixed on the wrought iron entrance gates of Emmett Darrian's impressive estate.

"I knew because that's all you ever think about. Food."

The D.C.I. shook his head and grinned. "Not true. I think about women as well."

"I can't argue with that one."

Suddenly Craig grabbed for the binoculars, peering through them at the gates.

"Someone's arriving. Make sure the tape's rolling."

They watched as a van that looked as if it should have contained supplies pulled up to the entrance, and then as a suspiciously elegantly clothed arm emerged from the driver's window to press for access.

"Unless the grocers around here wear tuxedoes I think we've just met our first guest."

Liam shrugged. "Could be a waiter."

Craig shook his head. "Listen to that voice."

As the crystal-clear diction of wealth rang through the air requesting entry, Liam was forced to agree. When the gates opened Craig pointed to the video-cam in the D.C.I.'s hands.

"Did you get him?"

"Yep."

Liam turned the screen towards his boss, smirking as he did.

"Recognise that mug?"

Craig's eyes widened. "That's the British Home Secretary, Basil Hartnell!"

"The little weasel himself." Liam's guffaw was so loud that it almost shook the car. "Dirty wee devil. Exactly how high does this stuff go?"

Craig response was to glance at his watch. "Kyle should be inside by now, so hopefully we'll soon find out. The party's definitely here, so stand the Gardaí down. At least someone will have a relaxing Saturday night."

While his two bosses were stuck in a cramped car Kyle Spence's experience of the evening was proving far more luxurious, the only drawback being that as Veronica Lewis' designated bodyguard he couldn't help himself to a drink. And there was a lot of it, from the champagne that had greeted them on the removal of their blindfolds through to the assortment of aperitifs and spirits being carried on trays by passing girls. Alcohol wasn't the only thing that the girls were carrying; their assortment of tablets, powders and spliffs saying that Emmett Darrian had planned a high old night.

The ex-Intelligence Officer watched as the madam fluttered protectively around her girls, wondering why Lewis did what she did. He could understand when she was younger and had needed to survive, but she had a legitimate fashion business now and could easily leave all this behind. He was running absentmindedly through possible reasons ranging from greed to feeling trapped, when the man that Liam and Craig had spotted entering just seconds earlier walked past him into an oak-doored room. Kyle recognised the Home Secretary in a heartbeat and it brought him sharply to alert. Men like that didn't arrive at parties until they absolutely had to, so something was about to kick off.

He knew that he'd been right when seconds later Joshua Loughry and Trevor Rudkin strolled through the front door. When they entered the same room, followed by several men whose faces appeared on the TV news each week, Kyle's finger itched for his gun. The corruption had penetrated the top levels of politics, celebrity and business! Could all these men *really* be so anti-Europe that they would collude in murder to get the UK out?

The D.I. shook his head; he wasn't there to judge them, that was the job of the courts. He was there to get the photographs and recordings that would throw the lot in jail, and to do that he had to access where the group was meeting. He was just withdrawing to the veranda to check the floorplan he'd brought with him when Leonard Montgomery sidled up.

"Don't bother with that room. It's not the one."

Kyle led the MLA further away from the house, reaching the veranda's stone balustrade before he turned around.

"The one with the oak door? But I saw Basil Hartnell go in there." His eyes narrowed. "You're not trying to tell me he's not involved."

Montgomery shook his head. "He's up to his eyes in it, but they're not meeting yet. That room's just a gathering place for the VIPs. The real stuff goes down once the party's in full swing." He turned to leave. "Trust me. I'll give you the nod."

Kyle grabbed the politician's arm, hissing at him. "I wouldn't trust you as far as I could spit, Montgomery!"

A flash of arrogance lit the official's eyes

"I don't give a damn if you trust me, but you should at least trust your own man, Rudkin. He's going to tell us where they'll be. When the rest of the guests are too drunk or stoned or busy to notice, *that's* when your little group will slip away." Montgomery ripped his arm free. "Believe me or don't believe me, I really don't care, but nothing will happen for at least three hours."

It proved an accurate prediction. At six-thirty Craig and Liam had been joined by Andy and Jake, dispatched to another vantage point at the back of the estate, and by nine-thirty even Bill McEwan had grudgingly contacted them to find out what was happening. Not a signal that he'd forgiven them for pointing out his men had missed Beatrix Hass' hiding place but a sign that even a man with a capacity for silence such as his could eventually be worn down.

Meanwhile, Kyle had spent almost four hours resisting alcohol and trying to look like he was protecting the escorts, who by and large seemed to be more in control than their male guests.

Finally, at ten-thirty Trevor Rudkin appeared by his side.

"Loughrey's sloped off."

Kyle dropped his glare at a minor celebrity who was shoving Bolivian marching powder up his oversized nose and turned to face the civil servant.

"Where to and when?"

Rudkin answered him glassy-eyed, and Kyle had a fleeting thought that perhaps he should tell the informant to wipe his face. He thought better of it. It would serve the little bastard right if his upper lip was snow covered when Armed Response kicked down the door.

"Just now, to a different room upstairs. I don't know where."

Kyle was off on 'upstairs', slaloming through bodies in various stages of undress until he'd reached the bottom of the mansion's elegant staircase, where a remarkably sober looking Leonard Montgomery was standing what appeared to be guard.

"I'm going up there, Montgomery. Don't try to stop me."

"Wouldn't dream of it. I volunteered to guard the stairs just for this reason."

The MLA gave him access with a sweep of his hand, adding "Corridor on the right, the fourth room down" before he sauntered away.

When Kyle was halfway up the stairs he turned back, just in time to see the MLA lift his first drink of the evening. What he didn't notice was a late-comer to the gathering, a silver-haired man who'd been approaching the stairs when he'd spotted Kyle, sussed exactly what he was and slipped out into the summer night via a side door. A call five minutes later to Beatrix Hass told her that they'd been blown and it was time to run.

Kyle took the final three stairs up to the landing in one stride and found himself standing in a wide space, empty apart from some plants and a chaise longue, with a corridor running off either side. He swerved quickly into the right hand one, following Montgomery's instructions, and then slipped off his shoes and padded quietly the rest of the way, coming to a halt outside the fourth door and placing his ear gently against the wood. The voices he heard were unmistakable; all male, all cultured, but all speaking in a language he didn't recognise.

Logic said that it was probably Latin or Greek of some period, but any speech at all was his signal to record. He placed one cufflink against the door and held it there for what seemed like a life sentence, glancing over his shoulder at intervals for guards and praying that no-one opened the door and made him fall in. The spy's heart was thudding in his chest and sweat was trickling down his back, but he felt exhilarated; alive in a way that he hadn't done for months.

He just hoped that the recording would provide enough evidence for court, but either way, between the teams outside filming and what he'd captured with his links, they could prove that representatives of every parliament in the British Isles were in a house where drugs were being dealt. That scandal alone should stop their referendum plot in its tracks.

When he thought that he had enough conversation recorded, Kyle turned back the way he came, making it safely down the staircase and onto the veranda before a now alcohol-mellowed Leonard Montgomery reappeared. He went to say something but Kyle shushed him into silence, quickly retrieving the phone and Glock McEwan's man had planted in the flower-bed the night before. The mobile only held one number and when the D.I. dialled it he was answered instantly by Craig.

"What have you got?"

Kyle dropped his voice to a whisper.

"They're in a room upstairs. I can take you to it. I recorded a bit of what they're saying, but I think they're speaking ancient Greek."

Montgomery's eyes widened and he flopped down on a step, shaking his head. This was all beyond him. All he'd ever wanted was a good time to obviate the boredom of his marital bed.

Craig was nodding at the other end. "Makes sense. OK, good work." He meant it. "Now, walk out the front door as if you need some air. Take Montgomery and Rudkin with you if you can, but get out now."

Spence didn't need to be told twice. He motioned the MLA to haul ass, but Trevor Rudkin was nowhere to be seen and he couldn't afford the time to go looking for him. The civil servant would have to look after himself, snow nose and all.

Craig lifted his radio and made the call, and in a coordinated attack that saw the front, rear and both borders of the estate either abseiled over or crawled through in silence, within five minutes there were uniformed and plain clothes police officers swarming wordlessly all over Emmett Darrian's grounds.

Craig left Andy and McEwan to clear the house, while he and Liam were led by Kyle up the carpeted stairs to the first floor. When they reached the indicated door, Craig drew his gun and nodded the ex-spook to step back, then he and Liam kicked hard in unison, breaking the door's lock and shattering the wood. They dropped to their knees and covered both sides of the high-ceilinged room, scanning the hands and faces of its stunned occupants, and identifying the likelihood of two guns that weren't theirs.

"POLICE! THROW DOWN YOUR WEAPONS."

Ignoring the warning saw Emmet Darrian receive a shoulder shot. The second shooter dropped his handgun on the floor hastily and kicked it across to Craig.

"Liam, cuff Darrian."

Craig did the same to the second man. When they were both anchored to chairs, Craig took his time surveying the scene, ignoring the now very vocal objections of the remaining guests. Liam found the noise harder to ignore and resorted to a deafening "SHUT UP!" that had the desired effect.

Kyle meanwhile was struggling to hide his shock; the group was a who's who of Northern Irish society, with a sprinkling from the Republic, London and further afield.

Craig wondered if the man who'd phoned Beatrix Hass was amongst them, but time would soon tell. He stood in the centre of the room, smiling.

"The Zeus Circle, I presume."

The mixture of widened eyes and stunned expressions was as loud a yes as he required. He could see the men's, and they were all men, minds racing with questions, top of the list 'how the hell did they find out?' Craig answered even though it hadn't been asked out loud.

"We have very clever people working for us, gentlemen, as you'll find out in the coming weeks."

Just then a uniformed sergeant entered, looking very pleased with himself.

"All secure downstairs, sir. We've nicked quite a few on drug possession and the CSIs are on their way. I only wish I could un-see some of the anatomy on display down there." It earned him a dirty laugh from Liam as he continued. "I've vans coming for that lot. Thought I'd send them to the nearest station, Bangor, to be processed and released, if that's OK? What do you want me to do with this bunch?"

His thumb jerking towards the Classics group indicated just how far the mighty could fall and made Craig laugh. The gesture had said it better than he ever could.

"Call an ambulance for our host, please, Sergeant. He's

to be kept under guard the whole time. And ask D.C.I. Angel to come up here, please."

Between them the detectives split the circle's members between High Street and Stranmillis and after three hours of booking and arguing with expensive briefs everyone was held.

It was one a.m. when Craig suddenly realised that Annette and Rhonda were still outside Terry Harrison's flat.

"Oh, God! I'm a dead man! I left Annette still watching Harrison and he hasn't moved all night."

Liam was unsympathetic. "You think you're in trouble? Danni was cooking me a flipping steak!"

\*\*\*\*

## Demmin, North Germany.

The two officers had been watching the house for hours, feeling useless. They could see the lamp shining in the ground-floor front room, so they knew that their target was there. Beatrix Hass had made no attempt to hide the fact, parading past the window several times in the previous hour, once even standing right in front of it as if she was looking out into the night.

They'd thought it was defiance, knowing that she was a quarry but certain that she couldn't be touched. One had even speculated that she could see them, crouched down in their cold surveillance car, with nothing to heat them but the dying steam from their vacuum flasks.

But that was nonsense; there were no overhead lights in the small side-street and she was too far away to see. It was only after midnight when the light should have moved to the woman's bedroom and closed curtains signalled that she was settling down to sleep, that Beatrix Hass' blank-eyed gazing at the street suddenly began to make sense.

The low, black car that passed them only inches away had windows that hid the faces inside, so when a man emerged and tapped the front door of the house, smiling towards the window where Hass was standing, the surveillance officers' shock at the car's appearance was compounded by astonishment at who they were staring at. Gleb Solokov, the right hand of the Eugenov Mafia. Rarely seen outside Berlin, they hadn't believed the rumour that he was Beatrix Hass' lover, but now here he was.

The younger officer whispered nervously.

"What do we do, Lukas? He's got a gun. I saw the bulge. And you can bet that his driver is armed as well."

His companion nodded curtly, his mind racing as he made his choice. He was the senior officer and it was his choice now whether they lived or died. After only a second spent considering he answered by sliding well down in his seat.

"We watch for now, and later we have them tailed to see where they go."

He said 'they' because the one thing he was sure of as the upstairs light came on and the curtains were quickly drawn, was that after Solokov and Hass had had their sordid reunion, they would be leaving together in the sleek, black car.

\*\*\*\*

## The C.C.U. 2 a.m.

"Aw shit."

Andy Angel rubbed his eyes hard and peered at the camera again, his hope that the action might somehow have eradicated the image in front of him dying in his chest. There was no two ways about it, the chief wasn't going to be a happy boy. The D.C.I. glanced at his watch, wondering if Craig would be unhappier if he found out about the photograph now or tomorrow morning. He plumped for tomorrow; if the chief knew tonight he could at least begin the pursuit.

It meant rousing other people who sensibly would have been in their beds for hours, so Andy nodded Jake to start the round of calls and prepared to summon Craig himself. Thirty minutes later the analysts had joined them in the squad-room, and a yawning Davy was already hard at work when Craig appeared.

"OK, Andy, what's the bad news?"

It was a sensible conclusion; no-one in their right mind would insist their boss returned to work at two a.m. just to shout 'surprise'.

The D.C.I. reached for the digital camera on Davy's desk. "You finished with this, Davy?"

On the analyst's nod he passed it to Craig, who had a bed head that would have made Ash proud. If Ash had been awake enough to notice that was; at that moment the junior analyst was drooling on his desk. When Jake went to waken him Davy shook his head.

"Wait till I have a clear enough image for him to search. It'll be another ten minutes at least."

Craig said nothing. He was too busy squinting at the camera though exhaustion reddened eyes. Andy filled the silence nervously.

"We had men all over the perimeter, chief, but it was four miles around, and some of the estate backed on to a wood, so-"

Craig cut him off without looking up.

"This man escaped."

It wasn't a question but Andy answered anyway.

"Yes. I'm sorry, boss."

Craig still didn't look at him.

"Who was watching that stretch of the perimeter?"

His tone said that he already knew, making Andy's immediate instinct to protect another officer redundant. Even so, the D.C.I. answered reluctantly.

"Three of... Commander McEwan's men. They'd offered to help guard the south side."

Craig did look up this time, accompanying the movement with a roll of his eyes.

"It would seem that our Commander has a problem with basic search and surveillance tactics. They missed Beatrix Hass at the Travis and now they've missed this man."

Just then Davy pressed save and nodded Jake to wake up Ash. The analyst's Mohican hadn't survived his desk and his head popped up with a horizontal wedge of hair jutting out.

"What?" He gazed around him, alarmed. "Why am I at

work? What time is it?"

Jake handed him a hanky. "Time you wiped your mouth and got back to business. Davy's got something for you."

As the image started to process Craig beckoned the two detectives across.

"OK, whoever this guy is he wanted out of there fast. That *could* mean he was just a local trying to save his reputation, or it could mean something else. Jake, work with Davy to get this image to ports and airports. He has a head start, but we might be lucky. Andy, bring the camera. You and I are going to pay a call."

He turned towards the exit and then turned back, remembering something.

"Anything at all on him, call me. I might have more information for you in an hour's time."

It seemed that no-one was sleeping after the raid. When the two detectives reached Veronica Lewis' apartment they found her wide awake and cleaning up.

"Makes me feel better having a tidy place." She stripped off her rubber gloves and headed for the kitchen. "Tea or coffee?"

It was a very different attitude to when Craig had met her in Tobermore and he said as much.

"Why so cooperative now, Mrs Lewis?"

She waved them to a low sofa and brought in a tray.

"Because you kept your word. None of my girls were arrested and you took all that lot in. I hope you throw away the key on the bunch of them! Bloody parties. All that drugs and kinky stuff was no good. It was never what I wanted."

She poured out the drinks and took a seat. "They forced me into it, you know. I used to run my own parties, just on a small scale and no drugs or kinks, then one evening one of my regulars, an MLA, and no, I won't give you his name, asked if he could bring a visiting friend."

The madam shuddered so hard that she almost spilt her tea.

"Nasty bastard, I knew it right from the off. But once he heard about my clientele he forced me to keep running the parties and made them even bigger, then he added all that sordid stuff." She took a sip of tea. "I refused to run them any more, but, well, you saw what happened to me when I tried that." She glanced meaningfully at her still bruised wrists. "So-."

Craig interrupted the speech, the instinct that had brought him there practically shouting at him now.

"Can you describe this man, please, Mrs Lewis."

The request seemed to frighten her. "Didn't you arrest him?"

"So he was definitely at tonight's party?"

Her eyes widened at what the question meant. *"Yes, he was there!* You mean you didn't catch him? He could still come for me?" She jumped to her feet and started to pace. "He'll kill me if he knows I helped you!"

Craig spotted her impending meltdown and rose as well, gripping her shoulders firmly to calm her down.

"Show her the photo, Andy."

As the D.C.I. obliged Veronica Lewis gasped and tried to pull away.

"Is that the man, Mrs Lewis?"

As she struggled Craig could feel her fear in every tightened sinew. His voice grew more insistent.

*"Is it him?"*

Her answer emerged as a shout. "YES! Yes, that's him. Oh God help me, he'll kill me! He'll kill Rupert! He said he would."

Craig drew her down beside him on the sofa. "He won't kill you, I promise. In fact, it's probable that he's on his way out of the country already."

The madam wasn't appeased. "You don't understand! He'll come back. That's what he does. He comes in and out of Ireland all the time."

Craig seized on the information. "From where?"

She shook her head. "I don't know. Europe somewhere. He had an accent."

He doubted it was from the west.

"And he'll come back again. He always does!"

Andy tried to calm her. "He has no reason to return to Northern Ireland again. We believe that whatever he was tasked to do is almost over."

She turned to Craig for confirmation, his nod making her

relax but only for a second.

"Do you know his name, Mrs Lewis?"

She was staring straight ahead now, and Craig watched as her thoughts raced across her face, all of them fearful. Eventually the madam answered in a small voice.

"He said I was to call him Colonel."

Craig was puzzled. "Colonel? Colonel of what?"

She shook her head, and as Craig watched exhaustion suddenly etched every year of her half-century on her face. He signalled to Andy that they were leaving, reassuring the madam before they did.

"I'll post officers outside your door for a few days, until we catch him, and we have officers watching your son as well."

Her mouth opened to object but Craig shook his head.

"At a distance. He doesn't know they're there, and he'll never know how you earn your money, I promise. As soon as we know where this Colonel's gone, I'll make sure that you're informed." He smiled kindly at her and opened the front door. "Get some sleep, Mrs Lewis. You're safe."

By six a.m. Craig knew exactly how safe Veronica Lewis was. There'd been no point trying to get back to sleep, and he couldn't have done anyway, not while his men were still at work, so when his phone rang in the staff canteen where he'd been sitting bantering with a bunch of undercover drugs officers, he knew it had to be coming from the squad-room and immediately raced the three floors up.

"What have you got for me, Davy?"

The analyst shook his head to say that it wasn't good news. "He got away, chief. Facial recognition has him at Dublin airport an hour ago, boarding a flight to Germany. Frankfurt."

East Germany. It was exactly where Craig had expected him to run to, that or Russia.

"Under what name?"

"George Harrison. Must be a Beatles' fan."

It could have been worse. While their fugitive was still in Europe there was hope that they might retrieve him. Ash piped up, interrupting the detective's thoughts.

"I'm running him through Europol and Interpol

databases, chief."

"Good. What passport did he fly on, by the way?"

"British. But maybe it was a fake?"

Or maybe not. The presence of people like Basil Hartnell at the party said that accessing any passport for one of their associates would probably be an easy task.

"OK, leave those running, Ash, please, and just do one more thing for me then you can all go home. We'll be briefing tomorrow but not until two."

Ash poised his hands above the keyboard. "Fire ahead, chief."

"Send that picture to Vala Raske at BPOL."

\*\*\*\*

## Berlin, Germany. 7.a.m. Local Time.

Vala Raske wasn't woken by the beep of her smart-phone because she was already seated at her desk, staring in despair at an image that had been sent to her two hours before, that of a limousine's rear number plate as it disappeared onto a ferry at Wolgast on the Baltic Sea. Her men had tailed Beatrix Hass and her lover to the port and then had to watch impotently as the mafia man and his moll had waved them a two-fingered goodbye. Next stop Baltiysk in Kaliningrad, the Russian province between Poland and Lithuania, courtesy of her boss making her back off.

The chief inspector didn't know which she was more depressed by, losing the bastards or having to tell Craig that his assassin was out of reach, so when she opened the message that Ash had sent part of her wanted to cheer that she might still be able to help. The other part of her was in shock.

The silver haired man staring back from her screen was dead, or at least everyone had believed so. Oberst (Colonel) Maximilian Weber, a notorious Stasi Officer, tried in nineteen-ninety for crimes against the German people and sentenced to ten years, suspended by the Bundesgerichtshof (the German Federal Constitutional Court) who had overturned the convictions on the basis that the Stasi was acting on behalf of a sovereign power at the time of its offences. Weber's particular talent had been Zersetzung, the State's infamous decomposition technique; the process of psychological harassment and terrorising people, while barely even raising your voice.

However, the Stasi's men hadn't got off scot-free; negative public perception of them in unified Germany meant that some of them had suffered badly, although not half as much as their victims had. Many others had simply disappeared or died of old age, and Weber had been thought one of them.

The Ministry for State Security or the State Security Service, commonly known as the Stasi, had been based not far from where she now sat. The official state security service of the German Democratic Republic, the old East Germany, the Stasi had been one of the most effective and repressive intelligence and secret police agencies to ever exist. Its motto had been '*Schild und Schwert der Partei*', Shield and Sword of the Party, referring to the then ruling Socialist Unity Party of Germany or the SED.

They were events rarely discussed now, things that had happened decades before when she was in her teens, but that was no excuse for her naiveté. The experienced police officer slumped back in her seat, shaking her head in disgust. How could she *ever* have believed the SED would have allowed its top men to be put out to pasture? After all, many senior Nazis had remained in the country, unprosecuted and working in plain sight, so why not the Stasi five decades on? She wondered exactly where Weber had been all the intervening years. The KGB and Stasi had worked closely together and it would have been an easy trip for him across the border to communist Russia. But more than that Vala wondered what he had been doing in Belfast.

She lifted the phone to call Craig and then suddenly remembered the time. Better to let him sleep and call him tomorrow, hopefully when she had something more useful to say. Meanwhile she would post her loyal men at Frankfurt airport, despite her seniors' instructions to stand down. Maybe she couldn't lock Weber up herself, but she could ensure that Craig got his chance.

# Chapter Seventeen

**Whitehall. Sunday morning.**

"Damned incompetence! One week to go and the group gets exposed!" The elderly man shook his jowls. "Idiots all of them! Worse than idiots, if I could think of the right word!"

The silver fox was unperturbed, more engrossed by the spectacle of the normally controlled mandarin becoming emotional than by the arrests of dispensable men. He swallowed his mouthful of whisky smoothly and set the crystal tumbler down by his side.

"Why are you so worried? It wasn't the inner core, just a regional branch. Everything is as it has always been. Nothing will divert us from our path."

His host stared at him, angrily at first at being disagreed with and then with a grudging smile. Perhaps there was more to the foreigner than he'd first thought. He knew how to hold his nerve at least. After a moment saying nothing he nodded.

"They mustn't be allowed to talk."

The subtext was clear. He wanted the Zeus Circle's incarcerated members taken out. Even though The Fox had half-expected it, the politician's ruthless ability to kill men that he'd worked with for years still took him aback. He shook his head.

"Too risky, and it's unnecessary to kill all of them. One will be enough to scare the others into silence."

"Darrian?"

"No. Already injured. They would just assume that his death was linked with that. Someone with a higher profile would work better. I already have someone in mind."

The Whitehall mandarin smiled maliciously, knowing exactly who he meant.

"Do it quickly, and make it painful. That bastard climbed over my nephew on his way up."

He would do it, and then he would get the hell out of the UK, before the remainder of the group decided to do the same to him.

\*\*\*\*

## Ken Smith's Apartment. Eglantine Avenue. 10 a.m.

Relief was the ex-soldier's first thought when he heard Craig's greeting over his intercom, his second was chagrin that he'd missed out on what had obviously been an exciting operation the night before. His third thought was how quickly he could brew some coffee to accompany Craig's freshly baked croissants.

When two each had been devoured he finally asked why the detective was there. The question made Craig smile.

"Can't I just drop by with some housewarming croissants?"

"You can, but you really didn't. So, what is it that you need?"

Craig pondered how to put his request for a moment and then decided to defer it with some thanks.

"Thanks for understanding why I called you last night, but don't tell my folks or Lucia. They don't need reminding that my job is dangerous."

"OK. So?"

The lack of frills made Craig chuckle. "You get straight to the point, don't you? OK, but this can't go beyond this room. You're not in the force yet, and you're not on my squad even if you were."

"I understand. Shoot."

In the next few minutes Craig outlined everything that they knew about McManus' and Regent's deaths, Beatrix Hass their assassin, The Zeus Circle and the previous evening's raid.

Ken puffed out his cheeks, astounded.

"Bloody hell! You really think they're trying to influence the referendum vote?"

"Convinced of it. We haven't got them all, not even the ones working here, but there's nothing I can do about that right now. Our primary job is to solve two murders, and I know for a fact that the two people responsible have got away. Beatrix Hass is in Germany being watched by a friend of mine, and the man she was recorded talking to wasn't amongst the men we lifted last night."

Ash had stayed at work doing voice matches on the prisoners, without him even having to ask.

"So how can I help?"

Craig swallowed hard, knowing that he could trust Ken but still never one hundred percent sure that he could trust anyone. He decided to take a punt anyway.

"One of the men we lifted last night was Basil Hartnell."

Ken's jaw dropped. "Home Secretary Basil Hartnell?"

"Yep. Look...I'd like you to use your contacts through the MoD to find out what you can about him. You know how Whitehall gossips."

From his experience of working in London the place was worse than a knitting circle for passing rumours on.

Ken found his voice again. "But can't Ash find-"

Craig's headshake was emphatic. "He can only find what's in the official files and I want the dirt. The real stuff that never gets written down. Who has Hartnell pissed off? Who wants him out, who wants him in? Who's he sleeping with? You know the kind of thing."

Ken shrugged. "I can probably get it, but will it really help you?"

"God only knows, but the smallest thing could be something right now. If it's any comfort I've other people doing the same for the TDs, MLAs and business people we lifted, but as Hartnell was the only English Minister there I thought of you."

Ken slid off his stool, walking to the window to gaze out at the street. It was a sunny day and he could see dog walkers in the distance. His desire to be one of them added to his vagueness as he spoke.

"I'm not high up the food chain, Marc. It's not like I can ring the Chief of the Defence Staff and shoot the breeze."

Craig stood up. "Trust me, I'll take any leverage I can get right now. We have two dead men, a Machiavellian group that's lawyering up with people whose headed paper I couldn't afford, and a killer who's miles away." He opened the front door. "Just do what you can and let me know."

The detective's exit was interrupted by his mobile ringing.

"Yes? Liam? Where are you?"

"High Street, and you'd better get down here 'cos Jack's chucking his toys out of the pram."

Craig waved goodbye hastily and made for his car. Fifteen minutes later he saw exactly what Liam had meant. Jack Harris was storming red-faced around the station's reception, muttering to himself. When Craig appeared, he pointed towards the staff room and shooed both the murder detectives in. No sooner had the door closed than the sergeant turned on them.

"A journalist, a thug, and now a dozen of the so-called great and good, all baying for my blood and threatening me with law suits!" He took out a hankie and wiped his forehead. "It's a Sunday morning, for God's sake! Quiet, sleepy Sunday. A day of rest, or it was till you two started!"

Craig sat down, hoping that the others would follow. Like all the best body language it worked. First Liam and then Jack took a chair, still wiping and muttering to himself. Craig leaned forward, speaking in a soothing voice.

"OK. So... Let's bail Wilberforce and brief Reggie to keep an eye on him on the Demesne. Mercer will have to stay, I'm afraid-"

Jack went to object but Craig waved him down.

"The whole thing will hit the evening edition if he's released, Jack, and *whatever* you do don't let him see who's in the other cells. He'll start writing profiles on them."

He sat back slightly before speaking again. "However..."

The sergeant's face lit with hope.

"How many of the others have lawyers?"

Jack prefaced his answer with a sigh. "All of them except one. That bloke Hartnell. Some posh solicitor from London's coming specially this afternoon."

It made sense.

"And what are the other briefs requesting?"

"Bail or released on their own recognisance."

Liam shook his head.

"R.O.R.? Not a chance! With that bunch's resources, they'd skip the country and we'd never see them again."

Craig nodded. "I have to agree with Liam. Charge them, get them arraigned and then tagged on bail. House arrest preferably, and their passports need to be seized. Liam, post some uniforms outside their houses."

Jack narrowed his eyes, puzzled. "With all due respect, sir. Charge them with what? Sitting around at an orgy talking Greek?"

Liam scoffed. "Have you *seen* the drugs haul from that party, Jack? Charge them all with possession and intent to supply until we can suss out who did what."

Craig nodded. "I want Loughrey and Burke held on conspiracy to murder as well. Kyle's informant, Trevor Rudkin, can confirm they were in on McManus' murder plot. But I want him charged with the others to keep his cover intact."

Jack was almost appeased. "I'll get Loughrey and Burke held on remand at Maghaberry, but that'll still leave Mercer and Hartnell here." After a moment's consideration he sniffed, conceding that it was an improvement. "OK, I suppose I can live with that."

"Just keep them apart while you're sorting things, please. We're off to Stranmillis to check on the others, but I warn you, Jack, I'm inclined to bring any of their remnants that can't be bailed down here, just so we've got them all in one place."

At that point, the sergeant's muttering turned rude.

On the way to Stranmillis Liam asked the question that Craig had been hoping to avoid.

"What's next, boss? We can't get past their lawyers to get information from any of them, so the chances of anyone *admitting* there's a plot to highjack the referendum are zilch."

Craig gave a non-committal grunt that failed to silence his deputy. Liam had always been talented at talking to himself.

"And even if they *did* admit they'd been exerting influence, how could we stop it? At the end of the day, if the actual referendum vote is handled properly and double-checked, and we can easily tip them off to do that, then it's not a crime to influence the way people think. If it was then every TV advertiser would be in jail!"

This time Craig did have words. "They've attacked army

bases, incited hatred-"

Liam cut in. "And whoever did that on the ground should, *will* be arrested and charged, but proving a direct link from this bunch to street-level thuggery is a hell of a stretch, boss. Even if we could do it, it would take months, so back to my original question...in the cases of our two murders, what's the next step?"

Craig turned left off the Malone Road into Chlorine Gardens and parked up behind Stranmillis Station before he replied.

"Did anyone ever tell you you're a pain in the ass, Liam?"

"My lovely wife, every single day. But you still know that I'm right."

Craig climbed out of the car, talking as he walked. "That's what makes you one. You *are* right, but the only answer I can come up with is one you're not going to like."

He pushed at the station's heavy rear door and entered, looking for Jack's equivalent John Maguire and going through the same plan with him. By the time they'd finished and were drinking tea in the staff room, all but two prisoners had been sent for arraignment and those two were being ferried down to Jack.

Craig couldn't avoid Liam's question any longer.

"OK. The next step is that I'm going to Germany to get Beatrix Hass."

Liam shook his head instantly. "Not on your own, you're not! You get yourself shot at here often enough, so God knows what you'd manage over there."

Craig smiled. "I was hoping that you'd say that. Glad to have you along."

Liam sighed, that evening's Sunday roast becoming a lost hope.

"So when are we leaving?"

"Not for a few days."

The roast was back again.

"I want to know more about our mystery man, and see what we can get from the others, if anything. Plus, Davy's still working on that code."

He stood up, a sudden light-headedness making realise how tired he was.

"Get some rest for a few hours and we'll regroup at two. If we're lucky we might learn something useful over the next couple of days."

\*\*\*\*

## Annadale Embankment, Belfast. 1.30 p.m.

John Winter was just settling into his Sunday post-lunch snooze when he thought that he heard a knock on the front door. It was faint and only once so he wondered whether he might have imagined it, and after a moment of dozy listening that included no repetition of the sound he turned his face into the sofa and began to fall back to sleep, only to be woken again seconds later much more abruptly, by a hammering on the living room windows and a shout of, "JOHN, GET UP."

The pathologist sat bolt upright and rubbed his eyes, convinced that the sight of Craig's girlfriend pressing her face against his French Doors was some sort of anxiety-generated hallucination. He was so worried about Natalie that he was imagining seeing her best friend now! It took several thumps of Katy's small fist against the glass to make him concede that she was really there, and he opened the doors hurriedly, adding "I thought you were a dream."

"At least you didn't say nightmare."

Which is what he was likely to be thinking in around five minutes time.

Katy glanced glumly towards an armchair and the pathologist nodded her to sit, suddenly remembering his manners and rushing into the kitchen to make tea, leaving her alone with her thoughts.

She knew Natalie was going to kill her for coming; that was if she ever spoke to her again. She'd spent the two days since the fiasco at the geneticist's office trying to persuade her friend to return there, only to be told in varying shades of language to 'bugger off and stay out of my affairs'.

But the problem was, it wasn't just Natalie's affair, anything that she did would affect John as well, just as her moodiness had been doing already. She really liked the pathologist and he was Craig's friend, so she couldn't just stand by and do nothing, especially as a simple test could tell Natalie whether she had anything to worry about or not.

While Katy was busy torturing herself, John was spending the time while the kettle boiled wondering why she was there, but nothing could have prepared him for what he saw when he returned with the tea tray.

Katy's glumness had been replaced by a tearful nervousness, and instead of sitting sedately like a guest she was now pacing a hole in his rug, gesticulating wildly and muttering to herself.

When the pathologist eventually persuaded her to sit down and explain why she'd come, the previous few weeks of his life finally started to make sense.

\*\*\*\*

It didn't take that long for Craig to learn something, although useful wasn't the word that he would have used. Vala Raske had got as far as she could through research so it was time to tell him what she knew.

She disturbed the detective as he was lying with one arm dangling over the edge of his sofa and a cushion on top of his face, mid-doze.

"Sorry, did I disturb you, Marc?"

"Don't worry, I was just napping. It was a long night." Craig sat up quickly, ignoring the loud buzzing in his head. "I take it you got the photo we sent?"

"I did, and I couldn't believe my eyes. He's an ex-Stasi officer called Oberst, Colonel, Maximilian Weber who was sentenced to ten years when the Stasi collapsed in nineteen-ninety, until he was freed by the courts. He disappeared after that."

They'd found Veronica Lewis' Colonel, and he was German, just like Beatrix Hass. But the Stasi... Things were either about to get more confusing or just starting to make sense. Craig decided not to dig into the man's background, preferring to see him in custody first.

"You spotted him at Frankfurt?"

The chief inspector made a face. She'd really wanted to

give Craig some good news before she told him about Beatrix Hass, but it wasn't to be.

"Sorry, no sign of him. Weber didn't get off that plane or any other plane from the UK or Ireland this morning."

Craig sprang to his feet. "That's impossible! Facial software puts him boarding the Frankfurt plane at five-fifteen, under the name of George Harrison."

She would have laughed if it hadn't been so serious.

"Sorry, Marc. He gave you the slip somehow. I would get your analysts to go back over the tapes. I've no doubt that Weber travelled somewhere this morning but it wasn't to Germany."

They'd lost him. Craig palmed his face, his mind racing when suddenly the NSA's taped call from Whitehall started to make sense. Maximilian Weber had gone to London, not Germany! The cabal and its plot wasn't dead yet.

Vala was still speaking.

"My guess is Weber will come home eventually. Where else can he go? Russia maybe, but East Germany is the natural habitat for these old communists. I'll keep an eye on all our access points and let you know."

Davy and Ash would be doing it as well.

"Thanks, Vala. I know you were told to back off, but have you heard anything more on Beatrix Hass?"

The pause before she answered told Craig it was more bad news, so he wasn't surprised when she outlined Hass' escape.

"Sorry again, Marc."

"It's not your fault, Vala. You've gone above and beyond, especially after being told to back off. We were always unlikely to get Hass with her connection to Solokov, and risking your men against the mafia makes no sense at all."

She swallowed hard, wondering whether there was any point passing on the next piece of information. She decided to do it anyway.

"You know I was warned off Hass."

"By your boss."

"It came down through her, but the way she said it made me think it was official."

Craig guessed what was coming next. The crime-fighting

partnership across Europe was fine in theory, but on the ground it was money that dictated what got done in each country, or not. He aired his thoughts, expecting a grudging acceptance of the budgetary realities, but Vala Raske had other ideas.

"No way. Normally once it's confirmed a German citizen has committed a serious crime in another country, partnership approaches alone say we should rush to give them up, but instead I was told to back off even watching Hass. So, if someone in our government realised you were onto her, or onto the whole plot you've uncovered..."

Craig saw where she was going.

"Either they didn't want Hass lifted because they're in bed with the mafia, or-"

"Someone in the German government is involved in your plot. Given Weber's part in this I'm starting to wonder if some old Stasi warhorse hasn't worked their way into a position of power here."

It wasn't as far-fetched as it sounded but they'd need time and resources to find out.

"Don't take any risks, Vala. This bunch are killers and if they find out you're onto them..."

The words tailed away as Craig realised he needed to be in Germany sooner than he'd thought.

"How do you feel about having visitors in a couple of days?"

"Excellent. But, visitors plural?"

He chuckled, wondering how she would cope with the culture shock that was Liam. "You've never met my deputy, but he never lets me go anywhere alone."

\*\*\*\*

## The C.C.U. 2 p.m.

"Thank you all for coming in on a Sunday, especially after such a long night." He gestured to Liam. "Liam will take you through the events since yesterday's briefing and I'll cover the next steps."

*After I've had enough caffeine to keep an army awake.*

As Craig did that and took a call from Ken Smith, Liam brought everyone up to date. He handed the briefing back with a one liner.

"Seeing as our Armed Response colleagues obviously couldn't find their asses with their elbows, you have my permission to tell them so when you next meet."

Aidan nodded in agreement. "Just make sure their guns are holstered first."

Craig shook his head hastily, restarting his headache. "Ignore those two! I'll speak to Commander McEwan."

"No matter how one-sided that conversation might be."

"Thanks for that, Liam. OK, next steps everyone. I've taken some interesting calls this morning, the most recent of which was five minutes ago from ex-Army Captain Ken Smith, who as of yesterday was out of the military and about to become one of us."

He waved down the short cheer that followed.

"However, he does still have contacts in Whitehall, at the Ministry of Defence, so I asked him to ask around about one of our guests at High Street, the Home Secretary, Basil Hartnell."

Kyle had been staring lethargically out the window, now he suddenly became animated.

"The Home Secretary? I didn't know we'd managed to hold him!"

Liam's answer was droll. "That'll be because you were out of that estate so fast your ass was in flames last night, leaving the rest of us to do the donkey work."

The ex-spy shrugged. "I had a date."

"In the middle of the night?!"

"What can I say? The ladies want what the ladies want."

The words were accompanied by a combined shrug and leer that emerged as a jerk, just like their owner.

Craig interrupted the exchange.

"That's enough. Kyle, you did good work last night but you should have stayed behind to help, and you'll be doing most of the paperwork on the party to compensate."

He ignored the immediate groan.

"Right, Ken Smith. He contacted someone at the MoD who's friends with Hartnell's son. He's in the navy. Anyway, rumour has it that Hartnell is one of a group of right-wing MPs who have been vocal about their desire to leave the EU for well over a decade and becoming increasingly frustrated, both about the lack of movement to leave and the general Pro-EU feeling across both sides of the house."

Liam nodded knowingly. "So Hartnell decided to help things along."

"Looks like it. I've got people asking about the other politicians who were lifted last night and I'm expecting to hear the same about them." He took a sip of coffee and made a face. "Someone put fresh coffee on, please. Kyle, that means you."

As the D.I. slumped off Craig continued.

"OK, I also spoke to Chief Inspector Raske in Berlin this morning and unfortunately our assassin Beatrix Hass is now out of reach. She crossed to Kaliningrad by boat early this morning with her partner, Gleb Solokov, a senior player in the Eugenov Mafia family, based in Berlin. I doubt if Hass will return to the west in the foreseeable future, and even if she does BPOL have been warned off."

Aidan Hughes gawped at him. "You're saying the German government is involved in this plot as well!"

"Possibly, or they're in bed with the mafia. If they are involved with the cabal I imagine it will be in much the same way as the other governments are. That is, some of their individual members, but not the governments as a whole."

"But why? What's in it for them?"

"I'll come back to that in a moment, Aidan, because it *is* something that I want to discuss. But before then..." He glanced across at the now bubbling percolator. "Help yourselves to coffee and biscuits, and take five."

While Aidan and Kyle raced to the roof for a cigarette and Liam raided Nicky's stash, Craig used the time to phone High Street.

"What's happening with Hartnell, Jack?"

Jack Harris had been savouring the Sunday newspapers when the phone rang and he was determined that Craig wasn't going to ruin his newly calm mood.

"Good afternoon to you too, sir."

It made Craig smile, acknowledging that his people skills

fell by the wayside when he got caught up in a case, but it didn't change his question.

"Yes, great. So? Hartnell?"

The sergeant answered the question but not before he'd sighed pointedly down the line. "His solicitor is due in thirty minutes."

"Excellent. Call me with what he says."

Craig made some more calls, ending them just as a coffee was set down beside him by an unusually caring Liam.

"OK, let's get back to it, everyone. The other thing Vala told me was that our suspect, the man we've been calling George Harrison, the man that we know pressured Veronica Lewis into allowing her parties to be used for subterfuge, kink and drugs, is actually a Stasi Officer called Colonel Maximilian Weber, who disappeared in nineteen-ninety."

Davy's eyes lit up. "The Stasi? Those boys had disinformation down to a fine art."

Liam raised an eyebrow. "You say that like it's a good thing."

"Good or bad, they w...were the best at it."

Craig broke up the debate.

"OK. Weber's background labels him as a state communist, Hass' is a right-wing terrorist, and most of our other plotters are pillars of the British, Irish and possibly German establishment. The ones we know of so far mostly belong to the right wing, but not all of them."

Liam nodded. "The Earl's a liberal and more interested in a United Ireland."

"Correct. We'll discuss *why* this coalition of the willing all seem to want the UK out of the EU in a moment. But first." He turned to Davy. "Sorry, Davy, but Weber gave us the slip. He wasn't on any plane entering Germany this morning."

"But we s...saw him at the departure gate!"

"He must have guessed he was being watched and changed destination at the last moment, so I'd like you to find out where he really did go after the briefing. My money's on London. We've no doubt he will go home eventually so Vala's going to monitor all entrance points into Germany and let me know when he appears."

He took a sip of coffee and turned back to the group. "OK, theories please. Why would all these different groups want the UK out of Europe?"

He lifted a marker ready to write on the board, and within five minutes it was covered with a range of suggested motives, covering: a weakened EU leading to increased commercial opportunities and profit for Russia, and decreased security obstacles for their criminal mafia; Germany wanting to lead the EU without opposition from the UK; the desire to break away from EU control for the UK, plus limiting immigration; the potential benefits of weakening the EU market for the rest of the world; and the instability of Northern Ireland and its border increasing the chances of a United Ireland for the TDs.

"And the German right-wing and Stasi? What's in it for them? Anyone?"

It was Jake who answered. "Surely the German right-wingers want the UK out because they really want Germany out as well. One, so there'll be controlled immigration and because they want a more sovereign, Reichsbürger Germany. And two, so that East Germany can realign with Russia against the rest of the world."

Davy concurred. "The Stasi worked closely with the KGB back in the day. And there's another thing, chief."

"Which is?"

"When the Stasi folded, thousands of its officers got jobs within the reunified Germany."

And how many of them had worked their way into senior government positions was anyone's guess. Vala's blocked pursuit of Beatrix Hass was starting the make sense.

Aidan nodded. "There's another reason to throw in as well. With the UK leaving, perhaps someone believes other countries may not want to remain in the EU and it could completely collapse."

Liam snorted just as the telephone rang. "I doubt that. We're not that important. But I suppose some nutcases could believe it."

Craig answered the phone call to the sound of a team argument about to kick off.

"Murder Squad. Craig speaking."

It was Jack Harris calling back sooner than he expected, but the sergeant's tone said that it wasn't with good news. The tone of the words he managed to squeeze out that was.

"He's...it's..."

"Calm down, Jack. What's wrong?"

The question made the argument stop mid-flow as everyone turned to listen.

"It's the Home Secretary, sir. He's dead!"

\*\*\*\*

## High Street Station. 3.30 p.m.

"How the hell did this happen, Jack?"

Liam's undisguised accusation made the sergeant rear up in his face.

"Say that again, Cullen!"

The implied threat didn't scare Liam but it did take him by surprise; he and Jack Harris had known each other since training college and they'd been personal friends for the three decades since.

He realised the offence his question had caused and raised his hands in apology.

"Sorry, Jack. I didn't mean anything by it."

Harris didn't budge. "The hell you didn't! This wasn't down to me!"

Craig glanced up from his hunkered position beside the Home Secretary's abnormally pale, even for a corpse, body, and barked at them both to shut up, following the words with a nod for everyone to quit the cell. Once past the police tape and in the staff room, he made Jack go over the previous few hours again.

"I've told you. I checked on Hartnell at two o'clock and told him his brief was coming about three."

That would be the solicitor who was currently pacing the small carpark behind the station, yelling at some subordinate on the phone. Craig jerked a thumb in the direction of the shouting.

"What time did he get here?"

"About five minutes after I called you."

"So, before the ambulance?"

Jack shook his greying head. "They arrived at the same time." He kept shaking it. "I'm not sure why I even bothered calling them. I knew Hartnell was dead as soon as I opened the cell door."

Liam frowned, trying to place things on a timeline. "And you opened it because...?"

Jack answered with a loud tut. "To collect the man's bloody lunch tray of course!"

Liam understood his irascibility. If someone had died on his watch in the six months he'd managed to stick being a custody sergeant then he'd have been irritable as well.

Craig perched on the small room's windowsill, thinking. "OK, so you saw Hartnell at two o'clock and informed him his brief was coming after lunch. How long after that did you take in his tray?"

"Ten minutes at most. The delivery came just after two so I stuck it in the microwave to reheat it and then took it straight in."

The timing made Craig frown. "Two o'clock's a bit late for lunch, isn't it?"

Jack shrugged. "Not really. It can come anytime between one and two-thirty. Depends which van's making the rounds. Sunday's always a bit slower as well."

Liam risked asking another question, expecting to get his head bitten off again.

"Had Hartnell ordered something special?"

To his surprise the sergeant answered him calmly this time, his anger obviously spent. "They only get a choice of three meals, so it would have been one of those. Chicken curry I seem to remember."

Something occurred to Craig. "How long before did Hartnell make his selection?"

"At breakfast, so around six hours ago now. The meal arrived here five hours after I phoned the order through to the firm."

"And these are the same caterers you always use?"

Harris nodded. "Not just me. They have the contract for the whole force. We can't go making individual meals for the prisoners with everything else we have to do-"

Liam cut in, trying to lighten the mood. "Not to mention the fact you can't cook. I've tasted it, remember."

It produced Jack's first smile of the hour. "There's that too. Anyway, I reheated it, put it on a tray and took it in."

"At ten-past-two."

"Yes."

Craig nodded. He'd known Hartnell had been poisoned as soon as he'd seen his body, but he also knew that the death of a British Home Secretary was going to rain all sorts of crap down on Jack so they needed everything sewn up tight.

"What did the doctor say?"

"It was that new wee M.E. The GP from the Woodstock Road. She said she reckoned Hartnell had been poisoned but she would have to wait for the P.M. to say what with."

Craig turned to his deputy. "You've called John?"

Liam nodded. "Aye, and Des to identify the poison."

It was Craig's cue to stand up straight. "Right, Jack, unless you'd been psychic there was nothing you could have done to foresee this. Someone wanted Hartnell dead and they'd messed with his food before it had even reached here. Just pass the body to John, write up your report, and get ready to fend off officials and reporters for the rest of the day. I'll send Jake down to help you. Andy and Annette will get onto the caterers, although I doubt they'll know anything either. Someone wanted Hartnell dead, and while he was locked up his food was always going to be the easiest way. They could have tampered with it any time in that five-hour window and my guess is the culprit is already long gone."

He turned for the door but Jack immediately blocked his way.

*"Why?"*

Craig nodded, understanding immediately.

"Because Hartnell might have talked and someone very powerful didn't want that. And probably also to put the fear of God into the rest." The detective shook his head as he realised what that meant. "No-one will talk to us now."

Jack stepped back. "Find the bastard who did this. I've never had a death in custody in twenty-five years."

It was a matter of professional pride.

****

Craig pulled up outside the C.C.U. and nodded Liam to get out of the car, but the D.C.I. remained stubbornly in place.

"Not until you tell me where you're going."

It made Craig laugh. "No-one's allowed to ask me that unless we're married."

Liam simpered. "I thought you'd never ask. But seriously, boss, you're not gonna go all Rambo on me, are you?"

Craig raised an eyebrow. "On who, exactly? The people I want to beat up are unfortunately out of my reach. I've a loose end to tidy up and then I'll be back. Meanwhile, you're going to task Jake, Andy and Annette as we discussed." He leant across and opened the passenger door. "Now, get out before I push you out."

It was enough to pacify Liam for now, but as he watched Craig's Audi race away down Pilot Street, the D.C.I. was already running through a list of possible destinations in his head.

He needn't have bothered, because Craig would tell him everything once he was done. Twenty minutes later he was waiting patiently in Sean Flanagan's outer office, waiting for the big chief to rouse himself from his Sunday afternoon television and appear in response to his call.

When Flanagan did arrive, Craig gave him a ten-minute update that saw the C.C.'s eyes grow further with each new revelation, but it was at the end of the report that the detective uttered his most important words.

"That's where we are right now, and there's a lot more that will come out, I have no doubt. But before it does, sir, I need to ask you something."

Flanagan nodded, his face returning to its normal serious but affable mould. "Ask away, and if I can answer you I will."

It wasn't a promise but it would have to do. Craig swallowed, not from nerves but because he was furious and struggling not to let it show. Flanagan had got them involved in this sodding case yet done nothing to help steer their way. He'd embroiled them in a political plot that stretched across two continents and risked lives in the process and now he really needed to know why.

"Why did you ask us to investigate Veronica Lewis' disappearance, sir?"

Half of him was hoping that Flanagan would fess up to some sexual peccadillo and his fear of it leaking to the press, even though it didn't fit with his image of the man. Or even if he'd said that he'd *known* about the cabal and sent them in hoping that they would blow it wide open, he could have lived with that, although a warning to wear Kevlar would have been nice.

In fact, either answer would have been OK, not wonderful but acceptable, but Flanagan's answer was stranger than either of those possibilities.

"Because First Minister McManus asked me to. Discreetly." He saw Craig's mouth open and raised a hand. "But before you ask me why, I've no idea, and as the poor man's dead now we can't ask him, so perhaps we will never know."

*Peter McManus?* Peter McManus had asked Flanagan to investigate Lewis' kidnapping, knowing it would lead them to the sex parties and blow the whole referendum plot apart?

As the pieces dropped into place, Craig fell back in his chair, torn between laughter and astonishment.

"My God!"

Flanagan sat forward, knowing the detective had just worked out the answer that eluded him.

"Why did McManus ask me to investigate, Marc?"

When he received no answer the C.C. asked again, his tone more intense.

"*Answer me, Craig.* Why did McManus-"

Craig cut him off. "Because he really *was* Pro-EU but he knew the rest of the IBP was just paying lip service to it."

He shifted to the edge of his seat, raking a hand through his dark hair.

"McManus *knew* what was happening within his own party, *and* within The Zeus Circle. He'd *been* to those parties, so he probably knew all about the German and Russian connections as well and just how far they would go to swing the referendum. For whatever reason, maybe he thought they would kill him or harm his family, McManus didn't want to take the risk of calling them on it publicly. But by getting *you* to investigate Lewis' kidnapping, and thereby involving the police...he hoped that *we* would bring everything out."

Confusion and realisation combined on Flanagan's face. "But they killed him anyway. Why?"

"Arrogance. He was an obstacle they needed rid of and they thought his killing would be blamed on Billy Regent, a disillusioned squaddie, and that no-one would ever find them out. But it was a very stupid move on their part because it just made us dig deeper. Now we know what they were planning and we can make it more widely known."

Flanagan's eyebrows shot up. "You're suggesting we tell the press?"

"And the media."

"But until we have proof-"

Craig shook his head. "That'll take months and by then it'll be too late, sir. There're only four days until the vote. It *has* to be now." His thoughts flew to Ray Mercer, sitting in a cell. "I know a man who can get it out there tomorrow, and he discovered most of it on his own, so we'll just have to fill in a few gaps."

"Anonymous source says?"

"Of course."

Thirty minutes later Craig was sitting opposite Ray Mercer feeding the journalist details he could never have dreamed of, and hoping it would be enough for people to still make an informed choice.

\*\*\*\*

**St Mary's Hospital.**

"It was none of Katy's bloody business! She had no right to tell you anything!"

The words were punctuated by Natalie thumping each

hard surface that she passed, in a way John was certain wasn't good for a surgeon's hands. He stood up to join his wife, who'd been storming around her on-call room for most of the thirty minutes since he'd arrived. He said most, because the first five minutes she'd spent asking him why he was there, only to cut him off halfway through his explanation with threats of grievous bodily harm against her best friend.

John stood directly in his wife's path, hoping to make her stop. All it achieved was a body swerve that would have done a footballer proud, so he had to follow her around the room instead.

"She was worried about you, Nat. She was worried about both of us."

That stopped her. Natalie turned towards her partner, hands on hips, and said the words that he would never forget.

"*Us?* What has this got to do with *us*?"

John was all for a woman's right to choose, but that was taking it too far in his view. The man of few words, and all of them softly spoken, yelled back at the top of his voice.

"I'M YOUR BLOODY HUSBAND! IT'S MY BABY TOO!"

The effort almost exhausted him so he fell back into his chair, adding sombrely.

"You can't cut me out, Natalie. Please don't cut me out. I need to be there for you, you're all that I have."

No-one watching the exchange would have blamed John if he'd started sobbing at that moment, but the only sobbing in the room came from his feisty wife, as Natalie Winter suddenly realised two things: One, she was John's only family in the world, and two, while she had to make life and death decisions at work all alone, marriage meant that didn't need to be true in the rest of her life.

"I'm sorry, John. I didn't think of your feelings."

The pathologist gave a weak smile. "At least you're honest. You were confused. It's understandable."

Except that it wasn't really. It wasn't the first time that Natalie had done exactly what she'd wanted without any thought for him, and it probably wouldn't be the last. John pushed his own feelings aside for a moment and took his wife's small hand.

"You're not alone in this, Natalie. We'll do everything together, starting with returning to see the geneticist."

She went to object but then reconsidered, shrugging instead.

"OK. I'll remake the appointment."

Then her expression darkened.

"But Katy betrayed my confidence and I'm *never* speaking to her again."

There was repair work to be done all around.

\*\*\*\*

## The C.C.U. Tuesday 21st June.

The thirty-six hours after the party were spent finishing interviews and statements and dealing with the fallout from Basil Hartnell's death in custody, from what John and Des had identified as poisoning with cyanide. The oldies were always the best.

Liam had grudgingly given Ray Mercer his interview as an unnamed D.C.I., and the reporter's exposé in the Journal, revealing details of the cabal's plan to swing the referendum outcome their way and headed 'Your Free Will Bought and Sold', had been picked up by every other newspaper in the UK.

Meanwhile, the logo on Hass' bag had turned out to belong to a fringe group in Moscow and Davy had plumbed the depths of his book code, but it had yielded little more than what they already knew, except that the Russian involvement in the plot clearly extended much further than the narrow financial interests of its criminal mafia, to its military's desire for supremacy and their hope that a weakened EU might one day lead to a weakened NATO too.

The trail on Maximilian Weber had led the analysts to Heathrow instead of Frankfurt, but he'd been lost on the London Underground, reappearing as predicted in East Germany a day later where Vala and a small team had been tailing him, still unofficially, since he'd arrived.

By Tuesday there was only one thing left to do, and Craig was in his office finishing some notes when Liam burst through the door carrying a book and a travel bag.

"You ready, boss?"

Craig kept typing, answering without looking up. "We've still got a couple of hours before our flight."

Liam thudded into a chair. "Aye, but I fancied having a mosey around duty-free. I need a new watch."

"And there I was thinking you were going to buy Danni some perfume."

The D.C.I. didn't rise to the jibe. "Pointless on the way out."

Craig finished his sentence and glanced up. "What's the book?"

Liam's response was to open it and read aloud. "German phrase book. Wie viel für ein Bier? That means how much for a beer?"

It was the best idea he'd had in days and Craig's cue to get a move on. Four hours later they were landing at Dresden Airport, Liam's new watch and all. Craig smiled at the tall, slim brunette waiting for them at the gate, stepping forward to greet her.

"Vala! How are you? Chief Inspector Vala Raske, this is Chief Inspector Liam Cullen."

The niceties were cut short by the anxious look on the German officer's face and the pace at which she ushered them to her car.

"We have Weber under surveillance but he's on the move. He checked out of his hotel four hours ago and rented a car."

Liam was puzzled. "Why don't you just lift him?"

The BPOL officer shook her head just as they reached her BMW. "I've been warned off."

Craig frowned. "Again?"

"Yesterday. This time it came with the threat of demotion."

They threw their bags into the boot and climbed in. As she started the engine Raske added.

"You need to remember that a lot of the top echelon of government here still have sympathy with the old guard."

Liam leaned forward between the seats, trying not to notice that they were driving on the wrong side of the road.

"You're saying there are Stasi thugs high up in parliament here?"

It made Craig laugh. "As opposed to the choirboys we have in ours?"

Raske shrugged, glancing at Craig. "I've been digging since we last talked, Marc, and it seems we have remnants in parliament, justice and the police here. They might not all have been named as Stasi members when it was disbanded, but everyone knew their beliefs. And there are plenty of ordinary Germans who have sympathy with the UK's referendum to leave as well. They feel the EU's power has grown too much and that immigration is uncontrolled. Plus, lots of these people are Reichsbürgers."

"As opposed to other types of burgers?"

Craig ignored the joke and nodded her on.

"Reichsbürgers or Reich citizens aren't an organised group. It's more a belief system, and although most of them are right-wing not all are. They just honestly believe that the Federal Republic of Germany was *never* a legitimate state, because Germany didn't sign a peace agreement with the Allies. So anything that threatens the post World War Two order in Europe is OK with them."

"Including the breakup of the EU."

"Yes."

The small group descended into silence for they reached the outskirts of Görlitz, a small town on the Polish border. Raske pulled up at the side of a narrow country road and pointed towards a quaint, white shuttered house.

"Weber was seen entering it three hours ago."

Liam was puzzled. "Why here?"

"Because he can pass through Poland and the Ukraine into Crimea in less than a day."

Craig nodded, scanning the quiet area. "Are your men still here watching?"

She shook her head. "I had to let them go. If they get caught they could lose their jobs."

"So could you, Vala. Thank you for everything you've done, but Liam and I can take it from here."

She shook her head emphatically. "You've no jurisdiction."

Craig reached into his jacket and produced a document. "We have a European Arrest Warrant for Weber, for his part in dealing drugs and organising prostitution in the UK."

She seized the paper, scanning it quickly. It was legal.

"OK, but you're still supposed to cooperate with local forces, and I'm all you've got. We're sticking together."

Just then a silver van pulled up at the front of the house. Its side panel slid open to reveal two short but seriously steroid enhanced men. As they entered the small house Liam broke the tension with a quip.

"At least we're bigger than them."

Vala wasn't so confident. "But we're not bigger than their guns. The second man had a MP7." A Heckler and Koch machine gun.

Craig thought for a moment and then took charge. "OK, if we try to enter the house they'll have the advantage. It's far easier to defend territory than break in. I say we wait until they're mobile and then run them off the road. With a bit of luck, the crash will weaken them and help us."

Before the chief inspector could respond Liam was out of the car and across the street, strolling along the pavement opposite as if he hadn't a care in the world. The BPOL officer gawped as the D.C.I. stopped to admire a tree half a block behind the van, and then as he restarted his constitutional, unhurried, admiring each garden as he passed and taking time to nod to a pretty fräulein who was walking the opposite way.

When he'd passed both the van and the house Liam crossed the street again and turned left, disappearing for five minutes to circle the block on the other side. Eventually he returned to the BMW and as he clambered back into the back seat Vala leant over to whack him on the leg.

*"Scheisse!* What the hell was that? You could have got yourself shot!"

Liam rubbed his thigh dramatically. "Here, have you been taking unarmed combat lessons from my wife?" He turned to Craig with a smile. "No driver in the van and no keys, so there's only the two men and Weber in the house makes three."

Vala shook her head. "You can't say that. There might be someone in the back of the van."

Craig disagreed. "If there was they'd have left the leys in the ignition in case he needed to make a quick getaway. Liam's right. It's three against three and we have the initiative. Good work, Liam."

Just then the front door of the house opened and the two bulked-up men reappeared. Wedged between them was the man they'd caught on camera at Emmett Darrian's house. Vala hissed beneath her breath.

"Weber."

"OK, wait till they're three hundred metres up the road and then pull out, Vala. Stay three car lengths behind until I signal."

It was a long five minutes before Craig did, but finally, on a broader stretch of road with hedgerows on both sides and a ditch that might have been dug especially for the event, he signalled Raske to speed up, praying that the windowless back door of the van meant that by the time their adversaries finally spotted them in their wing mirrors they'd be so close it would be too late.

He was almost right. Everything was going to plan until the BMW had pulled out halfway along the van. Then, as had always been the risk, the van-driver spotted them and swung out to side swipe their car before they could do the same to him.

With a sickening thud Raske's head smashed against the driver's window, knocking her out cold. Like a synchronised swim team Liam moved behind her seat and lifted the BPOL officer wholesale out of her seat-belt and into the back with him, while Craig slid across into the driver's seat and slowed down the car to regroup. Meanwhile Liam laid the unconscious chief inspector down and took up Craig's vacated position, opening the passenger window a crack and inserting his Glock ready to fire.

"Give them a whack, boss!"

Craig accelerated so they were lined up with the van's front bumper, then he torqued the wheels so hard the BMW's rear end swung around and tipped the van forward and over into the ditch.

Liam whooped as they passed the now recumbent transit van.

"Nice one. Chuck a U-ey and go back. I'll keep my gun on them."

With that he slid his window the whole way down and leant out, ready to fire at the first thing that moved. He'd reckoned without the natural barrier that the van afforded their opponents and halfway back to their target Craig heard a series of cracks.

"Machine gun! Get down."

Liam slid back into the vehicle and both detectives dropped their heads.

"Pull up there and let me out, boss."

As Craig obliged, Liam slipped out and took up position behind his open door, firing off six rounds that saw the machine gunner fall. Craig did the same on the other side of the car, praying that Vala didn't choose that moment to wake up.

"Two of them left, Liam. Can you see anything?"

"A pair of feet down the side. I'll going to aim for those."

He was as good as his word. Two more shots cracked out followed by a loud scream and foreign words that even he knew were rude.

Craig decided to call the men out.

"Maximilian Weber. This is the police from Northern Ireland. We have a European warrant for your arrest. Come out with your hands up."

More swearing followed by English.

"I can't walk. You bastards shot my feet."

As Liam sniggered, Craig shouted again.

"Tell your friend to throw out both your guns and any one still alive raise your hands."

For a moment there was no movement, then they heard two loud clatters as the guns hit the thankfully deserted road, followed by four hands appearing above the horizontal van. Liam shook his head, whispering.

"Don't go out there, boss. I don't trust them."

Craig agreed, but what was the alternative?

"We'll both have to go to cuff them, Liam. Are you up for

that?"

The D.C.I. edged slowly around the BMW in response, watching the men's elevated hands all the way. When he was behind Craig Liam whispered again.

"Something's off. I can feel it."

"We've no choice."

They reloaded and then Craig moved around the car door until he was in the open. Just as he did Liam put a name to his doubt.

"Machine gun!"

The dead man's machine gun was still in play, and in the second Liam called it the second bodyguard dropped his hands, grabbed the weapon and releasing a spray of bullets their way.

As the bullets hit the air, Liam rugby tackled Craig, pulling him to the ground. Both cops hit the tarmac with a thud as Liam aimed his Glock in the gunman's direction and squeezed off six more rounds.

They hit their mark, and the second guard joined his buddy in the grave. Maximilian Weber yelled over the ringing in everyone's ears.

"Don't shoot! I'm unarmed."

Liam could feel his finger twitch to shoot the Stasi Colonel but he controlled the urge and turned towards Craig. The sight that greeted him made his heart sink. The detective was lying face down on the road with blood covering the left side of his head and a hole in his left thigh. Liam turned him over frantically, checking for a pulse. It was there but it was thready and a charred gash on Craig's skull was spurting with blood.

Liam reloaded his Glock and raced towards the van, his fury making him want to put a hole in the German. He screwed his barrel hard against Weber's temple, picturing the way in which Billy Regent had died. The D.C.I.'s mouth was dry with adrenaline and the desire for revenge and the sight of the aging communist's terror was doing nothing to deter him, only the thought of having to explain Weber's death well enough to avoid getting locked in a German prison made Liam eventually retract his gun.

He cuffed the man to the van's front bumper as roughly

as he could and raced back to the others, reaching for his phone and hoping the emergency services spoke enough English to understand his words. He checked on Vala Raske and then thudded down on the tarmac beside Craig, praying that he survived long enough to reach a hospital.

Three hours later Max Weber was in a prison ward with both of his feet in casts and Vala Raske was under observation with the promise of discharge the next day. Craig was back from theatre without the bullets lodged in his skull and leg but still comatose, with the doctors refusing to give a guarantee of his survival or what abilities the detective might have if he ever woke up.

It was the middle one of the three scenarios that Liam had imagined: Craig dead, comatose for who knew how long, or wide awake and joking, but now that he had a title for his condition he'd couldn't put off making the calls.

The D.C.I. removed Craig's mobile from his plastic possession bag and copied three numbers onto his own phone, trying to choose the best order to call them for the least distress and the most support. In the end, he plumped for dialling Craig's father, Tom, and then Katy, reckoning that between them they could work out how to tell Craig's mum.

# Chapter Eighteen

**Dresden. Monday, 27th June 2016. 6 p.m.**

*"You're telling me the UK voted to leave the EU anyway?"*
Liam rolled his eyes at the question. Glad as he was that Craig had finally woken up, it had to be the tenth time that he'd asked it, and he couldn't keep putting the repetition down to the hole in his head. Denial was obviously not just a river in Egypt.

The D.C.I. lifted a grape from the bedside cabinet and popped it into his mouth.

"Look, boss, what can I tell you? The media told people all about the cabal and the conspiracy and they *still* voted for Brexit."

He planted himself at the bottom of Craig's bed.

"When you think about it, Weber and the rest could have just saved themselves the trouble of all that plotting, couldn't they? 'Cos obviously enough people wanted out anyway."

Craig shook his still-bandaged head. "I'm astounded. I really am." Suddenly a frown covered on his face.

"*What?* You've just thought of something, haven't you?"

Even Craig couldn't believe what he said next. "What if they did something else and we missed it, Liam? Something more than the bent politicians and whipping up nationalist fervour."

"Such as?"

The reply was preceded by a sigh of despair. "I don't know, that's the problem. We know that there was someone in Whitehall involved, someone that we didn't get. It must have been them that ordered Hartnell's death." He ended the sentence with a defeated shrug. "We'll keep looking for them but we might never know what else they did."

Liam decided that it was time to cheer him up. "OK, so do you want some *good* news?"

Craig couldn't imagine what good there could possibly be in the situation so he responded with a grunt. Liam was unoffended.

"Harrison's story checked out. He's in the clear."

Craig wasn't impressed. "I thought you said it was good news! That means we're stuck with him."

"Ach, that was just a teaser. OK then. Bakar Dudaev."

Craig frowned again, making his head hurt. "What about him?"

"Well, it turns out Weber wants to make a deal and he's offering us Dudaev in exchange."

Craig gawped at him. "How the hell does he know Dudaev?"

"It seems our little Chechen has been touting his stolen satellite codes for sale around Europe. Weber won't give us any more detail unless we agree to deal."

Just then the hospital room door opened and a smiling nurse appeared, brightening the mood.

"Herr Craig, your father and partner have gone to their hotel for dinner and will return to see you later."

When she disappeared again it was Liam's cue to leave. He produced something from his jacket pocket before he did. A CD case.

Craig eyed it doubtfully. "What's that?"

Liam rolled his eyes. "It's a Lamborghini. What the heck do you think it is?"

"I meant what type of music, smart-ass."

The D.C.I. shook his head, struggling not to laugh. "It's a surprise. But you'll like it, honestly. It'll keep you company till your dad gets back."

He put the disc on to play and headed quickly for the door, as the strains of a country and western song about someone's favourite pony began to play.

Craig's groan was almost as loud as the music. "Turn it off! You know I can't get out of bed."

But the detective was already out the door.

"Liam! Get back here now!"

Liam was too far away to hear. Just as well or he would have heard himself being threatened with the sack.

**THE END**

# Core Characters in the Craig Crime Novels

**Superintendent Marc (Marco) Craig:** Craig is a sophisticated, single, forty-six-year-old. Born in Northern Ireland, he is of Northern Irish/Italian extraction, from a mixed religious background but agnostic. An ex-grammar schoolboy and Queen's University Law graduate, he went to London to join The Met (The Metropolitan Police) at twenty-two, rising in rank through its High Potential Development Training Scheme. He returned to Belfast in two-thousand and eight after more than fifteen years away.

He is a driven, compassionate, workaholic, with an unfortunate temper that he struggles to control and a tendency to respond to situations with his fists, something that almost resulted in him going to prison when he was in his teens. He loves the sea, sails when he has the time and is generally very sporty. He plays the piano, loves music and sport. He lives alone in a modern apartment block in Stranmillis, near the university area of Belfast.

His parents, his extrovert mother Mirella (an Italian concert pianist) and his quiet father Tom (an ex-university lecturer in Physics) live in Holywood town, six miles away. His rebellious sister, Lucia, his junior by ten years, works as the manager of a local charity and also lives in Belfast.

Craig is now a Chief Superintendent heading up Belfast's Murder Squad and Intelligence Unit. The Murder Squad is based in the thirteen storey Co-ordinated Crime Unit (C.C.U.) in Pilot Street, in the Sailortown area of Belfast's Docklands. He loves the sea, sails when he has the time and is generally very sporty. He plays the piano, loves music by Snow Patrol and follows Manchester United's and Northern Ireland's football teams, and the Ulster Rugby team.

**D.C.I. Liam Cullen:** Craig's deputy. Liam is a fifty-one-year-old former RUC officer from Crossgar in Northern Ireland, who transferred into the PSNI in two thousand and one following the Patton Reforms. He has lived and worked in Northern Ireland all of his life and has spent thirty years in the police force, twenty of them policing Belfast, including during The Troubles.

He is married to the forty-one-year-old, long suffering Danielle (Danni), a part-time nursery nurse, and they have a five-year-old daughter Erin and a three-year-old son called Rory. Liam is unsophisticated, indiscreet and hopelessly non-PC, but he's a hard worker with a great knowledge of the streets and has a sense of humour that makes everyone, even the Chief Constable, laugh.

**D.I. Annette Eakin:** Annette is Craig's Detective Inspector who has lived and worked in Northern Ireland all her life. She is a forty-seven-year-old ex-nurse who, after her nursing degree, worked as a nurse for thirteen years and then, after a career break, retrained and has now been in the police for an equal length of time. She divorced her husband Pete McElroy, a P.E teacher at a state secondary school, because of his infidelity and violence. They have two children, a boy and a girl (Jordan and Amy), both teenagers, and Annette also has a baby daughter with her new partner, Mike Augustus.

Annette is kind and conscientious with an especially good eye for detail. She also has very good people skills but can be a bit of a goody-two-shoes. Since her marriage broke down, she has acquired a newly glamorous image and is now in a relationship with Mike Augustus, a pathologist who works with Doctor John Winter.

**Nicky Morris:** Nicky Morris is Craig's thirty-nine-year-old personal assistant. She used to be PA to Detective Chief Superintendent (D.C.S.) Terence *'Teflon'* Harrison. Nicky is a glamorous Belfast mum married to Gary, who owns a small garage, and is the mother of a teenage son, Jonny. She comes from a solidly working-class area of East Belfast, just ten minutes' drive from Docklands.

She is bossy, motherly and street-wise and manages to

organise a reluctantly-organised Craig very effectively. She has a very eclectic sense of style, and there is an ongoing innocent office flirtation between her and Liam.

**Davy Walsh:** The Murder Squad's twenty-eight-year-old computer analyst. A brilliant but shy EMO, Davy's confidence has grown during his time on the team, making his lifelong stutter on 's' and 'w' diminish, unless he's under stress.

His father is deceased and Davy lives at home in Belfast with his mother and grandmother. He has an older sister, Emmie, who studied English at university. His girlfriend of almost three years, Maggie Clarke, is a journalist and now News Editor at The Belfast Chronicle. They became engaged in early 2017.

**Dr John Winter:** John is the forty-five-year-old Director of Pathology for Northern Ireland, one of the youngest ever appointed. He's brilliant, eccentric, gentlemanly and really likes the ladies, but he met his match in Natalie Ingrams, a surgeon at St Mary's Trust, and they have been happily married for almost two years.

John was Craig's best friend at school and university, and remained in Northern Ireland to build his medical career when Craig left. He is now internationally respected in his field. John persuaded Craig that the newly peaceful Northern Ireland was a good place to return to and assists Craig's team with cases whenever he can. He is obsessed with crime in general and US police shows in particular.

**D.C.I. Andrew (Andy) Angel:** A relatively new addition to Craig's team and its second D.C.I., Angel is a slight, forty-one-year-old, twice divorced, perpetually broke father of a six-year-old son, Bowie. A chocoholic with a tendency towards lethargy, he surprises the team at times with his abilities. His spare time is spent collecting original Irish art and the constant search for a new relationship Romantic subtlety isn't his strong point.

**D.C.S. Terry (Teflon) Harrison:** Craig's old boss. The fifty-eight-year-old Detective Chief Superintendent was based at the Headquarters building in Limavady in the northwest Irish countryside but has now returned to Docklands where he has an office on the thirteenth floor. He shared a converted farm house at Toomebridge with his homemaker wife Mandy and their thirty-year-old daughter Sian, a marketing consultant. Mandy has now divorced him, partly because of his trail of mistresses, often younger than his daughter, so Harrison has moved to an apartment in South Belfast.

Harrison is tolerable as a boss as long as everything's going well, but he is acutely politically aware, a snob, and very quick to pass on any blame to his subordinates (hence the Teflon nickname). He sees Craig as a rival now and is out to destroy him. He particularly resents Craig's friendship with John Winter, who wields a great deal of power in the Northern Irish justice system.

# Key Background Locations

The majority of locations referenced in the book are real, with some exceptions.

**Northern Ireland (real)**: Set in the north-east of the island of Ireland, Northern Ireland was created in nineteen-twenty-one by an act of British parliament. It forms part of the United Kingdom of Great Britain and Northern Ireland and shares a border to the south and west with the Republic of Ireland. The Northern Ireland Assembly, based at the Stormont Estate, holds responsibility for a range of devolved policy matters. It was established by the Northern Ireland Act 1998 as part of the Good Friday Agreement.

**Belfast (real):** Belfast is the capital and largest city of Northern Ireland, set on the flood plain of the River Lagan. The seventeenth largest city in the United Kingdom and the second largest in Ireland, it is the seat of the Northern Ireland Assembly.

**The Dockland's Co-ordinated Crime Unit (The C.C.U. - fictitious):** The modern high-rise headquarters building is situated in Pilot Street in Sailortown, a section of Belfast between the M1 and M2 undergoing massive investment and re-development. The C.C.U. hosts the police murder, gang crimes, vice and drug squad offices, amongst others.

**Sailortown (real):** An historic area of Belfast on the River Lagan that was a thriving area between the sixteenth and twentieth Centuries. Many large businesses developed in the area, ships docked for loading and unloading and their crews from far flung places such as China and Russia mixed with a local Belfast population of ship's captains, chandlers, seamen and their families.

Sailortown was a lively area where churches and bars fought for the souls and attendance of the residents and where many languages were spoken each day. The basement of the Rotterdam Bar, at the bottom of Clarendon Dock, acted as the overnight lock-up to prisoners being deported to the Antipodes on boats the next morning, and the stocks which held the prisoners could still be seen until the nineteen-nineties.

During the years of World War Two the area was the most bombed area of the UK outside Central London, as the Germans tried to destroy Belfast's ship building capacity. Sadly, the area fell into disrepair in the nineteen-seventies and eighties when the motorway extension led to compulsory purchases of many homes and businesses, and decimated the Sailortown community. The rebuilding of the community has now begun, with new families moving into starter homes and professionals into expensive dockside flats.

**The Pathology Labs (fictitious):** The labs, set on Belfast's Saintfield Road as part of a large science park, are where Doctor John Winter, Northern Ireland's Head of Pathology, and his co-worker, Doctor Des Marsham, Head of Forensic Science, carry out the post-mortem and forensic examinations that help Craig's team solve their cases.

**St Mary's Healthcare Trust (fictitious):** St Mary's is one of the largest hospital trusts in the UK. It is spread over several hospital sites across Belfast, including the main Royal St Mary's Hospital site off the motorway and the Maternity, Paediatric and Endocrine (M.P.E.) unit, a stand-alone site on Belfast's Lisburn Road, in the University Quarter of the city.

Thank you for reading this book. If you enjoyed it, why not leave a review on Amazon and recommend it to your friends?

Discover the other titles in the series at:
www.catrionakingbooks.com

Printed in Great Britain
by Amazon